A Delightful Life

Gail,

Thank you for the pretty pen the class gave me. I will treasure this for a long time.

Please enjoy this book which was written for my grand-children, because they never knew their grandfather.

Caroline J. Cross

A Delightful Life

Caroline Jones Cross

Caroline Jones Cross

HILLSBORO PRESS
Franklin, Tennessee

TENNESSEE HERITAGE LIBRARY
Bicentennial Collection

Printed in the United States of America

02   01   00   99   98   1   2   3   4   5

Library of Congress Catalog Card Number: 98-73722

ISBN: 1-57736-075-3

Editorial Consultant Dimples B. Kellogg

Cover design by Gary Bozeman

Published by
HILLSBORO PRESS
An imprint of
PROVIDENCE HOUSE PUBLISHERS
238 Seaboard Lane • Franklin, Tennessee 37067
800-321-5692

To my children, Amy and Jim,
to my grandchildren, Madeline and Will,
and to the memory of my husband, Billy,
without whom my life would have been
much less delightful.

Contents

Introduction

> *May the Integrity, Courage, Charity, Hospitality*
> *and Patriotism set forth in the Records of Our Family*
> *be reproduced in all future descendants;*
> *and may the Christian Faith of their forefathers*
> *be re-incarnated in their lives.*
> *—Anonymous*

My life has been one of pure delight. Don't misunderstand, I have had my share of trials and tribulations. But the blessings have by far outweighed the burdens.

Faith and family have been the solid foundations of my life. Both sets of grandparents were strong people of God who came from generations of church members. Their faith passed on to their children and eventually to me and my sisters and our cousins. The extended family is sizable, providing a special kind of security for all its members. We all know that the family is there for us in the good times and the bad times. And sometimes family members tell us what we need to hear whether we want to hear it or not.

I told my children that they are very fortunate in today's world to have had a mother and a father who loved each other and were true to each other. Billy and I never thought of getting a divorce or of becoming interested in another man or woman while we were married. We loved God and our children too much to have broken our marriage vows. They were raised in a very traditional family with an emphasis on traditional values of honesty, integrity, and hard work. They had one set of grandparents living nearby and another within an hour's drive from Franklin. Grandparents can often say things to children that are more meaningful than when the parents say them, and they sometimes have more influence. In our mobile society too many children don't see their grandparents very often, but my children got to benefit from all that close contact.

At the last prayer breakfast held by Governor McWherter, Elizabeth Dole spoke of her grandmother, who was her mentor. She said her grandmother taught her that she couldn't change the world, but that she could change the things around her. If all of us could change ourselves as well as others, the world would be so much better. That speech and those sentiments made me an admirer of her.

This book presents stories and traditions of our ancestors. It also tells about more recent events in which the family has been involved. Middle Tennessee, especially Williamson County, has been home to us, and I like to think that we have given as much or more to the community than we have taken from it. That idea has been strong on all sides of the family—the Joneses, the Jordans, the Harrises, and the Crosses. Preserving family history and other history has become even more important to me as I have discovered gaps in information about the family but no one is left alive to fill them in.

These events are told the way I remember them. Other people may not have the same recollections. My four cousins, the Batey sisters, can get together and recall the same event, yet they all saw it differently. My sisters may see the events described in this book differently, but what I tell is the way the events affected me. To me, that's an important reason to write this book. We need to realize that we have an influence on others, but we don't often realize how others interpret our words and deeds.

Delight yourself in the LORD
and he will give you the desires of your heart.
Psalm 37:4

A Delightful Life

CHAPTER 1

The Sweet, Simple Things of Life

> *I am beginning to learn that it is the sweet, simple*
> *things of life which are the real ones after all.*
> —*Laura Ingalls Wilder*

"Hello, world!" That's what Aunt Amy reported I said as a very young child when I pulled up to the window and tried to look out. I greeted the world July 16, 1931, in Murfreesboro, Tennessee, at the local hospital. My parents named me for my great-grandmother on my father's side, Nancy Caroline Smith Jones, and my mother's grandmother, Nancy Newsom. (For some reason, Caroline is pronounced as if it was spelled Carolyn.)

Both of my parents, Ruth Forrest Jordan and Tom Fox Jones, were born in Rutherford County, Tennessee. Daddy was from Eagleville, and Mama was from a little community near Smyrna called Stewarts Creek. Mama came to Nashville to attend Lipscomb as a boarding student during high school. She stayed and finished two years of college; Lipscomb was only a junior college in 1927. She then went to what is now Middle Tennessee State University (MTSU) and finished her education with a major in music. Daddy only went to the eighth grade, but that didn't hinder him from being a good businessman and a good teacher to his children.

Mama had coal black hair, but by the time I started to school she was prematurely gray. I promised myself that if I had children, I would not have gray hair when they entered first grade. That's why I have dyed my hair since before Jim was born. She had brown snappy "tight" eyes that were characteristic of the Elliotts; when members of that family smile, their eyes almost close.

3

Gathering of the Jordans in fall 1931 at Uncle Bryan's house in Smyrna. First row, left to right, Amy Jordan, Sue Batey Baker, Maggie Batey holding Thomas, Ben Batey (on arm of chair), Arch Wood Jordan, Evelyn Batey Sigmund, Ettie Elliott Jordan, and Ruth Jordan Jones holding me. Second row, left to right, Ernest Jordan, James Benjamin Batey, Evelyn Ward Jordan, Herbert Jordan, Margaret Batey, Ann Batey Whitley, Alvis Huddleston, Minnie Jordan Huddleston holding Robert Alvis Huddleston Jr., Katie Rhea Jordan holding Dorothy Jordan Balfour, Roy Jordan, Dixie Owen Jordan, and Bryan Jordan. (Absent: Tom Fox Jones.)

Daddy was just under six feet tall, but he always seemed taller than that to me. He had curly brown hair—that's where my curly hair came from—and blue eyes.

Both Jones and Jordan grandparents were members of the Church of Christ. My Jordan grandfather adhered to the Bible teaching that said to be "given to hospitality." Grandma said she never knew who he was going to bring home after Sunday services. She would stay home and cook instead of going to church. Granddaddy Jordan invited Daddy Jones to hear a certain preacher at a gospel meeting at the Smyrna church. Granddaddy and Grandma Jordan were then living in Smyrna, having moved from the farm. My daddy drove his father over to the service; Daddy and Daddy Jones stayed for Sunday dinner; and that's when Daddy met Mama. Uncle Ernest, one of Mama's older brothers, met his wife, Amy, in similar circumstances. (Aunt Amy and Uncle Ernest had no children, but they treated their nieces and nephews like their children.)

Both grandfathers saw to it that their children—the boys *and* the girls—received as much education as possible. Granddaddy Jordan sent his children to Lipscomb, beginning with Maggie. Daddy Jones also sent his children, except Daddy and Uncle Buster, to Lipscomb. An interesting point is that I never realized until adulthood that other families made a distinction between education for the boys and the girls.

Mama and Daddy were married in 1929, and I was born two years later. Mama was crying when she was pregnant with me because she knew it meant a big change in her lifestyle. My great-grandfather Moon (we called him Granddaddy Moon—my daddy called him Grandpappy) was a doctor, and he said, "Why, Ruth, what did you expect when you got married?"

The February before I was born, Mama's older sister, Minnie, who married Alvis Huddleston, had had a son, Robert (Bobby) Alvis Jr. Uncle Alvis kept telling Daddy, "You've got to have a boy." In my baby book there is an envelope with a card addressed and mailed to Miss Nancy Tom Jones because Uncle Alvis was teasing Daddy about my not being a boy. I still have a little black Eskimo brand electric fan (and it still works) that Daddy bought to put in my room because it was so hot that summer. Mama and Daddy lived in Kingwood Heights, a subdivision, in Murfreesboro, and there are pictures of me and Nodie, the black woman who worked for them, outside the house. For my first outing, Mama took me when I was just a few months old to Aunt Maggie's for a luncheon, and Nodie went along to look after me.

People noticed me because of my curly hair, which looked like Shirley Temple's although I didn't particularly resemble her. Maybe because she was popular in the movies then, people made comments about it. Getting the tangles out when Mama washed my hair was torture, and the brushing of it when it was dry was the same way. Mama took me to Nashville to the beauty shop, and invariably a man cut my hair and kept it fairly short. Men were considered the epitome of hair cutters for women then. We washed our hair—once a week only!—in rain water that we caught in a big tank. My grandmother believed in washing hair in rain water and rinsing in lemon juice or vinegar to make it shine. A blonde was to use lemon juice; a brunette was to use vinegar.

Growing up, I had an idyllic situation. Maybe every child thinks that, but I didn't know anything about a dysfunctional family. Granddaddy Jordan died when I was five. My mother had always promised him that she would look after my grandmother, so we moved to my grandmother's home in Smyrna from Murfreesboro. Having two generations right there was a wonderful opportunity for me, and that opportunity has spanned more generations. My children grew up near their grandparents all their lives, and now my grandchildren are on this farm living next to me.

Mama was one of eight children, and Daddy was one of ten. Many relatives came to Grandma's house during the week and ate supper. Most of them came on Sunday for lunch. Billy and I carried on that tradition by having our children over for Sunday lunch after church, and I still have them over when I'm in town. The family members would gather around the piano and sing parts—soprano, alto, tenor, and bass—which partly comes from learning to sing at church with no instruments. To this day we get together and sing.

Next door lived Aunt Dixie and Uncle Bryan. He was my mother's older brother, and he was ten years older than Aunt Dixie. Their house, built in 1929 or 1930, was probably the finest house in Smyrna at that time. My mother and Dixie had been roommates at Lipscomb. When Aunt Dixie died, Billy and I went to her funeral in San Antonio, where they had moved years earlier. The preacher had asked Aunt Dixie how she and Bryan met, and he learned the story he shared at the funeral service.

Dixie had gone home with Mama one weekend. Bryan was a co-owner with Will Coleman of the Smyrna Lumber Company, then one of the largest cedar and walnut brokers in the U.S. Their office was across the railroad tracks from Grandma's house. Mama was proud of her big brother, and she took Dixie over to the office to introduce her to him. It was summertime and the windows in the office were up because there was no air-conditioning. The young women couldn't get Bryan's attention because he was too busy talking on the telephone, selling walnut and cedar to no telling whom or where. When all else failed, they started singing and dancing the Charleston. Was I surprised to hear that! I got home from the funeral and asked Mama about that event: "Mama, you never told us that you could do the Charleston." She sort of drew back and said, "Well, sure I did."

Uncle Bryan and Aunt Dixie had two girls very quickly after marrying; only a year separated Ettie Lu and Frances Owen. Ettie Lu was a year younger than I was. Since we were all so close in age, they were like my sisters. I cried every morning on the way to school because I didn't want to leave my cousins.

Mama and Daddy had the hardest time getting me to school, even though it was just up the street. That poor teacher, Mrs. Lorraine Ward, had to have the patience of God to put up with me. I was disrupting the whole class, but I didn't care. I wanted to go home. I sometimes wondered if my parents should have kept me back and let me start with Ettie Lu, but I realize now that would not have worked since Aunt Dixie kept Ettie Lu back so she and Frances Owen could start together.

Mr. Waller was the bus driver of the only school bus, and he was the father of my teacher, Mrs. Ward. The principal of the elementary school was J. E. McCrary. The elementary school classes probably had no more than seventy-five to eighty students in all.

Smyrna Elementary and the high school were in the same rock building. The right side of the building was the elementary school with eight grades. In the middle was the auditorium where chapel was held once a week. All twelve grades were together for chapel, but it was still a small auditorium. On the left side was the high school, which was the only high school in Smyrna. The home ec department was in the basement. Counting the principal, who taught classes, there were seven teachers for the whole high school.

When I was in first grade, I was asked to carry the crown for the homecoming queen on a pillow. I will never forget that special honor. Now I look at those football suits and what all the boys wore—their helmets and all—and they look like something out of outer space.

We children carried our lunch or came home for lunch until the lunchroom was built by students, teachers, and parents, sponsored by the WPA (Works Progress Administration). The three women who worked in the school kitchen were widows or their husbands made very little money. They were paid by the WPA program. Eating in the lunchroom cost fifty cents a week. My family was one of the few able to pay a dime a day. Other children got free lunches—it was hot food too. (Statistics I've seen indicate that 75 percent of the students received free lunches while only 25 percent could pay.) The money was used to buy items that the WPA didn't provide.

During the Depression years, people didn't have jobs or money. Children in that school were from low on the totem pole to high on the totem pole. That didn't really matter to me about my or their circumstances. Mama especially encouraged us to "never get above our raising"; she kept reminding us that everybody was equal. She meant that we weren't better than others in God's sight; however, it was important for us to go on and make something of ourselves.

The federal government provided commodity foods to the lunch-rooms. We had big porcelain-coated dish pans full of pecan halves. To this day I don't particularly like white beans because we ate so many of them. And chicken—I can't eat it because during the war, chicken was about our only meat. I can see Mama or Effie, the cook at Grandma's house, wringing the chicken's neck, and I can smell the scalding water they poured on the feathers before plucking them. I have never cut up a chicken, much less dressed one. I may be hungry enough and have to do it, but I'm very peculiar about eating chicken to this day. I only ate the pulley bone because it had no skin on it; I refused to eat the skin of a chicken. My feeling must have been prophetic because usually the disease of a chicken is in the skin. My mother wouldn't skin a chicken because she thought it didn't look pretty fried unless it had the skin on it. Believe you me, when I bought a chicken for our family, the skin came off, and Geneva, the cook for Billy and me and the children, showed me how to fry a pretty chicken without the skin.

Eventually the home economics department at Smyrna High School started cooking meals. Miss Henderson, the teacher, rounded up all the mothers who could afford to pay, and Mama sent me over there to eat my lunch. It wasn't because I was too good to eat in the lunchroom, but the home ec department needed to make money to carry on its programs. Miss Henderson hired a cook—Hattie, a little black wiry woman who was fast on her feet—to do some of the cooking for the lunches. One day Hattie asked me if the food was too hot. I replied, "No, it's just right." She said, "Well, I mean hot with pepper or hot with fire." That struck me as funny. Miss Henderson had to teach the entire department, and every girl took home economics and learned how to sew and to cook. I imagine Miss Henderson did more teaching in sewing and left the cooking to Hattie. (Later on in this book Billy is quoted about his theory of home economics and its importance.)

All the Batey cousins lived in the country. The girls were going to high school in Smyrna, and they stayed at our house on the weekends to date. Not all boys had cars, so they must have had to double-date, and my cousins didn't want the boys to drive so far out in the country to pick them up. Also, they might have thought Mama and their grandmother would let them come in later than their parents would.

Evelyn Batey, who now lives in Lake Charles, Louisiana, was dating Bill Barnett. Bill and my daddy were working at Vultee together during the war and carpooling. One night when Bill came to pick up Evelyn, I had already had my bath and was wearing my pajamas. I was sitting in Daddy's lap, and he must have been reading to me or we were listening to the radio. Bill teased me by saying, "Why don't you go with us on a date tonight?" I was out of Daddy's lap like a flash, and I was heading to the stairs to put my clothes on and go. Daddy said, "Hey, you come back here! You're not going anywhere." I was so disappointed; I wanted to find out what happened on a date. Dates were mysterious to me at that age.

My piano lessons began while I was in the first grade. The principal allowed me in the middle of the day to walk to Mrs. Ridley's home, which was near the school. My teacher, Carolyn Manley from Nashville, rode the Greyhound bus to Smyrna and used Mrs. Ridley's piano in the living room to teach lessons. Mrs. Manley in turn gave free piano lessons to Mrs. Ridley's daughter. In those hard times many services were bartered.

Mrs. Manley teamed me with John Norman Barnett. Recitals were always held in the Presbyterian Church. My first recital occurred when I was six years old, and John Norman, who was a year older, and I played a duet on one piano. In years to come we played duets on two pianos, and then Mrs. Manley joined us on a third piano. Precision and timing were essential to play together in duets and trios. John Norman and I played together until I moved away in 1942.

My favorite subject in elementary school was geography. Studying about foreign countries, from the towns to the agriculture, held my interest. As it turned out, I have managed to travel frequently as an adult. The love of geography is still there.

The Song of Russia, a movie with Robert Taylor and Susan Peters, made a deep impression on me. The life of Tchaikovsky, who was one of my favorite composers, was discussed in the course of the movie. Taylor was an American conductor who fell in love with Peters, a musician. They married there in the Orthodox Church, and I recall a crown being held over the man's and woman's heads during the ceremony. From the time I saw that movie I wanted to go to Russia. That desire was fulfilled in the spring of 1992, but I was so disappointed that I never want to go back. Getting to see Tchaikovsky's grave was a special moment, however. (I'll provide more details of the trip later.)

Looking back, I see that I was a homebody. I couldn't keep from crying anytime I was away from my parents. We'd go on a vacation— my two sisters, Mama, Daddy, and me—and I'd even cry to go home. As a youngster, I tried very hard to spend the night with Mama and Daddy Jones at their house, but in the middle of the night Daddy would have to drive from Smyrna to Eagleville and pick me up. I hope my Jones grandparents never thought I didn't love them as much as Grandma Jordan, but I felt I had to get back to where everybody was. Although I'm an active traveler now, I continue to feel the strong need to get back home to the family.

Discipline was fairly strict in our household. Mama spanked me for minor infractions, but Daddy used a leather strap for major infractions—and I'd have to wait for him to come home to do the spanking. I admit that I was a stubborn child, and I had to be disciplined often. Threats of discipline were sometimes enough. However, my parents sometimes punished me for what they considered my talking back to them. They misunderstood my need for explanations of things as my questioning their authority. Based on my childhood

10

Bertha Moon Jones, my paternal grandmother, and Leslie A. Jones, my paternal grandfather.

experience, I tried to be more explicit in explanations with my own children when they came along.

My parents were very entrepreneurial people. They didn't sit around and moan and groan over what we didn't have; they got up and did something about the situation. During the Depression, both of them had means to bring in extra money.

My mother was a good cook. She had many friends in Nashville, and word got around that she made wonderful fruitcakes. Her unusual recipe included buttermilk, which kept the fruitcake moist. By George, she soaked those cakes in the best Jack Daniels she could buy, and bourbon was also an ingredient in each cake. The family didn't drink liquor, but we cooked with it.

Mama would go to the wholesale house and buy the fruit. The citron, shaped like an avocado, was already glazed, but it was not cut up, so we had to cut it as well as the pineapple and the cherries. Because the English walnuts and the pecans were in the shells, we had to crack them and pick out the meat. We did that at night—and no hulls were allowed. Mama steamed the cakes like a plum pudding, then wrapped them in cheesecloth soaked in whiskey and put an apple in each tin box to let them age and keep their moisture. Mama was quite artistic. She made flowers out of the cut fruit and put them on the cakes, wrapped them in cellophane and tied ribbons around them, and delivered her orders in Nashville, many in the Belle Meade area. She charged one dollar per pound, and she sold forty to fifty cakes varying in size from two to ten pounds.

My daddy on his days off went to Bond and Chadwell, a storage company in Nashville. People stored furniture there in the big buildings—floor after floor of cubicles. During the Depression, they couldn't pay for a place to live, so they had to store their belongings. Then things got so bad that they couldn't pay their rent for storage, and their belongings went up for sale. I'd go with Daddy in his Ford pickup, a Model A or T. One auctioneer was balding and had a big white mustache. He asked us not to move or gesture unless we were going to bid. Well, I waved or did something one day, and he knew I wasn't bidding, but he asked if I was. That really embarrassed me.

Daddy bought barrels at Bond and Chadwell, paying a dollar for each one and knowing only that small things were in them. We had a smokehouse, and he put a floor in it and built shelves around the walls. We opened those barrels in there, and going through them was like opening gifts on Christmas. Some of the finest cut glass the family has today—Bohemian glass, turn-of-the-century items—came from there. He sold some of the items to people he knew; he didn't go out and peddle them as such.

That's probably where I get my love for selling antiques. I used to go to auction sales because I never knew what I would run across. Those days are mostly over since people have a better idea of the value of their things, and I find few bargains.

When I decorate houses, I'll rummage around in people's cabinets and pull out things they've inherited or received as wedding presents. I use these items to decorate their shelves with accessories. Seeing what people have stashed away is fun.

Granddaddy Jordan enjoyed taking me to Nashville. Mama got me all dressed up in my hat with the velvet trim, a coat with a velvet collar, and leggings. Leggings were wool pants that fit very tight, almost like jodhpurs, and they had zippers from the midcalf down to the ankle so that we could pull them on. They had a strap like stirrup pants to go across the arch of the foot. They were fitted around the waist with a zipper or buttons, and we little girls wore them under our dresses until we reached a certain age—probably eight or nine. Mama bought our winter coats from the Ruby English Shop on Sixth Avenue and Union, where now stands the office building across from the Hermitage Hotel. Ruby English faced Union. Grandma and Granddaddy took me to eat at Shacklett's Cafeteria on Third or Fourth Avenue. When Shacklett's closed—it was where the new Cain-Sloan building *was* on Fifth and Church—they took me to Kleeman's on Sixth Avenue. (I have recipes from there for apple pie and chicken on egg bread.) When Mr. Shacklett moved up on Church Street and I went there as a young married woman, he still remembered me as a child with all my curly hair.

Grandma and Granddaddy Jordan would bring me and a few of my cousins to the state fair where the fairgrounds are today. Seeing the animals was always a favorite part of the outing, although I'm afraid of most of them. The animals looked so well groomed and tenderly cared for.

Some of my most special memories are of my early years in Smyrna, and they tell something about that time in Middle Tennessee. We always had a telephone in our home. Granddaddy had been listed in the Smyrna telephone directory since 1917, and the phone number was 97. You would have to ring the phone to get the attention of the operator, then give her the number, and she would get your party for you. Until after World War II, you could call long distance, say to Chicago, and if the person you were calling wasn't at home, the operator would keep trying the number and call you back when she finally got the person on the line. That was really service from the telephone company. Long-distance calls were rare; they usually meant someone had died or was dying.

The railroad track running through the middle of town was an important route from here to Florida; the railroads were the L & N and N.C. & Saint L. Passenger trains as well as freight trains came through and stopped in Smyrna.

Something needs to be said here about the railroad track and where people lived. Just because people lived on the "other side" from where we lived didn't signify high class or low class or good or bad houses. The track physically divided the town but didn't socially divide it. Equally nice houses and families were on both sides of the track.

Before the freight train came through Smyrna every afternoon (maybe at four o'clock), the station master, Mr. Shumate, took a long bag of mail and hung it on a tall iron post. The man in the mail car on the train stood in the open door with a long gaffe to hook the mail bag. Many a time I've seen him hook the bag and rip it off and all the mail would go flying everywhere. We children helped the station master pick up the mail when that happened, and he bundled it up again for the next day for another try.

Sometimes Mama and I would get on the train in Smyrna and ride to Murfreesboro to shop, then return home with Daddy. Other days we'd eat lunch, take a nap, have our baths, and get dressed again. (The main meal would be supper in the evening when Daddy came home.) If we weren't going calling with Grandma, we'd sit outside under the shade tree and wait for folks to call on us.

One day in 1937 or 1938 we were all dressed up and sitting under the tree, and both Mama and Grandma were busy crocheting. Down the street came a girl in "men's pants" riding a bicycle. That set Grandma on fire. The bicycle rider, Arabelle, happened to be a distant cousin's child. Well, Grandma got up, went in the house, and called Nell, her mother: "Nell, you get Arabelle off the street. She is wearing men's pants." Poor Grandma would be having her eyes opened up today with the clothes young women wear.

We children weren't allowed to wear pants or shorts. We had romper suits or play suits—the blouse and the shorts were sewn together. We had skirts to put over the shorts, and we were never to leave home without the skirts. One day Ettie Lu decided that she, Frances Owen, and I were going out to the Sam Davis Home for a picnic. She hooked up Lady, the mare, to the buggy. However, our parents didn't think we should take Lady; they thought we should walk the mile, even though we would be on a main highway. That was the first time I'd ever walked a mile in my life. We got so hot on the walk that we unbuttoned our skirts, but we still had them on. We didn't want to get caught without them.

We had our picnic by the creek near the house. As we were coming out of the entrance, a big Cadillac pulled up and stopped.

Somebody in the car said, "Oh, there they are." They were Truman and Mary Ward of Nashville, the ones who owned Maryland Farms and WLAC radio. Our old friends had Andy Devine and his wife in the car with them. Truman had brought the Devines to Smyrna to see us. They had come to our houses, and when we weren't there, our parents told them where we had gone. That was the first time I met a movie star. Andy Devine was in his heyday then.

In many ways I grew up with the advantages of both farm and city life. Daddy had a farm, but we lived in the city with Grandma. A family lived on the farm and took care of it. My grandfather also owned a farm in the same neighborhood where Mama was raised in the Stewarts Creek community. Uncle Roy lived on that farm for many years. Both farms had dairy cows and sold milk to a dairy in Murfreesboro. Eventually Daddy put in a milking machine, which was an oddity to us.

We always had a vegetable garden, and we had fruit trees, so we canned and preserved food. Helping with all those chores was like play to me. The smokehouse had a shed on it with a slanted roof. Grandma sent one of the black men up on the roof, and he put down a clean sheet and placed the fruit on it to dry. He picked up the sheet and fruit at the end of the day and brought it in to keep the dew off. Each day he spread it again until the fruit was completely dry.

Next to the house was a barn for Daddy's horses and cow and Mama's chickens. Daddy would turn up one of the teats while he was milking and squirt it in the other children's mouths, but I never did like warm milk. We'd strain the milk on the back porch. My job every Saturday morning was to churn and make the butter as I got older. We'd have to feed the animals and gather the eggs every day. Putting my hand under a chicken to gather eggs scared me to death. One time a hen pecked my hand, and it went all over me. You'd have thought I would have been afraid of chicken snakes, but snakes have never bothered me—as long as I have a hoe in my hand.

Ettie Lu was very adventuresome, and she had a mare with a walking pony beside her. Uncle Bryan, who didn't know anything about horses, wanted my daddy, who had horses, to help Ettie Lu and teach her to ride. A black man trained horses for Daddy. Daddy always thought black people had a rhythm of training a horse that white people didn't. Back in 1935 and 1936 and 1937, a black man could put a "lick" on a horse that a white man couldn't. Daddy and this black man helped Ettie Lu ride the mare, and the men were breaking the pony, which wanted to go back to the barn every time someone got on his back. He had to be "barn broke."

Upstairs in the loft of our barn were hoboes who jumped off the trains coming through town. We never thought about those men harming us. They never showed their faces while in the barn, but we knew they were there. They would come in the morning to the back door and ask for food. If nothing was left over from breakfast, Grandma, Mama, or Effie, the cook, would fix them a full breakfast and serve the food on china plates to them as they sat on the steps. (Today those concrete steps are left standing, although the house has burned. To me, those steps are a monument to Mama and Grandma.) Then they'd stay the night at the barn and the next day they'd hop on another train.

Age six months, wearing a dress with hairpin trimming made by my paternal great-aunts, which is still in the family.

Caroline Cross

The house, at 124 South Front Street, had been built in 1895 and burned around 1995. Granddaddy had added on a sun porch and had done extensive remodeling. After it was no longer used as a residence, it had become an insurance agency and then a day care center. Frances Owen, who used to live next door, and I stopped by the site one day, and seeing the remains of that burned-out house made me feel as if a part of my childhood had gone up in smoke too. Although both of us had on sunglasses that day, each could see tears rolling down the other's cheeks.

Effie Smith, a widow, came to work as a cook for Grandma before Mama and Daddy and I moved to Smyrna. She made five dollars a week and worked seven days a week, except on her Communion Sunday, which was once a month. She arrived every morning while we were eating breakfast and stayed through supper. We ate supper in

James William Cross III about two years old.

17

the dining room every night with a tablecloth on the table, but for breakfast and lunch we ate in the kitchen. Daddy was a big tease and was always cutting up with Effie. Especially on Monday after the weekend, he'd say, "Who got killed at Basham's Store?" Basham's was a general store between the white and the black sections of town. Effie walked to work, and her route from her home, which she owned, to our home took her by that store each day. Sure enough a lot of killings happened there—both black and white.

Effie worked for Grandma ten or twelve years in all; she no longer worked for the family after we moved in 1942. Effie's brother owned a barbershop on Lafayette Street in Nashville, and in later years after she retired and we lived in Nashville, we would go there and pick her up and bring her out to the house on Sterling Road to visit.

Lily Bee was Effie's daughter, and she had two children, Forrestine and Bubba. Effie sometimes brought them to work with her, and Frances Owen, Ettie Lu, and I played with them. Lily Bee had a wild streak. One night she was out with a man and she was stabbed. She did recover, and Mama helped Effie get a lawyer for Lily Bee. One morning Effie brought with her a big cardboard suit box filled with Lily Bee's bloody clothes. I desperately wanted to see those clothes, but I was too young, and they wouldn't let me. I wanted to go to the trial in Murfreesboro, but I wasn't allowed to do that either. Lily Bee lived mostly in Chicago, and that's why Effie often had the grandchildren. There was a pattern even then. Those strong black women kept the families going because the men were absent. (In my lifetime black people have used at least four means of identification for themselves: colored, Negro, black, and African Americans, in that order historically. I prefer to use "black.")

Watching Effie cook fascinated me. One day she was preparing cornmeal muffins in fluted iron muffin pans. She had mixed up the batter and was about to pour it when I told her that she had forgotten the soda. I was quite young, but I had watched enough to know the ingredients. Effie or Mama would give me batter when she made cakes or cornbread so that I could cook in a little electric stove for children. I haven't seen a stove like it since then.

The wood stove stayed in the kitchen until we moved. We cooked on it only when the electricity went out. We had an electric stove, too, but with electricity being so new, Grandma could not bring herself to trust it. The first refrigerator had that round thing on the top. My parents must have had an ice box at some time, but I don't remember one. I do remember the first electric coffee percolator that Grandma bought; it was a huge porcelain percolator at least two feet tall. Mama, Grandma, and I went regularly to the programs put on by the TVA home economists. That early influence must have had something to do with my determining to major in home economics in college. The cooking demonstrations were my favorite parts. The TVA was beginning to heavily promote the use of electrical appliances. After Aunt Minnie, Mama's sister, remodeled her house, which was built in the late 1920s, her "modern" kitchen was the focus of TVA ads. Now its "modern" features would be laughable because kitchen conveniences have come so far.

Reuben and Hazel, a black couple, worked for Uncle Bryan and Aunt Dixie. Reuben kept the yard, helped Ettie Lu with the horses at the barn, and did the housework. Hazel was the cook. Uncle Bryan and Aunt Dixie often had people such as the governor and other dignitaries over for a meal. Daddy knew that Aunt Dixie was to have a highfalutin dinner party one evening. Reuben wore a white coat when he served, and Aunt Dixie got him all groomed up for the party. Daddy, with his strong sense of humor, must have been trying to put Aunt Dixie in her place because he took Reuben out to the barn and got him so drunk that he couldn't serve at the party. This event, I fear, seems to be harder on Reuben than on Aunt Dixie, however.

Daddy befriended two black brothers, Ernest and Sam Cage Cannon. They couldn't hear or speak. Daddy didn't know sign language, but somehow he communicated with them. They were the best workers and were good with horses. They lived in their own house if you could call it that. One Sunday morning I went to their house with Daddy, and even as a child, I was bothered by how they lived. But Daddy was good to them and helped them as much as he could. Our family was always looking after the unfortunate. They worked for Daddy for many years. I don't know what happened to them. Maybe they got better jobs or moved away, or maybe we moved away. They were probably in their mid-twenties to thirties at the time.

Mama often drove to Murfreesboro to shop or visit, and sometimes Effie and I went along to go to the movies. We had to sit in the third balcony reserved for blacks because Effie couldn't sit below with me. Much of what that meant in society escaped me then since I was so young. I do know that we had horrible seats up there, and I couldn't understand why Effie couldn't sit with me where I wanted to sit. After all, Effie was like a part of our family. I'm glad conditions are better now.

For one Christmas, Mama and Daddy bought me a pair of male and female black dolls. They were composition dolls with painted-on hair. I named them Forrestine and Bubba for Effie's grandchildren, which shows my affection for them.

My first doll's name was Polly Peaches. She probably wasn't famous like the Shirley Temple doll, though. I did have a Deanna Durbin doll. Frances Owen got a doll of Sonja Henie, a famous ice skater, and Ettie Lu got a Madame Alexander doll of Princess Elizabeth, who is now the queen. We all had paper dolls too. Frances Owen and Ettie Lu had a table-sized dollhouse in their attic, and we had many good times with it.

At the hardware store Daddy bought me little rooms of painted metal furniture that cost twenty-five cents per room. During the Depression, that quarter must have come hard for him. A dollhouse was high on my "want list," but that want wasn't met until after I married, and Billy and I had a large dollhouse, about eight by ten feet, built for Amy out in the yard.

Ettie Lu, Frances Owen, and I made a teepee out of tow sacks (heavy burlap sacks). We went across the street to two feed mills that ground wheat and corn, and we got the sacks from them. Then we asked the men at the mills for long needles and took twine and sewed the teepee cover together. Reuben made the poles and wrapped the sacks around them. That was our first playhouse.

We used to hang sheets on the clothesline with the middle of the sheet over the line. It looked like a tent, so we children ran through there and played. We were pleased with the simplest and most basic playthings. After winter was over, it was like a tent city when Mama and Grandma hung out all the blankets to air before putting them away for the summer.

My first bicycle was from Montgomery Ward. It had skirt guards on the back tire, so my skirt wouldn't get caught in the spokes. Remember we were not allowed to wear pants. As far as I was concerned, those guards looked awful, but Daddy was being protective as always. In our neighborhood were sidewalks, which made it easy to ride bikes and roller-skate.

Birthdays were not celebrated in any major way—no cakes or parties at my birthday or at anyone else's. I did get presents, however.

We children went to the post office twice a day because there were two deliveries. Our family had a box there, but I never learned the combination; to this day I'm not good at combinations. It was 1952 before Smyrna had home delivery of mail. Miss Nell Coleman was the postmistress, and she handed me the mail. Miss Marguerite Coleman, Miss Nell's husband's cousin, worked in the post office with her. Marguerite and I celebrated our birthdays together. Marguerite did beautiful monogramming by hand, and I still have tablecloths, napkins, sheets, and handkerchiefs that she monogrammed for me over the years.

In my younger years in Smyrna there were two grocery stores. Later there were three. But there was no dime store or anything like that. We didn't have any money to spend, like children have now. My parents didn't pay me for doing chores around the house, and there were plenty of them.

The family had helpers—whether white or black—at home and at the farm, but my parents and my grandmother participated in all the work. The family really did hire people to be helpers and not doers of everything that needed to be done. They taught me that I was to be in there doing the work with the helpers, and that's a lesson I've learned well.

The washing was done in a washing machine with a wringer out in the smokehouse. There were no plumbing connections. A hose brought in the water, and a pipe drained the water out in the yard. We had hot water in the house but none for the wash, so the hot water to wash in had to be boiled. A washerwoman named Queen also did the ironing for us; she did Aunt Dixie's laundry too. Sometimes Ettie Lu, Frances Owen, and I hitched up Lady to the buggy and took the washed clothes to Queen's house, and later we picked them up. We had to ford a little creek to get there.

Daddy and/or the men killed hogs at the farm. After our marriage, I told Billy I would love to do that, and he thought I was crazy as a bedbug. Killing hogs is a lot of work, but nothing tastes any better than the tenderloin right after the hog is killed. At the same time my grandmother made lye soap in a big black pot outside with a fire under it.

We made our own sausage with a sausage mill. Mama sewed the sacks for the sausage out of brown domestic material. She folded the material, stitched it at the bottom and up one side, and left the tops open so that the sacks could be stuffed. Then we hung the sacks in the smokehouse. Billy and I made sure that we had a smokehouse at Tuck-A-Way, and we smoked sausage and hams. We bought the sausage at the packing house in cloth bags and gave it as Christmas presents to customers, which is a tradition I continue. The packing house uses a mouth-watering recipe.

In general I was a cowardly child who was afraid to try many new things. Ettie Lu led Frances Owen and me, but even still I was reluctant to go along with some of her ideas. I probably saved her life many a time by holding back.

For example, I never learned to swim properly. I almost drowned when I was walking in the pool at the Cedars of Lebanon State Park and slipped and fell. We were there for a family reunion. Mama was in the pool—and she didn't swim either—but she picked me up. Fortunately we were in shallow water. Daddy didn't want me to learn to swim; he was afraid I would have an accident and drown. He told us that he would never own a swimming pool because as a young man, he was crossing the campus of what is now MTSU and saw a child who had drowned floating in the pool. In college I managed to jump off the diving board and swim to the side of the pool, which was enough to pass the course and get credit, but that is the extent of my swimming ability. I'm scared of water, even though I love to tarpon fish in Florida. Mary and Linda did learn how to swim.

From the time I was born I went to church. Belief in and obedience to God were integral in the lives of both sets of grandparents. In 1922 my grandmother and grandfather, Ettie and Arch Jordan, and their children—Bryan, Minnie, Ruth, Herbert, and Roy—were listed as members of the Smyrna Church of Christ, which was built in that year. The other three children—Ernest, Maggie, and Charlie—had left home by then. Granddaddy Jordan literally believed that what you had belonged to God, and that idea passed down to his descendants.

In those days in Smyrna the church didn't have a preacher every Sunday for the morning service, and there were no Wednesday night services. There was no Sunday night service on a regular basis either. Most of the preachers who came from Nashville to Smyrna were professors at Lipscomb. Each congregation did then and still does its own hiring and firing of preachers; it's an autonomous body.

During a gospel meeting, which lasted one or two weeks, the preacher and his wife stayed at our house. The meeting featured two daily services—one in the morning and one in the evening—held at the church. There was always a Sunday evening service then too. The men were working and were not really expected to come in the morning; that service was more for the women and children.

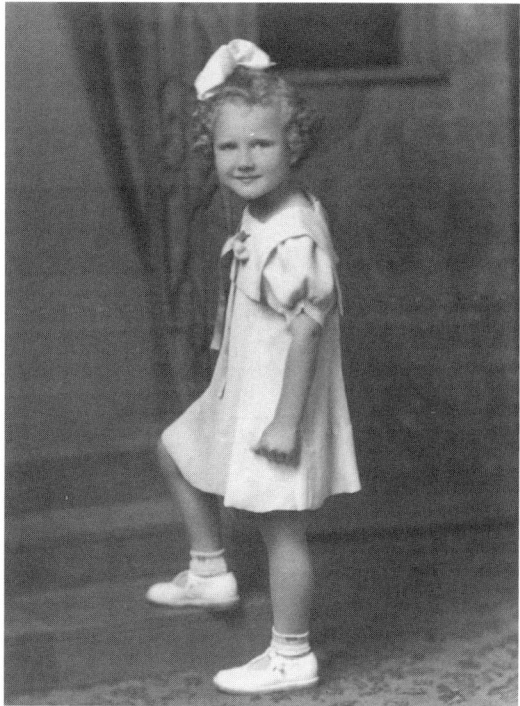

Age four—note the curly hair like Shirley Temple's.

The Smyrna church didn't have vacation Bible school, but it did have Sunday school. Churches in the larger cities may have had vacation Bible school. Things changed everywhere during the war, so it's hard to make comments in general about what was happening even in Middle Tennessee.

Going to church was an integral part of my early years, and it has continued to be throughout my life. Everything revolved around church. I went to school with the people I went to church with, my parents worked with people who went to our church, and they were our neighbors. Being a member of the church was an extension of being a member of the community. Some people may not have chosen to stay in the church they were reared in, but I have. The churches in Smyrna included Baptist, Methodist, Presbyterian, and Church of Christ. All of them had their own church buildings. We'd go to their gospel meetings and they'd come to ours. It wasn't a divided-across-the-denominations issue. There were no Jewish or Catholic or Episcopalian places of worship, but there were the Holy Rollers (I realize that's a politically incorrect term, but that was what they were called at the time).

The bus ran up Old Highway 41 coming from Nashville, and Smyrna was about a mile off that highway. Mama's younger brother, Uncle Roy, was coming home from Lipscomb one weekend on the late bus. He was walking by the Holy Rollers' church, and the people were shouting and rolling in the floor. He was so scared that he ran the rest of the way home—and there he was a college student.

Right behind the Holy Rollers' church the first water tank was built in Smyrna, and the city's name was written on it for all to see. The city felt as if it had arrived!

Later on when I was older and living in Nashville, I participated in the youth groups at church. They were fun. I never felt that I *had* to do those things. Our family never thought of churchgoing as a duty; it was a part of our lives.

Grandma prepared the Communion service every week for the Smyrna Church of Christ. She made the grape juice from grapes, which then fermented, and she made the Communion bread. On a weekday we went to the church and picked up the Communion cups, which were little individual glasses; my job was to wash them, scald them, and dry them. Then we'd go to the church on Saturday and set up the Communion table. There was a white cloth on it, and we'd cover up the wine and bread with another white cloth. We had Communion every Sunday then as we do now.

When Mama was growing up out in the county at Stewarts Creek, the church had only one cup, a silver chalice. I don't know where that is now. People would go to the front of the church to the Communion table instead of men serving it to the congregation in the pews. The oldest Church of Christ in London, which is more than one hundred years old, still uses a silver chalice, but that is a rare practice these days.

Most family members were married at churches, but some were married at home. They were probably married by the same minister who married their parents too. When Ettie Lu married in San Antonio, Uncle Bryan and Aunt Dixie sent back for S. P. Pittman, a professor at Lipscomb and the minister who married them. Uncle Bryan met him at the airport and took him to be outfitted in tails, which all the men were to wear in the wedding. Professor Pittman truly was like the proverbial absent-minded professor who never cared about his looks. He was very educated, read Hebrew and Greek, and taught both. He did love the champagne fountain and tested it out at the reception.

We had a welfare system as such in the early 1930s. Several families in Smyrna were getting commodities, and Mama volunteered to be the one to distribute the commodities. Looking after people seemed to be her calling. Again the giving of self, typical of the family, became evident. People from the state brought big sacks of rice, beans, flour, and such and also brought smaller sacks that we had to fill. We divided the commodities equally among the families whose names were provided by the state of Tennessee.

Going to those houses really made impressions on me. As I recall, many of the recipients were women and children but no men. There were some older people. They lived in tar paper shacks. No indoor plumbing. No water. I went to school with children who barely had shoes on their feet and not many clothes. This early example of Mama's helping the less fortunate made me aware that I was clothed, I had food and shelter, and both parents lived at home. This experience showed me how the other half of the world lived. One of Grandma Jordan's favorite expressions was, "One half of the world doesn't know how the other half lives—and they don't much care." But our family did care and tried to do something about it.

My two sisters are Mary, who is five years younger than I am, and Linda, who is ten years younger. Mary Virginia was born in Smyrna at home on January 7, 1936. It cost too much to go to the hospital then. The town had two doctors who made house calls, and Dr. Shipp delivered her. Mama and Daddy sent me next door to stay with Aunt Dixie and Uncle Bryan. Mama's pregnancy was not kept from me, but they didn't let me stay at home during the actual birth. Mary looked exactly like Daddy and had dark hair. Both Mary and Linda were bathed in a portable table-height bathtub called a bathinet. It was rubber and could be folded up. I thoroughly enjoyed helping at bath time. Mama let me pick out their clothes—the day gowns and booties to match. Grandma didn't like for Mama and Daddy to correct Mary and then later Linda. We grandchildren could do no wrong. Mary started school while we were living in Una.

Linda Ruth arrived January 6, 1941, in Murfreesboro Hospital, where I was born. (The facade on that hospital is the same as it was when I came into the world.) Daddy Jones died that year. Linda had auburn hair and looked like Mama, except for her eyes. That is, Linda had auburn hair when it finally grew in. She took forever to grow her hair. I used to rock her on our sun porch in one of the high-backed wicker rockers, and she would turn over and stick her head down in the crook of my arm.

We left Smyrna after I finished the fifth grade. I remember all my teachers there. I've told you about Mrs. Ward, my first grade teacher. My second grade teacher taught me the love of birds. On the Arm and Hammer soda boxes there used to be colored pictures of birds with information about them, their habits, and so on. Miss Elizabeth Everett Lowry, a small, wiry woman, was my teacher. She also taught us about the Leaning Tower of Pisa. In my mind I can still see the picture of it that she put on the bulletin board; forty-three years ago I finally saw the real thing in person.

The summer after I was in her second grade class, she gathered us children up, and we walked through town looking for birds and

My childhood home in Smyrna. It looked like this just before it burned in 1995.

trying to identify them. Today I'm scared of birds, but I love them from afar. I have a book in the breakfast room so that I can identify birds at the feeders.

My third grade teacher was Miss Gladys Potts, who was also my Sunday school teacher. I had a double dose. I couldn't do anything wrong; I had to march a straight line that year at school and church. Mrs. Ruby Goodman was my fourth grade teacher, and my fifth grade teacher was Miss Davis, who later married Charles Hodge.

My piano lessons continued through my grade school years and beyond. When we moved to Una because of Daddy's job there, I caught the Greyhound bus on Saturday to go to Mrs. Manley's studio in Nashville, on Eighth Avenue above Claude P. Street's Piano Company.

In sixth grade I entered Una School, but somehow I wasn't prepared for that year. I went there for seventh and eighth grades too. I was the most unhappy camper you have ever known. I hated living there. We didn't have the closeness of the little town that I had known in Smyrna, and most of all I didn't see Ettie Lu and Frances Owen as often as I liked. The school had the sixth and seventh grades in one room, which was a new—and unpleasant—experience for me. Una was growing then in the war years, and Vultee was making planes for the war and bringing in people to do the work. My sixth

2222ок

grade teacher was Miss Lenora Harrell, later the principal of Palmer School and headmistress of Harding Academy.

Mrs. Ellis was my teacher in the seventh grade. She was diagnosed with cancer, and I had substitute teachers nearly all year. Then Mrs. A. H. Roberts, daughter-in-law of the former governor A. H. Roberts, came to fill the position. She didn't teach us anything, but she was like a breath of fresh air with her big diamonds and beautiful clothes.

In the eighth grade the principal was my teacher. Her personality wasn't conducive to teaching younger students (she was more geared to working with senior high students), so I didn't learn anything that year either.

Our family did become close to several families in the church in Una—the Neals, the Andrews, the Ezells, and the Hogans. If it had not been for those families and more, we would have been even unhappier there.

In Una our newly built house sat on six acres, and that allowed Daddy to have horses. He also chose to have goats and calves. Daddy bought the calves not weaned from the mothers, and we fed them on a bottle until they were at the veal stage. Until that time he had milk cows with calves. He always said that all he could have were baby girls and male calves. He wanted a heifer calf. Raising the calves was a hobby for him because he loved to fool with animals.

While we were living in Una, Mama and Aunt Dixie, who came from Smyrna, would turn Ettie Lu, Frances Owen, and me loose in Nashville, and we would usually go to the movie. Loew's would not let patrons bring in any food; the theater didn't even sell popcorn. The Krystal was new, and nothing smelled any better to me than a Krystal hamburger. They'd put the buns on top of the hamburgers with the onions and all that grease—out on the street you could smell them cooking. On one outing we decided to buy some Krystal hamburgers. Well, Ettie Lu, being the daredevil, thought we could take them to the movie with us. She said, "They'll never know we have them." The ushers descended on us the minute we opened that sack, and they took our hamburgers away from us! I kept telling her, "I told you so!"

CHAPTER 2

Years of Transition

> *There are many things worse than war.*
> *Slavery is worse than war.*
> *Dishonour is worse than war.*
> *—Sir Winston Churchill*

The history of World War II and that period has always intrigued me. That may sound morbid—what with all the devastation and deaths and the Holocaust. Being in Europe in 1955, I saw all those places I had heard about as a child. Very little had been rebuilt in most cities even then.

Everyone, adults and children alike, hung by the radio during the war, and I was no exception. H. V. Kaltenborn was the news commentator. Uncle Bryan and my daddy listened to all those reports. No one was to utter a word; we were to sit there and listen to the radio. Our radio was a big Philco floor model, the latest thing available, and Daddy bought it before the war started. Thank goodness, he did because after war was declared, only war-related items were built. We could hear shortwave reports from all around the world, even Hitler's speeches. We couldn't understand a word he said, but we could tell that he sounded like a lunatic. We used a globe to follow where the people were and the places being mentioned.

Aunt Dixie and Uncle Bryan sailed to Europe in the late 1930s, first class on an ocean liner. Aunt Dixie had an evening dress for every night on the ship, and Uncle Bryan had his tuxedos and dinner jackets. Upstairs in one of her bedrooms she had all her clothes laid out for us to see before she packed. She had the purse, shoes, and hat to match each outfit.

At age six or seven, my first piano recital. The dress was Mama's that she wore when she sang solos at events.

They were on trains where Hitler's car was attached. They were just getting out as he was marching in to Poland, Hungary, and Austria. Their experiences whetted my appetite to want to go to Europe. Aunt Dixie came back and spoke about their trip at the school and other places. All attention was focused on Europe.

Despite our listening to all those radio reports, I never heard anything about the Jews being persecuted. I learned about it, though, before I went to Germany to live. Jimmy Gentry, who lives in Franklin, was among the first troops to enter Dachau, and to this day, he can barely talk about it. I asked him if the American people or the soldiers, for that matter, were aware of the Jews being persecuted. He said no. Reports I have read indicate that Roosevelt and government officials knew it; their failure to tell the American people about it really bothers me.

In 1941 on the day when the Japanese attacked Pearl Harbor, we had been out to Mama and Daddy Jones's house for Sunday lunch. We came back to our house, not knowing what had happened. There was no radio in the car, and we had not been listening to the radio at my grandparents' house. As we walked in the door of the house, Grandma Jordan said, "Did you know that there may be a war on?" All of us gathered around to hear the radio and discuss things.

During World War II, Daddy was declared 4-F because of a problem with his knee. He was sent to Vultee to do defense work instead of active duty in the service. In my early life, he was in charge of the public works in Rutherford County, keeping the roads maintained and the weeds cut. He lost that job because of political changes, and the draft happened about then. He was put on the flight line to swing compasses, that is, he would pull the planes off the assembly line and set the compasses. He was very ingenious and kept coming up with new ideas, and Vultee rewarded employees for ideas to make work more efficient. Daddy received several five- and ten-dollar prizes for that. He was concerned about the pilots because a lot of them were crashing in their planes. He was such a sensitive person, I don't see how he stood the trauma.

Grandma said, "In World War I, I sent two fine sons off." One was Uncle Ernest, a conscientious objector who served in the Hospital Corps. When a bomb hit the French hospital where he was on duty, he was buried under dirt and debris, but someone knew where he was and dug him out. He had shrapnel in his ankle that was never removed. The other son was Uncle Charlie, who was in the navy. He was in a battle on the water at the same time there was a big storm. He was not mentally ready for all that war involved—the dying and the killing. Before the war, he was a professional baseball player.

Later on, Grandma said she felt that we could never trust the Germans because they plotted war all the time. She had been through both world wars, and her two sons suffered as a result of war. One recovered mentally but had physical damage; the other one never recovered mentally. At the end of the war Uncle Charlie and Uncle Ernest came back to work on a farm that Granddaddy bought for them. Their parents thought that working the land would help them after their experiences and they could find themselves again.

31

Uncle Ernest did, but not Uncle Charlie. Uncle Charlie spent many years in the Veterans Hospital, and he died there. He was a very distinguished man who dressed in a suit and tie every day. He looked just like his father.

During World War II, some families chose to hang a silk banner with a red border in the window. In the middle was a blue star for each son that the household had sent to war. When one was killed, they took off a blue star and put up a gold star. More than one gold star hung in some windows, and seeing that, even as a child, did something to you. Families received a telegram when a relative died. Some of my girl cousins had husbands in the war, and we were fortunate not to lose any family members in death.

A frequent sight was the train cars filled with scrap iron going by on the railroad near our house. Before World War II the scrap iron was sold to Japan—and it might have even been made into armaments. That was big business for people coming out of the Depression. We wouldn't have emerged from that Depression for many, many years if it had not been for World War II.

FDR did some things that have caused the people a lot of misery—financial misery—in this country. However, I don't think he intended for some of the programs he created to go on forever. Social security was a great thing when it was set up, but now the politicians are borrowing from it, which goes against the intent of the fund. In the final analysis, FDR was our savior. Too many people today don't remember how bad off we were after that Depression. Based on what I have heard about and read about the Civil War, we probably were in just as bad a time with the Depression.

Going to Nashville was really a trip. The Old 41 Highway was two lanes but in pretty good shape. Grandma said she'd live to see the day that Murfreesboro and Nashville would meet. They have done that, and she almost saw it. It probably took us an hour or an hour and a half to drive from Smyrna to Nashville when we had a good-running car before the war. After the war started was a different story.

This generation knows nothing about rationing. In the war years Mama would drive from Una to Smyrna to see about Grandma. We worried that the old car might not make it, but we couldn't get parts or buy a new car. To make sure that Mama had enough gas to get home, Daddy acquired some black market stamps for extra gas. The car would overheat on the Old Murfreesboro Road, and we would have to get water from a nearby house to pour in the radiator. The tires wore thin, and we could only get them retreaded. Tires and gasoline were on the rationed list, and each household had ration cards that allowed the purchase of only certain amounts of certain goods.

Sugar, meat, and coffee were rationed. People who wouldn't usually think of raising their own vegetables started victory gardens to supplement their diets, but our family was used to doing that.

Silk stockings were virtually impossible to obtain, and nylon stockings were not yet available. To get them repaired, Mama took her silk stockings to a woman who sat in the back of the old Cain-Sloan building (it was in what is now Saint Cloud's Corner). The stocking repair lady was near the post office by the drinking fountain. She had a harsh light with a magnifying glass, and she used a pick to grasp the silk thread and reweave it all by hand. It probably didn't cost a quarter a run to repair.

My parents cautioned me not to put my mouth on a drinking fountain, and I obeyed them. Nevertheless, I got trench mouth at the drinking fountain in Cain-Sloan. There must have been a germ in the water coming up over the spout. My parents brought me to the dentist in Nashville to be treated. I can't remember what he did, but I still hate going to the dentist. Later on I had to have my wisdom teeth painfully extracted because they were growing in horizontally, and I'm sure that didn't improve my attitude toward the dentist. It's difficult to deaden my mouth or any part of my body.

We children didn't dare leave food on our plates. That was a sin in my grandmother's eyes. Our parents and grandmother constantly reminded us of all those poor starving children on the other side of the world who were suffering because of the war. If we had a weight problem, we blamed it on those poor starving children.

Everyone did something for the war effort. Although we didn't call it recycling, we children gathered tin cans and smashed them flat. Then we carried a grocery sack full of them to school. Whoever brought in the most was awarded an $18.75 war bond, which matured to $25.00. Cigarette packages had aluminum foil, and we'd separate that out and make blocks of foil. We also carried in all of our papers.

At school each week we bought war stamps and put them in a book until we had enough to buy a war bond. My uncles bought war bonds, and I tried to get to them to buy one from me before somebody else did because my school could have credit for that. One uncle bought a $100 bond, and that was like $1 million to me.

People, probably local celebrities, came to the schools to hold war bond rallies. I don't remember any movie stars coming to Middle Tennessee, but I recall when Carole Lombard was killed on a trip to sell war bonds.

Women started wearing pants acceptably during the war years because they had to go to work and take men's places. It was better and safer for them to wear pants, and a uniform was cheaper than a dress.

Nashville was packed with soldiers. Because Middle Tennessee has a terrain like that of Germany and much of Europe, much training occurred here. With the maneuvers they were all over the place. We'd go out the back door while we were still in Smyrna and see soldiers getting water out of the hydrant. We'd see them in convoys. Some soldiers bivouacked on our farm, and our family often invited soldiers to eat with us. We never knew much more about them than their names; we just knew they were lonesome young men. Mama and Grandma thought that if they were their sons, they would want someone looking after them.

Nancy Newsom Morton, who later married Constantine Jordan. I was named Nancy for her.

The Smyrna Air Base began construction just before we moved to Una. Engineers and contractors were coming in from all over the country, but there were no motels in Smyrna to provide a place for them to stay. Grandma had an

34

extra bedroom and rented it to Keith Taylor, a Vanderbilt graduate who worked for a construction company in Memphis. He was courting some girls in Nashville. We children hid nearby and eavesdropped on his conversations with his girlfriends while he talked on the telephone. In those days, like most families, we had only one telephone, and it was in a prominent place in the house, which didn't permit much privacy.

When the war was winding down, our family underwent a major change. Daddy became interested in real estate with his farm background and all of his knowledge of construction (he worked on the War Memorial Building as a young man). He started selling real estate for Uncle Herbert's company, and he went on to become a land developer and a builder. He first was into residential building in Nashville, then got into industrial and commercial building, including truck terminals in Nashville. From Una we moved to Sterling Road off Golf Club Lane in 1944.

Uncle Herbert had married Evelyn Ward from Elkton, Kentucky, whom he met at Lipscomb. In the late 1930s or early 1940s, Uncle Herbert bought the Folk Real Estate Company, started by the Folk family, and he renamed it the Folk-Jordan Real Estate Company. He and Evelyn had no children for the first ten years they were married, but then had Dan, who is now the owner of Folk-Jordan. Uncle Herbert let me start working at age sixteen in his office, doing office work and answering the telephone. This was at 214 Union Street, the old Rogers Caldwell Office Building.

I thought I was really something—riding the bus to my job downtown, getting to eat lunch downtown with all the other workers. Uncle Herbert was so patient with me. I knew how to type just a little, but it was my first learning experience in an office. I loved it; I had the job for three years in the summers until he became one of the commissioners of a new state commission, the Tennessee Real Estate Commission. That was when they started licensing real estate men and women as salespersons or as brokers. Uncle Herbert realized that would be a good place for me, so in my senior summer I went to work in the Commission office.

While I was in college, I continued to work during school vacations; I had the month of December off at Lipscomb, and that was the relicensing month, so I had plenty of work to do. I helped grade the tests that the people took and also went to the three sections of the state with the commissioners when they put on seminars to explain all the new procedures in regard to real estate sales. They were trying to bring professional status to the real estate industry. Uncle Herbert was the commissioner for Middle Tennessee. He also served in local, state, and national positions in various real estate organizations. His son, Dan, has followed in his footsteps. Uncle Herbert and Aunt Evelyn would include me in a lot of things they were doing.

Unfortunately Uncle Herbert died in his middle fifties. He was on Old Hickory Lake on his houseboat. He had eaten supper, told Aunt Evelyn and another couple that he was going to take a walk while the women cleaned up the kitchen, and left. He was going over the gang-plank, had a heart attack, and fell over—dead by the time he hit the water.

Every Saturday I went out to the buildings or houses Daddy was building, and I helped him by writing checks and keeping books with the plain old debit and credit system. His books were little ledgers he bought at the dime store, and each house had a separate ledger. It was a basic system, yet efficient. His houses were brick and sold from $17,500 to $25,000 in the late 1940s and early 1950s.

Daddy, Uncle Herbert, and Uncle Roy were the first to develop in Donelson, and two areas were Merry Oaks and Donelson Meadows. They weren't in partnership: Uncle Herbert developed the lot, Daddy bought the lot and built the house, and Uncle Roy sold the real estate. All business enterprises were separate because in families it's not always wise to do business together.

Starting to Hillsboro High School, I was really behind. The other students came from good schools such as Stokes, Woodmont, and Parmer. I was a lost ball in high weeds, and it hurt. I hadn't had the solid background I needed to do well in high school. If I had stayed in Smyrna, I might have been able to make the move better. Remember, Una was a poor educational experience.

Where Green Hills Shopping Center is now, fields were surrounded by a stacked stone fence. The area was not yet built up at all. Students were only allowed to cross the road and sit on that fence;

we weren't supposed to roam far from the school. There was a honky-tonk or hamburger joint near where Richard Jones Road is now. The boys would go down that way and smoke, and maybe some girls too.

In my freshman year I was eligible to ride the school bus. Mama's oldest niece, Margaret Batey, had moved with us to the Sterling Road house. She taught Spanish at Hillsboro High where she always had students in the Spanish contest, both local and state. Margaret and I walked together from Sterling Road to Medial Avenue and down to Woodlawn to the bus stop. Later the mileage limit was changed and we were not eligible to ride the bus, so Daddy took Margaret and me in the morning and Mama picked up in the afternoon. Margaret lived with us for my four years in high school. (Then she went to Mrs. Caldwell's boardinghouse on Twenty-first Avenue. Much later she went to the Stephen Foster Apartments, and from there she moved into her first condominium, which she bought in her later seventies.)

Riding the school bus in Una or in Nashville was my least favorite activity in the world. In Una my parents told me never to get in the car with anybody who would stop; they never told me why, though. People would stop while I was waiting at the bus stop and insist that I let them take me to school or to my piano lessons. I might have even known the people, but I'd never get in the car because my parents told me not to.

Riding the train was a different story. Aunt Amy took me, her sister's child, Andrea Rogers, and Margaret Batey on a trip to New York and Washington, D.C.; we set out in July 1946 for a three-week excursion. I had just had my fifteenth birthday. When Daddy put me on the train in Union Station under that big shed, he cried like a baby because I was leaving him. He never did like for me to leave.

Ten-year-old Andrea wrote an account of the trip, and excerpts are included here. We started in Niagara Falls at Uncle Jess's house (he was Daddy's oldest brother). Andrea noted, "Caroline's Aunt Mable was a little woman who used funny expressions like: 'something the cat dragged in and the dog refused' or 'something that jumped out of King Tut's tomb backwards.'" I apparently spent a lot of time looking for a husband for Margaret Batey on the trip because Andrea remarked about it in her account.

The next leg of the journey was the train ride to Albany, New York. We were to leave late at night, so we had sleepers. Andrea wrote,

> We rang for the porter but there was no porter, so Aunt Amy decided she didn't need a ladder to climb to the upper berth,—we seemed to have the whole car to ourselves as far as we could see, so Aunt Amy took up her gown (Uncle Ernest had told her to wear pajamas on the trip but her gown was newer) and she scrambled and scratched around and nearly fell. Finally we gave her a boost and she made it. We had a lot of fun seeing somebody nearly a hundred years old turning into an acrobat.

We got off in Albany but nearly lost our bags. They were put off the train while we were in the ladies' room.

We took a boat on the Hudson River. Andrea commented that "white people and colored all ride together up North on trains, boats and street cars." We ended up in New York City and stayed at the Taft Hotel. We went to Radio City and sat in on a radio broadcast. We saw the plays *Song of Norway*, which was the music of Edward Grieg, and *Harvey* with Frank Fay playing the part of Elmo P. Dowd. (To this day, I love the story, but I think the movie with Jimmy Stewart was much better than the play.) We also took in Sak's, the Empire State Building, and Macy's.

Next we went on to Philadelphia and then Washington, D.C., where we stayed at the Statler. Andrea called it "the finest hotel in Washington." We did the city with museums, galleries, and the Capitol. While there we saw President Truman. That trip was an educational experience of a wonderful sort.

Hillsboro and West were two of the best public high schools in the area. Hillsboro was a county school, and its curriculum was tougher than that of most other schools in the county. The feeling was that everybody at Hillsboro would likely go to college, so the students needed to be prepared. For example, students were required to take two years of Latin before we could take French or Spanish, and we had to take three years of sciences and math. The requirements applied to everybody, not just students on a special academic track.

A family picture of the Jordans and the earliest picture of Mama; she was seven just before Ernest and Charlie left for the war in 1914. First row, left to right, Minnie, Arch, Roy, Ettie, and Ruth (my mother). Second row, left to right, Bryan, Ernest, Maggie, Charlie, and Herbert. Taken at W. G. Thuss Studio in Nashville.

Today the courses would be identified as college preparatory level. All of high school was hard for me. I had to repeat algebra because I knew nothing about it. The other boys and girls had a good background in it.

Dorothy Jean, a first cousin (Uncle Roy and Aunt Katie's daughter), was in high school with me for a while. Her family moved to Florida, though, after a year or so. Dorothy Jean had been in Donelson before moving to the west side of town.

My activities showed my early leadership abilities. I was in the Junior Civinette Club, which promoted citizenship within the home, school, and community. Membership was limited to junior and senior girls of good standing, and I was an officer in the club.

The students had a carnival to raise money to build a stadium at Hillsboro. That thrilled me to death because we competed to raise money. My fund-raising probably started then. Daddy gave a nice amount, and other people gave me contributions too.

Anything musical appealed to me, and the operettas were no exception. I loved singing and being in the chorus. We did *HMS Pinafore* and the *Pirates of Penzance*.

In my sophomore year the doctors thought I had appendicitis, but the problem was an ovarian cyst. They performed surgery and managed to save the ovary. That event caused me to get behind in my schoolwork, so I had to discontinue piano lessons with Mrs. Manley. I had taken lessons from her since the first grade, you recall. She didn't allow her students to play popular songs; we were to concentrate on classical music. Tchaikovsky was my favorite; I loved the bass—you just pounded it. One regret is that I was unable to give a piano recital on my own. That would have indicated I had arrived at a certain level of achievement, according to Mrs. Manley. She had taken piano lessons from a German man in Nashville, and her schooling in classical music probably came from her work with him. I'm sorry now that I didn't take more lessons later on because I really loved playing.

Everybody thought Margaret Batey was my aunt, but she was my first cousin. She tutored many of the football boys and basketball boys at our house. Everybody thought that having all those boys coming to the house was great, but it didn't faze me. Margaret invited the teachers over to play bridge, and they taught me to play, but I never did like it. Bridge is too passive; I feel I should be doing more, and having to concentrate so hard on a game takes the fun out of it.

My grandmother lived with us too. She had what was called hardening of the arteries then, now known as dementia or Alzheimer's. Mama still wanted to look after her mother. With five bedrooms at the Sterling Road house, there was room for us all. After her mind failed, Grandma wanted to "go home" and tended to try to walk off. We had to watch her carefully.

Finally my uncles purchased a house in Murfreesboro, and Grandma went to live there with Mrs. Ward, a retired nurse. She reverted to her childhood and played with dolls. She would call Uncle

Herbert Arch because he looked like my grandfather. She had been such an active, energetic woman, and to see somebody go down like that was very sad and tragic for me.

Older women who called on one another during those years used calling cards. (Even after I married, some of the older women used them in Nashville.) Mama had friends such as Mrs. Spence McGavock coming to call, and some had chauffeurs, who would bring the calling cards to the house and then the ladies would be invited in. Mama fed the chauffeurs in the kitchen while they waited, especially if her friends came for lunch. Serving food or tea or coffee was not essential to a visit; people came just to sit and talk.

Across from our place in Una was a larger farm owned by Miss Addie Brent. Albert and Maggie Roberts—we children called them Uncle Albert and Aunt Maggie—lived there. They had a house full of children. All the children went to school, and the older ones went to Haynes High School near Whites Creek. Haynes was the only black high school. Margaret, their daughter, came over to the house one summer day and asked if Mama needed any help. Mama first asked Margaret what she would like to do, then they decided together that she would help with doing housework and looking after Linda, who was two or three at the time, and Mama taught her how to cook. She worked every afternoon after school and on Saturdays.

When Margaret graduated from Haynes High School, we then were living on Sterling Road. She said that she wanted to go to college, but she didn't have any money. Daddy paid her tuition to go to A&I (Tennessee Agricultural and Industrial College), and she worked for us after her classes. She rode the bus to the end of the line, and Mama picked her up. Daddy didn't want her riding the bus at night, so he took her home. By that time the Roberts family had moved closer to A&I (now Tennessee State University).

Daddy had helped Aunt Maggie and Uncle Albert with obtaining a house and the closing process on it, and their children helped them pay for it. Margaret worked part-time in the school year and full-time in the summers for us until she graduated. She then found a job in Missouri as a teacher and married there. The university eventually bought her parents' house, and they moved to Clayton Avenue. Whenever she was back in town, Margaret would come out and see

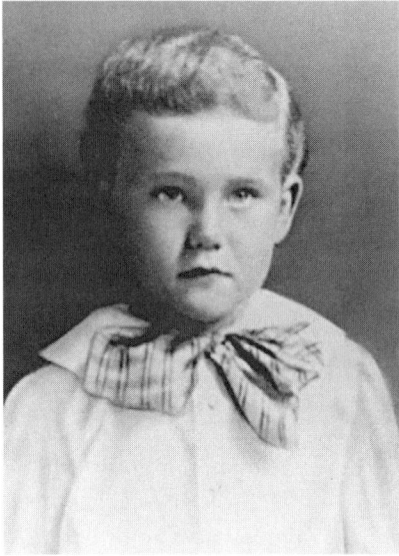

My daddy, Tom Fox Jones, at age six. Taken at W. G. Thuss Studio in Nashville.

Mama and Daddy. After Mama died, Margaret called, and Mary, Linda, and I met her for lunch at the Sunset Grill. She always said how much my parents did to help her get through school. When the family wanted to sell the house on Clayton, Margaret called Amy to close out the estate. The relationship certainly covered many years.

Only when I moved to Sterling Road did I start having many friends. The extended family and its activities kept me so busy that I didn't have time for many friends before that. Several friends lived nearby. Jean Loftin lived up the street with her younger sisters, who were twins, and they were my sister Mary's best friends. The Allens had a son who was Mary's age, Jack, and they remain friends to this day. They also had a daughter, Alice, who now lives in Franklin. Down the street on New Natchez Trace was Lucy Bennett. Lucy's mother and Uncle Bryan had dated; I told Lucy that we almost became cousins. Years later my sisters and I were staying at a cottage in the Cotswolds, the lights went out, and we lit candles and spent quite some time talking about all the people in that neighborhood, taking them house by house.

Going in to town to the movie was a big deal in high school. We'd probably eat at the Krystal too. We rode the Hillsboro-Sunset or Sunset-Hillsboro buses, but we had to go to the corner of Woodlawn and Natchez Trace to catch the big buses. I still have nightmares about not finding a bus in uptown Nashville. Shuttles took us from Natchez Trace down Woodlawn toward my street.

Occasionally we went to Mr. Austin's grocery store to call Mama to pick us up at the end of the bus line. He had some walk-in trade, but most of it was home delivery to Belle Meade. My mother thought that home delivery was a luxury we should never afford. One day she went in to get something—she didn't buy a lot from Mr. Austin because she thought he was higher than the A&P or Piggly Wiggly—and she was bemoaning the expensive prices. Mr. Austin told her, "Mrs. Jones, you eat better than anybody in this neighborhood." She asked, "What do you mean?" He said, "You buy good cuts of roast beef and steaks." We cooked all our meat in a skillet, and Daddy liked it burned, nothing pink or rare. Mr. Austin said, "You'd be surprised, Mrs. Jones, the people I deliver to you'd think they'd be eating like kings and queens. But they skimp on their food budget to have things that show outwardly, which you don't. You buy good meat."

The need to have fine clothes and houses didn't bother Mama. It didn't matter to her what you wore as long as you were clean. My attitude about that was the exact opposite of hers. She wasn't a housekeeper either, and I am. Mama was always looking after other folks, hauling somebody to church or doing something for a poor family. She felt that was her calling, and sometimes we weren't the calling. But she had a good heart.

Mr. Austin had a point, though, because our family had regular, healthy meals. We sat down for every meal, and we never ate without having the blessing. My parents would hear nothing of this running in and out, grabbing meals on the way. When we had our family, Billy and I had the same rules. Even on Saturday morning the children had to get up and eat breakfast with us; they could go back to bed later. My opinion has been that eating together helps keep a family together, and recent research studies seem to bear that out.

Daddy had been wanting to teach me to drive, but I was reluctant to learn, even at age seventeen. I said, "I'll just have somebody drive me." When Lucy came driving up in the car to take us to Lipscomb, that was all it took for Daddy to start teaching me on a 1950 two-door Dodge. It had reverse and low gears. I never learned how to shift anything more than reverse and low. As soon as he could, Daddy bought a car with an automatic transmission.

To go to school, we girls wore sweater sets, skirts that came below the knee, and brown-and-white saddle oxfords with white socks folded down. The saddle oxfords, which had leather soles, had to be polished, and the shoe strings had to be washed regularly. In the warmer months we were never allowed to wear shorts or pants to school. That would have been unthinkable.

To go to church, we girls had Sunday dresses and white gloves in the summer and special shoes. My first high heels were sandals with two-inch heels, and that was when I started wearing stockings. Before that I wore patent leather shoes to church. Here's how we kept them clean: we took a leftover biscuit and split it open; the shortening was enough to shine the shoes. Later on Mama didn't think that was such a good method, so we used Vaseline.

Mama didn't like to shop. Daddy liked to go with us girls to buy our clothes, and he would buy more for us than she would. He had a good eye; he wore nice clothes and people told him that he was a natty dresser. He liked for us to look nice, too, and he loved pretty cloth. He picked out many of Mama's clothes.

Mama's fascination with hats defied her otherwise nonchalant attitude toward clothing. Even when it was fashionable not to wear hats on Sunday to church, she still wore them; she didn't feel dressed up without her hat. A good friend of hers, Maggie Miller in Donelson, made hats for her. When Mama died, my sisters and I had lots of hats to give away. Daddy used to say, "I'm going to buy your Mama a go-to-hell hat." The full meaning of that escaped us, but we do know at least that it meant a snappy hat.

The boys wore dress pants, probably khakis. Blue jeans were not allowed for girls or boys. My first pair of blue jeans were purchased when I was at Lipscomb. They had not been "in" before that. Keeping up with the latest trends was not for me anyway.

Mama and Daddy weren't crazy about the idea of my dating, and I was shy with boys anyway. I wasn't smitten by any particular boy, but I did date in my senior year. Lucy and I met two young men who were in premed at Vanderbilt and were five years older than we were. I dated John Derryberry, who became a doctor in Shelbyville and has just died. She dated Charles Branch, who ended up being a neurosurgeon in San Antonio. We had a lot of fun. They went to Hillsboro Church of Christ, where we were going, so we did things with the youth group. John drove his model T or A, and Charles worked the choke over on the right side of the dashboard. It was a coupe, and we four piled in one seat.

Hillsboro High School had distinguished young people who went on to make something of themselves. In my graduating class of 1949 one boy went to Yale and another to Harvard.

The building of Hillsboro High School that I attended burned during my freshman year at Lipscomb. Daddy was taking me to Lipscomb the next morning, and we drove by there and saw the smoldering ruins. We had heard on the radio that it had burned overnight. Seeing that was hard to take after all of us students had worked to raise money to build the stadium, which burned too. The wooden floors in the halls were oiled and oiled to a high gloss. Any kind of spark on those floors would have spread immediately. The Hillsboro students then went to Belmont, where they used some of the back part of the campus. Belmont had just bought the facility from Ward-Belmont.

In 1997 a house sold for $450,000 or $475,000 on Golf Club Lane; its backyard met the backyard of our house on Sterling Road. Daddy bought that Sterling Road house for $25,000 in 1944. Sterling Road and Golf Club Lane have been kept up and well preserved because of the doctors and professors wanting to live there near the hospitals and universities.

When I was still a child, Mama took the family to Lipscomb for a picnic held near the stacked stone wall where Acuff Chapel is now. Tables were put up, and everyone spread out food on them. Most of the people were alumni still living in Nashville. That was a highlight of our spring, and it seemed to be a big day for everybody involved. It was held in May, and May Day processional occurred then with a May Queen. The boys wore tuxes, and the girls wore long dresses that were all alike and of the same color. That event made me want to go to Lipscomb, and I did attend there. I participated in one of the last May Days, but it was held in the gym because of rain.

The background and props for the processional were set up in front of Elam Hall, which was a boys' dorm at the time. The girls came from Sewall Hall, the girls' dorm, and the boys came from over near Harding Hall. The boy and the girl came together and then went up the steps. Then they had the crowning of the May Queen, who was chosen because of her popularity and her embodiment of Christian womanhood (good morals and standards). There was also usually a pageant.

Steve Flatt recently talked about events and traditions he wants to reinstitute, and May Day is one of them. The idea is to promote traditions that strengthen ties to the school. Beautiful Day is another example; I believe it started in my junior year in college. The administrators kept secret which day it would be, so students never knew until it was officially announced. Chapel was held around 10:00 A.M. every day (and it is still held every day). Willard Collins, a vice president, was in charge of the students. He conducted chapel, and as he prepared to dismiss us, he announced that it was to be Beautiful Day. All of us then rushed to put on our blue jeans. The cafeteria people packed up the kitchen and went to Percy Warner Park and set up a picnic for the students. No classes were held that day.

Ettie Lu had come from Texas and started at Ward-Belmont. I talked to Mama and Daddy about changing from Lipscomb because I wanted to be with her, but Daddy really didn't want me to change. Ward-Belmont was only a two-year college then, and I'd have to go somewhere else for my last two years. During my college years I lived at home, except for one quarter in my senior year, and that experience was one I'll never forget.

A home economics major was my choice. Billy believed that was the best major for a girl. He thought I learned all I knew from college, which wasn't true. I was basically an organized person to begin with, but my home ec teacher really emphasized organization. We cooked meals probably four times a week, and then we ate them. She would open each drawer of each person's work station and check it for the utensils. Each spatula or turning fork or whatever had to be in order, and the work station had to be spotless.

My teacher, Margaret Carter, was our neighbor in Smyrna. Her father died when she was young, leaving her mother a widow with four children. My grandfather was a surrogate father to them, and Margaret was one of my mother's roommates at Lipscomb. After graduation Margaret got a job at the hospital in Chattanooga as a dietitian. Granddaddy gave her money each time she returned to Smyrna because he knew that she brought most of her earnings to her mother. He didn't want her to have empty pockets on the road.

All these details were unknown to me until after Billy died, however. Margaret knew how much money it took to look after Billy.

She had $35,000 coming due from a certificate of deposit, and she wanted to give it to me—all because of what my granddaddy had done. Don't ever think that what you have given will not come back, even though it may be two or three generations later. I told her it was the nicest thing to have happened to me in all my tragedy surrounding Billy's illness, but I didn't need it. I wanted her to give it somewhere she felt called to give it. She chose Lipscomb's home economics department. Billy and I had given money and land to establish the Caroline Jones Cross Chair and more money to redo the dining room, living room, and kitchen of the home economics lab. We did that in Margaret's honor because I was thankful to have had her and to have learned many things from her.

The last quarter of my senior year was a home management course. We didn't have an elegant house to live in like the students later had, which was given to the school by A. M. Burton. Behind the boys' dorm was a concrete building in which a maintenance crew had lived, and they cleaned it up for us a bit. We had two bedrooms, a little eating room, a kitchen, a bathroom, and a living room; there were four students and Margaret, the teacher, making a total of five. She had to move out of her apartment and live with us in that little place. Her mother was still living, so she had to go home and look after her on weekends.

Everybody else had a bed to sleep in, but I ended up sleeping with Margaret on the sofa that made into a bed in the living room. My classmates thought I was the logical one to sleep with her, since I got along with Margaret so well and she was a family friend.

We planned menus, and we stayed with them. With our weekly budget of ten dollars we had to buy food, toilet paper, washing powder—we had a washing machine—and household cleaning supplies. Little did Margaret know that I would sometimes go home and raid the freezer, which was full of vegetables and fruit. For the most part we managed to stick to the budget, though.

The demonstrating cooking parts of class that were for TV were favorites of mine. I did a Caesar salad that was so dramatic as my final exam. I don't even know how I got onto that idea.

When Billy and I were first married and living in Germany, all those lessons I learned from living on ten dollars a week came in handy. Billy made little money as a soldier, and I earned money from substitute teaching in the American schools and typing for an insurance company. We managed not to have to dip into our savings. It was a real eye-opener for Billy that I knew how to manage well.

The courses also honed the leadership abilities I was born with. The home ec department at Lipscomb then ranked high in the nation. The science and chemistry courses were really difficult, but getting my Bachelor of Science in Home Economics was worth all the effort. My teaching certificate, which I considered insurance, was the last certificate issued before students had to do additional work to be able to teach.

Majoring in home economics just made sense to me, but there were many job openings for home ec majors: country clubs such as Belle Meade Country Club needed people to schedule and coordinate events, TV needed people to prepare food for demonstration—like Julia Child did—and hotels and hospitals hired dietitians. Vanderbilt welcomed Lipscomb home ec graduates to be dietitians. Because of Margaret Carter's emphasis on nutrition, I probably learned more about it than doctors graduating from Vanderbilt.

The thought never occurred to me not to go to work. Following graduation in 1953, I went to Clarksville to work in the University of

My graduation picture, 1949, from Hillsboro High School, and Billy's graduation picture, 1950, from Clarksville High School.

Tennessee Extension Service. Then in 1954, I came back to Lipscomb and taught in the home ec department. There were always more people than Margaret Carter in the department; many were part-time, but I was hired for a full-time position. She and I worked together well. I loved teaching college students drafting, design, and the first year of cooking. For one quarter I went to Peabody to work on my master's degree because I thought I wanted to go on teaching.

Both of my sisters had a whole lot of boyfriends, more than I ever had, and they went out on dates younger than I did. Being the oldest, I had to pave the way. Mary and Linda went to many dances. Daddy took Mary to the dances at Sewanee Military Academy and Castle Heights and brought her home because the boys weren't able to drive yet.

Mary and Linda could go into stores such as Cain-Sloan and Castner-Knott and charge things on Mama's account. That was a luxury I didn't have. They always had the latest of everything, too.

Mary went to Woodmont Grammar School, then to Lipscomb High School four years. That's where she met Clive Anderson Jr. She started to college but didn't finish because they married. Clive's daddy was an auctioneer, and Clive followed in his father's footsteps. During high school Clive and Helen Huntley had a teen disk jockey program on WLAC.

Mary and Clive were married several years with no children, so they decided to adopt. Tommy was born January 15, 1964. I was in the old part of St. Thomas Hospital having Jim on January 16. I told Mary when they went to see Tommy, "If you don't like him, you don't have to take him home." Later I found out that in St. Thomas's nursery, on the back row, were babies from the Florence Crittenton Home girls. Jim and Thomas Edward (we call him Tommy) were in the nursery at the same time and ended up being first cousins. Tommy became very special to all of us. To me, adopted children are chosen and are clearly wanted.

That same year Mary became pregnant. On December 20, 1964, she had David Clive, and suddenly she was rearing two babies at once. It wasn't long before she was pregnant with Samuel Forrest. Then there was Mary Susan, and not much later there was the fifth one, Dan.

Billy and Winston, Linda's husband, used to tease with my daddy and say, "You know, we need to tell Clive what is causing this." That was not the thing to say to my daddy. You didn't talk about such subjects in polite company. But when Mary was pregnant with Dan, Daddy said very seriously, "Billy, I think you better have a talk with Clive and tell him what's causing this."

After Tommy went to his first year of school, Clive and Mary were instrumental in forming Franklin Road Academy (FRA). Those five children went all the way through FRA. Then all went to college, and all but Tommy graduated—he had other things to do.

Sam was one to save money, and he would loan money to his brothers. If he loaned one dollar, he wanted two dollars back. He was the banker of the family.

Tommy is a surveyor at Gresham, Smith and Partners, and he is married to Stacy and they have Kayla and Ashley Todd. David works with his daddy at the auction company, and he is married to Kathy and they have a son, John. Sam is an attorney, and he married Jennifer and they have a son, Samuel. Susan married Kent Burns and they have twins, Mary Jordan and Virginia Anderson; she is a homemaker. Dan is in the music industry; he hasn't married as of this writing.

Linda went to Donelson High School. Daddy and Mama moved to Donelson for a while because Daddy was building houses there, but nobody liked living in Donelson. Linda was a cheerleader and very popular with the other students. She went to college at Lipscomb, where in her freshman year she met Winston Biggs from Alabama. They were married after her first year.

They lived in a little apartment near Lipscomb. Linda got pregnant and dropped out of school and had the baby. The little boy named Leland Calvin Biggs lived two days. The problem was similar to hyaline membrane disease.

Because Winston was with Billy on business somewhere in Alabama, Daddy and I took Linda to the hospital. We barely made it to St. Thomas in time because when the baby entered the birth canal, he dropped and was born quickly.

After the baby was born, I returned home; later that afternoon I took Daddy back to the hospital with me. Mary had stayed with Linda. I walked down to the nursery to look at my new nephew. He was beautiful. However, I could see that his little chest was laboring for him to breathe. I talked to the pediatrician; he called the nurses in the nursery, and they said the baby looked fine. Well, about 4:00 A.M. St. Thomas called me to come and get the baby because something was wrong. I took him to Vanderbilt Hospital to Dr. Mildred Stahlman. The people at St. Thomas had also called the doctor. Losing the baby was devastating to Linda and Winston and the rest of the family.

Linda recovered and went back to school to get her degree in home economics. She had a good relationship with Margaret Carter too. After graduation she and Winston moved to Sheffield, Alabama, where Winston's father owned a trucking company that hauled chemicals. Linda soon became pregnant, and she had Leigh Forrest. My mother was named Forrest for Nathan Bedford Forrest because my grandfather thought that he was a wonderful general. She had no problems with that pregnancy.

Leigh was about five when Linda became pregnant again. She had the baby in Alabama in a local hospital. Mama, Daddy, and I drove down to see the baby, Mary Winston. I went to the nursery and saw her breathing like that first baby. She was two or three days old. Daddy called me Nancy; he said, "Nancy, don't you say anything." Winston called me before the week was out to call Dr. Stahlman because they were on their way with the baby. That was my first experience with a feeding tube. Trying to give Linda a break, I kept little Mary a week before she died at the age of six months. Winston had to go somewhere on business, so Linda went with him. Mama and Daddy kept Leigh.

Linda and Winston adopted a little boy later on, and they named him Winston but called him Winn. He had a tragic automobile accident as a student at the University of Alabama. The injuries required many operations, and he still has a limp. When Winn was in the hospital in Alabama, I called Joe Ross at Vanderbilt and asked advice on where they should move Winn. Eventually he went to Gallatin at the rehab center there.

Now Leigh has three children—two sons, William and Gray, and a daughter, Mary Winston, named after her deceased aunt. Her husband, Brian Reames, from Richmond, Virginia, is in the real estate business in Nashville.

51

CHAPTER 3

The Adventure of a Lifetime

> *Successful marriage is always a triangle:*
> *a man, a woman, and God.*
> *—Cecil Myers*

I first met Billy when I was at a 4-H camp for young people in Columbia, Tennessee, and was working for the University of Tennessee Extension Service. Camping has never been a favorite activity—I like my creature comforts—but it was a part of the job. Billy's brother was at the camp in my group, and when he became sick, we had to notify the parents. It turned out that he had polio. Billy drove his parents to Columbia to get the brother and take him to Vanderbilt.

It was June or July, and I was back in the kitchen with my hands in a dish pan full of flour making biscuits. I looked like homemade sin: I had no makeup on, my curly hair was going every which way, and I was hot and sweaty. We couldn't wear shorts, so I was wearing a summer dress. That was the first time Billy saw me. He wasn't impressed at all with our first meeting. I don't remember much about him, what with his brother being sick and me working hard in the kitchen. It was far from love at first sight.

My job with the extension service was based in Montgomery County, and I rented rooms in Clarksville. All the eligible males checked out the female employees of the extension service. Billy had seen me in town one day in Clarksville while he was there doing something for his daddy. He worked on his daddy's farm. I know I looked a whole lot better then than when he first saw me. There were two Bills calling me at one time. The lady I rented from told me that Bill had called, and I said, "Which one?" Billy's full name was James William Cross III; I called him Billy, but he was known as J. W. to friends and business associates later on.

We dated from that summer of 1953 until he went into the service in 1954, but I almost didn't go out with him because I found out that he was divorced. I knew the Church of Christ's position on divorce—only for adultery if you remarry—and our own family had very strong feelings about divorce. Aunt Dixie and Uncle Bryan had been the first to divorce in our family, and that experience was shattering to all the family members. After the divorce Uncle Bryan retired and took the children to San Antonio. Years later he and Aunt Dixie did remarry. Billy and his wife had no children, though. It had been a high school romance, and the marriage lasted only a few months.

The third time he called I agreed to go out with him. He had said to himself that he wouldn't call me again if I refused that third time. I dated other people for a while, too, but I think we both knew that this was it. From the beginning a real attraction between us was evident.

We went square dancing a lot after he taught me how. We had a good time dating, and I was pleased that my family liked him.

His mother and I went to Fort Stewart in Augusta to see him after he was drafted. All the young men were marching in from the field, and she said, "There he is." I said, "That can't be him." He was so tanned that he looked like a black man. The men from the North were falling out in the heat, but it didn't bother Billy because he had been working outside on the farm all those summers.

He was in a division of engineering, and he enjoyed it. He was only a private but went on to become a specialist in that division. At the outset of the Korean War, he was sent to Germany. It was a close call—he almost went to Korea.

Billy was drafted into the army for two years. We had planned to marry in June, and I was going to take another trip with Aunt Amy to Europe. When he was shipped to Germany, we decided to marry there. Few people had done that, and as we were to find out, we broke new legal ground.

Looking back, I think that marrying him in Germany and living abroad a while were wise moves. We had such close-knit families at

Billy's mother, Pearl, with Ray Harris, his only uncle.

home, but we had to depend and lean on each other over there. We learned how to manage a household with little money. We didn't write home for our parents to send money either. Thank goodness, I learned from that experience. Then I didn't know that I was being prepared for what happened with Billy later on.

Billy's father, James William Cross Jr., was state director of the ASCS (an agricultural conservation service) in Eisenhower's administration. He was traveling and doing other jobs but not farming directly. He needed somebody like Billy to look after the farm. Billy's grandfather had set up a college account for him, but Billy chose to work on the farm along with his brothers. Their father really taught them all the work ethic. Their mother was Pearl Brandau Cross.

Billy's grandfather, Dr. James Monroe Harris (called Docca by Billy), had given him a lot of attention. Mama Lula, Billy's grandmother, was a tall woman, as was Billy's mother. Billy was six feet four inches tall, and Docca was taller. After Billy learned to drive, he drove for Docca on his rounds because Docca never learned to drive. Until Billy was old enough, Docca hired boys from Nashville to drive for him, and they lived at his house. Unfortunately I never met Docca; he died before I married into the family.

Mama Lula's father was Thomas Stewart, and the family lived not too far from Dr. Harris's house. Mama Lula had an automobile, one of the first. One day she was speeding into Clarksville, and an officer stopped her. He said, "Miss Lula, do you know how fast you're going? I'm afraid I'm going to have to give you a ticket." She answered, "Sonny boy, you give me that ticket and give me another one because I'm going out like I came in." She also learned to shoot. She sat on the back porch,

Billy's maternal grandparents, Dr. James M. and Lula Stewart Harris, with a friend of the family (on the left), and Billy's mother, Pearl.

My paternal great-grandparents,
Martha Dryden Moon and Dr.
James Pleasant Moon.

had the hired helper line up tin cans, and shot them with a pistol.

Dr. Harris insisted that someone live in with Mrs. Cross and her family because she had four boys in five or six years. That's how Zenobia entered the family picture. Zenobia Hudgens was from a big family living out in Palmyra. She and Mrs. Cross had gone to high school together. Mrs. Cross had been sent to school in Clarksville, and she boarded with a cousin of my mother's who kept girls coming from the country to attend school. Zenobia didn't board. During the Depression she needed work, so Dr. Harris persuaded Mr. Cross to get Zenobia to live in. Gene is the only surviving brother now, and she started work when Gene was a baby.

When Mr. Cross died, Zenobia stayed to look after Mrs. Cross on the farm. But Zenobia got sick with cancer, and Mrs. Cross was driving her to Nashville for treatment. Billy insisted that his mother sell the house and a few acres Mr. Cross left her. Billy bought the house and the acres and later sold them. He built Mrs. Cross a house in Maplewood so that she would be close to Vanderbilt to take

Zenobia to the doctor. We all ended up looking after Zenobia, but at the last we had to put her in a nursing home.

The first Cross to come into this area was Richard Cross, who arrived with the second boatload of the James Robertson group and settled down on Broad Street at Second Avenue. (He gave the land for the Old City Cemetery in Nashville.) He had a son, William, who received a land grant in Clarksville, but William never lived there. William had a farm out where the old Berry Field is and lived there. When he died very young, his widow sold the land in Clarksville. Then years later, probably in the 1920s, Billy's grandfather bought the same land, and Billy's father added to it. That was an ironic twist of family history. My genealogical research uncovered all that information; the Crosses never knew it before then.

Two of Billy's brothers died tragically. Wayne and his son, Greg, were on the farm cutting walnut. (Wayne had inherited the farm at his father's death.) The tree fell wrong and was going to hit Greg. Wayne tried to get Greg out of the way, and he was hit, paralyzing him from the waist down. He lived one and a half years. Wayne's wife was diagnosed with cancer of the brain and died shortly thereafter. The farm left the family after that.

Gene in his early forties had a serious heart attack followed by heart surgery. His wife is named Patsy, and their children are Ricky, Linda, Jerry, and Margaret. He worked for us a long time at Century Construction and Cross Properties until I closed Cross Properties, and he was a vital part of the two companies. Then he had a second bypass. Barton Campbell was his cardiologist as well as Billy's. Dr. Campbell said that probably another of Gene's brothers had a similar condition, so they were all tested. Billy must have been the one with a similar condition. At the time Billy didn't show signs of heart problems, but eventually he had cardiac arrest. That is a whole story unto itself to be told later.

Maurice married Edna Jenkins right out of high school, and they adopted two children. He was the sports star of the family. He played football and several colleges made offers for him to play, which he turned down. He chose instead to work at the Ford Glass Plant as one of the first employees. He and Edna lived in Ashland City. He collected antique motorcycles and decided to ride a motorcycle to

Moon family reunion in 1946. Left to right, Mrs. Henry Holmes, Ernest Moon, Mrs. John Wiseman, Mrs. A. L. Jones, Urbine Moon, Mrs. Ervin Sanders, Mrs. Homer Powell, John Moon, and Sandy Moon. (Absent: Dr. Jim Moon.)

work on the night shift at Ford. We think he must have had a heart attack on the road because the truck driver said he was coming right toward him. He survived the wreck and was taken to Vanderbilt. That day I was returning from a trip out of the country. David Grimes, who worked for me, said when he picked me up at the airport, "Mrs. Cross, don't get upset, but Maurice has had a bad accident. He's getting ready to go in the operating room right now." David was to drive home a friend who was with me, so I decided to go to the hospital the next day. Maurice died on the operating table as a result of his injuries. .

That is a bit of background about Billy's family, but I need to return to his and my story.

While Billy was stationed at Fort Belvoir, my sister Mary and I went to Washington, D.C., and stayed at the Statler Hotel where I had stayed with Aunt Amy years earlier. It just wouldn't do for me to visit Billy there by myself and stay in a hotel. Mary had never been to Washington before, so the trip was a treat for her. Billy had met in basic training a boy from Atlanta named Bill Cowart. Bill was a fine young man who was drafted too. We all had a good time on their leave.

Mary came home and told Mama and Daddy that she thought I was the happiest I had ever been. That was a good thing for my parents to hear and to get them prepared for my marrying Billy.

Following my resignation from my job at Lipscomb, I prepared to sail to Germany in January 1955 aboard the SS *United States.* Daddy drove me to New York in my car, which was shipped with me, then he flew home.

That voyage is unforgettable for several reasons, not the least of which is that most of us on board were seasick for a few days. A big storm hit the first day, January 13. By the third day I was feeling better and could enjoy talking with some of the passengers. I met a Swiss doctor and a newspaper editor from Baghdad, among others. The entertainment included movies and bingo.

The ship docked on January 20 at Bremerhaven, forty-eight hours behind schedule; apparently it was the worst voyage in twenty-one years. Billy met me there, and we had the car registered in his name. The roads from Bremerhaven to Heidelberg were icy; I'm not sure that I ever got used to Germany's severely cold weather.

Getting married in Germany is somewhat different from getting married in the States. Billy and I were in for some surprises, and the most notable one was that we were legally married but didn't know it.

There is no book in the U.S. to record marriages out of the country. Only my passport and the army records show that we were married. It took us from Monday until Thursday to get all the paperwork done. A complication was that some of it had to be translated. Few American soldiers and civilians had been married as we were doing. The closest similar circumstance involved an American soldier who married an American employee of the U.S. government. Neither the German nor the American authorities had a good idea of how to go about it. A friend, Ann Dearing Hale, came over later and married while Billy and I were still there. She benefited from our experience.

Billy and I went to the Stadt Halle to get the marriage license—at least we thought that was all we were doing—and we had a picture made there. As it turned out, we had a civil wedding ceremony. The

"Wedding" photo at the Bürgermeister's office, Stadt Halle, Heidelberg, Germany, January 27, 1955, 10:35 A.M.

Bürgermeister, who is the mayor of Heidelberg, married us. He performs marriage ceremonies only one day a week, and he is brought to the Stadt Halle in a decorated carriage. We saw the carriage as we entered the Halle but didn't know what it meant. Because no friends were with us, his secretary and the janitor were our witnesses. That was Thursday, January 27, at 10:30 A.M.

Billy had found an apartment for us through some friends at the Heidelberg church. Merle and Joe Diaz, the previous renters, had moved into government housing because he was a sergeant. The apartment was quite small. Well, small is an understatement. In what had been the dining room, twin beds were pushed together so we could get in the room. We shared a kitchen with two other families.

We had a shower and a lavatory downstairs. I shared the tub bath with the other two families in the upstairs bathroom.

Billy was still on leave. He took me to the apartment, and he went back to the base after the Stadt Halle ceremony. We planned to have the religious ceremony on Saturday at the Church of Christ. To us, that meant we were officially married.

The next morning when I went into the kitchen to fix my breakfast, Ruth Westermann, our landlady, was in there. She was a beautiful woman who reminded me of Ingrid Bergman. She looked at me in horror and asked, "What has happened? Have you had a fight?" I said, "No, we haven't had a fuss. What are you talking about?" She said, "Where is Billy?" I answered, "He is back at the base. We're not getting married until Saturday." She told me, "You got married yesterday." I stated, "That was just a formality. We didn't get married." She responded, "You are married by German law."

It was a rude awakening for me and Billy.

Even Germans have two ceremonies, one civil and one religious, whether they are churchgoing people or not. Later, I learned a bit more about the custom. Next door were three families living in one house. That was not unusual because of the war's creating a housing shortage. One couple had two little children. One day I saw many people going into the house. No cars, of course. People walked. Then I saw a bride and a groom. There were lots of flowers, and the front door was decorated. I asked, "Ruth, what is going on?" She said, "So-and-So got married today." I said, "Married? They've been married and have two children." She said, "Oh, no. They hadn't had the church ceremony." That's how things were.

I stayed two nights without Billy at the apartment, even though we were legally married. Then we had the church ceremony at the Church of Christ in Heidelberg on Saturday, January 29, at 2:00 P.M. It's a beautiful little building on a main street, Steubenstrasse 17. Some friends from church and even some Germans from the German-speaking church group joined us. There were about twenty-five people in all. I carried lilies of the valley and one pink camellia, and I wore a suit. As long as I could remember, my plan had been to have an elaborate wedding; at least I could say that I had two ceremonies.

After the "real" ceremony at the Geminde Christi (Church of Christ), Heidelberg, Germany, Saturday, January 29, 1955.

We took our honeymoon later on in the year. On the Monday morning after our Saturday ceremony Billy had to leave early to drive to work. I started right in on the laundry, which I had to do by hand. During our stay in Germany I spent much time washing and ironing the old-fashioned way. Eventually I found a place to get Billy's shirts done, and that was a big help.

Ruth's first husband was named Heck, and they divorced after World War II. She said he came home wearing the Nazi officer's uniform and carrying the officer's crop. He was a true Nazi who couldn't believe they had lost the war. Ruth couldn't take it anymore. In that day and time when people got a divorce in Germany and there was a son in the family, the son always went with the father—no matter what the circumstances. That woman suffered terribly over the loss of her firstborn, Peter. Sabine was the next child, then Uschi.

Ruth and Hans (her second husband), Sabine, and Uschi came to our wedding. We kept up with the family through the years. Sabine is a teacher for Pepperdine's year abroad program in Heidelberg, and she teaches German to the American students. She has been there since the school started thirty years ago. When she was swapping with the language department head in Pepperdine and was on sabbatical in the States, Sabine came by our house, knowing that Billy was very sick. She was here with us the day he died. That is full circle—from marriage to death. She had to leave before the funeral, however.

Billy and I would never have had the relationship with that family if I had not gone to Germany. Ruth was like a surrogate mother; she looked after us, and she loved Billy. He wasn't crazy about some of the tarts and cakes she made for him, but he didn't want to hurt her feelings. We threw them away, but she'd find them in our garbage.

Ruth learned to do all kinds of things during the war that most people in her position would never have dreamed of doing in usual circumstances. She had been raised in an upper-middle-class— almost upper-class—German home. Having to come down and "live like a peasant," as she called it, was hard for her. Ruth said she had stolen apples off a tree to feed her children. I saw her rip up wool sweaters and knit new ones with the reused wool yarn.

Ruth's father was an elected official in a very high position in Karlsruhe. After the war ended, the Americans made her father sweep the streets of Karlsruhe to get his pension. Ruth loved Americans, but the only words I ever heard her speak against them concerned their treatment of her father. The French soldiers took over her parents' apartment and used it in the war. A lot of damage was done then.

One Sunday morning Ruth and Hans were cleaning out the garage; that was the day for extra garbage pickup. They were going to throw out pieces of a beautiful Victorian chair made from French walnut. I took that chair, which had belonged to Ruth's parents, in pieces and wrapped it in twine, sent it home, and told Mama and Daddy to get Mr. Reinhart and Mr. Heins to put it together. Daddy said when he found those pieces, "What has Nancy sent home now?" I also have the mug that Ruth's father kept at the Red Ox Inn as a student at the University of Heidelberg.

Heidelberg is on the same latitude as Minnesota and Wisconsin. The winter was cold with frequent snows, and German houses were not kept as warm as American houses. All I could do was to wear multiple layers of clothes. American army wives had to present ourselves in the best light. We had to abide by a list of rules for women who were not actually in the service, and wearing pants was forbidden. The German people had terrible images of some soldiers and their wives, and I was determined that Billy and I would present a good image of Americans. Some soldiers drank too much, and many half-American children were left behind when the soldiers returned to the States.

I did typing for Bill Leavengood to earn some money, and by the first part of February I had completed arrangements to be a substitute teacher at the school at USAEUR Headquarters. I had to be registered with the police and obtain an AGO card in addition to all the papers for the U.S. authorities.

Driving in the snow was impossible for me. I'd walk in snow up to my knees to catch the OEG (streetcar) to get to school. Naturally I taught on the bad days because somebody was sick. My suede fur-lined boots didn't help much in really deep snow. I carried my high heels in my pocketbook, and I'd change when I reached school. The idea of teaching in high heels seems impossible to me now.

The OEG took me into the center of Heidelberg where I got off and walked a block to catch a taxi to the school. Army buses ran all the time, but I couldn't seem to get on their schedule since we lived so far out.

Most of the students were officers' children. It was the first time I taught black children. The first day I sat down in the cafeteria in the faculty area, the first person to join me was a black woman who remained my friend throughout our stay. A lot of teachers stayed only one year. Most of them had taken a leave of absence in the States to come over and teach these students. I subbed from seventh to twelfth grades in no particular subject.

A teacher who was supposed to be at our school in Germany ended up in Japan because of a too typical army entanglement of papers. I taught her class for about a month before she finally showed up. I started with them at the very beginning of the year.

The principal took me to the class of seventh graders. He stopped me before we opened the door and said, "We cannot keep a substitute for these students. They are incorrigible. Don't feel bad if you can't handle them." I thought, *They can't be that bad.* Well, they were. They were hanging out of the windows and throwing erasers out. The principal told them that I was going to be their teacher until the other one got there, then he left. One of them went over and threw something out the window. I grabbed him by the collar of his shirt and plopped him down in his chair. He said, "What are you doing?" I said, "My name is Cross. You needn't push me to be cross." I put on the meanest face I could. He said, "Send me to the principal." I stated evenly, "I don't send my students to the principal. You will stay here." I got them under control. All I had to do was threaten to call in their daddies, and that was not good for daddy's record to be called in about an unruly child in school. We teachers had a lot to hold over their heads.

Teaching in that school was an enjoyable experience. My next assignment was a typing class for several months. I had never taught typing, although I could type. I had to read the books and make my lesson plans.

While in Germany, Billy and I didn't eat fresh vegetables as a rule because Germans used to spray vegetables with liquid from the honey wagon (the truck that collected human waste). The lettuce had to be soaked in a powdery liquid before we could eat it. We ate out of cans, and for two southerners used to having fresh vegetables, that was a hardship. We seemed to make endless trips to the PX to buy food. By March the need for a refrigerator became apparent because our food kept spoiling, so we bought one. Ruth and her family had never had a refrigerator until then; they repaid us for it with a credit on our rent each month.

In the summertime we opened the windows to cool off—certainly no air-conditioning then and not even a fan. The problem was huge horse flies. The Germans had no screens, so Billy ordered screen wire from the PX and Hans made the screens. On Sunday afternoons when the German people took their walks, they would stop and stare at the "oddities" on our windows. They had never seen anything like them.

We went to church as often as we could, and Billy was baptized in the church at the end of June. Other than going to church, we would see movies at the base or have friends over to play cards or eat supper. We had little time for much entertainment what with me working and Billy sometimes out late at the base.

For a weekend in May we drove to Holland and to the Hague. That was our delayed honeymoon.

July proved to be an interesting, busy month. We took day trips to Worms and to Mainz. For my birthday Billy took me to supper at Perko's. Era Mae Rascoe, a college friend, visited, and Uncle Bryan and his family came to Heidelberg.

We took off about a week in August and went to England. In London we saw the play *Crazy Gang* that was supposed to be Princess Margaret's favorite play, but we thought it was terrible. At the Douglas House army hotel, we had a bedroom with four single beds, a baby bed, and a bath for two dollars a night. It was next door to Claridges. Little did Billy and I know then that we would be regular guests at Claridges until his death—but never for two dollars a night! We shopped at the silver vaults where the government was selling silver and bought much silver with our wedding money.

In November we spent a leave of about two weeks in Italy. We saved up out of my salary and his to make the trip. Milan, Rome, Naples, Capri, Pompeii, the Vatican, Florence—we saw all those places. La Scala was most impressive. Carnegie Hall may be the best, but nothing can compare with this one. The stage is larger than the auditorium, and more than eight hundred people can be on the stage at one time. Driving in Italy was an experience that Billy didn't care to repeat, though. The drivers scared him to death.

In the Straw Market in Florence, Billy loved to negotiate with the vendors. He would even argue about a lira, about twenty-five cents at that time. We were buying a green leather gold-tooled box to hold playing cards—two decks fit in it, and I still have it. There we also met a general, the father of one of my students. In Europe, you never know when you'll bump into friends or acquaintances.

We stayed at fine hotels, and Billy negotiated the price of the rooms, usually five dollars a day. Now the same rooms in those hotels are more than two hundred dollars a day. We bought meals at the nice restaurants only once a day. We had instant coffee with us and ran hot water in the tub to make it, then we'd go to the bakery and buy hard rolls for breakfast. Pasta for lunch was really inexpensive.

For holidays we did what we could to have traditional celebrations. We had Thanksgiving dinner for several guests at our apartment, with turkey, dressing, sweet potatoes, and pumpkin pie. At Christmas we decorated a tree. We didn't care that it crowded us in that tiny apartment because seeing it and smelling it made the holiday seem more like the Christmases we had known at home.

Before Billy's tour of duty was over, we started talking about what he would do when we went back home. We knew for sure that we would return to Middle Tennessee. His father would have liked for him to return to the farm, but Billy wanted to do other things. Daddy wrote and asked us, "Why not come back and build houses?" He and Mama were living in Donelson, and he was building houses there. I didn't want Billy and Daddy to be in business together, however. I wanted it to be a hands-off thing with no mixing of money between relatives, and that was what happened. Daddy was a very patient teacher, and Billy was an apt learner who soaked it all up. He had leadership qualities and a work ethic that helped him succeed in business.

Back in the States in April 1956, we moved into the house in Donelson that Daddy built for us. He gave us the equity, and then we made the payments on it. Billy started right into the construction business.

CHAPTER 4

Starting Our Businesses

> *Honesty is the first chapter*
> *of the book of wisdom.*
> *—Thomas Jefferson*

Billy and I worked together from the very day he started building houses. Daddy had some lots lined up for Billy and had him set up to get construction loans at Fidelity Federal. Billy had an office at home in the basement, and I kept the books and paid the bills. I taught for a while, too, and that income was paying-the-bills money for food, the house note, and insurance. In the construction business, you don't know what is coming in when or how much.

Mama and Daddy had taught me about feast and famine in this business. Little dips were certainties, and I was determined that we would always eat. When we first got home from Germany, we had a huge vegetable garden, and I froze everything. I'd make our rolls and biscuits and put them in the freezer, then at dinnertime I could just heat them up. The opening of Shoney's Big Boy was a noteworthy event in Middle Tennessee. Still there weren't many places to eat out, so we had little choice but to eat at home. We probably had more nutritious meals as a result instead of fast foods from paper sacks typical of too many homes today.

We were lucky to have a car that was paid for. The Ford Victoria went with me to Germany, and it came back home with us. We could have sold it for a lot of money in Germany to either Germans or Americans because it was a sporty car. I wrote Daddy that we would probably sell it. Daddy responded immediately: he wouldn't hear of it. To him, that was like leaving a child there. I become attached to houses that way, but not to cars.

The Ford had scrapes on the sides from German bicycles' handlebars. Later on Daddy decided that we needed another car, and he traded it in for a Chevrolet for us. Billy used a truck for his work. Before being shipped to Germany, he had sold his sporty Chevrolet for $1,300 since it was still nearly new, and he put that money in the bank.

After two years of teaching I saw that I was needed more in the business. Business has always fascinated me. Billy and I didn't look on what we did as "careers"; we were building our business, and I was helping my husband. Billy considered what he did a job—working for himself, which is much harder than working for somebody else. You can't help taking it home with you.

Century Construction was incorporated in 1958. Billy was president and I was secretary/treasurer. The lawyer may have had one share—there had to be three to incorporate. At the very beginning of our company Billy was always on-site coordinating the subcontractors and suppliers. Somebody had to be there to keep the work ongoing. He had no job-site trailer, radio, or cell phone like Jim has now. Billy left home each day with a pocketful of dimes for the pay phones, and he'd have to stop all along the way. His truck was his job-site office.

Billy and I moved to Brentwood from Donelson in 1959 because we missed living on that side of town. My parents moved at the same time, and we built houses next door to each other. My children have never known what it's like not to have grandparents next door.

The children knew where I was every day, being at the office. I was not playing bridge at somebody's house or playing golf at the country club. If the children were sick, the school knew to call me at the office. Billy and I could take off any time to go to the children's games or programs, and I stayed at home with them when they were sick. I told some young women who asked me to speak about careers, "My situation was much different from that of many young women. I feel sorry for these women who are punching the clock every day and have to be on the job. They have to work—maybe a single parent or the husband's income isn't enough to support the family."

The business was more or less laid out for us from the beginning. Some years there were little recessions, and we'd have houses on our hands with the interest clock running. It was not all perfect, but basically we were fortunate—and we continued to work hard.

Billy stayed in residential building for a few years. Then he could see that the money was really in the commercial/industrial side and more money was in development. Daddy taught Billy about development, and Billy did a lot of commercial building for Daddy when Daddy was building truck terminals in Nashville and leasing them. Billy got his contractor's license in 1958.

Century Construction was always the construction company. When Billy and Daddy decided to work together on developing some projects in Franklin in 1964, they created Tower Real Estate and Development. Windsor Park was just Billy and my development; Ellington Park, Oakwood, and Redwing were Billy and Daddy's. Daddy was retiring, so Billy and I formed Cross Properties in 1964 for developing land for residential and commercial use.

Early on Billy recognized the need and the practicality of prefabricated metal buildings. We had the INRYCO, a division of Inland Steel, franchise for more than twenty years, and it was very lucrative for us. An article in the *Review Appeal*, June 26, 1975, stated, "Century Construction Co. has the unique distinction of owning and constructing the first building produced by Inryco's new building systems plant in Cullman, Alabama." It was an eight-thousand-square-foot office and warehouse for Cross Properties. Our company built buildings for Kusan on Elm Hill Pike and for Kusan in Kentucky and in South Carolina. Kusan was only one of many of our clients.

At one point the metal building division of Inland Steel was going through rough times. Several of the dealers across the country decided to get together and buy the metal building division from the Bloch family. Inland decided not to sell, but instead set up an advisory council of those men. Billy was on the first one, and he remained on the council for several years. They had four meetings a year, going to nice places like the Cloisters in Sea Island and Greenbrier. He and I went on those trips, even though my way was not paid by Inland. All of us wives became very close since most of the men were reelected each year. We tried to take different employees to the Inland conventions over the years. Billy's brother, Gene, always went.

We didn't bid government jobs because those jobs were too price sensitive. We didn't like to bid if price was the bottom line. We wanted to work with people who wanted a quality product. We avoided low-bid jobs because contractors lose their shirts that way. Our construction business was the design/build concept.

In the meantime Geneva came to work for Billy and me as a day worker. After Amy was born in 1958, Geneva became our full-time cook. Annie Mae, Geneva's older sister, was a live-in cook for Mama and Daddy, and she told us about Geneva. Their family, the Browns, was from Pulaski. Daddy asked their brother-in-law, Albert, and sister, Janie, to move to Nashville, and Albert worked for Daddy. Geneva had married a Clark and had a child early on, but her child died and then her husband died. She did not remarry. The only way to track her birth was to find a listing on some white person's farm in the census. She was born April 15, but we don't know the exact

Amy, age three.

72

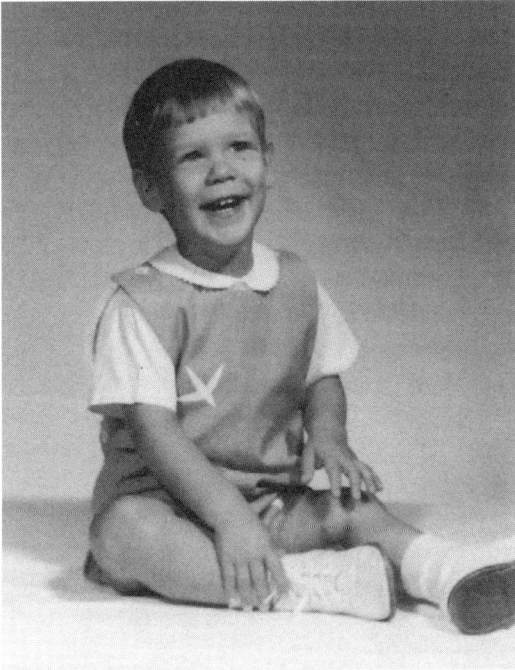

Jim, age three.

year—probably around 1915. She was in her late thirties when she came to work for us, but she did not live in until we moved to Brentwood. Geneva was a good cook who didn't use too much grease or salt or sugar, and nobody made chocolate pies like her, according to Jim.

When Mama and Daddy sold their house in Donelson and moved to Brentwood, Annie Mae chose to work for and live in with Mr. and Mrs. Herbert Grissom of salad fame. Geneva lived at Tuck-A-Way Farm with us until she was sixty-two. Although she started drawing social security, she told me that she wanted to work some. That was music to my ears. She would come on Thursday or Friday and stay through the weekend because she wanted to see Amy and Jim on their visits home from college. She always wanted a gold watch, so Billy gave her one for Christmas, but she wouldn't wear it because she wanted to keep it nice. He thought so much of her that he left her money in his will too.

Three generations of James William Crosses.

The four Brown sisters wanted to buy a house, and I went with them to close it. There were four X's on the deed since not one learned to read and write. Despite her lack of formal education, Geneva had a sharp mind and would have been a good business-woman. I opened a bank account for the sisters and they sent me their cash; I put it in the account, wrote the checks, and paid the loan and utility bills.

A not-so-honest remodeling contractor got to some of the sisters, but not to Geneva. They signed a contract that caused financial woes, and I had to pay off a second mortgage to save their house. Amy and I were Geneva's powers of attorney. In her mid-eighties, she entered the Bordeaux nursing home because her inability to read and write became a problem. She had a home health nurse who divided her medicine according to the days she was to take it, but she kept getting it mixed up and forgetting what she had taken. She had a stroke while in the nursing home. Geneva died December 31, 1997, and the memorial

74

service was held at Woodlawn Cemetery on January 3, 1998.

Billy and I had seven-day-a-week help at home for many years. After Geneva semi-retired, Minnie Johnson did the cooking and the laundry. David Grimes lived on the place for twenty years to take care of the yard and the house and do the cleaning. Amy and Jim's generation won't be able to have the help that we had, but I'm glad that they could see and benefit from those wonderful people.

In many ways Billy and I worked to provide favorable conditions for our children to grow up in, whether in our home or in our county. Orderly growth is good for Franklin and Williamson County. A project has to be a win-win situation for both parties or else it's not successful. Growth has not caused the quality of life to go down, but we do have to keep a watchful eye to maintain the quality of life.

Everybody thought that Billy was crazy running water and gas out to areas that were all farmland. At first everything was a trial here in Franklin and Williamson County because no one wanted any growth. Later after people had seen that Billy did what he said he was going to do and lived up to his word, the fights were not so hard, and people were more willing to accept his ideas.

The way Billy walked down the hall when he came home told me whether he had gotten what he went after that night from the planning commission. It was devastating to him when he was put off to the next meeting or required to do additional things. He finally got everything through that he wanted, and if there was anything the town was ever unhappy with, we didn't know about it—and I'm sure there were some things.

An article written in the Nashville paper after Billy's illness reported his prediction that we would have rapid transit from Williamson County and we could use the Franklin Interurban Rail tracks. If they ever get the shed repaired in Nashville at Union Station, trains could arrive there and then people could take buses across town. The foreign students who came to live with us were shocked that we had to take cars everywhere. In their countries they can walk a short distance from their homes to public transportation or to a shopping area.

We Americans don't want to live that close to each other. We don't want a grocery store in our community, we don't even want a school, and because of that, we have to bus children too far from their homes. Until we have an attitude change in how we want to live in society, this is going to be a problem.

This morning, September 3, 1997, the local paper notes that administrators may have to think about year-round schools. We can't keep building schools and leaving them empty for three or four months. The change will be hard the first time it is done; it will take work, but it can be done effectively. Somebody needs to get to work and just do it because it is inevitable. We're not thinking enough to the future. I saw the year-round school concept work in Germany more than forty years ago.

Billy's feelings about development were summed up in an article in the *Review Appeal*, July 1, 1976:

> In order for Franklin to be a great place to live . . . we must have the best of three worlds. Number one will be to preserve and restore the historic homes and buildings of interest, because we have a great potential for tourism. Number two rests on the fact that the National Historical Sites has designated 300 sites in Williamson County to be historically significant enough to preserve, and number three is that Franklin must provide industrial and commercial development of a nature to help the people locally. . . .
>
> I do pledge to the community that I intend to return my personal resources and business abilities back to the community.

The motto for Century Construction reinforced his position: "The decisions you make today must be the right ones for tomorrow to be better."

If word had leaked before the Saturn deal was completed, prices would have skyrocketed higher, and growth would have been chaotic. Maclin Davis was the attorney that Saturn had hired to do its work. He was breeding his steeplechase horses to our Thoroughbred stud, and we saw him fairly often. Nevertheless, he gave us no inkling of that deal.

Our company owned and subdivided a commercial and industrial park where part of the battlefield was; we didn't know that then. If the people interested in preserving battlefields had come to us then and wanted to buy it, we would have asked for the going rate of commercial property. The preservationists do not need to take advantage and seek a price break. They should pay what the land is worth—not necessarily as a battlefield but what it is worth to the community.

Farms in Williamson County are disappearing, but we can't tell a farmer *not* to sell the land; that's his nest egg. He can't sell it as a farm; appraising farms in this county is difficult because nothing comparable is left that has been sold as farmland. It's not fair to the farmer to appraise farmland as if it is industrial or commercial or residential property for tax purposes. The poor farmers were going to be taxed out of business until the tax structure was revised to protect them.

The year 1997 was my third year on the Franklin National Bank Scholarship Selection Committee that gives $1,000 a year to a graduate of each high school in the county, private or public. Hearing those young people talk about their families and their future plans is inspiring. Other board members include Charles Inman, brother of Gordon Inman, chairman of the board; Ed Moody, Moody Tire Co.; Eunetta Kready, a lifelong resident; and Mike Sullivan, the youngest in the group. We all have pet questions. My pet question is, "I know that you have told us what you want to do in life, and that is not etched in stone. The answer to this next question isn't either. Where will you live and what will you be doing after graduation?" They all say they'll come back to Williamson County because of the quality of life.

Eunetta told me that if I had asked her that question when she was sixteen or seventeen, having been born and lived all her life in Franklin, she'd have said to get out of town as quickly as possible. It amazed her that all the students wanted to come back. They weren't necessarily born and bred here either—some were here because of Saturn and some from Nashville and elsewhere. The people moving here with Saturn don't want to go back where they came from; that was evident from the students' comments.

In talking to the students whose parents came here to work at Saturn, I've asked about the schools: Are they too easy in Franklin compared to schools in the areas they came from? They said as a

77

whole the education is as good or better than where they came from. An added bonus is that they find the people more friendly. I thought to myself, *We have to preserve that*.

Ed Moody asks, "Other than your mother and your father, who has been the greatest influence on your life?" The answer is grandparent, teacher, or Sunday school teacher, something to do with the family, school, or church.

Mike asks, "In this century who do you think has been the most influential person in the world?" The students give a variety of answers, from Gandhi to Roosevelt. One young person said, "Hitler." That answer indicated deep thinking; the question didn't specify that the influence was necessarily *good*.

Counselors and teachers select these top-notch students and submit the names to us. Not all are in financial need. One didn't need the money, but he was eligible because he was top in his class. He was very wise to be interviewed even though with his affluence he didn't need the money, and he admitted that he had no financial need but wanted to compete anyway.

We meet five or six nights at the end of school to interview and choose these youngsters. The task is hard because all the applicants are winners; for example, in one school two students were one-hundredth apart in grade averages. They are not all from ideal homes, meaning there has been divorce or problems in the home. Some fathers have no jobs because of downsizing. Yet the children seem to have overcome the problems and are well-adjusted. That restores your faith in humanity.

Eleanor Fleming was an outstanding student and a poised young lady. She was the first person to be interviewed the first year I was on the committee. She was the valedictorian at BGA and received a full scholarship to Vanderbilt. Her father is a masonry contractor, and her mother, Barbara, works at NationsBank on the square in Franklin. Eleanor's response to Ed Moody's question about an influential person in her life was her grandparents. Everybody in Franklin knew her grandfather as a good man who did good things for the community. Ed reinforced that to the committee. Eleanor sent me a copy of her valedictory address, and in it she went back to how she was raised and the things that she had garnered from her family—just as I'm trying to do in this book.

Franklin needs to do hard thinking about its college graduates. They want to come back home, but there is not enough work for them. The town needs more companies like Primus to hire employees. If Jim and Amy had not had their businesses, they couldn't have come back here. People need to work and play and go to church and go to school and live in the same community. This makes for the quality of life we in Williamson County want for generations to come.

Two young girls who came before the Franklin National Bank Scholarship Selection Committee want to be dairy vets. They already know something about that because their families have dairies. In answer to my question about whether they would be coming back to Franklin after graduation, both said they didn't know if they could come back. There might not be any business for dairy vets since the dairy farms are disappearing.

When Billy and I first moved to Franklin, there wasn't much industry in the county. From a list provided by the State of Tennessee Economic Development Department, Billy looked through names of possibilities. He and I traveled at our own expense to Germany, Switzerland, and Holland to bring companies to Williamson County. We were selling land and building buildings for the new companies. Franklin and Williamson County were beneficiaries of all the business activities. My opinion is that if the new families hadn't moved in, we wouldn't have such a good school system and many of the improvements in the county. The new families had experienced better things, and they wanted—even demanded—better things. That's why growth is good. They brought us many new and better ways to put in place, especially in education.

Billy was named Man of the Year for 1983 by the *Review Appeal*, and the front page of the newspaper, December 29, 1983, had this to say about him:

J. W. Cross III has done more to help develop the economy of Williamson County than probably any other individual in the past 20 years. . . .

Cross was responsible for bringing a number of major industries to Williamson County, including Pelikan, Inc. [of Germany], Precision Tubular Heater Corp., Doug Nash Engineering and Equipment Company, Prime Colorants, Black and Decker, Parsons Company, Advanced Coating Technology, Inc., Bomas & Company [of Holland], and Emerson Electric. . . . Officials of the state Department of Economic Development have shown prospective industrialists sites here since Franklin has been one of the few communities with developments all ready with roads and utilities.

Billy was clearly a leader in economic development in this county and state. Jim and I saw that something had to happen to fill the void after Billy was stricken with his illness. We had land that we needed to sell—this was just the beginning of the recession—so I got busy and called Governor McWherter, knowing of his involvement in economic development. I explained that I would like to have a breakfast at our office for people who could generate economic development in the county. He said that he would tell me who needed to be involved at the state level and he would send some representatives. (That was before Franklin had an economic development committee.) He asked if he could come too. Somewhat taken aback, I said, "Sure, I would love for you to be there." I never dreamed that he would have time or would want to join in. Getting all those men— twelve in all, including the governor—together was a feat. I-840 was announced the day of the breakfast, and it would come right through our county. That seemed ironic timing because 840 should contribute to economic development. Following that meeting—but not necessarily because of it—leaders of the county and the city developed the economic development division of the county.

A big company wanting to move to another market will sometimes hire a site consultant, who will pick out a site that best suits its needs as far as labor, shipping, and related business concerns. The Williamson County Economic Showcase was started by the Economic Development Committee to showcase the offerings of the city and the county. The vision was to invite consultants to entice companies to send representatives and look over the area. Our Cross-owned companies contributed to the Showcase in time and money because we recognized the importance of the effort. The committee wanted to have a nice dinner at the conclusion of the Showcase, so Jim volunteered to have it at my house. Seventy-five to eighty people attended. I held the dinner for three years, and two of those years Governor McWherter was here. The Showcase is an excellent, though costly, concept. We need to stop and evaluate the results; the likelihood is that it doesn't need to be held every year.

The year I was chairman of the Showcase—the third year—we had to raise all the money because neither the city nor the county contributed at that time. Some money needs to be kept back each year so that the next year less money has to be raised. There was $25,000 in the coffers when I finished my year, and I asked that it be put in a trust fund or a savings account. The idea of stewardship can't be overemphasized in the handling of these funds.

Being around the men as they are talking of business has been enjoyable to me. I learned much, and I missed those discussions when Billy got sick. Most people didn't really know how involved I had been in the business. They tended to view me as a figurehead, which I certainly was not. Billy made the basic decisions, but we discussed the pros and cons of each issue.

Someone asked me whether I felt put down being a woman in the construction and development business. Did I have any untoward advances or remarks? The answer was no; I was always treated like a lady, maybe because I always tried to be one. They knew where they stood with me. When the women's liberation movement started, I didn't feel that I was being liberated; I was already my own person and felt liberated.

Women have more opportunities now with a better pay scale, and that's good. I still think, though, that some jobs are for men and not for women. For example, women should not be in combat. When Margaret Batey graduated (she is my oldest cousin and is now in her eighties), she had limited choices of career of teaching school or being a secretary—but she had a master's degree in education—or of being married.

For a period of time the business had an airplane. Billy bought a small plane that seated six. Then he decided he wanted a bigger one, so he sold the small one. The King Air 200 seated ten. Billy let me pick out the interior and the colors for it. Everything was brand-new from the inside out when we bought it. The hulls don't change. I had to have a potty in it; I think I only used it once, however. We'd go on fun trips as well as business trips.

He used to take all the men who worked in the field for Century Construction Company to Florida on a fishing trip. They'd go to Panama City on a chartered Greyhound bus and leave all the women at home. The secretaries and I were sitting in the kitchen in the office one day, and somebody was bemoaning the fact that the women were left behind. I said, "Y'all be good to Mama, and I'll see that you get a trip." Over the years we went to the Greenbrier, the Homestead, and Sea Island. When we took our plane to the Greenbrier and the Homestead, the pilot made us weigh ourselves and also weigh our luggage to make sure we weren't too heavy for the little plane because he had to land on top of a mountain on a short runway. I was sitting up in the cockpit to have room in the back for the others, and he just barely landed it on that mountain.

Having the plane available at Stevens Aviation at Metro Airport was nice. Our pilot had his commercial license, and he later went to work for Eastern. When we weren't using the plane, we'd lease it out. The plane stayed pretty well in the air.

After Billy got sick and I saw the wheelchair for him, I knew we couldn't get it on the plane. I sold the plane a year later and made a profit. Jim was upset with me about it, but I told him, "We can't go anywhere in it because we're all working. Daddy can't enjoy it because he isn't responding." I went to the hospital and told Billy that I had sold the plane. That was the only time he seemed to recognize what was going on, and he became very upset with me. I said, "You gave it to me, and I made money on the sale." I repeated the story for the doctors to see his reaction. We never talked around him as if he wasn't going to get well. We weren't sure what he was hearing.

The saying that something good often comes out of tragedy applied to the life of a woman who became one of the company's long-time employees, and our family can't say enough good about her. Let me give you some background information. The assistant headmaster at Ensworth was Jim Brown. The children at that school came from affluent families, but some of those children longed for attention that they were not receiving at home. All children need love and attention, and children with problems need even more. Jim Brown could get those unruly children to behave, and they loved him.

When Amy was in the seventh grade, Jim kept having pains in his legs; it was bone cancer. Amy said, "Mama, the Bible says if you pray, all things will be given." She prayed so hard for Jim Brown to be well, but he didn't make it. That was the first real test for her faith. She just knew that her prayers and the other children's prayers would help him get well. He was such a fine man and a positive influence on many children's lives, we have to wonder why he was taken.

Hazel, his wife, stayed with him at the hospital, and some of us took lunch to her as a diversion in her day. When he died, we weren't sure what to do for her. We decided to start a scholarship fund for their daughter, Kathy, who was going to high school at Lipscomb. We knew Kathy's parents could afford to send her to college, but some of us parents felt in some small way we could repay Jim for all his good works.

One day while Jim Brown was still alive I took food to Hazel and told her that Billy and I wanted to talk to her when things settled down. We wanted her to work for us; I wanted to cut back on what I had been doing in the business because the children needed me to do things for them. She had been working at Ensworth in the office and

Hazel S. Brown with Billy. Her "trial basis" as an employee of Century Construction has lasted more than twenty-five years.

commented that she knew nothing about the construction business. I said that anybody who could answer the phone, bandage a knee, and look after an irate parent all at the same time could fill our bill. Hazel and Jim, her husband, discussed it, and he told her that starting something new would be good. He knew he wasn't going to live. Hazel agreed to come to work on a trial basis, and she has been with our company for twenty-five years on that initial "trial" basis. Hazel and Kathy moved into our house anytime Billy and I traveled out of town, even though Geneva was here with the children. Kathy is a teacher at Lipscomb and is married.

Joe Ewing is a superintendent who has been with our company for more than thirty-five years and has been in charge of our steel erection. We gave him and his wife a trip to Hawaii for his twenty-fifth anniversary. Our company had black superintendents long before the government stepped in to vigorously encourage hiring of black employees.

We have many longtime employees still working, and they are like family to us. Among them is Rosemary Smithson, who had worked for our dentist, Tom Covington. Billy wanted a personal secretary, and about that time Rosemary decided she wanted to make a job change. She worked for Billy until he got sick; she stayed on at Cross Properties until I closed it. She came to work for me—she had for years been looking after our personal business, and my children and I needed her to keep doing that. She worked here at my house every day for about two years until Amy opened her law office. Four days a week she is in Amy's office, and one day a week she helps me.

Gene Cross was an actual family member who came to work for Billy and me just after he had married and had one son, Ricky. (Ricky is now in the residential construction business in Brentwood. Ricky went to Memphis State, majored in construction management, and worked for Century Construction until he went out on his own.) Gene was Billy's right-hand man for many years in the construction business as well as in the development. Having been raised on a farm, both of them knew land and how to put in roads and subdivisions. But because of his ill health, with recurring heart attacks, Billy brought him into the office instead of being out in the

Rosemary Smithson, employee of Cross Properties, and Billy Hamilton, employee of Preservation Interiors.

field, and because of the eventual closing of Cross Properties, he retired. Gene was a valuable member of our whole team. When he had been with the company twenty-five years, he and his wife, Patsy, received a trip to Hawaii. There was also a dinner in his honor at the City Club.

Our company is one of the oldest of its size. We used to have more employees—probably fifty or sixty. We weren't the largest, but in our category we competed well in volume. Most construction companies don't last this long. People have trusted us, and we have had many repeat customers.

Billy did many cost-plus jobs. People have to have confidence and trust that you're not going to "do them in." He always told people, whether it was a house or a commercial building, "You're going to get the best building on this cost-plus deal for the price, but you've got to trust me." And they did. The first house built on a cost-plus basis was for JoAnne and Dick Mchaffey. When they wanted to enlarge their house, they contacted us. We weren't doing residential construction then, so we sent them to a man we felt was trustworthy and would give them a good product. During Billy's illness, JoAnne called again for more construction and said that the man we recommended was no longer in business: Where could they find someone to rearrange some rooms and tear out some walls? They wanted to redo the house

Caroline and Carter Williams, M.D., at the twenty-fifth anniversary party for Century Construction held at Tuck-A-Way Farm.

since their children were gone. There was a slump in business, and Jim was trying to keep all his employees on the payroll. I talked to Jim about it, and he took on the job on a cost-plus basis. (Cost-plus construction means that the contractor bills to the customer anything that is a direct cost and then adds a percentage that is his profit.)

To celebrate the twenty-fifth anniversary of the company, Billy and I had a black tie party here at Tuck-A-Way Farm, and it was a big one. We had invited the Mchaffeys. Billy told the group about the relationship between them and our company and ended by saying, "We're still friends after all these years."

The *Nashville Banner*, May 31, 1984, ran an article by Mary Hance, celebrating the twenty-fifth anniversary of Century Construction Company: "When Cross and his wife, Caroline, moved to the sleepy little town of Brentwood in 1960, there was not much there—a post office, drug store, tiny grocery and a couple of service stations. . . . But now, with much of the credit going to Cross and his companies, Brentwood and Williamson County are booming."

In honor of that anniversary Dortch Oldham wrote to Billy, on December 26, 1984:

Congratulations on making it through 25 good years. Not only have you had a successful company, but you've meant an awful lot to Williamson County and to the entire Nashville area.

The family at the twenty-fifth anniversary party.

Let me also congratulate you for having made a wise decision in choosing a wife. You really do have a lovely family in every respect and when all is said and done, that's even more important than being successful in business, isn't it? . . .

J. W., it's been a pleasure working with you during these past few years. I'm sorry it hasn't been more profitable for both of us, but even though it hasn't been profitable in dollars and cents, it has been in many other ways for me. You're a real gentleman and a credit to your profession. The world needs more people like you and I mean that in all sincerity.

You can't buy your reputation.

I'm very much a fan of Ronald Reagan, and I think he'll go down as a great president. But that 1986 tax law—if it had been grandfathered in, we would have had a better real estate market. That caused many of us to lose a lot of money.

The August 1988 issue of *Advantage* magazine featured Billy, and it noted that he had a "$25 million-a-year conglomerate that includes land development, housing, design/build commercial construction, interior design, even janitorial service." Even then the struggle between pro-growth and anti-growth factions in Williamson County was getting attention because the reporter commented on it.

A DELIGHTFUL LIFE

Billy and his brother, Gene, at the twenty-fifth anniversary party.

Some years Century Construction Company may be doing auto dealerships. Other years Century Construction Company may be doing bank construction. We did more metal buildings while Billy was still involved in the business, and we did more manufacturing buildings. Jim is now restoring the Jamison Plant as a cost-plus job. Calvin Lehew, the owner, had enough faith in Jim to hire Century, and I was pleased that, like Billy, Jim is creating his trustworthiness.

My business interests took a turn from what I had been doing, yet it was an area that seems to have been perfectly suited to me. Amy had been asked to build a house for the Parade of Homes in Hearthstone in Brentwood. She chose to build a $200,000 to $250,000 Victorian house and wanted me to help her furnish it. "No problem," I said with all confidence. "We can borrow furniture from stores like Bradford's. I have some furniture, and so does Mama. We can piece it together." It turned into a problem, however. Bill Rowland of Bradford's had loaned furniture to another house in the Parade of Homes the previous year, and somebody broke in and stole all the furniture. The insurance company wouldn't let him do that again. I started buying up furniture, knowing that Amy had a 2,850-square-foot house to furnish, and I even covered some furniture belonging to Mama and me. Amy and I persevered until the job was done. She won the award.

Then we had to dispose of the things I bought, and a garage sale seemed the obvious answer. Then Billy asked me, "Why not open a shop in part of our office building?" It was like Topsy from then on, and Preservation Interiors was launched.

88

While in England in 1980, I read about a company called Passport. You hired the company, they sent you a driver (courier) and a car, and the driver took you to wholesale places, usually warehouses, where the English trade bought antiques. Then Passport shipped the antiques for you. They even loaned you money if you needed it.

That arrangement appealed to me, except the borrowing money part. Billy and I went over four times a year and brought back forty-foot containers full of furniture. We shipped everything from London, and from London it was trucked to Ipswich. Then it would come in to New Orleans or Mobile, and a Customs Office would clear it there. Today the Customs Office in Nashville clears the shipment. From the time the shipper gets a shipment until I receive it may take about two weeks by air or a month by water. The shipper price is from their door to my door, not just the port.

The shop was a good diversion for me during Billy's illness. Six or seven girls worked for me when I was furnishing model homes for contractors. Builders would build, and I'd help their buyers pick out interior and exterior finishes. I loved dealing with the people.

You never know who has money to spend. Mama and Daddy taught us never to look down on people—in business or in personal relationships. In Houston, Texas, a very casually dressed woman sailed by my booth in an antique show, made an abrupt about-face, and came back to check out my Mason's china on display—just like a sailfish does when he strikes your bait. She didn't even ask how much it cost. Between her and her daughter, they spent thousands of dollars with me. The name was recognizable after they introduced themselves.

Furniture makes the money; but fine porcelains are so expensive they can sell for as much as a piece of furniture. Porcelain is my favorite item to buy and sell. Antiques go through cycles of popularity, and what is popular shoots up in price. Every design book now features majolica, and that's why the price is through the roof. Flow blue china was that way. I bought it to satisfy my customers even though I'm not crazy about it. It looks like a mistake and was a mistake when it was first made. In general I buy the things that are unusual and the things that I like. Occasionally I'll look for specific items for people, but I tell them that they're not obligated to take them. They will be items that I'm certain I can resell.

Some people at first protested and said my prices were too high. Nashville is a peculiar market—peculiar because people want to go to New York or London or Paris and buy the pieces there and bring them home. But they can buy the same things here much cheaper; for example, in New York the prices would be three times as high as my prices. However, that attitude changed before I closed my shop.

At Opryland's Heart of Country Show put on by Dick and Libby Kramer, I was the first English formal dealer to be allowed to set up a booth. Most of the other dealers' pieces were primitives. A man across from my booth came from Wisconsin, and he was selling canoes and oars and such. He said, "There are only two sayings in the South that you women know. These little old ladies come in and say, 'Oh, my grandmother had that, or what's your best price?'"

Preservation Interiors was open Monday through Saturday, and it featured antiques, some new furniture, fabric, and wallpaper—a full-line design studio. Nobody wanted to work on Saturday, and I didn't want to work on all Saturdays, so I closed it after Billy's death.

A forty-foot moving van took the furniture from the shop to New Orleans for an auction sale. Everybody thought I had lost my mind to

Inside Preservation Interiors, which I closed following Billy's death.

90

gamble on an auction sale. I chose Neal's Auction House in New Orleans after some people from that firm came here to look at two period pieces that I wanted to sell. I wasn't going to give them away because I knew what they were worth. One of the men from Neal's asked if I had ever thought about selling my whole shop at auction; I had told him that I was going out of business. "No, the thought had not occurred to me," I said. "But I'll think about it."

The men were to be in town overnight because they had other pieces to look at in the area. As a matter of fact, I liked their approach—they wouldn't take just anything; they wanted to see pieces in person. Overnight I came up with what I had in the goods. Then I asked the man the next day what all the costs would be in the sale—the expenses of the sale, including photos for the catalog, special insurance, moving the furniture to New Orleans; the commission; and anything else. He took the time to figure it all out, and I told him that I wanted to get back what I had in the inventory, the expenses, and a bottom-line figure at the end of it all—and a signed contract specifying the details. It was a very good deal, and I felt that I was working with a reputable company, owned by John R. Neal from Columbia, Tennessee. My contact with Neal's came about through my acquaintance with Paul Cross (no relation), who was an employee of Neal's.

My goods were grouped with some smaller sales; the best items went first. I went to the preview of my things and then sat through the whole sale. The low bid on a great piece made me cringe, but some other things sold for six or seven times what I had paid for them. It helped that I understood auction sales from having a brother-in-law in the auction business. The results could have gone the other way; I couldn't have been happier with the outcome of the sale.

The antique shows I was doing were upper-end shows, set up as room settings; they ran from Thursday to Sunday and could be very lucrative. The best sponsored shows were—and are—for charities. I was doing fourteen a year for a while plus having the shop and doing design work. Keeping all of that going was hard, but it was good for me because I didn't feel guilty leaving Billy at home. He had good nurses who knew where I was, and they could get in touch with me at any time.

A Delightful Life

The majority of dealers have integrity, and they're not going to take advantage of their customers. There are too many repercussions to do otherwise. My policy is, if you buy it and you find out that I have misrepresented something, I will take it back and refund your money. Of course, a misrepresentation would never be intentional, but on some pieces, such as ones that are "married," accurately determining what has been done to them is difficult.

Billy Hamilton drives the truck and unloads the furniture at the antique shows, and he also helps me sell on the floor. Billy came to work for Billy, my husband, and me after he retired from the air force. His wife's cousin, David Grimes, had worked here at the house for us. David asked if I knew anyone who needed a jack-of-all-trades. I talked to Billy, my husband, about it, and because we were moving our Cross Properties offices to another building from downtown Franklin, we were no longer close to the bank or the courthouse, so we would need someone to go into Franklin. Billy became like a porter for the business, and he has been with us ever since. He eventually worked more with Preservation Interiors; he has been my right-hand man.

The *Review Appeal*, February 28, 1997, had a feature article on him. William Hamilton was the son of a brick mason, who was a strict father role model. "He had his morals in the right place," Billy observed. Billy was one of nine children. He is a retired air force flight engineer; he has the Distinguished Flying Cross and is a Vietnam vet. His wife, Hester, is involved in Community Housing Partnership and Leadership Franklin. Billy is the bus driver for Leadership Franklin.

We used to go up and down the East Coast for antique shows, but I do only four shows now, and that is all Billy wants to do. He and Hester do a lot of good work in the town. They tutor children. They are very devoted to their church, where Billy is a Bible study teacher. He is a people person, and everybody loves him. He dances around all the time—just full of energy—he has such a positive outlook on life.

Some antique dealers want to go with me on buying trips so that I can train them, but I'm not ready to give away my secrets yet. When my Billy was sick, I didn't go to Europe on buying trips four times a year. I went only once or twice. In 1996 I once again went four times. The pickings are getting slimmer, but they're not going to run out.

Caroline Cross

A room I designed and furnished for the Junior League Showcase House, which belonged to the former president of Peabody.

People are getting older and dying or scaling down. Museum houses will likely take the oversized furniture, which I'm not interested in. Some of the things on the market now are more massive than in my earlier days of buying.

For many years in London my driver was a young fellow trained in the art world. Before we went into a place, he usually had scouted it out while he was with other clients. He learned the kinds of pieces I wanted. I gravitated to inlaid furniture—Sheraton and Hepplewhite periods and styles. He could almost spot me on porcelain. Now I have a woman driver named Ann. She told me, "I have never seen anything so unbelievable. You can find more in these places when you come in." I admit I've found some rare things; I don't always know at first what I've got because no one can know everything about antiques. I can't keep all the information in my head about specific pieces. I buy with my eye; if I like a piece and it's pleasing, it will please somebody else.

Shopping in the States isn't cost-effective. For example, one year for their birthdays I took my sisters to Adsmore in Kentucky, which is a house museum open to the public. After we left we decided to shop our way home and take the back roads. We didn't find a thing. It would take me a month in the States to find the quality and the amount I find in England in a week.

93

Leaving Dorset Square Hotel, London, ready to go on an antique buying trip in the country, 1996.

Even with the expenses of airfare, meals, and hotel, I come out better in England. I usually stay in London and work out of there: I can cover a lot of "antiques territory" in fairly short distances. My driver picks me up early in the morning, at 7:00 or 7:30, and drops me off at 9:00 or 9:30 P.M. At the little hotel called Dorset Square they know where I'm going and my driver's name. They have wonderful room service, so that when I come in and am filthy dirty, I can relax, have a hot bath, and not have to go out again. I go to open-to-the-trade houses, which are converted barns or chicken houses in the country, and nine times out of ten when I find a piece it has not been touched as far as refinishing. But those places are slowly drying up, which is a mystery to me because the goods are still available. They must be refinishing faster than they once did.

94

There goes Auntie Mame, think people when they see me and my luggage. I never know what I'm going to do or who I'm going to see, so I pack enough to be ready for anything. Some trips I don't tell my friends in England that I'm coming; other trips I may take time to see them. I pack dresses or suits to wear to the nice restaurants or homes of friends, although women today can wear almost anything. The men are still required to wear a tie and coat.

My English bank was Barclays, but it was so antiquated in its business practices that I wanted to change banks. Through First Union here in the States, my bank officer, Mark Yawn, put me in touch with the private banking division of National Westminster Bank called COUTTS. When I told my driver, Ann, that I was changing banks, she knew immediately that COUTTS was the queen's bank. Mr. Cannon is my private banker, whom I met for the first time in January 1998.

I have to go through a set procedure when I buy items to ship. The shipper gives me my papers, that is, a book with original and three carbon copies and the stickers. The stickers have the name and address of the shipper, Hedley's Humpers, and my name and address. I was the first American Hedley's shipped antiques for. He had been shipping household goods and art to the States but not antiques.

Hedley's Humpers was using bubble wrap to protect furniture during shipping, but if a piece has been refinished and hasn't had the proper drying time, the bubbles make indentations and the piece has to be redone. (Refinishing doesn't hurt most pieces, in my opinion.)

To solve this problem, Steve Hedley, owner of Hedley's Humpers, and I came up with a blanket wrap that is waxy brown paper on the outside and gray insulation stuff inside. Each piece is wrapped and then goes in the container. Air freight is not more economical than sea transportation, but the shipment arrives more quickly. On the sea a problem is that pieces can pick up moisture sometimes.

There are no customs on goods more than one hundred years old; however, there is a charge for the release of the goods. My account book is filled out with the description of the item—for example, one mahogany breakfront circa 1860—and the amount paid and date purchased. I have never tried to pull anything over on Customs officers. Life is too short. They are producing things in Europe now that

Behind the desk in my office, all set to work.

I could sell as authentic antiques—the average person would not know that they are reproductions—but I can't do that. I went into one of the warehouses to see them make the reproductions. The carcasses were made in Greece, then shipped to England to be refinished. As a rule I didn't want to mix in antiques and reproductions; an exception was a dining room table. An antique dining room table is prone to warp when it gets in an American house. While the furniture was being unloaded in my warehouse, I asked the Customs officer to look at the pieces that I paid duty on. I asked if he could tell whether they were antiques or reproductions. He said, "Lady, I'm not interested in that. I'm interested in drugs."

In a little town outside London I bought a lady's writing desk and a pair of old Paris compotes. The shippers picked up the writing desk but forgot the compotes. The lady who owned the shop called and told the shippers to pick them up the next time they were out there. The records showed that they picked them up, but they couldn't find the compotes to ship them to me. Hedley's Humpers called me and deducted the amount I had paid for them from my shipping bill. A few days ago they called to say that they had found the compotes. The English people are very honest.

For several years I did the antique show at the Belle Meade Mansion. A couple wanted to buy wicker furniture for their porch, but they didn't know whether it would all fit. I'm a great believer in letting people take the furniture home on approval and delivering it to the house for them. If they don't buy it, I charge only a small handling fee. They never forget that, and most times the furniture doesn't come back. The man asked if we made house calls, meaning would I come and help arrange the furniture, and I agreed. They ended up keeping the furniture too.

Carol Vance, who worked for me, said that she had never seen anybody enjoy selling as much as I do. The buying part is equally enjoyable to me. Since my daddy and Daddy Jones were always buying and selling things, I guess that is where I get my love for the business.

CHAPTER 5

Hearth and Home

Mid pleasures and palaces though we may roam
Be it ever so humble, there's no place like home.
—John Howard Payne

Our first house was the one that Daddy had built for us in Donelson on Dellrose Drive. Billy and I lived there a year. Then we built a larger house also in Donelson. To reach the school where I was teaching in Goodlettsville, I had to drive through Nashville. There were no bridges from Donelson to Gallatin Road, only a ferry, and I felt uncomfortable taking the ferry every morning. After having taught there for two years, I resigned to help Billy in the business, but a big surprise was that I was pregnant with Amy. Before long, I was balancing a baby with one hand and running an adding machine with the other hand.

We moved to Brentwood on Old Smyrna Road when Amy was one and a half years old. Tom Batey, my cousin, is an architect, and he drew the plans for that house. He later became the first architect for Hospital Corporation of America; he is now retired.

To me, houses are like people, and I become attached to them. I have never gone back to a house that I have lived in; I think that is a painful experience. I get emotional when I move; therefore, I haven't moved too much. I should have sold this house, Tuck-A-Way Farm, when Billy died, but now it's in trust for my children. I'm hoping that Jim, Amy, or another family member will move in my house at my death. My strong wish is that it stay in the family because of the way it has been deeded. The children own the block of land here, which includes their houses and mine.

99

Jim, Jenny, Madeline, and Will lived in the apartment downstairs while their house was being built. Amy also lived here while her house was being built. Both Jim and Amy sold their houses before they had time to build on the property on the farm. I was determined that we were going to get along with no fussing or hard feelings, and that was accomplished. I hated to see them leave. Many mornings my grandchildren came up the steps, peeped around the corner of my bedroom, and said, "Are you awake, Grandmother?" Then they jumped in bed with me. I tried not to interfere with their parents' discipline of them because all I wanted to do was to hug them. I knew how my grandmother felt about the joy of being a grandparent. Billy would have been so happy to have had both children and both grandchildren under one roof.

The house where my parents lived is now owned by the Beatty family. We've all become so close that we call this the Cross compound; there are sixty-four acres including our original land plus the Beattys' land. That house is intricately tied in to my house with a private driveway between the two houses.

Aerial view of the house and part of the Tuck-A-Way Farm on Lewisburg Pike, 1989.

Billy and I took the plan of the house in Brentwood and started from there in designing the present home. The traffic flow is so important, especially in entertaining a large group; that was a point taught in my college home ec courses. Since I was raised with lots of family and company, it's a good thing that Billy liked having my family over for get-togethers and entertaining in general. Big rooms were important too.

The hallway is about forty feet long. It would look like a railroad track if it was narrow, so I wanted it five feet plus. When we were permitted to bring Billy home from the hospital in his wheelchair, the doctors were going to give us a few days to set up the house with hospital equipment and do what needed to be done to prepare for wheelchair usage. The wheelchair, an Autobach made in Germany, was very big, and Billy's legs extended forward. Turning corners was hard. We had wide doorways on all bathrooms and also a wide hallway. The house was already designed to accommodate a wheelchair patient. Having a wide hall, wide doorways, and large rooms was not done with the thought of preparing for a wheelchair, but it certainly worked to our advantage when we were presented with that challenge.

Tom Batey helped us at first with some of the architecture on the present house. Then we found an architect who took our drawings and did the structural part. A steel beam runs in the middle of the house because of its length. The house is sitting on a rock quarry, and there is sand underneath so it can float with the movement if there is an earthquake. After all these years the house has had a bit of movement.

The idea for the molding might have come from Uncle Bryan's house, which had walnut trim and handmade molding around the door facings. Billy and I ended up at Stephens's Woodworking in Nashville where they told us that the price would be prohibitive on some of the things we wanted. Driwood Moulding Company in South Carolina made molding and kept it in stock, so the man at Stephens's in Nashville handed us over to them. Mr. Mitchell, the owner of Driwood, and a young man came here with blocks of designs for us to make selections. I wanted walnut in the study, but real walnut cost too much; we used poplar and stained it with walnut color. Other people have been here to copy our study—Governor McWherter looked at it for his river house (Nashville Sash duplicated it as much as possible), and Dick Freeman used the design in the penthouse of Royal Oaks.

The rooms include kitchen, breakfast room, utility room, dining room, entrance hall, living room, playroom, study, and four bedrooms on the main floor; we also enclosed the porch for a sunroom. There is an apartment downstairs. Nine baths are in the whole house, and there are two working fireplaces. The house has 8,500 square feet on one floor; upstairs and basement make it 10,000.

In 1987 Tuck-A-Way Farm was featured in *Nashville Magazine*'s "At Home" section. The writer called it a "comfortably elegant blend of antiques and contemporary furnishings." We have it filled with family photos and portraits. We chose a gently sloping hill for the site, and the name came from a Tuck-A-Way house that I knew in Sewanee as a child.

David Grimes came to work for us part-time when he was at CPS (Chicago Printing String). David, a native of Williamson County, was my right-hand man at the house for many years. When Billy, my husband, died, David asked what was going to happen to him. I had told Billy Hamilton that I was going to close the shop but wanted to keep him working part-time with the antique shows, and that was fine with Billy. David knew I had talked with Billy about that, and he was wondering about his status. I said, "David, nothing is going to happen to you. I expect you'll stay here until I die." He was lonesome and unhappy. The farm managers were gone; the nurses were gone; there was no activity in a house that had once been full of people and daily activity. The two cooks, Minnie and Geneva, had retired. David had lived on a trailer on the farm, but when Billy got sick, the children moved him into the apartment in the house in case there was an emergency. We never did have to call him during the night, though.

One Thanksgiving David told me he had taken a job as a house man with Cal Turner. A wonderful couple now have taken his place to care for the house. Still, I miss my Geneva and Minnie. When God closes a door, he opens a window. He sent me a young man, Jason Hay, who takes care of everything outdoors.

Jim gets upset when I say the following because some people say it and don't mean what they say: we've been blessed to have this house and we should share it with other people. And I *do* mean it. In our early years in Franklin, there were few places to have events. The older houses may be large, but their rooms are small. We were always having some event—a fund-raiser for the Heritage Foundation or the Y. Many other events and other functions have been here, including dinners for political candidates. We and the house have always welcomed guests.

One Christmas season nearly one thousand people came through the house for a Christmas open house as well as a sit-down dinner for friends and family. We've always had caterers, and I'm particular about them. As long as I know the caterers and servers and they know my kitchen and my house, it works out.

The family tradition has been to celebrate on Christmas Eve. That worked out with all my generation so that the children could have Santa Claus on Christmas morning at their houses. We went to Grandma's or Mama's house on Christmas Eve. Now my children and grandchildren come to my house on Christmas Eve.

As far back as I can remember, 1935 or 1936, being at my grandparents' house for Christmas was the highlight of the holiday season. The family would come to Grandma's for Christmas Eve supper, and we would exchange presents. Granddaddy Jordan started the tradition of giving each of his children one hundred dollars and each of the grandchildren one dollar. You have to remember, that was the Depression, and that was a lot of money. He gave other gifts too. Gift giving was a part of my family. Giving is better than receiving, and I want my grandchildren to learn that lesson.

The smells of Christmas remain vivid. Nothing smells better to me, and reminds me more of Grandma's, than the smell of cornbread dressing cooking. Naturally the food and gifts appealed to us as children. As we grew older, there was more to that family gathering than gifts and food. It was the love of each other and the happy memories of grandparents and parents.

Grandma closed her home in Smyrna and came to live with my parents in Nashville in 1944. My mother assumed the role of host for this dinner until the 1960s. Grandma died in 1953.

After Billy and I moved to our present house in the mid-seventies, we continued the role as hosts for the Christmas dinner. The house was large enough to accommodate up to eighty people. In 1979, eighty-five gathered here. Our menu naturally follows the one of the 1930s that I remember. It consists of turkey, country ham, cornbread dressing, cranberries, sweet potatoes, green beans, hot rolls, boiled custard, and a variety of cakes. The boiled custard is served in a punch bowl with cakes beside it. Since whiskey was so forbidden in the family and we knew that there was a family weakness for alcohol, we didn't serve it—except at Christmas to go with the boiled custard. Mama put it in a vinegar cruet, and Billy teased her about that. Later I changed the tradition to whiskey in a cut glass cream pitcher.

Other celebrations at our house have included Mama and Daddy's fiftieth wedding anniversary and four weddings—the horse manager's daughter; Billy's niece; Jim and Jenny; and Amy and Rex.

The Jones family reunion now happens once a year, in July in Franklin or Nashville. Most of my Jones cousins scattered throughout the United States whereas more of my Jordan cousins continued to live in Tennessee. Nevertheless, all of the Jones kinfolks make an effort to get together and to keep in touch. Here is a summary of Daddy's brothers and sisters and their children; Daddy was born in 1906, between Nona and Ailene. Their parents were Artemis Leslie and Bertha Era Moon Jones. (The Moon line can be traced all the way back to the time of the Magna Charta.)

Jess went to Niagara Falls, New York, after college to enter the shoe business; he was born in 1899. His wife was named Mable; they had no children. He died in 1968.

John Robert was born in 1900; he was named for his grandfather, Dr. John Robert Moon. He lived and worked in Chicago as an accountant but retired in Nashville; he never married. He died in 1981.

Grace was born in 1902. She married Joe Priestly and had two daughters, Marjorie and Sue. Aunt Grace and Uncle Joe lived in Vicksburg, Mississippi, during his working years. Marjorie married James E. Duggan of Buffalo, Illinois, and Sue married Jess W. Moore of Dubach, Louisiana. Marjorie is the keeper of the records for the Jones family, and she was a schoolteacher. Sue was adopted by Aunt Grace and Uncle Joe.

Nona May, born in 1904, married John Butner of Winston-Salem, North Carolina. The first Sunday that my family went to West End

Family reunion of eight of ten Jones children. Front row, left to right, Tom, John, and Boyd (Buster). Second row, left to right, Onnie, Audrey, Sara, Nona (I was told as a child that I looked like her), and Grace.

Church of Christ after we had moved to Nashville, a man came up to me and said that I had to be Nona's daughter or niece. That was the first time anyone had told me that I looked so much like her. Everyone had always said that she was a great beauty, so I took that as a compliment. That man had been one of her boyfriends at Lipscomb. Aunt Nona had been trained to be a teacher, but since there were no jobs here in Middle Tennessee, she went to North Carolina. They have three children—John Jr., Joann, and Eleanor. John Jr. (we call him Johnny) is the second oldest of the grandchildren. When I was in high school, our family would drive to North Carolina in the summertime and go to the beach with Aunt Nona and her family. Her house was one that Cornwallis had slept in; she and Uncle John soon after their marriage bought the house in the village of Bethania and restored it. Uncle John was very talented in wood-

105

working and built the case for the pipe organ for the Moravian Church in Bethania, and he also built grandfather clocks for his children. His occupation was a jobber (that is, a wholesaler) of Blue Horse school supplies and other related supplies. Johnny married Josephine (Jo) Conrad. Joann (also Jo) is about my age; she was married to Tom Larose from Greensboro, and she became a teacher. Eleanor is a teacher in Charlottesville, Virginia.

Martha Ailene, born in 1908, was named for her grandmother, Martha Melinda Dryden Moon. She married Ernest Kapp, who was a chemist for R. J. Reynolds. Their children were Ernestine and Melinda. Ernestine went to Salem College on a scholarship because her father's ancestors were one of the founding families of Salem and the college. Any descendant from that Kapp family could get a similar scholarship. She majored in voice. Later she went to San Antonio, Texas, and met and married Stanley Studer Jr., an attorney. Melinda's married name is Pailetoril, and she and her husband lived with Aunt Ailene. Aunt Ailene died in 1998.

Sara Elizabeth was born in 1911. She married Marion Stem, her high school sweetheart who died in 1941. She and Marion married while he was still a student at UT, majoring in agriculture. That was almost unheard of at that time; most students waited until after graduation to marry. They lived in Knoxville while he was in school, and they had three children—Carl, Kathleen, and Beth—before he graduated. Uncle Marion worked for a federal agency involved in agriculture. Carl is my "best-educated cousin" on either side; his wife is named Linda. He graduated from Vanderbilt, then he went to England for a year on a Marshall Scholarship to Reading University and received an M.A.; later he got a Ph.D. in economics from Harvard. Carl has just retired from Texas Tech as head of the business department. Before that, he was with the World Bank in Washington, D.C. Kathleen was married to Bob McClaren; she is a teacher, living in Oak Ridge. Beth lives in Hendersonville; she married Jess King.

Audrey Oletta was born in 1913. While she was going to Lipscomb, she lived with the family of the president of the college, Batsell Baxter. She helped Mrs. Baxter with household duties, so she had room and board, and Daddy Jones had to pay only for tuition.

When Mr. Baxter was offered a job at Abilene Christian College, he and Mrs. Baxter asked Aunt Audrey to go with them and finish her last two years of college. Daddy Jones agreed to the plan. She met and married Clyde Ross, and they both were schoolteachers. Their children were Melissa (Mrs. David McCoy); Harvey; Rebecca (Mrs. John Zaun); Betsy (Mrs. Cannon); and David. Aunt Audrey has retired twice but still substitute teaches. She is now in her eighties.

Onnie was born in 1915. She married Jordan Redmon, who was her high school sweetheart. Aunt Onnie might have gone to Lipscomb one quarter. Their children were Barbara (Mrs. Everette Dennis of North Carolina), Larry, and Jess (J.J.) Jones. Larry farmed a while in Eagleville but retired and moved with his wife, Alice, to Atlanta to be near their only child and grandchild. J. J. married Sharon Futtrell and is a principal in Gallatin. Onnie and Jordan live in a retirement home in Gallatin.

Leslie Boyd (Uncle Buster) was born in 1917. He married Robbie Raulston and became a contractor. Their children were Leslie Robert and Ann Era. Leslie married Sara; he is a graduate of Georgia Tech and is an engineer, who went to work for General Motors. He is preparing to retire. His specialty has been setting up state-of-the-art assembly lines. Ann Era is special to me in that I brought her home from the hospital in my arms. Because Uncle Buster was out of town, Mama went to pick up Aunt Robbie and the baby, and I went along. Ann Era lives in Birmingham.

Marjorie Priestly, Johnny Butner, Jo Butner, and I were the four oldest grandchildren when our great-grandfather, Dr. John R. Moon, died. One of a set of four chairs was given to each of us at his death. Granddaddy Moon was a doctor in Rutherford County, mainly in Eagleville and Unionville. His house, which has since burned, was across from where the high school is now. It was a wonderful example of a Victorian story and a half house with two bay windows. Daddy remembered the square piano placed in one of the bay windows.

Our children, Amy and Jim, have always been joys and very mature for their ages. Maybe that was because they were raised around adults. Billy and I never talked down to them or used baby talk. If anything, they tired of hearing business discussions around the dinner table. We never had them leave the room when we were talking; we discussed everything in front of them. Amy was born December 23, 1958, and Jim was born January 16, 1964. Both arrived by cesarean section.

Amy and Leigh, her first cousin, played together often when Leigh came from Alabama to see Mama and Daddy. Their grand-daddy told them, "You know, I have two granddaughters and one of them is bad." He was a big tease, but that bothered Amy. One day Amy was playing with something, and Leigh wanted it. Amy wouldn't give it up. Leigh hit her, didn't hurt her, but grabbed that toy. Amy stood there very defiantly and said, "Now I know who is the bad granddaughter!"

Jim Brown tested Amy at Ensworth, which was my first outing after Jim's birth in 1964. Amy's test scores were high. He asked me why I hadn't taught her to read, and I said, "Mr. Brown, I was afraid to teach her to read. I've never taught in the lower school. I was afraid I would do it wrong." He replied, "Whatever you might have done wrong could be undone." Amy started in kindergarten; if she had known how to read at that point, she would have been placed in first grade. That school had levels to let the students progress at their own speed. Amy was doing second and third grade work when she was in kindergarten, and she loved it. That was the right school for her.

Billy and I were interested in the school activities of both children. Sometimes the children didn't want us at their games, though. Amy was self-conscious about our being there. She was good at playing basketball and field hockey. What's more, she competed with herself.

We told our children that they wouldn't be allowed to participate in some activities away from school that other children participated in, private parties and such. We brought their friends here to our house and saw it to that there were plenty of things for them to do. They had our backing and our blessing for all school-related events.

An outstanding student at Harpeth Hall, Amy was second in her graduating class in 1977. In 1976, she got the Sophia Dobson blanket, which was the junior year award for excellence in scholarship, as she had done in her freshman year. She was also named Lady of the Hall, probably the highest honor for a senior girl at Harpeth Hall. She was

*Amy following graduation from
Harpeth Hall, 1977.*

in the National Merit Scholar program, the Cum Laude Society, and
Mu Alpha Theta (math society). At various times she was business
manager and assistant editor of the school newspaper.

Amy graduated in three years, without going to summer school,
from the University of Tennessee with a degree in historic preservation. She was in the College Scholars Program. That is, a college
scholar is appointed a tutor, and with him, Amy and I chose her
curriculum. A college scholar can float from school to school at the
university. She had the grades to qualify for the program, and she
might have had to go abroad to study. She did manage to do all her
work in the States. Amy had taken so much advanced placement at
Harpeth Hall that in her first year in college she was taking sopho-
more-level courses. She enrolled in French I, which would enable her
to be eligible for Phi Beta Kappa. Her professor recognized that she
had taken French from grammar school through high school; he
asked her to take a test after about two weeks, and she passed with a

high score. He gave her credit for two years of French. Amy was honored to be Phi Beta Kappa, and she graduated cum laude in 1980.

Both children, I think, chose UT because they wanted to have the college experience of living away from home in a dormitory. Jim had become a UT football fan even in grade school, and that had something to do with his choice.

Amy was accepted at the University of Virginia but chose not to go there. Our ancestor, Dr. Thomas Walker, gave the land for the University of Virginia, and Francis Walker, his son, went to France to hire the first professors for the school at Thomas Jefferson's request. That family connection made it easier for her to get accepted; the university accepts few out-of-state students. The primary reason she turned the offer down was that there was no Church of Christ nearby,

Amy's restoration of her first house with Preservation Construction.

110

and she would have to drive many miles to church. Her church affiliation was that important to her. Laurel Avenue Church of Christ in Knoxville welcomed college students and offered programs for them, and both Jim and Amy attended there and enjoyed it.

In March 1980 Amy began Preservation Construction Company with her daddy, though she was still in school. Among the houses she worked on or restored were the German House; the 1810 House on Fourth Avenue North; an addition to Mary Frances Ligon's house on West Main Street; Harpeth Academy; and two phases on Carnton Mansion—the veranda cornice and other work. On top of doing all that she taught a course in preservation techniques at O'More College of Design. She received the Williamson County Heritage Foundation's annual award in 1982 for restoring the 114-year-old Heritage Federal Savings & Loan building. Amy was believed to be the state's largest-volume female home builder, according to an article in the *Tennessean* (December 30, 1984).

Amy comments, "One year I think I built seventy-five houses, and there were approximately one hundred building permits pulled in the whole city. Here is how I got started building houses: I was doing restoration, but Daddy was having trouble finding a builder, so he encouraged me to build just one house for him. Two hundred and forty-five houses later, I was still building houses in one subdivision— Maplewood. I have probably built more than three hundred houses to this point.

"From our early years our parents involved us in business. Daddy was criticized for turning so much responsibility over to my brother and me at an early age. But that was what he needed to do, especially in light of what happened to him. He really did let us do the work. Of course, we knew that he was there as a mentor or a guide, but he didn't monitor us on a day-to-day basis. He was very interested in what we were doing, but it was still our baby."

A diversion from her work was being a member of the court at the Bal d'Hiver held February 12, 1983, at the Belle Meade Country Club. It was a special honor to be asked by Kappa Alpha Theta.

Amy joined a law firm in Franklin after graduating from the Nashville School of Law; she was notified that she passed the bar in October 1993. She "will concentrate her law practice on real estate and small business matters." Previously she had Preservation Construction Company and Cross Roads Real Estate, reported the *Williamson Leader* (November 4, 1993). Later she went into practice in her own office.

Amy saw how much lawyers were involved in the business. That may have led her to get a law degree. To me, law seemed to be common sense, but Amy taught me that it was not.

Amy says of her career now: "There is some overlap in going from being a contractor and Realtor and preservationist to being a lawyer. I do construction law and real estate law. I sometimes miss being out in the field. I may do more construction in the future. Right now I'm a one-woman law practice; taking a day off is tough. I do title closings, contracts, leases, probate work, wills, some estate planning, and small business law, such as forming corporations. I don't do litigation or divorces or courtroom law." She searches titles for many in the black community, and she has succeeded in untangling some of them.

Amy and Rex Nance had been dating some time, and they announced their engagement in January 1998. Rex works for a manufacturing company in Nashville. He has two children; Whitney is twelve and Hannah is fourteen. The wedding in the spring of 1998 took place at Tuck-A-Way, and a large garden party followed. Madeline and Rex's daughters were attendants, and Will was the ring bearer. Amy and Rex asked their close friends, several couples, to stand up with them during the ceremony. Limiting the guest list was a challenge with all of our family members and friends and business relationships. They live in Amy's house, and Rex and his girls share Amy's love of horses. With Amy's marriage, we got three new family members at once, and when Amy and Jim and their families come for Sunday dinner now, we've had to move to the dining room.

In their younger years at home, Amy and Jim had chores to do. In fact one time when Robin Beard, our congressman, drove by, he saw us working in the yard. We couldn't keep grass in the ditch down the drive in front. It kept washing, so I thought the solution was to sod it. We got a sod cutter, went back on the farm, and cut sod. Amy and Jim and I put sod down the driveway. Robin told Billy, "You sure do work those children." They were always doing something, but then Billy and I were always doing something alongside them.

*Amy and Rex Nance, following
wedding ceremony.*

Both children have been good at handling money. Maybe they heard Billy and me weighing decisions of large purchases, and it made an impression. We never knew what we were going to be making. You talk about a gamble—the business we were in was a big-time gamble, and we were rolling some pretty big dice. We had to keep something back.

Jim played football from junior high through high school. He also was a shot-putter and did well in state-level track meets. He went to Battle Ground Academy and then moved to Brentwood Academy in his sophomore year. He had to lay out his sophomore year from football because he had played football at BGA, but he played during his junior and senior years. He was first string on the championship team— TSSAA ranked as AA then. Apparently if Jim sacked the quarterback,

113

Jim following graduation from Brentwood Academy, 1982.

his daddy would give him twenty dollars. They didn't tell me about that until much after the fact. Jim said that he learned a lot from playing sports; one lesson was to be a team player, which came from the coach and the other players. He elected not to play ball at the college level, however. Jim graduated from high school in 1982.

After two years of college, Jim told us he wanted to quit school and learn what his uncle Gene and his daddy could teach him. Little did we know that was a very good move because of what happened with Billy. UT was so full, Jim would have had to go five or six years to finish a degree in the major he wanted, business. He would go to the agricultural department and take a course in horse science, not because he liked horses but because the business classes were full. It was getting to be a waste of time, and he wasn't really interested in college either.

Before Billy got sick, we gave Jim a percentage of Century Construction that we started in 1958. He has been there ever since.

After Billy's death, I gave him the remaining interests.

An article in the *Nashville Business Journal*, March 9–13, 1987, reported that the company's sales more than doubled since Jim took over from Billy in 1985. A highlight for Jim was construction of The Legends golf clubhouse in 1991–92. It was a 26,000-square-foot structure.

Jenny Ann McCain, daughter of Mr. and Mrs. William J. McCain of Franklin, married James William Cross IV on September 12, 1987, at Fourth Avenue Church of Christ. Jenny was born in Donelson; her family moved from there to Georgia where she lived until she started to college, and then they moved to Franklin. Jenny has a degree in business management from the University of Tennessee in Chattanooga; she was employed with Access Data Services in Brentwood when she and Jim married. Jim and Jenny had known each other for some time before they started dating, and they owned condos in the same complex.

Billy and I had a buffet supper at Tuck-A-Way for five hundred guests for the wedding reception. We had such a good time, even though Daddy had died the day before; the memories are bittersweet. On a video of the wedding Billy told Jim to put Jenny on a pedestal

Wedding day at the Fourth Avenue Church of Christ— Jenny, Jim, and Geneva B. Clark, who worked many years for the family.

115

Billy and his mother on Jim's wedding day.

and never take her off, and he added, "I did your mother that way." My mother had some real sweet things to say on the video, and it was hard for her to speak because of grieving for Daddy. She was in a wheelchair for the reception, but she insisted on being escorted by an usher and walking down the aisle of the church for the ceremony. Billy was mingling and having the best time in the world with all the guests. We didn't have an official receiving line at the reception, but everybody was offering me condolences. Billy came up to me and said, "You've got to move on; people are backed up the drive down to the highway." Although we had a highway patrolman directing the traffic, the situation was becoming dangerous. That was as good a night as it could have been under the circumstances.

The day Madeline was born, July 11, 1991, we were all with Jenny in her room at the Williamson County Hospital, but as the birth was drawing near, only Jim stayed with Jenny. When he came out to the waiting room, he said it was a little girl. We didn't want to know before the birth what the baby was. Madeline was wide awake, looking around. I'm not talking from a proud grandmother stand-point either; I have never seen a baby so alert. She didn't have much hair, but had vivid eyes and beautiful skin. They named her Madeline Brandau. Madeline is not a family name, but Jenny's best friend from high school named her daughter Madeline. The Brandau was the middle name of Billy's mother, Pearl Brandau. Dr. Harris, Pearl's father, had a best friend named Dr. Brandau who practiced medicine in Nashville.

Jenny was pregnant when she went to London with me on a buying trip. As Jim brought Madeline out, I said that she had already been across the ocean to Europe.

The Gulf War started while we were there. I heard the TV in another room in our small hotel at two or three in the morning, and I told Jenny I was going to turn on the TV in our room. Somehow being so near to the war but not being in actual danger was exciting to me.

We were to leave that morning and fly to Dublin. At Heathrow, tanks were all around, and in the terminal were policemen with machine guns. They told us to keep our bags nearby as a precaution about bombs. Jenny was frightened, she later told me. She almost called Jim to tell him she was coming home.

Madeline was what we all needed, given the situation with Billy. Madeline has been a delight from the day she was born. She wants to know everything, and she has a good time wherever she goes. Her favorite parts about school are recess and lunch.

Madeline called her granddaddy Gaga. She was two when Billy died. We thought if he would become alert to anything, it would be her. On the way home from the hospital after her birth Jim brought her to our house to see Billy, but he did nothing to acknowledge her presence. Later on Jim would put her in the bed with her granddaddy, and Madeline would pat his face—somehow she knew he was sick. She has much empathy and sympathy and a caring attitude. We had to try to explain to her about death. She asked when Gaga was coming back, and I told her, "When you die and you go to live with God, you do not come back." She sort of accepted that. Now Will, at three, is asking about Gaga. Madeline and Will were with me in the car, and Will asked when Gaga was coming back. I said, "He's with God. It's a better place and he's not hurting anymore. He's feeling good. I want you both to know that I think he sees what you're doing and what is happening." I believe that. I don't think God lets those who have died know the bad things happening on earth. I have no basis for this belief, though.

A Delightful Life

When Linda, my sister, lost her first child, Amy was four or five. Amy asked, "Why did God take this baby?" I said, "That was the prettiest little boy. I think God felt that he couldn't live without him." That seemed to satisfy her. We adults may think we have to go into these long rigamaroles, but we don't. I had to relate it to something that I felt she could comprehend. I think Madeline was that way about Billy's death. When I told her that he had gone to a place where there wasn't any pain, that we had to feel good about that, but we were sad that he was gone, I said, "Aren't you glad that he doesn't have pain anymore? God looks after him."

On May 29, 1994, a Sunday, Jim was in the balcony of the church to serve Communion. When it was time for the men to go to the Communion table, Madeline trotted right along with her daddy and stood with him. One of the men told Madeline to sit with him and got her away from her daddy. There are so many experiences like this that we grandparents can tell.

Madeline dressing up in the dress I wore thirty-nine years ago on New Year's Eve, complete with mink stole and jewelry.

118

Caroline Cross

James William (Will) Cross V was born on August 31, 1994. Jim called me at 5:30 A.M. and said to come and pick up Madeline, they were on their way to the hospital. Jenny had no problems with either birth; she is fortunate to give birth easily. I told Madeline that by the end of the day she would have a baby brother or sister. She was very much a part of the pregnancy, and she has never been jealous of Will. Keeping her busy the day of Will's birth included giving her two cups of flour and some aluminum foil and the flour sifter. She sifted that and played in it quite a while. She had flour all over her and had the best time. Later Jim called me to bring Madeline to the hospital; Will's birth was imminent. Isn't it wonderful that younger children can now go to the hospital when a sibling is born?

I could not pick up Will when he was a baby because I had just had my spine fused. Jim came over to sit with me while I was recuperating and brought Will, and he put Will in my arms when I was sitting. That was the extent of my involvement with Will until my recovery was over four months later. Will has really curly hair, but Jim wanted it kept short because everyone thought he was a girl. He was just as pretty a baby as Madeline was.

Madeline and Will are always good with me. Madeline goes to the beauty parlor with me, and she gets her nails done. Then we have

Will dressing up in Gaga's English tweed hat, with binoculars and sword, getting ready to go "hunting with Mr. Beatty," the next-door neighbor.

lunch. Sometimes she'll run errands with me. She is inexhaustible. I asked her, "Why do you like to do these things with me?" She looked at me very seriously and said, "Grandmother, you are fun!" As far as I'm concerned, that is a million-dollar compliment.

We like to eat at the Picnic in Belle Meade Drug Store. Madeline orders for herself. Before we got there, I told Will on his first trip to the Picnic what Madeline likes to have, but he could decide what he wanted. I impressed on him that we had to be very good in the restaurant because few children were there. They didn't make a peep and were perfect examples of model behavior. Other people commented about how good they were, and that made me feel like a queen.

Madeline will eat boiled okra, and I cook it just for her. Geneva taught me how to cook okra so that it's not slimy. Madeline tells everyone, "Don't eat my okra. Grandmother cooked it just for me." She and Will like to help me in the kitchen. Everything takes longer to do, but that's the nice part of having them with me.

Jim and Amy would help Geneva and me in the kitchen when they were young. Jim likes to cook. He and Amy made recipe cards for such things as hot chocolate. We were not a family for eating fried foods, but Jim would make donuts from scratch. Geneva let him do anything he wanted to, but I didn't want him cooking with all that grease for his donuts if we were away from home because of the danger of fire. To this day, the recipe cards that Jim and Amy wrote are still in my recipe box.

Madeline asked me one day when we were making pies, "Grandmother, are you going to live to see me married?" I said, "I sure hope so. I'm going to ask God from now on to let me see your husband." She asked, "Well, what about Will?" I said, "There are three years' difference in your ages. I'm not sure God will spare me that long, but I will ask." That's deep thinking for a youngster.

Jenny has always said not to say anything in front of the children that I don't want repeated. I don't keep anything from them.

Madeline and Will have no first cousins, but my sisters' grandchildren will act as their first cousins, and Jenny has first cousins with children also. I hope they'll have the same kind of relationship that I've had with my first cousins.

Billy said before Mama died, "We're not going to keep this Jordan family together when Aunt Maggie [Mama's oldest sister] dies." He meant coming to our house for family Christmas. I thought he was wrong, and it proved to be that way. Billy was in the hospital for the first Christmas after he got sick. On Christmas Eve 1990, which was the second Christmas after he became ill, the nurses and doctors thought he was dying, and I prayed to God that he wouldn't die on Christmas Eve and leave that memory. The nurses asked me to call the children to be here just in case. He did pull through that time, and a prayer was answered.

Over the years foreign students stayed with us; two were associated with the American Field Service (AFS) program, and two were family friends. We never officially applied for a student at AFS. We got them after they had been in an unhappy situation in the U.S. The exchange program of AFS was organized in 1947; its goal was to stimulate international understanding by placing students in typical home situations across the world. Expenses are funded in part by the student's family and by organizations in the student's future home. The students gave us more and we learned more than they learned from us, I think. It was good for Amy and Jim and for Billy and me to learn tolerance of other people. Other cultures can teach us things.

Jac (Jacqueline) Reiners was sixteen when she came here from Krefeld, West Germany. She attended Harpeth Hall with Amy for the 1975–76 school year. She is now a small animal vet in Krefeld, and we keep in contact with her.

Elena was going to Franklin Road Academy. She was from Helsinki, Finland, where her father was an international attorney.

Simon Brooks-Ward was from Hertfordshire outside London. We had met his father, Raymond Brooks-Ward, when we traveled to the horse show at Olympia in 1980. Simon had a twin, James, and we told them to come and see us if they visited the States. Jackie Adams went with us to England; Sherri Dietz was there; and they and Jim and Amy all chummed around together on that trip with Simon. A year later Raymond called and said that he needed to do something with Simon. Simon had a royal appointment in the army—he would have

Graduation day at Harpeth Hall, 1976, for Jac (Jacqueline) Reiners from Krefeld, West Germany.

to serve a year or two—but he was about to be drafted. James, his twin brother, had been placed in Australia. Raymond wanted to know if we could take Simon until June or July. I told him that we would with stipulations—no driving, no smoking, no drinking, etc. We had the same rules that AFS had, even though he was not coming to us through AFS.

Simon was to work around the farm, not for pay really. He had trouble getting through Atlanta and on to Nashville because he didn't have a return airline ticket and he didn't have a green card. When the officials asked him if he was going to work, he said yes. That raised a flag. The officials called me, and I explained the situation: the boy's father was a renowned BBC equine commentator and had been knighted by the queen; Simon would certainly be going home to serve in the army; he was only going to work unofficially around our place. That satisfied them. Simon was a year older than Jim, who was then a senior in high school; Simon had already graduated from the equivalent of American high school.

Students at Brentwood Academy took Simon under their wing. We had a party for him at our home before he left. Simon stayed upstairs in the little suite, and he took forever to come down that night. The wait was worth it because he walked in wearing his tuxedo. Before he came to live with us, Simon had asked if he should bring his tuxedo, and I said, "Yes, you might go to the prom or other places to wear it." When Simon walked into the room where the party was being held, he said, "I brought the damned thing. I might as well wear it."

Raymond Brooks-Ward has since died. In addition to being the equine commentator for the BBC, he ran a horse show promotion company. Raymond did the commentary for the BBC at the LA Olympics for the horse events. Simon is now in the horse show promotion business. He has a wife and two daughters.

On one trip to England, I had dinner with Simon and his wife, Katherine. I asked if they were going to send their two little girls off to boarding school. Very quickly both Simon and his wife said, "No. They'll be schooled near our home." That meant they would go to day school, and I was thankful for that. I think Simon learned from coming here how important it was to be in a home situation, especially to sit down to meals as a family. We didn't make a big deal out of the way we lived, but he saw by example how the family interacted on a daily basis. He didn't have that experience as a child. From the age of six he was shipped off to boarding school. In his social stratum in England, that was the way children were raised. He didn't want that to happen with his children, however.

Sabine came to stay with us in 1960. She is ten years younger than I am, and we have the same birthday. She was here a year and a half and went her first whole year to Lipscomb. She learned to improve her English by watching TV. She had the basics in written English, but not spoken English, when she arrived.

In Heidelberg after Billy and I first married, we had a very good relationship with Sabine's whole family. Her mother, Ruth, said to me one day when we were about ready to come back home, "Would you take Sabine? Her father and I will pay for her education, but will you let her live with you and help you for her room and board so that she can go to school where you went?" I asked, "Why? What brings you to that?" She answered, "You can cook and sew and type and teach school. I want her to go to a college like that. We don't have anything like that in Germany." Most of their colleges teach students to be professors or doctors or psychiatrists. There is no general education or teaching of practical things.

I said, "Ruth, the only thing is that it's a Christian school. The students go to chapel each day and take a Bible class each day. That's part of the rules and regulations. And it's strict on things that the students can do. I don't think Sabine would have a problem with that

123

because she has been reared very well. But I know that religion is not a part of your life." They were more like agnostics, not atheists.

Ruth believed in a Supreme Being but had no use for organized religion. Having come through the Nazi regime and losing everything, she was very down on religion. She was knowledgeable about the Bible but said, "The Bible is just history." Her mother and father were not religious people. Hans, Sabine's stepfather, was not either, and he was a learned man. Ruth was quite intelligent and spoke seven languages.

Sabine was seventeen and in Germany had just finished the equivalent of the first year in an American college; she got her Abitur. She had no idea what she wanted to do after college. Given Sabine's background, I was very careful in helping her select the teacher for Bible class: Mack Craig, who had a good rapport with the young people. No pressure was put on her about going to church. I had told Mama not to pressure her either. Putting any kind of pressure on her would have created a negative experience, but I did explain that most Americans went to church, especially in the South. When it was time to go to church the first Sunday, I said, "Sabine, we're going to church and Sunday school. You're welcome to go, but if you choose not to, that's your choice." She didn't want to go. I said, "Okay." Later on in the week we were in the car, and she said she'd like to go to church with us. I said, "Fine," then I dropped the subject.

Some time later Sabine and I were again in the car coming from Lipscomb. We were on Franklin Road, near the First Presbyterian Church and Tyne Boulevard. She asked me, "What are you going to be doing on Saturday morning?" I answered, "I don't think anything special. Why? Where do you want to go?" (She had learned to drive, but we wouldn't let her drive because of the insurance costs, and she wasn't familiar with the area.) She calmly stated, "I want you to take me over to the Charlotte Avenue Church. Mack Craig is going to baptize me." I could have driven off the road. She had never said a word earlier. I asked, "Sabine, are you sure this is what you want to do?" She said, "Yes, I'm sure."

Sabine had been confirmed in the Lutheran Church in Germany. She didn't want to be, but her mother insisted. Billy and I were in Germany for that, and we bought the material for Ruth to have her dress made because we wanted to do something special for her on that occasion.

Hans is still living. He was and still is a very good stepfather to the girls. One morning in February 1992, Sabine called me and asked if I was sitting down. I was. She said that her mother had committed suicide by jumping in the Neckar River. She had left a note. Ruth had become a closet drinker for a few years and was very depressed. That was a year before Billy died in August, and I had just gotten back from London on a buying trip. Sabine said not to come: "The body hasn't surfaced, and they tell us that the bodies don't surface for a long time in cold weather." They had no funeral. I wondered what people do when there is no church connection. Ruth never was connected with a church, other than the state religion, even though her son-in-law (now former son-in-law) and daughter were members of the Church of Christ. She was pleased about Sabine's connection with religion, but it wasn't for her. They had a memorial at the house with only the family. They had no visitation. They don't bring food and do other things as we do in the South or other parts of the United States.

Sabine was here visiting one year, and Jac surprised us and came in from Germany also. I was looking out the kitchen window and here came Elena. No one had coordinated the visits. What an unexpected treat to have three out of the four foreign students here together!

————•◦•————

In October 1997 one of my older cousins, Ann Batey Whitley, went to Monteagle with me. She reminded me of something that happened while our family was still living on Sterling Road and I was probably fourteen. Her husband worked for Libby, McNeil in Norfolk, Virginia, then. Ann would come back home to visit all the relatives, and on one trip she and a friend, Eleanor Thornton, came by our house before they went to the country to Ann's parents. They were sitting and talking to Mama about their husbands and said, "You know, our husbands like to go with us to buy our clothes. They love for us to dress well." I piped up and said, "I sure hope I get a husband like that." And I did get one like that. In fact I got a husband with many more special qualities.

125

A DELIGHTFUL LIFE

A successful marriage is integral to a sound home life and the rearing of well-adjusted children. How do you have a successful marriage? Some of it is just luck. A lot is give and take. Billy and I were both very strong individuals, and usually that doesn't make for a good marriage. The man is head of the household; nevertheless he shouldn't usurp that authority. God wanted marriage to be a partnership, and the husband and the wife need to respect each other's opinions.

My intuition sent Billy into orbit because he was so logical. He'd ask, "Why don't you think we should do this?" I'd say, "Something tells me this isn't the thing to do." We had our biggest arguments over that—but not getting mad and falling out with each other over it. He couldn't understand it, and I couldn't understand it either or explain it. Sure enough, more times than not, my intuition paid off.

An example of how we worked out differences was building the house at Monteagle. Billy was raised with a screened porch off the bedroom end of the house, but I never had a screened porch and I wanted one. Billy considered the whole idea a nuisance because all he could remember was having to take down the screen wire that rusted and redo the screens. Later people who came to the house commented on what a wonderful porch we had. You'd have thought it was his idea. I let him go on and think it, but I had to fight to get that porch. Some things I'd hold my ground on; normally we made a decision together; other decisions it didn't matter to me.

Halloween 1997—Grandmother (Caroline) as Miss Piggy, Madeline as a princess, and Will as a cowboy.

126

This being the head of the household—I've run in to some of that in doing my design work. Some men really want to get in there and decorate the house, but they don't have one clue as to what to do. If the men showed a talent for decorating, I would listen. They really intimidate their wives. I told one man, "This house is her domain. I think she should have her say in it." My father was not that way, and neither was Billy.

Mama and Daddy felt that when you were married, you didn't come running back home anytime something went wrong. You had to work it out yourselves. With all their sons-in-law, they would probably have taken their sides against their daughters.

When we girls married, we were young and hadn't had many experiences in life. Yet somehow we made it and had happy marriages. Parents need to set a good example, and my sisters and I benefited from what we saw day in and day out, year in and year out, in our parents' marriage. Daddy always said that the Lord lost the pattern when he made Mama. In many ways Mama was a real individual. You don't just preach it to them; you show it to them. Somewhere I read that love is something we need to *do*; falling in love implies that love just happens to us. Staying in love and staying married require work. We girls never saw the example of people walking away from a marriage when things got demanding.

Mama taught us our duty of being there for our husbands. Cooking good, nutritious meals. Keeping an orderly house. Working men and women are sometimes in stressful situations. Although it's getting a little better today, there was a period of time when it was considered terrible to be a homemaker. That's the highest calling for a woman. I know that some women have to work, and I'm not saying that it's wrong. But if they're working to have more clothes and a nicer car and a nicer house at the expense of the children, that's not good. Women should know how to manage the money and try to make the best of their circumstances.

Being a homemaker and rearing children are stressful. Even though women are born with more caring and nurturing aspects than men have, the men need to take more responsibility when they come home. There are things he can do, such as take the children and get them out of her hair while she cooks dinner.

Day care has become a necessity in many families, but I wouldn't want to leave my children with just anybody to raise. My grandchildren don't have to have day care, for which I am grateful. Jim and Jenny agreed that she would be home with the children, and both grandmothers are always standing by to help.

CHAPTER 6

Tennessee Walking Horses and More

> *The association has strived to improve, expand*
> *supervision, and promote the Walking Horse*
> *on a national and international basis, with the*
> *well-being of the breed foremost.*
> —*Walking Horse Owners' Association*

D addy was a charter member of the Tennessee Walking Horse Breeders' Association. The association has kept records of all registrations and transfers concerning the breed since 1935. In the early days Daddy and other men had the responsibility of determining whether your mare or stud was foundation stock. Many of the early foundation books are now stored in my home. Although I was very young, I can remember the excitement of going with him when he examined the foundation horses.

Some early horse shows were associated with county fairs, and some community organizations held shows too. Probably three hundred to four hundred people attended. The shows often had ten classes, each with five or six horses. Middle Tennesseans' growing interest in horses increased the demand for more elaborate horse shows.

My daddy, Uncle Bryan, and other men in Smyrna decided to have a horse show in the summer of 1936—seventeen classes with first, second, and third prizes for each class. It was held on W. R. (Will) Coleman's property, and the money raised went to the Smyrna Parent-Teachers Association.

Within the next year, a Smyrna Horse Show Association was created. A steeplechase was added to the show, with the *Nashville Banner* offering a fifty-dollar prize to the winner. Eight horses participated that year. The Sloan family and the Houghland family, among others, were steeplechasers, and Calvin Houghland won that year.

One class in early shows was a ride-a-thon. They were judged as to how the horses endured at the flat-foot walk over a twenty-mile course. Uncle Bryan had asked Gordon Browning to come to the horse show, and he was to ride Dixie, a Walking Horse that Daddy owned. She had just had a foal, and it had to go with its mother because it wasn't weaned. Governor Browning had a meal with my aunt and uncle before participating in the horse show.

A Mrs. Martin from Murfreesboro showed her Standardbred horses in fine harness and cart; the spokes of her cart were silver and would shine when she went around the ring. She was dressed to the gills with a hat and gloves and twin silver fox furs, their tails flowing behind her.

We had the best time. Our family had box seats, and we children sat in little chairs and could look under the railing of the ring. That was about as close to the horses as we could get without being in the ring with them.

People from the community worked together to make the show successful. Local people as well as people from out of state brought their horses of all breeds. Each year, from 1936 to the beginning of the war, the show got bigger and better. At one point the Smyrna Horse Show was billed as the "largest one-night horse show." Estimates are that three thousand people attended in 1939. Later on—maybe just before the war—the show might have gone to two days. It stopped when the war started and never did pick up again. Perhaps Smyrna would have become the recognized center of horse events if the war had not disrupted American lives.

Daddy found Haynes Peacock, a gelding, working out in the field. He didn't have the money to buy the horse, so Daddy told Mr. John Haynes about him. Haynes Peacock became the second World Champion. Mr. John was wildcatting for oil and struck oil in Louisiana. He and his wife purchased a farm, Haynes Haven, in Maury County. My parents and I visited there many times and often had lunch. Miss Mec (her full name was Americas) was from Mama's neck of the woods, Stewarts Creek. When Haynes Peacock died, he

The only picture of Daddy on a Walking pony.

was buried on the farm with a tombstone. That must be where I got the idea to have a tombstone for our stud horse. Haynes Haven had a lot of good horses in its day, and the rock barn is still there as well as the house.

Harlinsdale is another big barn that was built in those early days and is still going. Billy and I bred most of our horses there over the years.

Daddy loved to fool with horses and to have them around. He had horses when we lived in Smyrna. After our move to Una in 1942, we still had a barn but only one horse. He did have a mule, and that was my one and only time to be around a mule.

My friend Sir John Miller in England knows all breeds of horses. He said that the Tennessee mules were the smartest animals he had ever been around. He became acquainted with them in Washington, D.C., during World War II, and he always wanted to come to Tennessee and drive a team of mules.

My parents' house on Sterling Road in Nashville had no place for horses. While in Donelson we had a few horses, but when both families moved to Brentwood, we all had more than enough acreage to expand our ownership of horses.

Both Daddy and Billy rode; I never did. To my knowledge, Daddy never showed a horse in his life, but Billy started showing in his late forties or early fifties. Amy says that "the first time I was on a Tennessee Walking Horse was when I was two years old. I rode with my grandfather in Donelson." Her love of horses has been there ever since. Billy got into it big time because he loved the mixing of the bloodlines; his interest was in both Walking Horses and Thoroughbreds. If Daddy and Billy had a good enough horse, they would put it in training.

Billy started showing at age fifty—his first win in the fifty and over class at the International Walking Horse Show.

While we were still in Brentwood, Billy and I had a mare named Corinna, and she was bred to Midnight Sun. When we discovered that she was not in foal—and Midnight Sun had died in the meantime—we were heartbroken.

In addition to Premier Delight (to be described in detail later), some of our other horses that deserve a special mention include Pride's Copper Penny, which was the weanling filly World Champion in 1976, and Ace's Super Honk, which was a World Champion yearling in 1978. In 1980 Jim won first place on Heir's Black Rascal at the Franklin Jaycee Show; then he won the North American Championship for seventeen years and under in Baton Rouge, Louisiana. One of Daddy's top horses, Pride's Royal Master, didn't become a World Champion, but he became a nationally renowned stallion. We Crosses raised but sold Man of Pride, which won World Championships and is a breeding stallion, and we also raised the

Jim on Heir's Black Rascal, winning the North American Championship at Baton Rouge, Louisiana.

mother of a three-year-old World Champion, Skywatch, which is a top breeding stud. Pride's Delight K. won championships as a two- and three-year-old, and he was bred to twenty-eight mares in 1985. Premier was insured at his death, and we used the insurance money to buy Pride's Delight K. and some mares.

The first Celebration, held in 1939 at the high school football field in Shelbyville, was a far cry from what it is now. Daddy took the whole family, and I've been going ever since.

Billy and I decided that we wanted to go more than one night to the Celebration, but we couldn't get a box seat. It was the year I was pregnant with Amy—1958. My doctor said that I shouldn't go because I was having a problem pregnancy, but I told him not to worry. Dr. John Derryberry, whom I had dated in high school, could take care of me if there was a problem. We did get a box seat when Amy was one and a half, and we still have it. You could say that Amy has been going to horse shows since before she was born.

Amy rode at age eight or nine in the Celebration's Walking Pony Division. In the ring, the pony automatically cantered when the announcer called for a canter. He was what is known as a push button. Watching her in the arena made me uptight. The night she won the World Championship with her yearling, Ace's Super Honk, Amy observed that I wasn't nearly as upset watching her lead the yearling. There is a big difference to me in watching her ride or lead a horse; she couldn't fall off if she was on the ground.

Nevertheless, watching her with a stud horse going around the ring made me a nervous wreck. Steve Beech, a breeder, had the filly that year, and Amy had the stud. It was hard to beat a Beech in the ring, but Amy did. She won numerous blue ribbons with that yearling, Ace's Super Honk. It was a record at that time and may still be a record. That win was a culmination of a good year with the horse, which turned out not to be worth two cents under a saddle. You can't tell for sure what a horse is going to do, even one that seems to have promise.

As part of the family's commitment to community activities, we helped a group of young Jaycees put on a horse show here in Franklin. Amy and Jim and their daddy worked on the grounds for the show at Jim Warren Park. Billy was in the Rotary Club and had helped put up

Amy's winning the Yearling World Grand Championship with Ace's Super Honk. She set a record for blue ribbons with the yearling.

the bleachers for the rodeo sponsored by the Rotarians, so he knew the details that could help the Jaycees with the show. Billy was given the Distinguished Service Award, which I had to accept for him because he was in the hospital for a few days for a checkup. He regretted that he had to miss it. (Some time later with my encouragement, the Jaycees took on the project of helping an AFS student, especially with making cultural adjustments. The upshot was that they gave me the Distinguished Service Award in 1979. Our family was thus doubly honored.)

The situation in the Walking Horse industry kept getting worse and worse in regard to the soring of horses. Several men and women did not want to see the breed destroyed. The federal government, specifically the USDA, was pretty hot on the industry's train, trying to clean it up. The soring of horses was so blatant that we could see the bleeding from our seats in the arena. There was no need of that.

The Millers, the Whitmires, the Womacks, the Johnsons, the Dunns, and our family, in addition to many other families, put their efforts and their resources into trying to save the breed and trying to get the industry on the same sheet of music. All these years later I'm sad to say, I don't think it ever will be on the same sheet. They started the Walking Horse Owners' Association (WHOA) to represent the owners of horses; they didn't feel represented in the Breeders' Association. In my opinion if it had not been for WHOA, the breed would have been destroyed.

The Walking Horse Owners' Association of America was organized in 1975 with the paramount goal to promote integrity in the breeding, the sale, and the exhibition of the Tennessee Walking Horse. The membership of the association comes from almost every state in the U.S. and certain foreign countries. WHOA started its own newspaper and registry.

The association has strived to improve, expand supervision, and promote the Walking Horse on a national and international basis, with the well-being of the breed foremost. The association works very closely with humane groups and the USDA to educate the horse public pertaining to the Horse Protection Act of 1976.

WHOA had to fight to get established. The USDA was uncooperative in general and applied different rules to WHOA than to the Breeders' Association. The agency put WHOA in a catch-22 position of trying to comply with a set of vaguely defined regulations; final regulations were promised the last of March 1979. In the meantime members of WHOA were involved in a series of meetings to try to clear up some issues.

On January 4, 1979, in a Washington, D.C., hearing, members of WHOA protested that the group was not being credited by USDA for efforts on behalf of the horse. WHOA wasn't there to disagree with the new Horse Protection Act; WHOA disagreed with the USDA interpretation of regulations and the lack of cooperation with the group. Jesse Helms, a congressman, and Herman Talmadge of Georgia were prominent at the hearing.

A second meeting was held March 14 or 15, 1979, in Washington, D.C. Representatives of Howard Baker, of Congressman Ed Jones, of Jim Sasser, of Robin Beard, and of Al Gore Jr.; Robin Beard; Ed Jones;

and Richard L. Reichmann for the American Horse Protection Act came over to sit with us. They came to our rescue in what was really a federal, not a state, issue.

On March 29, 1979, there was a meeting with state officials. In attendance were Tom Beasley, Bill Walker, Charles Overby, staffers of Governor Lamar Alexander, John Dunn, Dr. Ben Shelton, Dr. Bob Womack, Dr. Lois Hinson (a vet and a friend of the Walking Horse industry), Jim Rowland, Mary Miller, Dr. Jerry Williams, and Billy and me. Dr. Ben Shelton was president of WHOA.

Some people thought that WHOA started having its own shows to put the Celebration out of business. I can honestly say that no one can put the Celebration out of business; if they're put out, they'll put themselves out. Two WHOA shows, held in August, made money to keep the group going. The first one was in Louisville, Kentucky, at the state fairgrounds because it was enclosed. The possible sites in Tennessee were not enclosed.

The first show in Tennessee after bringing it from Kentucky was held in the Ellington Agricultural Center, and the next one was at Murfreesboro's Old Stone Park. The lack of facilities was a serious problem: tents used for stalls, not enough seats, no barns. To improve the situation, WHOA appointed a committee to consider buying land—again out of members' pockets—to build an arena and head-quarters.

Billy was the chairman of the committee that focused on possible sites in Murfreesboro. Murfreesboro seemed a logical choice because it was close to Nashville, Hickory Hollow Mall, motels, and restaurants. People come for several days with their families to attend a show. Shelbyville is at a disadvantage with crowds because of the lack of housing and restaurants. WHOA also wanted to be close to MTSU, which has an equine science program.

The more the men and women worked on the idea, the more they could see how expensive the venture would be. A few years before that, a small arena had been attached at MTSU with a small ring and limited seating. After a WHOA board meeting, Billy and some men met with Cliff Gillespie, of MTSU, and others at the arena. I went along, and I could see the wheels in Billy's mind turning when he walked into that arena—he was visualizing how to enlarge it to meet

WHOA's immediate needs. It's a state university, so the state had to be involved with the plans to enlarge the arena. John Bragg, the local state representative, was invaluable in getting the funding for the addition. Also assisting in the effort was Andy Womack, a state senator for that area and son of Dr. Bob Womack.

Billy had to stand WHOA's ground with an advisory committee from the state. One member couldn't see putting the state's money into an arena for a horse show. Billy pointed out that it wasn't just for a horse show; cattle shows and other shows could be held at the fixed-up arena. The legislation passed, the arena was enlarged, and it has been booked up ever since it opened. It has been a boon to the town.

Before the first show at the arena, I raised money for purchasing silver awards for perpetual and challenge trophies. Competitors have to win the challenge three times to retire the beautiful trophy, and there are different qualifications for the perpetual trophy. Winners do not take the awards home and display them because we have had a hard time getting them back for the next year's show. In the new Miller arena (I'll explain more about that later on) will be

Saratoga Springs, New York, for Travers Race.

a permanent display case to show the trophies at all times, not only during the International Show.

Thurman Mullins called me, wanting to know if some horses could be donated for state park use. A lot of horses don't make it to the show ring, so I put the word out asking for gentle and well-broken horses to be donated. The owners had to have appraisals so that the horses could be tax deductible. Many horses and even the saddles and tack were donated.

In April and June 1980, the *Nashville Banner* carried stories about the use of Tennessee Walking Horses in the state parks. The patrol program began in 1974, but had recently taken off. A ranger from Montgomery Bell State Park said he could cover every inch of park with his horse, and horses could go cheaper on rescue efforts than helicopters. The cost of maintaining the horses was much less than the cost for vehicles, so the horses were cost-effective as well as efficient. Thurman Mullins, captain of the state's mounted rangers, said, "We've expanded the program, redefined it, and we've been getting some awfully good horses donated by the Walking Horse Owners Association."

New York City police use Thoroughbreds on the streets. The state of Tennessee hired a man from the city of New York to come down and train the horses for the special park patrol work. Because he was used to working with Thoroughbreds, I wondered how he would get along with the Walking Horses. He worked with the horses and riders a few days, and then they put on an exhibition. The man was very complimentary of the Tennessee Walking Horses and said they were very trainable. The horses are trained to cope with the noise of motorcycles and gunshots and the activity of children; they are used for riot control, parades, and day-long patrols. At command they are not to move. Opryland used to have Walking Horses in the park, and Walkers were at all the state parks. People seem more willing to talk to rangers on horses than in vehicles with blue lights. It's a win-win situation—the breed gets exposure, and the horses are good for the parks.

Eventually Thurman left and became the horse manager for Charlie Daniels. The program has not run as well since then, although the rangers and their horses were at the 1996

James William Cross IV driving Governor Ned McWherter and Franklin Mayor Jerry Sharber as part of StreetScape in Franklin, August 1991.

Celebration. That did my heart good to see the horses there in all their "spit and polish." I'm pleased that I had a hand in such a worthwhile program.

When Jim and Amy were at Ensworth, Jim got out earlier than Amy. I'd pick him up, and we'd do something until it was time to pick up Amy. One day we went to Temptation Gallery, an antique shop that was then on Belmont Boulevard. We had bought several antiques from there when we were furnishing our house. Jim had been eyeing a real horse's hoof that been made into an inkwell, so I had bought it for him on an earlier excursion; it was his first antique. We were looking around, and a salesman from Gorham, named Phil Gustafson, was in there. Jay Bradley, the owner of Temptation, told him about our interest in horses. The salesman said he had something in the car he wanted to show us, and he brought in figurines of spotted horses that Gorham had made of porcelain. I said, "Those horses aren't pretty to me." He replied, "Maybe Gorham should make a Walking Horse. Has anybody made one before?" I said, "No, not out of fine porcelain." I never did like to see the Walking Horse in a silhouette with feet walking without a rider because the beauty of the horse was lost.

Phil told us that Gorham had been representing Albany Fine China of Worcester, England, which made birds and animals of porcelain. Phil contacted the Albany men in England, and they sent their sculptor to Middle Tennessee. The company's directors were D. B. Lovegrove, W. E. Nicholls, and D. T. M. Palmer.

Here were Mr. Gustafson, a man I barely knew, and David
Lovegrove, a man from England, and I was to go all over Middle
Tennessee with them to show them what we thought were representatives of the breed, the Champions. Billy asked me, "Aren't you
afraid to be going all over the countryside with these men you barely
know?" The thought never occurred to me. It was a pleasant excursion for all of us.

On the first trip the sculptor made sketches and took
photographs. The mane came from Pride of Midnight. The coloring
for the chestnut came from Sun's Delight. The black was a combination. The sorrel with flax mane and tail was copied from one of our
horses.

David Lovegrove, the sculptor, came back again in March 1978
with a white clay model, and he sat and studied the horses and
sculpted more on it. Billy and I made two trips to England—once for
the original firing and then for the second firing to make sure that
the colors were right as the horses were individually hand painted.

*Number three figurine of the Tennessee Walking Horse designed by David Lovegrove of
Worcester, England. Left to right, David Palmer, David Lovegrove, Caroline, Billy, and
William Nicholls.*

The figurines were made in a limited edition of one hundred; the cost was $1,500 each. They were at Garrard's, the Crown Jewelers in London, the exclusive agent for them. Some sold in England, I sold many and bought a few, and the project was a moneymaker for WHOA. Gorham also made plates, and the company made limited edition plates of Delight's Bumin Around, which was the Millers' horse, Sun's Delight, and Super Stock. The owners gave seed money and got back money or plates to give away. The sales of plates made money for WHOA too.

Bill Nicholls was a painter and the business manager at Albany. They sold the company, but Bill bought it back after it fell on hard times. I didn't know that in October 1996 when I was in England spending a month and called the Albany firm to place an order for another figurine. The woman asked if I'd like to talk to Mr. Nicholls. I had lost track of him for ten or eleven years, so I was surprised to hear from him again. He had not known about Billy's death either. Bill picked me up and took me and my two friends to the factory in Worcester. They made a black figurine for me; black is the hardest color to get right, and Bill personally painted it. I don't think it's as good as the first one, though.

Later on the company did figurines for Thoroughbreds and Standardbreds. The Tennessee Walking Horse was the first American horse figurine to be done by Albany.

All that happened because Jim and I went in that antique shop one afternoon, and from that experience came one of our most exciting ventures with the horses. In a letter dated May 16, 1979, from W. E. Nicholls to both Billy and me, he wrote that "the highlight [of the trip] . . . was the marvellous hospitality which you afforded us on our visit to your beautiful home." He also expressed interest in our plan to exhibit the Walking Horses in England, and he would make "enquiries" about the feasibility of the plan. His "enquiries" got the ball rolling for us. Little did we know how complicated the process would be and how long it would take to come to fruition. We had hoped that we could make the trip in 1979, but that was not to be despite writing to Raymond Brooks-Ward and even meeting him in London.

In the spring of 1980, fifteen or sixteen English reporters came to Tennessee to tour the sights; representatives of the state hoped that they would go back to England and encourage people to come here, thus giving tourism a boost with international visitors. They had been in the state parks all day, and when they came to our home, they were casually dressed and very tired. State parks can't serve alcoholic drinks in their restaurants, and the reporters had eaten lunch at one. At our home they weren't served alcohol either. They could not understand that and were most outspoken on the point. They were used to having drinks at lunch, before supper, and with supper. I told them that they were having a typical southern supper, and we don't drink wine with a typical southern supper.

One of the English writers was Linda Christmas, who wrote in *The Guardian*, May 10, 1980, about her admiration for the Tennessee Walking Horses after learning about them on her visit. She was true to her word, and we saw her again in England that winter when she reported on the Walkers. She and her husband invited Billy and me to their home for supper.

The Grand Champion in 1980 received $10,000 cash and other prizes at the International Grand Championship Walking Horse Show, held at the Agricultural Center in Murfreesboro. There were eight hundred entries for the show that year, and the numbers have risen substantially since then.

A writer for *Southern Living* magazine came to our farm to do an article with photos highlighting the five-day festival surrounding the WHOA show. "A Show of Horses and Hospitality" (July 1980) emphasized the Walkers and food and entertaining for the show. As a result of that article Billy and I received this letter from the Board of Directors of WHOA, dated September 18, 1980:

> It is our opinion that each member who read the article sensed a new dignity surrounding the breed that has brought us all so much pleasure. . . . Your efforts in bringing the Walking Horse to the attention of so many readers is to be commended, and the publicity directed toward the Walking Horse Owners' Association has, and will, be of tremendous benefit in the future.

The three men from Albany kept saying that they loved the horses. How could the English people see them? The Walking Horse is ideal as a pleasure horse for riding in the country. He could pull the plow during the week; he got hitched up to take the family to church. He is so versatile. The Walking Horse has such a comfortable seat that men could ride over the plantation all day in ease.

Since Albany's franchise dealer was Garrard's, Bill Nicholls went to see Mr. Davies, director at Garrard's, and told him that we would be willing to take the Walkers to England for an exhibition. The ideal event seemed to be the Olympia International Show Jumping Championship held each December. It's the largest show in Europe, and it's held in Grand Hall, Olympia, in London. The president of the show was Lord Westmorland, who was also the earl of Westmorland.

Garrard's had a display at Olympia each year. Mr. Davies of Garrard's contacted Raymond Brooks-Ward, the director of the show. Then Mr. Davies put me in touch with Raymond. We wrote back and forth and talked on the phone about our horses appearing in the 1980 show.

Nothing happened easily for that trip. The people in the Walking Horse industry had never shown abroad. Governor Lamar Alexander wrote a letter to Raymond Brooks-Ward, September 19, 1979, encouraging him to permit the horses to appear at the show. I had to contact friends in the Thoroughbred business to find out about shipping and quarantine and so forth. More than twenty months of effort were required to get make the trip a reality. I developed tennis elbow from holding the phone and talking nonstop on it. All the arrangements were made at our personal expense too.

The invitation had to go before a committee at Olympia. Every year there is a special exhibition pertaining to horses. We were first turned down, but then they changed their minds and agreed to the appearance of the Walking Horses. A letter from James Black of British Equestrian Promotions Limited, Belgrave Square, London, dated June 10, 1980, informed us of approval to go to the show. I then had to sell the idea to the owners of quality horses to participate and ship the horses to London at their own expense; no horse organization offered financial help. Our Premier Delight and Sherri Dietz's

The Pusher, owned by Sherri Dietz, and Premier Delight, with David Welsh, in front of Buckingham Palace, December 1980. The photo appeared on the front page of The Guardian, *accompanying the article "Two Tennessee Walking Horses Take a Stroll in the Park."*

The Pusher were the two horses to go. Later Raymond Brooks-Ward issued the official invitation, and on October 30, 1980, Raymond wrote to inform us that the two Tennessee Walking Horses were to be stabled at the Royal Mews, Buckingham Palace, beginning December 9. We could hardly believe it!

Eight-year-old Pusher, a roan, was the current International Walking Horse Grand Champion and Reserve World Grand Champion Walking Horse. Pusher was also 1979 Tennessee Walking Horse of the Year. Sherri Dietz from New Castle, Indiana, owned him, and she was a student at Stephens College in Missouri at the time. Her horse was trained in Danville, Kentucky, by Bob McQuerry.

Premier Delight was our horse, a breeding stallion in service at Shadow Valley Farms in Shelbyville. Billy bought the Junior World Grand Champion from Dr. James Johnson, a neurosurgeon in High Point, North Carolina, who also owned Shadow Valley Farms. David

Welsh was Premier's trainer, working for Dr. Johnson. Premier was sired by Sun's Delight, whose grandsire was Midnight Sun and produced more Grand Champions than any other line in the Walking Horse world. Midnight Sun stood at Harlinsdale Farm in Franklin.

The horses needed various shots and health forms and checkups; that year there were problems with piroplasmosis and equine infectious anemia. Pegasus Air Transport had arranged shipment of the horses to England. Pegasus was supposed to pick up the horses in Kentucky and truck them to New York, but representatives of the company called us at the last minute and said that their van would be full of fillies going to be bred. Did we want to ship our studs with them? The answer was an emphatic NO. David Welsh picked up Pusher in Kentucky and took both horses to New York City in a horse trailer. Along the way he stopped in Pennsylvania at a woman's farm where he had worked before so that the horses could rest. He left the horses in her barn overnight and got a motel room for himself. Billy and I flew up two days later. Joe Dietz and his son and daughter-in-law met us there; Joe was Sherri's dad. Sherri, Jim, and Amy were to follow us later.

The horses were in quarantine for four or five days at JFK Airport. Everything was sterile in the stalls and the horse trailers. Before the horses left Kentucky, Dr. D. L. Proctor of Lexington checked them over, and then at JFK a USDA representative checked them again. The vets found no problems.

Transporting horses by air is not cheap; it was $2,300 per horse one way plus $425 clearance and delivery costs in England—Pan Am didn't charge for David. (On the trip back the horses were trucked and boated to Amsterdam and then flown on KLM at a cost of $3,200 per horse and $450 for David.)

David was the only one of us going on the 747 Pan Am cargo plane with the horses, and the two Walkers were the only horses on that plane. Billy, Joe Dietz, and I were there to watch them be loaded onto the plane at 3:00 A.M. Those horses, which had been mildly tranquilized, looked calm and alert. Joe said, "Those horses think they've died and gone to heaven." Billy went aboard the plane with David and spoke to the pilot. He asked if there was any way that

David could stay with the horses during takeoff. Although regulations called for David to sit in the cockpit, the pilot allowed him to stay back there. The plane was so computerized that even the pilot walked around during the flight. Our flight to London left later in the day.

Raymond told us that upon the horses' arrival in London, he would take over and send a horse box. (That's what the English call a trailer.) The horses were being unloaded at the Royal Mews in Buckingham Palace when we first arrived. They open the Mews only one day a week to the public, and they roll out the gold coronation carriage. Before I left the Mews, they let me sit in that carriage. What a treat! Billy and I had never visited the Mews before, although we had been often to London. They had out all the regalia and the men were in uniform to welcome us and the horses.

Reporters were everywhere, and our friend Linda Christmas was among them. We were interviewed the whole two weeks we were there. We had to keep our cool and guard everything we said because we knew we would face questions about abuse. We didn't want anything to be twisted all around in the press and leave a bad impression. The English had heard about how badly Americans treated the Tennessee Walking Horses. We knew the horses couldn't wear the big shoes because the English would never have understood; instead we used the one-and-one-half-inch pad at the heels like the ones our yearlings wear. They couldn't believe that the horses could do what they did without having something done to them. We used the rolled leather collar around their ankles, which did not bother the English since the gaited breed uses the collar.

We handled the publicity well, I thought. We had warned Raymond about the kinds of questions we might be asked. He had vets on hand to verify that the horses were not under any cloud. They examined the horses from top to bottom and affirmed that nothing was wrong with them.

We Americans did find it odd that the English people talked so much about cruelty to animals, but they had horses jumping fences that were so high, they broke their legs or otherwise seriously injured themselves and had to be put to sleep. Our horses are really pampered. We wash our horses, which is something that they don't

147

seem to do in England—at least their horses don't smell as if they have been washed.

We went to London a week before the exhibition because we wanted the horses to become acclimated. We carried enough of their food and water to last until they could get used to English food and water. That was a very important precaution to take. The exhibition was to take place from December 17 to 21, 1980.

The Mews employees treated us royally. That's how we met Sir John Miller, the equerry to the queen. We also met Lord Westmorland, who was to become the queen's Master of the Horse (he is now deceased). To this day Jim, Amy, or I can go to the Mews and some of the employees remember us and the horses. The Tennessee Walking Horses were stabled right next to the garages housing the cars of the royal family. One morning David was washing Premier, and a man asked him to move because they needed to get the Queen Mother's car to take her to Ascot. We saw the Queen Mother get in her car. British people were there to give her small gifts since it was close to Christmas. As she was taking the gifts, a valet pulled up with a sports car, and Prince Andrew jumped in it with his male secretary.

At Ascot later that day, Billy and I, Joe Dietz, and David were guests. The children hadn't arrived in England yet. We were permitted into the owners' circle, and I got very close to the Queen Mother, who had a horse running that day.

We made time for a few other activities. We toured Whitbread Stables where we saw a blackboard marked off in squares with horses' names and their type of feed and feeding times. Imagine our surprise to see 4:00 P.M. designated as tea time for horses—they were served barley and water. Billy bought a top hat at Moss Bros. that he wore when he drove the carriages here in Franklin in parades or for the Candlelight Tours. He was also measured for a morning suit for Ascot. Most of the men rent their suits from Moss Bros., but they own their top hats.

Two days before the show, the horses were moved from the Mews to Olympia's show grounds. The horses and riders needed that time to have rehearsals and dress rehearsals at the arena with the commentary by Alan F. Balch, vice president of the Los Angeles Turf

Club at Santa Anita Park, California. The first rehearsal was December 16 at 2:00; on December 17 they held a second rehearsal at 11:00 and the dress rehearsal later in the afternoon. The first performance was that night. Alan came to us through the Standardbred owners; Joe Dietz and Billy and I paid half of Alan's expenses for the trip. That was the beginning of a delightful relationship between the Walking Horses and him. Alan is now director of Madison Square Garden.

The routine went like this: Premier Delight—ridden by David Welsh—entered with the U.S. flag to "Stars and Stripes Forever." Horse and rider proceeded to the Royal Box, David tipped his hat, and they made one round at the flat walk and exited. Then they reentered abreast of Pusher, ridden by Sherri, and exited to "Dixie." The performance lasted about eight minutes, and they worked the three gaits—flat-foot walk, running walk, and canter. In all there were one performance on December 17 (evening) and two on each of the other days (afternoon and evening). Five American Standardbreds followed our Tennessee Walkers. In fact, the Tennessee Walking Horses opened the whole show.

To watch the show, Billy and I were in something that was the equivalent of a sky box. We were served dinner each night; for example, on December 18 we had salmon mousse, beef carbonade, peas, potatoes, fruit or cheese, and coffee. We wore badges to get into certain areas. Everything was very restricted.

One night we had an invitation issued by the queen to sit in her Royal Box. Raymond said that only Billy and I were to go, but I wouldn't hear of it unless Joe Dietz was also invited. Raymond said, "You damned Americans. You always want to be so fair." Mr. Dietz was invited another night.

Prince and Princess Michael of Kent were the queen's representatives at the show. The queen was already at Sandringham for the Christmas holidays. A woman called from the palace and told me what Princess Michael would be wearing, and I knew to follow suit. The men wore tuxedos. She told me that the princess would be wearing a tea-length black lace dress. Knowing we would receive the invitation, I already had my black velveteen cocktail suit. She also told us what time to be in the box. Everybody is to arrive before the

Caroline and Billy making a presentation at the Olympia International Show to Lord Westmorland, Queen Elizabeth II's Master of the Horse, December 1980.

royalty, and then the prince and princess come in and greet each person. Because of my independent American streak, I did not curtsy to them, however.

Lord Westmorland's wife and the princess were talking about who was going to be at Sandringham for Christmas. They were really chatty—as if they were saying who would bring the green beans or sweet potatoes—because they're all kin. Yet Lady Westmorland curtsied to the princess and took her hand when she left.

They seated me in the Royal Box at the front table beside the Duke of Beaufort, who was the Master of the Horse. Lord Westmorland took over between 1980 and 1982 after the death of the Duke of Beaufort. (The Queen Mother and her daughters had stayed at the Duke of Beaufort's place during the Blitz.) On the other side of me was Ambassador Lind from Sweden. Lord Westmorland was close by. Also there were Lady Camilla Fane, Mrs. Brooks-Ward, Sir David and Lady McNee, among others.

150

As the horses entered the ring, they saluted the Royal Box. (Even Prince Philip does that to his wife, the queen. We saw him ride at the Windsor Horse Show on another trip.) When David came into the ring carrying our flag, Billy and I stood up. Those men around us were squirming in their seats. They didn't stand up. David saluted by taking his hat off. He did not dip the flag; he stood in front of the box while they played "Stars and Stripes Forever." After he left the ring we sat down. Lord Westmorland leaned over and said, "Caroline, what were you doing?" I said, "Don't you have flag protocol?" I thought that the English had protocol for everything. None for the flag. When the real competition started, every horse had to come to the Royal Box and salute. One of the men leaned over and said to the duke, "You better stand up because you're the highest-ranking military officer here to receive the salute." That was an eye-opener to me because they had to tell each other what to do.

When our horse came in the ring on that first night, I was shaking like a leaf. Billy had his arm around me and asked what was wrong. I said that it was the culmination of all that work and we were seeing a dream come true. The dream was shattered on the last night because Premier was unable to show. David had planned to wave a small British flag and make one round as a thank-you. With all of the construction for the show, Premier picked up a nail in his foot, and he limped. It was a real letdown.

Governor Alexander had given us certificates making Raymond and Lord Westmorland Tennessee colonels. Billy and I made the awards down in the ring, and a representative of the American Standardbreds accompanied us. Lord Westmorland received his first because of his higher rank, and I shook hands with him. Then I gave Raymond his certificate and kissed him on the cheek. Lord Westmorland boomed, "Where is my kiss?" So I leaned over and gave him a kiss—and all of this was broadcast live on the BBC. The BBC broadcast the show in England and to the Continent twice a day, and at least 72,000 people attended Olympia that year.

That night there was a party at the show grounds for the American group given by the ambassador to Great Britain from the United States.

Taking the horses was one way to get Tennessee on the map. At that time the Department of Tourism for Tennessee had a Fleet Street firm to do publicity for the state. Every major newspaper in London had a story on us and the horses. Michael Williams's report of the show in *Horse and Rider*, February 1981, titled "Olympia—Best Ever" remarked, "The biggest talking point of the week was provided by the first appearance of the American saddle horses, notably the famous Tennessee Walking Horse with his bizarre gait and floating tail."

Olympia provided ideas for our WHOA horse shows. For example, when they put up the tall jumps, they brought out massive bouquets of fresh flowers and placed them at the corners. The flowers were flown in daily from Holland. We used bird baths at the corner of the center ring at the International with gladiolas radiating out in huge bouquets. We also landscaped the center ring in the front like a garden with greenery. At Olympia the judges were brought into the arena in a carriage and made a loop before going to the judges' box. From that came the idea to use our Bentley driven by Billy Hamilton to bring the judges into the center ring.

Linda Christmas and her husband, John Higgins, associate editor of the *London Times*, invited us to their home for dinner. Also there were Wendy Hanson, publicist at the Met Opera, who was "a touch upset by John Lennon's recent death," according to Linda (Wendy had been the first agent for the Beatles), and Clive Barnes, drama critic for the *New York Post*. Billy said he felt like a fifth wheel because the others talked all about the Beatles and Lennon's death and the new plays in London. We would never have had all those English connections if it hadn't been for the horses.

The KLM flight back to the States was rough. On the flight from Amsterdam the two studs were pawing the walls because also on board were French mares going to Louisville and Lexington to be bred. That had to have been a dangerous situation for David and the horses. David said it was so cold that ice formed inside the plane. The whole plane load of horses was quarantined at JFK. It was Christmas Day before our horses were released. David later told us that Billy and I would never have let the horses get on that KLM plane if we had seen the conditions.

In 1982 Billy and I were invited to the Windsor Horse Show. Raymond Brooks-Ward was the organizer for that show too. We were there a week, and we sat in the queen's box. Once the queen turned around and asked who we were, but we were never introduced to her. In the Royal Box, protocol demanded that no one left until the queen did. No one could leave for any reason—not even to answer the call of nature. She had to make the first move. (In 1997 Simon Brooks-Ward asked me to come back to the Windsor Horse Show, which he now promotes. He said that I could sit in the queen's box in celebration of the queen's fiftieth wedding anniversary. Thirteen hundred horses from around the world were to be on exhibit as part of the special event. I really wanted to go and take Madeline, but we would have had to miss the Fourth of July celebration at Monteagle, so I chose Monteagle.)

The Windsor Horse Show was somewhat like a country fair. Sir John told us to go to a certain location to watch Prince Philip drive the carriage and warm up the horses. Sir John had taught Charles and Anne how to ride and also taught Prince Philip his four-in-hand driving. Sir John is really the epitome of four-in-hand driving. Naturally Prince Philip, being married to the richest woman in the world, had the best horses, and I have to admit that he was a good driver.

The queen drove herself in her Land Rover from the castle to the show grounds, which are just below the castle. The queen, wearing a head scarf, tweeds, and brogans, was out in the field where Prince Philip was driving. I walked by her and didn't even know it. Billy could see what was happening because he was so tall. Two security guards in plainclothes with guns underneath their jackets watched over her. They obviously could tell that I didn't recognize her, and they said nothing to me.

At that horse show, I was asked to give an award with Prince Philip. He sat one seat away from me but didn't acknowledge my presence. He treated me like a bump on a log, not a person. His people skills are somewhat lacking, to say the least. And I was not to talk to him first.

One day I looked across the aisle from the queen's box where Billy and I were seated, and there sat my gynecologist-obstetrician, Dr.

Robert Chalfont, and his wife and a girl I went to high school with, Lacy Irwin Perry. We bumped into them after the queen had left. They asked, "How did you get to sit in the queen's box?" I told them, "It's all in who you know." The invitation was issued from the queen, but Raymond had arranged for her to invite us.

At Windsor Castle in 1982, they were preparing for President and Mrs. Reagan's visit. President Reagan was a good horseman, and he and the queen were going to ride. Mrs. Reagan was to be in the carriage with Prince Philip. When we went to the barns at Windsor one morning, Sir John had arranged for the queen's farm manager to take us over the farm. Billy talked to him about the cattle and such; having been a farmer, he could talk about those things. It was such a privilege to go on that tour. The queen regularly meets with her manager to discuss the direction she wants to take in the farm operation.

We left Windsor and checked into Claridges in London. We took a walk to cool off because it was hot and stuffy for May. Claridges wasn't air-conditioned then. We came back and saw that a message had been slipped under the door. It said to please call Mr. Allman and noted a phone number. I didn't recognize the name, so I called the number. Windsor Castle answered. Mr. Allman was the secretary to Sir John, as I found out. Mr. Allman had returned to Buckingham Palace, so the Windsor Castle operator gave the number for Buckingham Palace and I called Mr. Allman there.

Mr. Allman said that Sir John wanted us to have dinner with him at 0800 hours. (Sir John was from the military.) He told me, "Mr. Cross is to wear a lounge suit." The only thing I could think of when he said that was a double-knit leisure suit that was popular ages ago. I knew that *couldn't* be right. Raymond Brooks-Ward had told Billy that he wouldn't need a dinner jacket or tux for the Windsor Horse Show. I laid my cards out on the table and asked Mr. Allman what he meant by a lounge suit. He said, "A business suit." To dress accordingly, I thought that a Sunday dress was appropriate. He also asked how we would be arriving. I said, "By taxi." What a comedown to arrive at Buckingham Palace in a taxi when any other time we had a car and driver!

Sir John lived in the equerry's residence, a nice Georgian house, on the grounds of Buckingham Palace. The housekeeper answered the door and sent us to the drawing room to join a man who had judged the Windsor show, an old friend of Sir John. The housekeeper informed us, "Sir John is momentarily delayed by a phone call."

Before long Sir John came down the stairs wearing what we called Prince Philip slippers. I had bought Billy some for bedroom slippers because his old leather ones were so ratty looking, I hated for the maids in the nice hotels to have to set them out for him each night. The family had really teased him about his Prince Philip slippers, which were black velvet with a crest on top, lined with quilted red satin. Billy and I were really tickled at seeing Sir John in those slippers, and it was all we could do not to laugh out loud. Sir John had on a business suit with a crease that could have cut butter—there was the military influence.

Sir John and Billy started talking about the South and country hams. Billy told him that we cured hams in our smokehouse and explained the details of the procedure. Sir John knew more about Virginia hams, which are more sugar cured than Tennessee hams. Billy said that he would send Sir John a ham. Sir John pointed out that the queen might enjoy one, too, so we sent two hams from Early's with the instructions for cooking them. Today when you sell hams, your smokehouse has to be approved by the health department, and ours is only for personal use. Early's can ship all over the world. Sir John sent a thank you, dated November 1982, for both hams. We don't know if the queen actually ate hers or not.

Mr. Black, whom we met at Olympia, told us to go to Reading, which is known for its auction sales, and Billy bought a gig from Thimbleby and Shorland on that trip. The gig is a one-seater for two people, and its huge wheels mean that the occupants are up high. It was one of many carriages that Billy acquired.

The first time I went to Sir John's beautiful house after he had retired and moved from Buckingham Palace, one outstanding-looking mare was grazing out in the field as I came up the driveway. (This visit was after Billy's cardiac arrest; Billy never saw his house.) Sir John said that it was one of the queen's horses; she had some problems with it, and she sent it to him to straighten out. Sir John really knows his horses.

Because of the Tennessee Walking Horses, we have met people we might not have otherwise. Sylvester Stallone and Dolly Parton shot the movie *Rhinestone* in Middle Tennessee. In November 1983 they came to Tuck-A-Way Farm and rode our horses. Stallone stayed at the Inman home during filming.

Another famous person we met was Zsa Zsa Gabor. She came to our home for lunch, and we had Premier and one of Amy's horses for a mini horse show.

WHOA invited Zsa Zsa to come to the International Show to exhibit her pleasure horse. Her trainer—Scott Benham—came here to show anyway. The public relations firm we hired that year seemed to think that would be good for the show. (WHOA had her first, the Celebration got her later.)

WHOA paid for her and her secretary; they wanted first-class airline seats, and that was expected. She received no money, just had all expenses paid. Then she wanted to bring a prince with her who, unfortunately, had no money of his own. I told the agency that a

Following a luncheon for Zsa Zsa Gabor at our farm on behalf of the International Walking Horse Show: Caroline, Billy, Zsa Zsa, David Welsh on Premier, Amy, and Jim.

group of men and women underwrote the cost of Zsa Zsa promoting the show. If she wanted a prince to come along, she could pay for him.

Zsa Zsa had a list of demands. She wanted no photographers to meet the plane, which I thought was odd for a celebrity. She wanted a Rolls-Royce with a chauffeur at her disposal. She had to have a hairdresser every day and, of course, a nice place to stay.

Faye Snodgrass was handling the event for the public relations agency. She asked me if I wanted to meet Zsa Zsa at the plane. I had too many things to do for the show, and anyway Zsa Zsa said she didn't want any hoopla. As it turned out she was really perturbed when no press met her at the plane. It was a complete turnaround from what she said she wanted.

Vanderbilt Plaza gave WHOA a suite for her use. Zsa Zsa brought her shih tzu with her, and she ordered special meals for the dog. We didn't include her meals in the expenses-paid part, much less meals for the dog, because she had so many invitations for meals. She ordered vases and vases of flowers from the hotel florist to fill her room. We didn't pay for them either.

Zsa Zsa was to come to Tuck-A-Way for lunch as part of her promotion. The people who paid to get her here were to come, too, and major sponsors of the horse show. Gentry Crowell, secretary of state, was the representative for Governor Alexander, and he was to make her an honorary citizen and colonel. She hadn't arrived by the time we were supposed to eat, so I said, "Let's eat now anyway." The people were hungry, and making them wait longer served no purpose. Faye made several phone calls telling me that Zsa Zsa didn't want to come, but I told her that she had to. It didn't look promising there for a while.

Zsa Zsa did finally show up. We had already eaten, but people stayed to see her. Members of the press from Nashville and from the state papers were waiting to interview her. We requested that they not ask her for autographs, and they didn't. She was very gracious. She genuinely loves horses, and that became evident on her visit. She loved the mare and the foal of Amy's.

When all the people left, Zsa Zsa stayed on. She wanted to ride the horse loaned to her for her exhibition ride. Before she did, however, she sat out on our porch and ate the plate full of food we served her. She was as down to earth as she could be.

157

As we were walking down to where she was going to ride, I said, "Zsa Zsa, you are just ageless." I meant that, and she appreciated the comment. She said that of all the husbands she had had, there was one who was a good man she should have stayed married to. I didn't have the nerve to ask her which one, and I regret now that I didn't.

She was at the horse show for several nights, and her box was next to ours. A mobile home was provided so that she could change from riding clothes. Alan Balch did the show's commentary that year.

In a letter written from her Bel Air home in August 1984, Zsa Zsa said,

> You really made my stay in Nashville. I am so glad I met you. You are a lovely and intelligent lady, and I hope we are going to stay friends.
>
> I already put out my feelers about the horse that J. W. wants to give to the Reagans. As you know, the President is not allowed to accept any gifts, but Nancy already knows of your generous offer.
>
> The gorgeous horse [porcelain figurine] you gave to me is in a wonderful place in my home, and I shall always cherish it.
>
> Please stay in touch with me whenever you have a chance, and if you, J. W. or Amy want to be my houseguest, just let me know.

Unfortunately we were never able to take her up on her invitation to her house in Palm Beach or Beverly Hills. She has since sold the Palm Beach house. When you get beyond the movie star bit, she is very nice person.

Zsa Zsa came to the Celebration in a subsequent year, and they had similar problems with her that those of us at the International did. She stayed at a hotel in Murfreesboro. The Celebration had given her a box seat; I never dreamed I would see her, though. I was leaving my box when I heard her holler at me. She was there with her daughter Nikki.

Of all our horses, Premier Delight was the most unique. He did not require the big built-up shoes. He had more natural ability than we had seen in a horse in recent years. Premier was standing

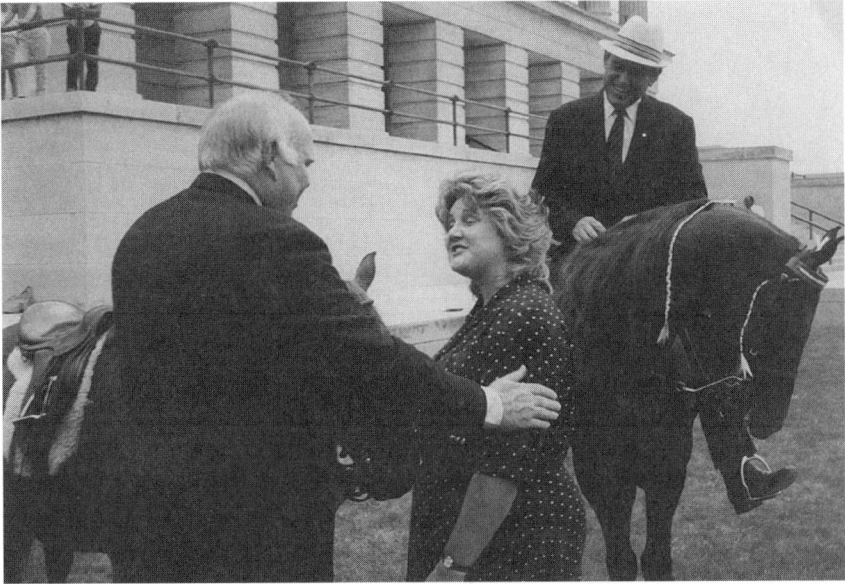

Amy issuing an invitation to Governor Ned McWherter to come to the horse show, with her proud daddy looking on (taken on the Monday before he was stricken).

public stud at Harlinsdale Farm here in Franklin. He was ridden every day to stay tuned up. They were bringing Premier in from the riding ring; the phone rang; the rider went to answer the phone, while holding Premier's reins. Apparently Premier put his front feet on the concrete pad by the phone and slipped because he had his show shoes on and broke his pelvis. He had to be put down. I cried a week and couldn't even talk about it on the phone. That was in 1986. We buried him on Tuck-A-Way II land and erected a tombstone. After the sale of that farm, we moved the stone to Tuck-A-Way I.

Upon his death we received a sympathy note from Luella Harlin, owner with Mr. Harlin of Harlinsdale: "Wirt and I are distressed over your recent loss and want you to know you have our understanding sympathy." She mentioned that when she and her husband lost Midnight Sun and Pride of Midnight, they felt as if they had lost family members: "To someone who has not owned a horse that seems a broad statement I know." We also received a sympathy note from Zsa Zsa.

Billy in the Classic Carriage Class at the Tenth Annual International Grand Championship with a pair of Walking mares. He won second place, the day before he was stricken.

Because a friend from high school called Amy asking for help, Amy became involved in the cerebral palsy therapeutic riding program. A report in the *Nashville Banner*, October 10, 1986, noted that the steeds Popeye, Black Beauty, and Sweet Pea were used. Amy was one of three adult volunteers. She can explain it better than I can because of her role in the early days of the program: "The program was just for people with physical disabilities, and primarily those with cerebral palsy. I assisted with lining up horses, volunteers, and the place to have the no-fee program. It was a year-round program with twelve- or thirteen-week sessions, and the children and adults would come once a week. The idea is that the horse's motion simulates walking, which stimulates the muscles of the rider. One little boy who participated went from using a wheelchair to using crutches; the horses weren't the only factor, but they certainly helped him. The

160

program gives the children an activity that is theirs; that helps when they have brothers and sisters who are active in baseball and dance and other things."

Amy is no longer involved in that program, but she has become a judge of horse shows. She had to attend seminars and judge three shows in an apprentice capacity before receiving her license. There are different levels of licenses based on experience. The National Horse Show Commission in Shelbyville issues the licenses for judges of Tennessee Walking Horses. She has judged shows in Tennessee, Wisconsin, Georgia, Kentucky, Ohio, and Indiana.

Our family's relationship with Tennessee Walking Horses took many turns that we could never have anticipated. The front page of the *Daily News Journal* (Murfreesboro), for August 14, 1988, had an article by Dan Whittle that summed up in a way I can't what happened at the horse show that year:

James W. "J. W." and Caroline Cross likely have had more hands-on effect on the International Grand Championship Walking Horse Show than anyone in its 10-year history.

Cross, who fell from his saddle during International show ring competition this week, was in critical condition Saturday at Nashville's St. Thomas Hospital. . . .

"There is just no way to measure Mr. and Mrs. Cross' contributions to the International. In terms of planning. In terms of financing. In terms of physical work. J. W. has been bound and determined that it would be one of the classiest shows of the nation," said Bob Womack, president of WHOA, which sponsors the International.

"People here agree this show is the classiest horse show they have ever attended. It became that this year," Womack said.

And attendance was up more than 50 percent.

That night is certainly one that our family will never forget. (I'll discuss it more in a later chapter.)

161

A significant family friendship that came about because of the Tennessee Walking Horses is going to have a major impact on the future of the horse in Middle Tennessee. Billy and I and the children would never have met John and Mary Miller if it weren't for the horses.

Mr. John, a true pioneer, was born in Morristown, Tennessee. Alaska was undeveloped when he first went there to work; he formed his own construction company and participated in laying the large pipeline and also worked on the Alaskan Highway. His company was Frontier Equipment Company and Pioneer Oil Field Service, Inc., based in Anchorage. In 1981 the firm had been in business for thirty-five years. The company's ad boasted that they delivered "Exactly as promised. On schedule. On budget"—with "savvy Frontier men."

The *Nashville Banner*, November 14, 1979, ran a story on the Millers. They divided time between Kentucky coal mining and Alaskan oil field contracting and Walking Horses and mules on farms near Lewisburg. Mr. John had been living in Alaska part time for about forty years; he was there while homesteading was the way to get land. He and Miss Mary met in Anchorage over a lost dog that he tried to return to her. They had been married for twenty-two years at the time of the report.

Our family was at a horse show in Jackson, Mississippi, and Mr. John and Miss Mary were sitting in front of us. Mr. John always wore a hat and his pants always had suspenders, usually red ones. Under Miss Mary's seat rested a pretty springer spaniel. Jim kept fooling with the dog, which was well-mannered. She said, "Jim, do you like this dog?" Of course he did. I told her, "You can't give that dog to Jim. I don't want dogs in my house." Their dogs were like children, so they stayed inside. She said, "I can't keep this dog. It bothers Bob." Bob was Mr. John's border collie, and he flew everywhere with them on Eastern Airlines. (As it turned out Mr. John died before Bob.) I asked how she came to have that dog. A young couple in Anchorage had the dog, but they were expecting a baby, and they wanted to give the dog up. Miss Mary took the dog, but Bob didn't like her. There was no question: the spaniel had to go. Miss Mary had flown both dogs from Alaska to Tennessee and then to Mississippi.

Jim had not been driving too long. We had given him a Blazer as his first vehicle, and a friend had driven down with him to the show. He and the friend and the dog went back to Franklin. We had her until she died.

One December 23, Mr. John called Amy from Alaska and gave her the stud fee for Delight's Bumin Around, then a World Champion, as a birthday present. However, the horse died before Amy could breed one of her mares.

Both Millers seemed to have a strong interest in our children. Mr. John would go to a horse show and whittle the entire time. (The day that he was buried Billy went into Mr. John's office and came out with some of the whittled sticks. He asked Miss Mary if he could have them. They're in our glass cabinets along with the whittling knives that Mr. John gave Billy.) Mr. John wouldn't look up from whittling during the shows, except when Jim or Amy or Sara Dunn, daughter of John Dunn, was riding. Mr. John would say, "Judge, there's your hoss!" That was a real compliment to those children.

Mr. John died instantly while he and Miss Mary were at their house on the North Slope in Alaska. She was there alone with him for quite some time before help could come and his body was shipped back to Tennessee. The man who gave the eulogy was his Alaskan lawyer. Mr. John was not a churchgoer, not by a long shot, and he likely knew few ministers. He was the best man in the world but used terrible language, although he was careful about what he said around the children. The lawyer was from Anchorage and had heard of Tennessee Miller, as Mr. John was called in Alaska, before he met him. Mr. John had contacted the lawyer about doing work for him— looking after his claims, checking that his taxes were paid, and so forth. One day Mr. John showed up at the lawyer's office with all his paperwork for his businesses in a beer carton. The lawyer had to sort through all that to straighten out all the businesses, and they were complicated ones. Miss Mary didn't know what he was worth when he died because he played his cards very close to his vest, even with her. The lawyer told all about Mr. John and how people in Alaska respected him. Mr. John made his money the old-fashioned way; he earned it. He was a true friend to our family, and he stuck by us. He felt strongly about the Tennessee Walkers and wanted them to get out of the muck and mire that had surrounded them.

The Millers were mainly in the breeding side of the business. Billy suggested that I ask Miss Mary for the money to speed up the program when he and the committee were trying to enlarge the arena in Murfreesboro; the arena would then be named after Mr. John. Miss Mary had gone to Washington, D.C., on behalf of the horse, and she was active in horse doings. I did as Billy asked and mentioned the sum of $3 million to her. She said, "Hell, no. I don't even know what I've got. I may be broke." In her generation the men didn't communicate to the women about finances, and she wasn't directly involved in any of the businesses. She really didn't know her financial situation. I gracefully accepted her no.

Dr. James Walker, president of MTSU, thinks that my inquiry planted the seed for her to give the $25 to $30 million for the proposed new arena to be named for Mr. John. However the seed was planted, I'm grateful that it took hold. Miss Mary continually called me and others in WHOA—Sam Stockett in Mississippi and Tommy Hall, WHOA's Executive Director—to ask about what was happening with the International Show while she was in Alaska trying to settle Mr. John's estate. I told her that we had a waiting list for box seats and that we needed more barns. John Bragg and Governor McWherter had arranged for more barns at the facility, but we had outgrown the arena. Apparently her questions and our answers were leading her to the decision about the arena.

Margaret Lindsley Warden had a collection of stud books for all breeds dating to the 1700s, many about Thoroughbreds. They needed to be in a special collection. After much negotiation between WHOA officials and Dr. Walker and Miss Warden, she gave it to MTSU to be put in the Miller facility. The collection will go in the house on the property, which had been built by Pete Gunnells, a Franklin native.

The money was given at Miss Mary's death. At the first meeting concerning the new facility, Dr. Womack said that he would like for me to tell the others about the Millers because I was the only one in the room who was close to them. I explained to the committee how the gift had evolved. She did not tell any of us she was doing it. The gift was a complete surprise. When the People's Bank of Lewisburg called First Tennessee Bank in Murfreesboro to inform Dr. Walker about the gift, Dr. Walker was told to get in touch with me because of our family's connection with the Millers.

The MTSU Foundation is to administer the gift. I am a member of the committee from the MTSU Foundation that decided to establish two chairs—one for her and one for him—in some specific part of equine science. They're planning eventually to move the whole department of equine science at MTSU to the facility. The will states that the money is to be used for the furtherance of Tennessee Walking Horses and for WHOA to have a place for the International Horse Show.

Most of the people on the committee that Dr. Walker appointed don't understand what has happened in the horse business that made the Millers have the feelings they had. The founders of WHOA have died off. The younger people don't realize the fight and the hard times the people in the horse business have had to keep the Tennessee Walking Horses.

Dr. Bob Womack is considered the historian for the Walking Horse. In an article noted earlier, he said that he had never seen such a classy event as the horse show that Billy and I chaired. That was what the Millers wanted. I hope the whole complex can be and will be run as the Millers wanted it to be run.

My speaking up for the Millers is essential because I think they would have spoken up for me if our situations had been reversed. They had no children to speak for them. That's a lot of money they worked hard to get, and their wishes should be carried out by the MTSU Foundation. That is stewardship.

The money of the family of John Haynes came from Standard Oil Company. Haynes Haven Farm is where the Saturn plant is today. Miss Mec (Mrs. John Haynes) said, "The biggest burden we have had as a family since becoming wealthy is that I worry about if I'm spending and giving my money where God would want me to." As I child I heard that. That issue weighed very heavy on her heart, and as I grow older, I can understand what she meant. We all need to be stewards of our money—no matter how small or how large the amount.

A Delightful Life

At the groundbreaking ceremony for the Miller facility, Charlotte Durdin came up to me and thanked me for helping Miss Mary when Mr. John died. I introduced her at the ceremony because she is a cousin, one of the few relatives of either John or Mary. On August 10, 1997, I received this letter from her:

> I am happy and proud I was at the Tennessee Miller Coliseum Groundbreaking Ceremony Saturday.
>
> You were the only person I knew who had been involved in the tremendous job, and I wanted to let you know one relative of John's was there to see what is being accomplished. You were sweet to want my presence acknowledged, but I was there in memory of John and Mary as I had been with them so much during their "Tennessee Horse Days."
>
> It had been sometime since I had seen you but I recall how sweet you were when John died. Also, I was with Mary at the International when Mr. Cross took ill, and my prayers were with you and your family during the years of his illness.
>
> You are an elegant and gracious lady. . . .
>
> I look forward to seeing the completed coliseum and grounds, and also attending the shows there.
>
> Thank you again for all that has been accomplished.

All horses scare me because they're so big, and I am especially scared of the highly strung Thoroughbreds. But I like the activities that go with them and the horse shows. People care for them like babies, and the Thoroughbreds live in such elegant surroundings.

Statues of black men in jockey uniforms stand out in front of Tuck-A-Way. State Supreme Court judges from across the nation were to come here for lunch. Some tour companies arrange to have a catered lunch here because there is no place in Franklin to serve ninety to one hundred people. They wanted me to move the jockeys because they thought the jockeys would be offensive to the black people on the tour. I refused. The men who worked here named them after themselves. I told the tour people, "You don't know history." Years ago black men were jockeys in Thoroughbred races and made extra money for themselves. I didn't move the jockeys, and the judges didn't come here. That was a shame.

Every year Billy and I went to the Kentucky Derby, where we had a box seat. Billy loved to visit the horse farms, although growing up, he was not a horse man. His family had registered herds of cows— Black Angus and Polled Herefords. Then when we married and had land, he bought Polled Herefords again. Daddy taught him to love the Tennessee Walking Horses.

We got into training, showing, and racing because some of the yearlings did not sell for as much as we thought they should. We were hoping to train them and then sell them. Tuck-A-Way II was the farm for our Thoroughbreds and Tennessee Walking Horses, and David Welsh was hired as farm manager in 1984 to deal with them.

Two of our Thoroughbred mares were a sister to Secretariat's dam and a sister to the mother of Vanlandingham and Temperance Hill. The October 1987 *Review Appeal* commented on Tattinger, our Thoroughbred, standing at stud. Tattinger was sired by Grey Dawn, which was a champion and won the Kentucky Derby.

Owning Thoroughbreds is a costly business. Billy and I were sitting at Keeneland in Lexington at a sale. One customer was on the left and Robert Sangster of England was on the right. The bids were being raised at $500,000 a bid, and our heads were going from left to right while we watched the action. Sangster had the final bid of $13 million for the yearling. When Billy and I were in Ireland at a farm owned by the Firestones (not the tire people), we asked the manager what had happened to the yearling. He said that it was in Ireland somewhere, but it never raced. It had to make a name for itself before it could be used for breeding purposes, so that $13 million went down the drain.

Princess Anne came to Nashville for the Royal Chase, which was part of the circuit of the steeplechasers. The profits from the event went to the steeplechase organization and to Princess Anne's charity fund in England. In that year, May 1988, what I call the "Royal

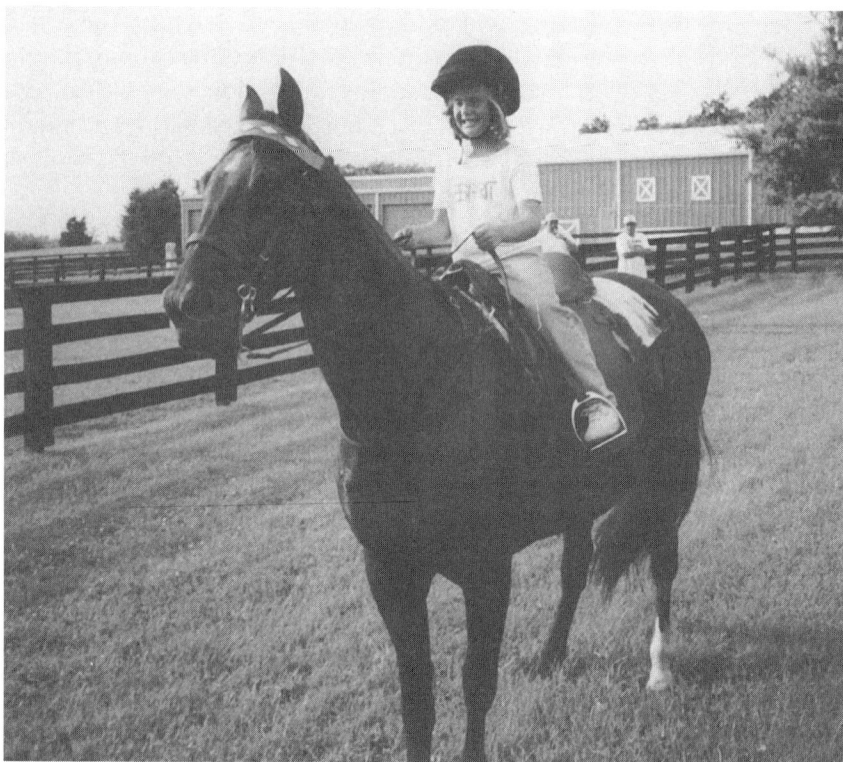

Madeline learning to ride, 1997.

Boxes" were added to the Iroquois. Until that year we had a meadow box; since then, we have had a "Royal Box." I wouldn't miss the Iroquois each year. George Sloan now lives in England most of the year, and I keep up with steeplechasing events through him. He wants me to come to Cheltenham—near my cousin's house in the Cotswolds—to the races, but I can't seem to find the time.

Billy was president of the Thoroughbred Association at the time of his illness. He was instrumental in getting Thoroughbreds started back up as a breed in this state, and he worked diligently toward the goal of pari-mutuel betting in the state. Many thought his work in that area was terrible since he was a church leader. My big gamble is my twenty-dollar fun bet at the track—whether I win or lose, that's as deep as I dig into my pocketbook.

David Welsh, our horse manager, helped me sell the Thoroughbreds through private and public sales after Billy's illness. The market was terrible, so selling them was not easy. Getting them off the farm was like being in a race against time. They consume constantly with food and vet bills costing money. The Walking Horses were sold too. Several in the ring at the International in 1997 were offspring from those horses we had raised. I got out of the horse business totally, and I sold all the cows, which were a herd of grade cows. An all-day auction at the farm sold off the equipment. Horses and cows would have required time I didn't have after Billy became ill.

Amy farmed out some of her horses. She has a few brood mares and trail horses on the farm here now.

Our family benefited in many ways from owning and showing horses, and we all enjoyed the activities associated with them. The differences between Thoroughbreds and Walking Horses are distinct, but the family's love has always been with the Walking Horses. Madeline is following in her great-grandfather's and grandfather's footsteps; she just loves the horses. The hope is that Will, too, will share that love.

CHAPTER 7

On the Road

> *The test of pleasure is*
> *the memory it brings.*
> *—Jean-Paul Richter*

Some years the family seemed constantly on the go. Football games and other sporting events for the children took us out of town often. Reviewing my daily diaries, I sometimes wonder when we stayed home. When Jim was playing football at Brentwood Academy, we were one weekend in West Tennessee and the next here in town and the next in East Tennessee. Participating in horse-related activities required a certain amount of time away from home. Geography and history have always intrigued me, as I mentioned earlier. Through all my travels overseas, my knowledge and appreciation of other cultures have broadened. And here in the States a highlight has been deep-sea fishing in Florida.

When Amy was eight or nine and Jim was three or four, we went to Williamsburg. Billy and I did genealogical research at William and Mary College, while the children rode bicycles or did other fun things. We always stayed inside the Williamsburg village where it was safe for them to be without us. Three times we took the children with us, and later just Billy and I went a couple more times.

One year the family drove to Kentucky and stayed in the Beaumont Inn and Shakertown and other old hotels. We toured all the historical sights.

For some trips we took the children out of school because we thought it was important for them to experience these things.

Sometimes traveling is more educational than sitting at a desk in school. We parents never flew on the same plane, however. If there was a crash, one of us needed to survive to raise the children and carry on the business.

Jim and Amy have been to Europe several times; Jim was six and Amy was eleven the first time they went with us. As a student at Harpeth Hall, Amy spent a month in England during their winterim (January). Both children were with us at the English horse show in 1980. Jim and Jenny toured Europe on their honeymoon.

We didn't make it out West with the children, but Billy and I went by car on the lower route to California. We planned to see Sabine and Herbert Luft at Pepperdine. About midway to California I said, "I don't know why in the world we fought the Indians over this desert." That country doesn't appeal to me in any way. We took the upper route coming home, and it wasn't much more appealing to me.

Daddy took the family to Mexico when I was fourteen or fifteen. We had been in Texas, and he wanted to cross the border. All three of

At Pepperdine University, Herbert and Sabine Heck Luft, with daughter Rebekka and son Sebastian.

172

us girls had on shorts, and even though I was in high school, I was in oblivion about what was going on. Daddy said he would never let us go over there again in shorts. The men really ogled us because Mexican women didn't wear shorts.

Deep-sea fishing has had me hooked ever since I went with Daddy while the family was in Daytona Beach during my high school years. The cost might have been $75 per day, and that was high then. Now it costs $500 a day. Mama didn't go, but I think Linda and Mary went along. Although it turned out to be a very rough day, I was a good sailor. I can take it even when the sea is a little bit choppy as long as I am outside and can see the waves. Inside I'm worse.

We had the whole boat with the captain and were fishing for bonitas, which are very swift sport fish. *Bonita* means "beautiful" in Spanish, and they are pretty fish that really glisten on the top of the water. I caught some good-sized ones, maybe thirty-five or forty pounds. I was catching them right and left, and the sport got into my blood. We threw all the bonitas back. Daddy always regretted that he didn't have one of mine mounted because I loved catching them so much. We were going to fish again the next day, but a storm came up.

It was after Billy and I married that I went fishing again. In Panama City once we went on a big boat where we hung our poles over the side, but I didn't like that at all. The fun is in fighting the fish.

Saltwater fishing was more our style than freshwater. On one trip Billy and I had fished for two days in Key West but caught nothing. We gave up our seats to some newcomers, and lo and behold, if they didn't catch a sailfish immediately. Billy finally got a sailfish, but I never did.

Our neighbors at Monteagle, Bill and Frances Reynolds, were from Tampa. Bill was in the shipbuilding business and sold a boat to Jim Mobley of Boca Grande, Florida. He introduced Jim to us as the "top fishing guide for tarpon." In January or February Bill wanted us to go snook fishing in the bayous. We had to cast for them, and in those mangrove roots the line became tangled up. I didn't know how to cast, so Jim or Billy cast for me. That kind of fishing was not nearly as much fun as fishing for sailfish, marlin, or tarpon.

Caroline and Captain Jim Mobley of Boca Grande, Florida, on his boat YoHo.

In the spring of that same year Billy engaged Jim to take us tarpon fishing. We found the most wonderful spot in the world—Boca Grande. Being on that little island was like going back to Monteagle—of course, one is wooded and one is beach. It was old-timey Florida, but now it is built up with condos and is getting crowded. My cousin Frances Owen from San Antonio, who would meet us there, said, "Don't tell anybody about this place." Nevertheless, word got around, and a lot of articles, including one in *Southern Living*, were published about Jim Mobley, who became very famous for his tarpon guiding.

For twenty-five years Billy and I fished with Jim, always in May or June because that is when the tarpon are the best. We went over to his house and got on the boat docked there on a little inlet. It took fifteen minutes to reach the fishing hole, which was a deep natural pass. We could see land all around us. There used to be a big dock where they loaded bauxite onto the boats. Oil tankers would come in too. The local people and the captains worked to preserve that natural area long before environmental people came to the fore, and they still work at its preservation.

Let me explain how to tarpon fish. You're sitting in a chair that has a socket in the seat. Only two people fish at a time. You hold the pole across your lap, out of the socket, until the fish strikes. While you're easing the pole into the socket, your partner is bringing in his line. Your bait is squirrel fish with a hook in it, and the tarpon crushes the squirrel fish. When that happens, the fish is hooked way down in its throat. Tarpon are very bony in the mouth. Then Jim starts backing the boat. You go down with the pole and then raise the pole back up and reel as fast as you can while bringing the pole up. When they jump out of the water, they're beautiful, sort of glistening. When you bring the fish to the boat, Jim takes the hook out and lets the fish loose. You fish from nine to noon and then come in for lunch and rest. Then you go back out at two—because of the tides—and fish till about five. It's an easy way to fish if it's not too hot.

By George, one day only Billy and I were fishing. The harder tarpon fight, the better I like them. I have fooled with one an hour or

Indulging my love of fishing.

175

longer. That day I had caught seventeen, and he had caught sixteen. I told Jim, "It's time to go in now." I didn't want Billy to beat me and catch another one.

Jim, our son, caught a 170-pounder when he was twelve years old, and it was a record that year. If he had been fishing in a tournament, he would have won. I had always told the children, "When you go fishing, don't you holler for your daddy or for me to take that pole. That fish is yours, and you've got to bring it in." Jim fought that fish so long and he got so tired that he had tears in his eyes. I wanted to help, but I had to stick to what I had said. We did hold the pole for a bit to rest his arms, but he fought that fish and fought it and finally brought it in.

On another trip Billy and I and the children were farther out than we had to go to fish for tarpon—maybe twenty miles out. We were standing up, and each of us wore a leather strap that has a hole in it to hold the pole. I got a cobia on my line. Jim Mobley said to let that thing go because he would kill it if it was boated. They don't eat

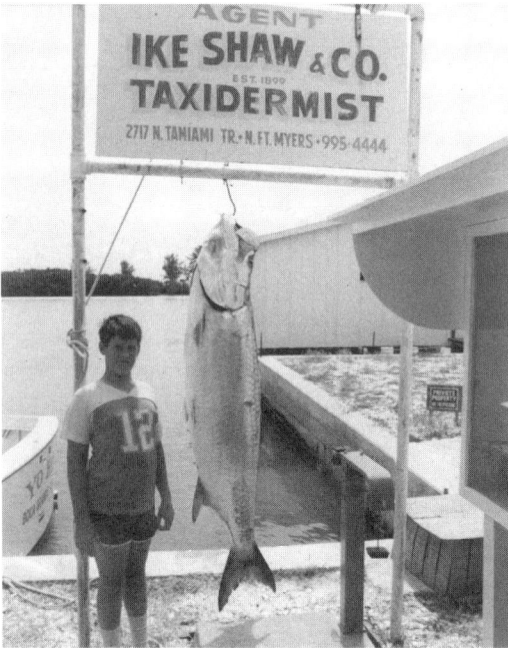

Jim and his record-breaking tarpon.

176

them; they're bad fish. I said, "Jim, I can't. I've told my children that if a fish is on the line, they have to bring it in." Billy said to me, "Let me try it." He wrestled and wrestled with that fish. Then I took it back, and we swapped it back and forth. We were determined to bring it in, and we did. Then Jim Mobley took a big mallet, conked it in the head, and killed it.

Three out of four of Mama's brothers died in or on water. Uncle Herbert, as I explained earlier, died in Old Hickory Lake, Uncle Bryan died in the swimming pool at his home, and Uncle Ernest died while he was out fishing in international waters. Uncle Ernest had just broken his own record for catching black tuna. (Maybe I inherited my love of fishing from him.) Uncle Ernest was telling the captain what a wonderful life that he and Aunt Amy had had and how many years they had had together; he remarked that he had been a lucky man. The captain was rebaiting the hook for him, but Uncle Ernest was dead by the time the captain was ready to hand him the pole. Billy and I had just returned from tarpon fishing, we picked up our suitcases, dirty clothes and all, and we headed to Norfolk, Virginia, to be with Aunt Amy. He had been fishing off the island of Ocracoke, North Carolina. The fishing captain met us with Aunt Amy and the car, while Uncle Ernest's body was being picked up; later Uncle Ernest and the rest of us flew back on the plane to Nashville.

Jenny went with us for the first time after she and Jim were engaged. Billy loved to take a nap in the cabin, where it was air-conditioned and comfortable. I never did understand how he could pay so much money to go fishing and then not actually fish. Jim and Jenny had just sat down in their chairs. Jim and I were discussing what to do if Jenny got a bite, and a fish hit her line! I hollered for Billy to come and help. She did well with it, though. Billy guided her through the process, but she brought the tarpon in. Billy then had it mounted for her.

The children and I went to Florida in 1994; Billy had died in August of the previous year. Even Amy, who was not much into fishing, liked that trip. I thought it would be a sad trip for me, but it wasn't. Because Jim Mobley has now retired, I'm not sure who will take us on future trips. To me, an ideal day would be to take my children and grandchildren fishing so that we can all be together and have a big time. Doing that anytime soon doesn't seem likely, and that makes me very sad.

All of us in the family mounted one fish. My daddy didn't want a big fish for his wall, so he mounted a little one. When my sisters and I divided his and Mama's furnishings after their deaths, I couldn't pitch that fish; it's hanging downstairs in the playroom along with the other trophies. Everybody who knows me thinks it's the strangest thing that I want to fish, but I love it.

My cousin, Frances Owen, and her husband, Leo, live in San Antonio. For several years they had leases on the King Ranch, and I went down there when they were hunting quail. We rode in a Jeep pulling a long trailer with eight dogs in cages. The Jeep was built up high, so we could watch the dogs work. Since Leo's eyesight wasn't too good, he asked me to watch the dogs for him, and then he would signal them. Grass is everywhere, and all the countryside looks alike to me. There is no road. Frances Owen has a compass in case she gets lost. What's worse, there is no bathroom! But I did enjoy watching those dogs work. I wish I had been taught to shoot.

On one trip to England, Billy and I and the children tried to trace Pocahontas's steps of when she married and went to England. We did find the churchyard near Lincoln where she is buried; a beautiful bronze statue of her is there. She was Billy's eighteen grandmothers back. The genealogical research has been done to document this fact. The line comes through Richard Cross, who was the first Cross to Tennessee and was a descendant of the East Coast Bollings (earlier spellings are Boling). Billy's great-grandfather was William Bolling Cross. In fact, Edith Bolling, second wife of Woodrow Wilson, was a relative.

Our German trips have been extensive and intriguing. Sabine married Herbert Luft, who was also a German. (Unfortunately they are now divorced.) His mother became a member of the Church of Christ right after World War II when Otis Gatewood went to Frankfurt and started mission work there. The church grew rapidly and constructed nice big buildings in the center of Frankfurt. Mrs. Luft first heard about the church because it was giving away food and clothing. Herbert was six when that happened, so he grew up in the

First trip to the States: left to right, Jim, Hans Westermann, Amy, Caroline, Ruth Westermann (Sabine's mother), and Billy on the patio of our Brentwood home.

church. His father worked backstage for the opera in Frankfurt. The entire family was enthusiastic about music. However, his father never had an interest in religion as his mother did.

When Sabine left Franklin as a young Christian, I wondered what we were sending her back to. The church in Heidelberg was made up mainly of older people, and the Germans are not religious people in general. Certainly her mother wasn't. She went to the German service, and a young German, Herbert, was preaching. He had received his bachelor's degree from Michigan Christian College. Then he went to California and got his master's and his Ph.D. from the University of Southern California. Pepperdine, the Church of Christ-sponsored school in California, helped put him through school. He returned to Germany to be a teacher. The saying is that when God closes a door, he opens a window. I knew that Sabine would be looked after. Herbert was appointed by Pepperdine as head of the

European program. Pepperdine has several schools in Europe: one in Florence, one in London, and one in Heidelberg, which is the headquarters. Sabine teaches there.

Herbert has always tried to broaden the field of the American students. One day he decided to go up to the villa in Heidelberg that Albert Speer owned, which is near the castle. He had seen Speer, who was a very lonely man, walking in the town.

Herbert asked Speer to talk to the students at the school, and he agreed. Somehow, though, Herbert had a falling out with him. Billy and I planned to travel to Heidelberg again in the late 1970s, and we wanted to meet Speer, but Herbert was unwilling to make the contact for us.

My interest in Albert Speer was probably stronger than Billy's. As I read books about him and about World War II, Speer seemed repentant of what he did, but he kept saying in the books that he didn't kill any Jews. Over the years, people in London told me that he knew all about what was happening to the Jews. The Germans I met didn't want to talk about it, however. Speer had a part in the coups that tried twice to kill Hitler, although he stayed in the background. He was the only aristocrat in the Nazi Party; the others were hoodlums.

About that time some articles appeared in the newspapers by the Associated Press about Speer; I called the reporter who wrote the last article I had read and asked how I could contact Speer and whether he thought Speer would see Billy and me. The man gave me Speer's address, so I wrote him and told him that I had read all of his books, that I was an admirer of his—but not of what Hitler did to the German people, the Jewish people, and the rest of the world. I wanted to meet him because he had said at the Nuremberg trials that he felt guilty, even though he did not kill a Jew, for being the head of the labor camps at the end of the war. He felt strongly that he should pay his debt to society. He was in Spandau prison for twenty years, the prime years of his life. I told him where Billy and I would be staying in Heidelberg and asked if he would call to let us know a time that he would see us. He wrote back that he would.

At our hotel, a pompous fat man was the concierge. He strutted around there as if he was still in the Nazi Party. He and Billy never did hit it off. He rubbed Billy the wrong way. We were peons to him, those crazy Americans. One day we had been out to Schwetzingen,

*Albert Speer and Caroline at his
home in Heidelberg, Germany.*

which is a village near Heidelberg where Billy was stationed with the
964th Engineer Corps. Returning to the hotel, I had seen a chimney
sweep on the street, which is good luck in Germany. I said to Billy,
"Speer is going to call today I bet, and we'll get to see him."

As we stepped into the hotel, the pompous concierge was bubbling
with news for us. Herr Speer had called and left a message. We were
to be at his house at a given time because he would love to meet with
us. We ate lunch; then thinking that Frau Speer would be there, I went
down the street to buy a bouquet of flowers for her. (As it turned out,
Frau Speer wasn't there.) While we were driving up the hill past the
castle, I was excited to think that it was all coming together.

Speer, dressed casually in corduroys and brogans, was very
hospitable and very gracious. I said, "I didn't come today to talk about
your Hitler days. I want to know about your architecture." Hitler was

enamored of architecture. Hitler wanted to put on all the extravaganzas in the amphitheaters in Berlin, and he planned the beautiful boulevards. Speer executed the plans. Speer said that only one of the buildings he designed was still standing, a little cottage in the Bavarian Alps near Garmisch-Partenkirchen. The Allies destroyed everything else. He and Billy talked a while about architecture and building methods.

However, Speer couldn't stay away from talking about the Nazi Party because it was such a big part of his life. His English was flawless (although it's interesting that his letters to us were sometimes in English and sometimes in German). He said, "You have to remember the conditions of Germany to understand what happened." His father was a medical doctor, and the house in Heidelberg was their summer home. It was a villa, the finest German house Billy and I had been in. Their regular residence was an apartment in Mannheim on the finest street. Speer had graduated from college, and I think he had married by then. It was the Depression and he had no job.

Here came Hitler, and Speer fit in with what he wanted. Speer said that he could have cared less about the Nazi Party, and he didn't have to join it initially. He was busy doing what he wanted to and what he loved—designing buildings—and money and labor were no objects in getting them built.

Speer eventually joined the party, but he and other officers knew that Hitler was on a path to destruction. They didn't want to see everything in Germany destroyed because they knew that the Allies would continue to bomb. They realized that they were going to lose the war. At the very least they wanted to preserve the autobahn system and other parts of the country. The men were visionary enough to know how much would have to be rebuilt. These were the reasons that the coups were attempted to kill Hitler.

Speer told us, "I know Hitler is dead. I know that some people say he is alive, but he is not. Yet if he walked through that door today with the same things he offered to me, package deal, I'd buy it again because of the circumstances of my life at that time."

I replied, "That's what I'm afraid of again with the German people." The German people were so proud; they could not stand to be defeated twice.

182

Speer said, "You're right. They have to be educated." Then we talked about what was being done to educate the German children.

Speer commented, "I've always loved the Americans, but I believed what your President Truman said, 'The buck stops here.' And I thought that the buck stopped with me. I needed to pay back my debt to society in some way."

His conscience seemed to be bothering him when he wrote his last book. He was smart enough and intellectual enough not to have been hanged or shot after Nuremberg. My opinion is that the judges and the lawyers at those trials probably saw that he was not one of the cruel, evil people of the Third Reich. I'm glad in a way that the judges spared him. All the Allies, except Russia, showed compassion.

Wanting us to know about other ways the Americans had helped him, Speer said, "Do you know what your government did for my family? I was your prisoner, but they took my oldest daughter to the U.S. through the AFS. She stayed a year in New York State. Wasn't that the kindest thing for them to do and let her live in their country?" (One of the sons is a building commissioner in Heidelberg now.)

Speer could not walk the streets of Heidelberg without hearing a sneering remark by younger people, not the older ones. Billy and I wanted him to come to the States, but he refused. He said, "No, I don't want to upset the Jews in any way." I said, "If you come to see us in Tennessee, no one will know you're here. They'll know *after* you've been here." He still declined. He went only to London to promote his books and evidently to see a woman. (Years later the great disappointment to me was that he had had an affair with a woman in London and he died with her in 1981.)

We were about halfway through talking to Speer and he was autographing my copies of *Spandau Diary* and *Inside the Third Reich* when he asked, "Do you have a camera in your car?" Billy answered, "No, we didn't bring it." We didn't take it because we thought that asking for a picture would have been an insult. He was more than willing for us to make some pictures. We had to go back to the hotel to get the camera.

As we were leaving to get the camera, I said to Billy, "Do you realize what might have happened if he and those men had succeeded in the attempt to kill Hitler? We Americans might not be in the position we're in." The men who were going to take over would have done things a whole lot differently. I think we still would have won the war. It might have been prolonged, or maybe the coup would have shortened the war. In any case the Germans' money was running out. Speer said the Germans never thought the Allies would transport gas across the English Channel. That was just one of many ways that the Allies outsmarted the Germans.

We weren't gone long to the hotel to get the camera. We returned and took several photos. The whole visit lasted about two hours.

On that trip to Germany, we also went to Berlin, Hitler's Eagle's Nest, and Dachau. Seeing both Speer and Dachau within a span of a few days was an ironic experience. At Dachau, I thought I could smell the stench of death. Later I was told that most of the original buildings

The last photo of Billy by himself, July 1988, in Ireland.

except the crematorium had been torn down, and the ones standing now had been rebuilt. It's an eerie place to visit, and everybody whispers. It's awe-inspiring in that people can't take in all that transpired there. I've been twice, and both times I've felt the same way. The second trip Billy and I took the children. Books about that period of history indicate that the people in the area had to know something was going on there. There had to be a distinctive smell with all the burning of the people and the smokestacks belching smoke constantly.

Billy and I and Joe and Isabelle Ross went to Ireland in July before Billy's illness in August 1988. Joe was to attend an international conference for doctors with specialties in chest diseases. I feel a real affinity with the Irish people, but Ireland isn't as pretty as I expected it to be. It's more rocky and craggy.

Billy, Isabelle, and I did antiquing while Joe was at the conference. I bought some things and asked the dealer to store them until October. Mr. Oman, who is kin to the families here in Tennessee, kept about six good-sized pieces for me.

Isabelle (hidden) and Joe Ross, M.D., and Caroline and Billy in horse cart in Ireland.

A Delightful Life

We had not been back from that trip a month when Billy got sick. Jenny helped in the shop while I was at the hospital with him. She called Mr. Oman and told him what had happened. We planned to go back to Ireland in October and take Amy and Jim and Jenny. We were going to tour; Jim and Billy planned to play golf on those challenging golf courses. Mr. Oman returned my money on some pieces and sent me a few pieces that I could air freight.

After I could start traveling again, I went back to that shop, but Mr. Oman's pieces weren't as fine as the ones he once had. Ireland was just being discovered when I first discovered it for antique buying. Now it is very picked over, and all the quality furniture is going to London.

On that trip with the Rosses we weren't staying in a very nice hotel. Two conventions were being held at the same time, so we had to stay at a place we normally wouldn't have chosen. In all of our walking around Billy and I found the Shelborne Hotel across from Green Park, which is where I stay now.

We met a lady at Kildare Antiques, close to the Shelborne Hotel. She was jolly and energetic, and she and Billy hit it off. He bought me a beautiful silver tray there for my birthday. It turned out to be the last birthday gift he would ever buy me. I see Nora occasionally now on return trips.

Not long ago I bought a piece of Mason's ironstone from Zane Moss, a dealer in New York. He knew that some of my good customers in Texas sought Mason's. (When I think of Mason's, I think of the country version, not the sophisticated type with turns and gold lid knobs.) At the show where I bought the tureen, he had sent John, an Englishman who assists Zane at some of the shows. John told me that Zane wanted me to look at a particular piece that he had had a long time in the warehouse. It was a sauce container, and inside were a note and photo that showed what the piece sold for in 1974 and where it was purchased then. It had come from the same lady I knew at Kildare Antiques, Nora Breen, and the price was about seventy-five dollars. Now it's worth more than a thousand dollars. Its mate is in a Dublin museum; Thomas Higginbotham was the dealer for Mason's china in Dublin, and a section in the museum features him and his wares. That was some coincidence of connection that I knew both Nora and Zane. This year, 1998, I sold the sauce dish.

Another woman, a widow of an ophthalmologist, was my picker in Dublin. Her shop on Anne Street was so narrow and so small and Billy being so big and Isabelle being with us, he just got out of there. The place was probably eight feet wide and maybe fifteen to twenty feet deep. It was wall-to-wall things, and I bought and bought there. She eventually closed her shop, but I managed to get in touch with her later. She wanted to meet me before she would let me go to her house. At her shop I had dealt only with her shop attendant, not her. Amy was with me on that trip, and we agreed to meet at an antique fair in Dublin's town hall. We walked around the fair, and I showed her the kinds of things I liked; she already knew what I had bought from her shop. Over the years she would buy things when she knew I was coming. She lived in the Black Rock section of Dublin in a very nice house.

My cousin Sue Batey's husband, Lamar Baker, was the U.S. congressman from Chattanooga during the Nixon administration. One Christmas when he came to our house, he told me that I resembled Margaret Thatcher. He was the first one to tell me that I reminded him of her—maybe not only in looks but in mannerisms and the way we do things. After that, people in the States and in England stopped me and told me that I looked like her.

Ann Batey and I were flying home from a trip. Stepping up in the plane's seat to get my bag down, I heard the man in the next seat declare, "My God! You look just like Margaret Thatcher." He was totally convinced that I was Margaret. I thanked him and took it as a compliment. Another time that Ann and I were traveling I was flagging down a cart to take us to another part of a terminal, and a man whistled a flirty whistle three times. Then he said, "Hey, lady!" I ignored him because I couldn't believe he was whistling at me or talking to me until he said, "Hey, lady!" When I turned around, he asked, "Has anybody ever told you that you look just like Margaret Thatcher?" I replied, "Thank you. You've made my day."

On one of our Florida fishing trips, Billy and I were coming from the airport and stopped to eat in a little restaurant we liked on Longboat Key. He had on a suit and a tie, and I was dressed up. In those days people didn't travel in casual clothes. Women at a table

My Margaret Thatcher impression in the garden of Ruth and LaGard Smith in the Cotswolds.

near ours were all in a titter over something. Finally one woman came over to us and said, "We're trying to decide if you're Betty Ford." They thought Billy was my bodyguard. That was a first!

My childhood dream of going to Russia was fulfilled after I became a board member of the World Christian Broadcasting Company. The story of how that came about involved our family's business ventures.

My Preservation Interiors shop was on the first floor of our four-story office building in Cool Springs, and we were trying to sell the building. The real estate agent called me and said that there might be interest from World Christian Broadcasting (WCB) in making the purchase, but she wanted to know if I would be interested in becoming a partner with WCB because the company didn't have the money for the whole transaction. I said, "No, I want no partnership. First of all, my husband said he only had one partner in his life and that was his wife, and he slept with her every night and had the board meeting at breakfast every morning. He didn't like partners." Billy was sick at that time, so I couldn't consult him about the issue.

Not long after that, I was eating lunch in the kitchen in the office, and I received a call from a friend, Larry Williams, who was then the owner of Williams Printing Company. He said, "Caroline, I have a man I want you to meet—Bob Scott from Texas." He could come at 2:00. An insurance man was scheduled to see me for that time, but I said that I could give him fifteen or twenty minutes. My first thought was that he was bringing somebody who wanted a donation for the church, and I was certainly in no position to donate to anything then.

Bob Scott was the president of WCB. When I met him, I realized that he was the one who had looked at the building with the real estate agent. Bob decided that WCB couldn't afford the building, but he did want to buy land and have our company build a new building. Well, that insurance agent got a call that I was tied up and needed to reschedule a meeting. During the recession, those kinds of deals were few and far between.

I buzzed Jim to come downstairs to my office, and we had a good meeting. WCB bought a lot in Crossroads Business Park, and Jim built the building for them. They are a great group of people to work with. My daddy always said that you don't need to do work for kinfolks or people you go to church with, but this was—and is—a nice association.

The headquarters had been in Abilene, Texas, before moving here to Tennessee. The headquarters made the move partially because the Church of Christ is strong in this part of the Bible Belt, but the main reason was that Middle Tennessee has Vanderbilt, Lipscomb, and Scarritt College with many foreign students studying for additional degrees. The broadcasting company wanted to reach people in China or Russia or the Philippines and to have the best speakers of the native languages. The broadcasters need to be knowledgeable and educated, although the scripts are written for them. As a means of checks and balances, somebody from WCB who is Chinese or Russian or Filipino pays attention to the broadcasts and knows that the broadcasters are saying what is on the scripts. The scripts are written to be inoffensive to listeners; it's not a preachy approach, and no listener has to buy anything.

Sending missionaries to foreign countries is very expensive. WCB started broadcasting to areas where missionaries couldn't go, such as Russia and China. (Voice of America buys time from WCB because of the powerful transmitter.) We can't ever forget about the power of shortwave radios in influencing people.

WCB broadcasts from the studio in Crossroads Business Park in Franklin that has a state-of-the-art broadcasting system. WCB owns a high-powered transmitting station in Anchor Point, Alaska. When that was built, thank goodness, the board members who started the broadcasting company were excellent businessmen and business-women. They saw to it that everything they did was the best. WCB may be the best-kept secret in Middle Tennessee.

The broadcasters talk about agriculture in China or Russia. Or about music, not religious music necessarily. Or about problems with teenagers and other social issues. Then they tell listeners about a good life. If listeners want to know more, they can write and receive free literature and Bibles. WCB has offices in Hong Kong and St. Petersburg, Russia. It's easier to send literature in bulk to them and let them answer the letters in those offices than to do it all from the States.

If WCB can raise more money to add more transmitters to the big antenna, it can broadcast into Europe. The long-range plans call for placing a transmitter in the Czech Republic. The broadcasts now touch some of the Muslim world. An important point is that the transmitters be on American soil or American territories, so that communications won't be disrupted by hostile governments.

The group I went with to Russia in 1992 had the mission of nego-tiating broadcasting contracts with Radio 1 in Moscow. The big needle building in Moscow is an antenna and also houses offices for Russian communications. The man in charge of that is Alexander Akhtyrsky; he was head for all of the old Soviet Union, and he kept his job after the breakup of the country. WCB had been buying time, and then Radio 1 gave WCB time because the Russian administra-tors were so impressed by what they heard. Women in Russia are very strong. They remind me of strong black women in families in the

United States. However, the men are very weak; they are alcoholics and womanizers, which means that they are not good husbands or fathers. The broadcasts do a lot of programming on how to be a good husband or father. The people we were meeting with knew little about the Bible or Jesus but realized the broadcasts would help the Russians. We visited only St. Petersburg and Moscow.

In St. Petersburg we went to the home of the young woman who managed the WCB office there. The young woman was also a member of our church. We took coffee, things in tins, and tea as gifts for her. That's a sad story—poor, cramped housing and sorry food and a single parent with a daughter and an aged mother. They supposedly lived in the best apartment house in St. Petersburg overlooking the Neva River, and they were on a lower floor, which meant they lived in a better apartment. They were allowed to live there because the aged mother was the widow of a World War II ace pilot. Imagine being recognized in a special way all those years because of his war record; war and its trappings still have a strong hold on the Russians. The stench from backed-up sewage lines assaulted us the minute we walked in the apartment house. There were only a toilet and a lavatory in her apartment, no bathtub or shower. Ed Bailey said, "Let's take the elevator," but it didn't work.

Another young woman we met was the director of the radio station in St. Petersburg where WCB was broadcasting, and she had a son. She, too, was a member of our church. She had divorced her husband, and her aged mother helped her look after her son. There were no grocery stores as we know them, so everyone had to stand in line to get food from a truck in the center of town or at a plaza. The older women formed a group, and one stood in line for potatoes, another stood in line for vodka or milk, and so forth. The young woman was very concerned about what would happen to her son when her mother died; no one could stand in line for food, since she had to work as a single parent. A friend of WCB got her son out of the country and put him in a boarding school in England. Then that man brought the young woman to the States, but she had to leave her aged mother behind.

The six of us in the WCB group decided that we wanted the young director of the radio station to join us for lunch one day at the Grand

191

Hotel in St. Petersburg. We had the best meal there on the whole trip. She was a very striking young woman; she had a driver and a car, which I thought was impressive. The hitch was that the car rarely ran, and that day she had to take public transportation to the hotel. During the meal, she slipped some of her food into her purse. That was a living social comment; there was an executive having to squirrel away food because of the pitiful conditions in the country.

St. Petersburg once was a beautiful city. They've tried to repair the damage to the Hermitage caused by World War II. I was disappointed with what I saw on exhibit in Memphis: the pictures didn't fit the frames; the gold coach looked like something from a bordello. That wasn't the Russia I had envisioned. Many people disagree with me and think the Hermitage is grand and glorious. Seeing the real thing, with the paint peeling and the floors sagging, confirmed my opinion of what I saw in the Memphis exhibit. Our U.S. museums wouldn't be like that. The Russians buried lapis lazuli urns during the war in an effort to preserve them, then dug them up and put them on display. The Communists sold off the majority of the art treasures. A few years ago IBM was selling computers to the Russians, but they didn't have the money for the goods, so they traded emeralds. I knew the emerald dealer who bought the emeralds from IBM when they were bartered to that company. All those Russian antiques were bartered out, and people like Marjorie Merriweather Post and Armand Hammer had a hand in the big sell-off.

St. Petersburg, to me, was a better city than Moscow. We had a guide and a bus, but I told the guide that she had shown us only monuments to war. I thought of my grandmother's statement I heard as a child about the Germans and wars. Grandma always believed that there would be wars and rumors of wars. The Bible says something to that effect. Her impression of the Germans from World War I on was that the towers they built were places for planning wars. The Russian people outdo them in that regard, however. Not a Russian designed any of the architecture; the architects were from Italy, England, and France. That was amazing to me. Anything built since the war by the Communists is a dump, a ghetto in our book.

Our church had to be registered with the Russian authorities to be allowed into the country. Before our group left home, we tried to decide what to take that would be useful to the Russians. I packed toiletries, personal hygiene products, and small bottles of lotions and shampoo. A young Russian officer at Customs looked through my suitcase with all the supplies, then he grinned and looked up at me and said, "Kotex!" He was so proud that he knew that word. KLM let us take as much humanitarian aid as we wanted at no extra cost. We also had medical supplies—hypodermic needles, penicillin, amoxicillin, things that we had gotten from some of the doctors' offices and hospitals here. A doctor, probably in his forties, from one of the hospitals met us at the airport and collected all the supplies.

In St. Petersburg, WCB held an open meeting in an auditorium rented for the occasion. The programmer for all programs, Dale Ward, was to be there and meet with listeners to find out what they liked to hear. Seventy-five to one hundred people showed up. We took literature and Bibles in Russian to give away. We didn't push anything on them, but it was available if they wanted it.

The doctor who had picked up the supplies at the airport came to the meeting. The children's picture books I had brought along were in English, but at least the children could look at the pictures. I thought I might want to go to the hospital and personally deliver them to the children, but I soon changed my mind. From what I had seen elsewhere I knew that would be too upsetting. Tears came to the doctor's eyes as he thanked us profusely for the medical supplies. I told him that was the least we could do.

Rubel Shelly from Woodmont Hills Church of Christ has been the ethicist for Vanderbilt Hospital. Rubel had taken a group of American doctors into the Russian hospitals, and he said, "I have never seen such sympathy and empathy from those Russian doctors." I told the doctor about Rubel's statement, and he said sadly, "That's all we have to give. Just sympathy and love of the patient." That was no vacation to see and talk about those kinds of things. I don't see how medical missionaries do it. Knowing what wealth had been in that country over the years and to see what I saw. . . . Reading about the Revolution and seeing the Wall come down made the significant point to me that without the presence of God for seventy years and without a middle class, the country suffered immensely.

Our group took the train from St. Petersburg to Moscow. We were to leave about ten o'clock at night, and the people we met from St. Petersburg insisted on seeing us off at the train station. They also brought us food for the trip because there was no dining car. I remarked to Ann Moran, the other woman in the group, that the people had made a sacrifice to bring us that food, but we couldn't eat it, so we left it untouched for the cleaners of the train. The compartment that I shared with Ann was clean, and the linen sheets, though ragged, were starched and clean. We slept in our clothes. The bathroom down the hall was a hole in the floor; I could see the tracks. There was no water, no method of hygiene.

In Moscow we had a driver and a huge bus that would carry maybe forty people, and there were only six—two women and four men—of us. Our hotel was a huge disappointment. We had been booked at a better hotel, but we were bumped. I zeroed in immediately on the happenings in that hotel. There were pimps everywhere outside, and some of the girls were only thirteen or fourteen years old.

Ed Bailey, who was president of WCB then, was standing beside me, and I told him that I had an uncomfortable feeling about the hotel. About that time we heard screaming on the elevator. It was stuck and wouldn't work. I told him that I wanted to be on a floor with one of the American men, and I asked that one of them knock on the door when he left his room so we could go down together. The same thing went for Ann. He asked why I was uncomfortable. I said, "Those are pimps out there. I have enough sense to know what is going on. The pimps aren't going to bother me, but what if somebody got shot?" He asked, "You mean you're upset in Moscow about this? Didn't you see it in St. Petersburg?" I said, "No!"

Eddie Miller, our preacher, is a runner, and he ran near the hotel at all hours since it stayed daylight so long at that time of year. He said that he was propositioned many times. Apparently the pimps in St. Petersburg were well concealed at that better class of hotel. Those men got a laugh out of me about that.

One morning in Moscow I heard a swish, swish. Looking out the window, I saw an old woman bent over with age. She had a broom made out of twigs and was sweeping the streets. For that poor woman, that was the only way she had to live.

We had a nice dinner for the Radio 1 people and the television people in Moscow because they went out of their way to help us. It was probably the best meal those people had had in many months or even years, and they were officials, not the peons of the company. Before I left home, Governor McWherter had given me certificates to make them honorary citizens or colonels of Tennessee. You would have thought that they came from the president of the United States or the queen of England. The certificates were framed the next morning and immediately hung on their walls.

Sometime before our trip to Russia, Alexander Akhtyrsky and his deputy of communications in all of Russia, who was named Lydia, had come to Franklin to see the broadcasting operation. WCB asked if I would have a reception for them. Because WCB is supported by people of other denominations, too, we wanted people who were active in other churches, and some from Franklin and some from Nashville attended. Billy was still living then, but they didn't go back in his room to see him. They knew that he was very sick and that it had been a lengthy illness.

When we left that dinner in Moscow that night, Alexander's deputy, Ludmita, said to me, "If I knew how to pray, I would pray for you and your husband." I told her, "You can pray. All you have to do is talk to God like you would to your father." Then the thought hit me that most of them didn't have a good father image. Eddie Miller, my preacher, was standing there, listening to our conversation. He said he wondered how I was going to explain that. It just came out of my mouth.

Our tour guide remarked that the members of our group were different. We weren't the typical loud Americans, we didn't dress garishly, and we didn't get drunk. All of us in the group took seriously the idea that we never know who we are influencing by our words and deeds. We explained to her why we were there and what we were doing and who we represented. The guide said, "My grandmother was very religious, and we had icons in every room." Her grandmother knew how to pray. Our guide went to the priest at the

Orthodox Church and offered him money to teach her to pray. He told her that he didn't do that. I thought, *How sad!*

Our two-week stay gave me a realistic perspective on the Russian condition. It was not a tourist trip. People who had traveled in Russia before the Wall came down had told me what beautiful towns, great hotels, and such that they had experienced. My experience didn't come close to that. The Finnish and the English hotels were only pretty good. The hotel in Moscow where we had the dinner was owned by people from another country, not Russians.

The food was so horrible that I lived off dried fruit and packaged food that I brought along and the Russian bread, which was tasty. The only fresh fruit I was served was a piece of kiwi on a dessert tart. Some of the other people were more adventuresome with the food than I was. I drank bottled Cokes or hot water and used my coffee bags. We all sampled some Russian white wine one night.

The Russian people are hospitable, and they want to give gifts, which we know are a sacrifice for them to give. That night at the dinner in Moscow they brought me a lovely shawl. Many of them were former Communists; they had to be to survive, so I can't blame them for that.

The government had taken over all the private houses and turned them into multifamily housing. Driving down the finest boulevard in Moscow, we saw a beautiful building with well-kept grounds. It was the home of Vasila Pashkov. He and Count Modest Korff in 1884 organized a gathering of one hundred Russian evangelicals. Immediately one of the men in our group—Ed Bailey maybe—said he knew of Pashkov: Pashkov had been disillusioned with the Russian Orthodox Church, and he started reading the Bible on his own. He was practicing before the Revolution a religion like that of the Church of Christ; they were called Gospel Christians. We didn't know this until our missionaries learned all about it. Pashkov was an influential man, who had a big following, and some of the converts are still living. Wesley Jones and Geoffrey Ellis from Canada documented all this and wrote a book about it.

There is a basis for Christianity in Russia, though not an extensive one. They say that the Bible was in Russia in the tenth century. Yet very few until the Wall came down knew that there was a Jesus. That's unbelievable to me.

As we were landing in Russia, Ed Bailey asked me, "What is your first impression of touching down?" I replied, "The runway needs to be resurfaced." From the beginning I didn't want to fly Aeroflot, and thank goodness, we didn't. At the airport we saw some Aeroflot planes with windshields and engines missing; the ground crew borrowed parts wherever it could.

The Russians live that way. For example, if a car stops running on the busy twelve-lane road into Moscow, they leave it and walk away. Getting parts and doing what we consider routine maintenance are like luxuries.

It's sad, sad, sad. It's going to take generations to bring them to higher standards of living. The Russian people have been looked after like babies for so long, they don't know how to do anything. They are well educated but don't know how to make a living. The Communist system has provided the food and the jobs for them. They have dachaus, which are little plots of land about the size of postage stamps with sheds, and they'll go out there and plant things to supplement their food. They have to ride the train out and then come back into town. They stay on the weekends—no bathroom, no running water, no nothing, just peasant living.

If WCB needed me, I would go back to Russia. Otherwise I doubt that I'll return. Our group did what we went to do and negotiated the contracts, and I'm glad to have met the Russians and had the opportunity to travel there.

WCB is doing a worthwhile thing, and the approach the company is taking is good. The programs catch people's attention by presenting the good life. Some people might be critical of that, but I think we win people that way. We're trying to teach them a better way of living. We're helping them, no matter whether they decide to accept the Bible and its teachings. We can never know what will come of it. God does work in mysterious ways. I do believe WCB has made a difference in thousands, even millions, of lives in countries where the broadcasts are heard. It seems now that Russia is closing its doors to missionaries, but the radio can still reach Russian people.

———•·•———

The last time I saw Paris was twenty-eight years ago. I had been twice before—once the year Billy and I married and then when Jim was six and Amy was eleven. My fall 1997 trip was really like going for the first time. I didn't realize how beautiful the city and its architecture were. My friend Deane and I elected not to go with a tour group; we did our own thing and met up with friends living in Paris.

When I was in France the first time forty-something years ago, the people were rude. Now they realize that Americans and Japanese are their livelihood. Oriental people were there by the busloads, and our hotel offered a Japanese breakfast buffet. One of our drivers told us that the government had campaigned to encourage the French people not to be rude to tourists. I had already decided that I was going to hand it back to them if they were rude to me.

We got in one cab after having been in the Louvre, and I gave my piece of paper with the name of the hotel written on it to the driver so there could be no misunderstanding my southern drawl. The driver was mad and pointed: Why didn't we walk? I told him that we were tired and would pay no matter how short the distance. He took us to a hotel, but it was the wrong one. From there he drove like a maniac to our hotel and tried to be a little nicer. We didn't give him a tip. I thought, *Bud, you split your breeches on that one*.

After two days in town antiquing, we had little luck. France right now is in a recession. The French dealers do not have much because there is not much buying. Talking with an American who lives in Paris and has an antique stall in a flea market, I learned that London is taking over the customers because of more merchandise and lower prices than Paris.

Deane and I were standing in line at the airport ready to come home, and they were offering $1,000 to give up a seat on American Airlines to Chicago and guaranteeing a seat on the next day's plane. Boy, that was tempting, but I was really ready to see my grandchildren. The lady behind me was going to San Francisco. She said, "I've been over here seven weeks. I guess I could wait one more day." I asked, "What in the world have you been doing for seven weeks?" She said, "Buying antiques." Naturally we struck up a conversation, and she said that she had been in the country. She looked long and hard

The "three merry widows," Mary Jo Loden, Caroline, and Deane Pigg, before dinner at the Manor House of Lower Slaughter, the Cotswolds, October 1996.

and kept thinking that the next day she would find something, but she didn't find that much.

We went to church Sunday morning at one of the two Churches of Christ in Paris. The whole service was in French. The preacher was a converted Muslim. His wife, an American, translated for us during the Sunday school portion. When they started singing the hymns in French, I couldn't remember the English words as well as I knew them; I was thinking French. My friend was doing the same thing. We didn't know each of us wasn't recalling the English words until later when we were comparing notes.

One night we went to a restaurant that a friend in Lake Charles had recommended to me—Le Souffle. It was a quaint little restaurant where the locals ate; I don't like to go to places for tourists. A mother and a daughter to my right were talking to someone to their right, who was from Cambridge, England. Later, they started talking to us: the mother and daughter were from Atlanta, but the daughter was in England studying fabrics and wall coverings. I said, "Oh, you're going to be in interior design." She said she didn't know what she was going to do. Her mother commented, "Maybe she will come and help me." I asked if she had a shop. The mother was Lisa Newsom, owner and editor of *Veranda* magazine. I said, "My goodness, Lisa, I've talked to you many a time on the telephone. I advertised with you." She said, "I had an advertiser—Preservation Interiors—from Franklin." I said, "That's me." When I'm traveling, I find so many people whose paths have crossed mine in the past.

Another night Deane and I were leaving the hotel for a restaurant where her former boss was to treat us to dinner. Someone called out, "Hi, Mrs. Cross!" It was Betty King—she was Betty Harlin from here in Franklin. Her daddy and mother go to church with us. When we boarded the plane in Chicago to take the last leg of our trip home, there was my neighbor from across the street returning from Athens, Greece. It truly is a small world.

CHAPTER 8

Community Involvement

> *When the well is dry, we know*
> *the worth of water.*
> *—Ben Franklin*

W e have to make contributions. We take so much from society that it's essential to give back to the community. Everybody should give of time and/or resources, and in resources I include money, mind, and might. As part of our family's contributions, we've raised funds for many worthy causes and worked toward encouraging and building leaders in the community.

Sometimes I tell people that I may put a pair of hands, with palms up, on my tombstone because I've raised funds for so many projects. They weren't my accomplishments alone, however. Whether it was a project that Billy or I initiated, all members of the family became involved as well as other people on committees.

Don't ever tell me I can't do something; that's all the challenge I need to move forward with a project. Challenges are needed whether you're six or sixty-six. Looking for opportunities to do things in new or innovative ways is a part of fund-raising. Some people want to keep doing things the way they've always been done, whether they're being done efficiently or profitably or not. Taking a negative approach and saying something can't be done without wading right into it are certain roads to failure. Making the attempt gets you more than halfway there. Setting precedents in the first year of a project or an event means a lot to its future. Persistence and patience play roles too.

Ego can get in the way of effective fund-raising, and the common good of a project is sometimes shoved into the background because of egos of participants. The positive side of ego may be that people who are singled out as potential givers and invited to certain parties and events like the recognition due their businesses for their contributions.

Raising money for a project is hard work. Nevertheless I've been more than willing to do fund-raising because of my commitment to the organizations and their goals. An ongoing problem is that after the money is made, some organizers tend to spend it too freely. Sending people to conferences and conventions and paying their way—when everybody could pay his or her own way—needlessly use up the money intended for other purposes. Even though I may be disappointed in some of the things that happen after the funds have been raised, I still have the love of what the organizations are doing.

People who have the occupation of being fund-raisers bother me because they receive such a huge percentage of the money raised. I don't mean that they should work and lend their expertise for nothing. A better approach would be for fund-raisers to teach local people how to raise funds effectively, and they could earn money from teaching fees. They don't know or have a connection with the movers and shakers in a community the way that residents do either.

To raise money effectively, you need to learn how to graciously accept what is given and how to graciously accept a no. I have never been apologetic about raising money because I am contributing to the causes too. Turning folks down goes against my nature, but I can't possibly give to all the good works.

When Amy was in kindergarten at Ensworth, Sissy McAlister asked me if I would like to be in charge of sorting through things received for the auction funding event and putting them where they belonged, for white elephant, for clothes closet, and so forth. Doing that was training for me. I learned the organization of the event, and I saw the importance of having a job description for each job. There was no official title for me at first, but I kept that job for the Ensworth auction many years. Later on I was chairman of the auction itself, not the overall event.

Ellen Harwell Sadler was on the board at Brentwood Academy when Jim and her son Russell were there. She called and told me that the board wanted to do a fund-raiser. I thought an auction would work well, so I planned one. It exceeded its goal of $35,000. Throughout the auction the auctioneer took rest breaks, and we announced the running total of proceeds to build more excitement. My brother-in-law, Clive, did the first auction for Brentwood Academy even though his children went to Franklin Road Academy; he also did several at Ensworth. I have assisted Franklin Road Academy and other private schools in the area in setting up their auctions.

Clive taught me about momentum in an auction sale. He could tell when the people were really into the bidding, and that was the time to bring on the best items to get the best prices. Before any auction, I knew the most valuable items and had them ready to bring on at that time. Another way I built interest was to have a big stuffed animal for the children to bid on as the first item at each auction.

People at fund-raisers such as this give their money, but they get some things in return—the item, a fun outing, the feeling of having participated in a worthwhile event in the community. Begging for money has no part in it; the project should be a way to tug at the heart strings of people.

The Heritage Foundation was begun to preserve houses and buildings that were going to be torn down in Franklin as well as throughout Williamson County. I was asked to be on the board, and my first assignment was a feasibility study to see whether having a ball would be a good fund-raiser. We found out that because so many women were in the workplace, there were few volunteers to do the work. That was a problem. Yet there were enough women to make it a viable project. The Heritage Foundation had had two balls before that; the first one was inside Magnolia Hall, which meant that few couples could attend because of size limitations, and the second one was at Carnton on the front lawn.

In 1974 I was made cochairman of the ball with Mary Frances Ligon. It takes a whole year to organize such an event. The morning after the event is the time for the new chairman to start working on the next year's ball. The momentum has to be kept going. Billy used to relate it to growing tobacco. Once you get tobacco in the barn ready to sell, you've started burning off the plant beds to set out the tobacco slips for the next season. It's a vicious cycle.

A Delightful Life

Mary Frances and I moved the ball from the front yard of Carnton to the cow pasture in the field beside the house. My children and I were out there literally removing manure from the pasture and mowing, trying to make the grass even and not have too much stubble. The house and farm were rented at the time.

From the Swan Ball came the idea of having a jeweler to exhibit jewels. His name was Richard D. Eiseman of Dallas. Alyne Massey told us about him, and I flew to Dallas to talk to him about coming to the ball and he agreed. Keeping all those jewels safe posed logistical problems. Two city policemen met him and his employees at the plane, and the jewelry, worth more than $1 million, was rushed to the bank vault at the Williamson County Bank, now NationsBank, on Main Street. There were armed guards for all related events, and the jewels were returned to the bank vault each night.

Several parties were held leading up to the ball, and the jewels were exhibited and sold at those events, which were like private showings. The country gentleman breakfast was held at our house. People who gave a certain amount were considered country gentlemen. Patrons who gave more money went to a cocktail party the day before the ball. The Heritage Foundation was given a percentage of the sales of the jewels.

Having a hand-served meal was becoming prohibitive in price, and it was a slow way for everyone to be fed at the ball. The caterer and I decided to have several buffet lines, and the people were served and seated in thirty minutes. We left plenty of room between the tables so that people could visit. The only downside was that the music was pretty loud. The younger ones wanted the bands to play longer because they were having such a good time and they were willing to pay the band, but I sent them home when the official time arrived. It was a truly successful event. Sometimes if you extend the time, things get out of hand.

The same year of that ball, Billy and I were at Williamsburg when they were getting ready for their Christmas celebration, which is a candlelight tour in the village. We thought that a candlelight tour would work for Franklin too. The Candlelight Tour of Historic Homes in Williamson County benefited the Carter House. It's an APTA (Association for the Preservation of Tennessee Antiquities) property and run with oversight of the Tennessee Historical Commission. The house had been restored but needed more work, it didn't have original furnishings, and the outbuildings required restoration.

Billy thought the tour of homes should all be on one street and we should ask the city government to close the street to traffic so that people could walk safely on the tour. He also wanted horses and carriages to lend a certain look to the tour and help older people get around. Today we can't get that many houses on one street, and closing other streets isn't feasible.

The houses have low light, not just candlelight. The tour is really charming, held the first weekend in December. Church choirs had people positioned around or walking and singing Christmas carols. They weren't in costume that year; that tradition started later on.

Billy and I had bought Amy two houses in Franklin to restore. Before the Candlelight Tour, they said, "Amy, why don't you put the little house on Fourth Avenue on the tour?" It's the oldest house in town, and Amy got it structurally sound. The house called for country antiques. A friend who was an antique dealer, Mrs. Yeargin, almost let us move her shop to furnish it for the tour. I got in there and cleaned out the grates in that house, hoping to have fires burning during the tour. I ended up all black with soot and came down with something like histoplasmosis. The furnished house was a big hit on the tour and looked good, but I was too sick to enjoy the whole event. That was one week, and the next week we were on our way to London with the horses.

As president of the Carter House board, Amy did some work with tour companies; for example, nine busloads of senior citizens came from Chicago for that year's tour. Going out of state to attract senior citizens is a good idea, and more of that needs to be done. Senior citizens have the money and the time to travel, and they could make a weekend out of it and see other sights in the area.

Offices and churches are also on the tour, not just houses. One year the first Cross Properties office, which was on Third Avenue behind the courthouse, was on the tour. We had just restored it.

Tuck-A-Way Farm has been on the tour two or three times. The tour eventually expanded to houses in the country as well as town. Carriages were discontinued except at our house. Today it isn't easy to find houses that people will open for tours, but the Franklinites come through for the Candlelight Tour. The tour is still going on and the money still goes to the Carter House and meets the original goal.

When I do antique shows from Southampton, New York, to Palm Beach, Florida, my sign is up with the name of the company, Preservation Interiors, and Franklin, Tennessee. There has not been a show yet but what at least ten people have said to me, "I know where Franklin is, and I have been there." We have done a good job through various organizations of publicizing the town.

In 1975 when I was president of the Heritage Foundation, we instituted a spring tour. It didn't seem to me to infringe on the Carter House tour because it was town and country, and held in daylight. It was a totally different concept that also proved to be successful, and it is still being held.

For several years (1975–79) I was chairman of the Carter House Antique Show. To give background on that, I have to go back to Aunt Minnie, Mama's second oldest sister. She was the epitome of the social southern lady who knew how to do everything "by the book." If people had a social or etiquette question, they came to her. She kept a wonderful house and gave great parties.

Aunt Minnie became involved in the restoration of Oaklands in Murfreesboro and had to come up with a fund-raising project. There again is the energy in the family devoted to doing for others. Aunt Minnie decided on an antique show, but where the idea came from, I'll never know because she wasn't as well traveled as some other family members. It started in1954 or 1955. In the early years she would drive from Murfreesboro to our house in Donelson, taking the back roads all the way, and then I would drive her all over Middle Tennessee to see antique dealers. She wouldn't take a dealer in the show unless she had been in the shop and seen the wares. The ideas were planted in my mind then, but I never dreamed that they would result in the beginning of two antique shows—one for the Carter House and then many years later one for BGA. I thoroughly enjoyed doing all the traveling to meet the dealers with her.

Aunt Minnie said, "When you put on a show like this [and she had nothing to go by], you remember that the dealer is the center of the show. If you don't have dealers who are dedicated, they are not coming back. You have to feed them, treat them like celebrities, wait on their every need." She saw that all of that was done too. People still remember her and her shows, and her involvement lasted more than twenty years. The Oaklands Show is still going on in Murfreesboro.

Aunt Minnie had her show at the Hobgood School, named after the superintendent. It was held in June when school was out, but it was so hot! The schools weren't air-conditioned then. Later the show moved to the Murphy Center on the MTSU campus, where it is held today.

In Franklin we knew we had to have the show when it was not so hot. I talked to the superintendent of the city schools, Emmett Strickland, who went to the board and got permission for the Carter House to use the middle school during spring holidays. To issue invitations to dealers, for example, in one day I flew to Atlanta and to Miami to see antique shows and visit the dealers, then flew back to Atlanta. This was on a cold-call basis; I hadn't met the dealers before. Like Aunt Minnie, I wanted to see the dealers and their wares before offering them a contract. The contract presents rules and regulations that the dealers are to abide by and other details. I came up with the contract, and a lawyer checked it.

Since we had to use the school over a spring holiday, many people were out of town. Nevertheless we made $1,000 to $1,500 the first year, and we saw the potential. The money made from an antique show comes from the selling of dealers' booth space (we don't take a percentage of dealer sales) and the selling of tickets to the show. We tried various ways to raise more money. We had a tea room. We had an exhibit of Tennessee silver as part of the learning process about antiques for the community. Tennessee silver is sought after because early Tennesseans as a rule were poor and there was little coined silver, but Franklin had several silversmiths. We borrowed a collection of silver from Dr. Ben Caldwell, a noted collector of Tennessee silver who has written books on the subject. The trophy cases at the school were perfect to display the silver pieces.

Dealers from all over the country participated. I didn't—and I don't—like to take local dealers with shops because people can go in those shops without paying. I did the show for five years running, and we made $7,000 or $8,000 the last year. Remember, it was a small show. Whenever possible, we got things donated to keep the show profitable. There were committees, but the women were getting scarcer and scarcer to work. The ones who participated were hard workers and enthusiastic about the project, though. I had too many other things to do, and I wanted somebody else to take the baton. Nobody seemed to be in the position to take it, however. One reason that an antique show didn't readily happen after I gave it up was that Franklin had no big gym or other space to hold it.

When Battle Ground Academy (BGA) had the opening of the new campus, my neighbors the Beattys, Don and Donna, invited me to go to the dedication. I was very impressed with it all, and as I walked in the gym, I was like Billy going to MTSU at the arena. The wheels started turning: it was an ideal place to have an antique show with many dealers. Everything was on one level so that trucks could back up to the exit doors. I could visualize the dealers' lounge; a variety of local chefs serving their specialties seemed an interesting method for the preview party. The floor could have been a problem. I spoke to Dr. Griffith, the headmaster, and asked if there would be a canvas, and he said it was already ordered. That was all I needed to get started.

I talked about my fund-raising idea for a spring antique show to Donna Beatty and to Barbara Harlin. Barbara and her husband, John, are copresidents in the parents' association for 1997–98. I told them that because I knew dealers whose merchandise should sell well in Franklin, they could save money by not hiring a promoter. It was a walled show, paper with a solid color, which means an upper-level show as opposed to a tabletop show, and the dealers used borders on the walls to dress them up. We supplied electricity because a lot of light was required.

The money raised from the show will be used to restore the 1820s house Glen Echo, which is on the National Register and sits on the school grounds. Having that house available for the students to learn from is a unique opportunity for them. Being able to sell the goal of where the money is going is three-fourths of the way to raising money. BGA administrators didn't want to take funds from tuition to use for the restoration. Antique dealers prefer to do shows that benefit a worthy cause, and for this show restoration and antiques go hand in hand. The show was a boon to the city and county too.

The Carnton House is another place that our family directed its energies toward restoration. Dr. Joe Willoughby, Virginia Bowman, Don Young, who was a former president of the Heritage Foundation, Billy and I, Curtis Green, Vance Little, and other people formed a group to encourage Dr. W. D. Sugg, who owned Carnton, to donate it. Thus, the Carnton Association was chartered as a tax-exempt organization. Carnton, the house built in 1826 by Randal McGavock, is located off Lewisburg Pike and is considered a local treasure. During the Civil War, John and Caroline McGavock were living there, and the house was such an integral part of the Battle of Franklin that it needed to be saved. Caroline McGavock was so upset by the soldiers dead and dying around their home that she and her black workers went out and picked up the bodies and buried them in the side yard with wooden crosses carrying the names. Later the bodies were moved to the Confederate Cemetery, which is the only private Confederate cemetery in the United States. At Carnton is the book in which she wrote the men's names, states, and companies. She must have been a tough, fine woman to do that and to allow the house to be used as a hospital. Five generals lay dead on the porch.

Curtis's wife was a family member of Dr. Sugg. Dr. Sugg, a native of Franklin, had moved to Bradenton, Florida, and had been trying to give Carnton to the state, but the state didn't want it unless a fund for upkeep and restoration accompanied it. Dr. Sugg and his wife donated the house and ten acres. Billy kept saying that more land needed to be given originally. Most of the people were afraid that Dr. Sugg would change his mind if we asked for more land, but in essence the association helped Dr. Sugg by taking it off his hands because he was in a dilemma about what to do with it and he received a tax deduction for it.

The association raised money for restoration work and struggled to get the roof repaired to stop the leaks. Preventing further deterioration was a priority. In the early years of restoration efforts the proverbial "women in tennis shoes" held bake sales, yard sales, white elephant sales, or anything they could to raise money to save many properties in Franklin. Only more recently have men become involved in these efforts. We should thank those underappreciated women for all that they have done. Some of them scrubbed floors or walls or did other physical labor to better the properties. Doing mundane tasks may not be a glorious way to spend a day, but they are essential. When the money isn't there to hire workers, those tasks still have to be done. The women personally invested in what they believed in.

The two parlors in Carnton were to be restored, but there wasn't enough money to do all the work. Amy was hired; she had just graduated with a degree in restoration and preservation, and she knew the preservationists and the carpenters who could do the job. Billy and I donated money to finish the parlors and to restore the entrance hall. John McGavock inherited the house in 1854, after he and Caroline married in 1848. The association's research indicated that was the high point of the house, and restoration efforts were directed at that era. Today they have decided to go back to a different period, and all that money used to paint or build or paper in keeping with the association's original intent might as well have gone out the window. Sometimes change is done only for change's sake. That has happened in other properties across the nation too.

The color Chinese red was in vogue at that time, and that is evident in First Presbyterian Church in Nashville. When Amy started taking off the layers of paint, she found blue marbleizing for baseboards and Chinese red on the trim of the arch in the entrance hall. One Carnton board didn't like the color red, though, so it was painted over. Opinion is sometimes taking precedence over historical accuracy. When a board decides to take a house back to a certain era, there should be a good reason to change it to another era and to do away with everything on which a lot of money has been spent. They should concentrate on getting the house stabilized and climate controlled so that the furniture and the building will be preserved.

The Carnton board took anything that people gave that was old, even if it was not of the period, because it could be sold later—if it was an outright gift—and furniture of the period purchased. I was the first acquisitions chairman.

The Carnton Association and historians think that the builder of the Hermitage built Carnton. There was such a close connection between Andrew Jackson and Randal McGavock, the builder of

Carnton. Carnton was not a grand plantation house like the ones in the Deep South; it was just a wealthy planter's house.

Mr. Brown of Brown's Antiques called me to ask about a full-length portrait that he knew was of a McGavock descendant, but he didn't know which one. A man in Colorado owned it and had it stored at Brown's, and he wanted to give it to Carnton. I found out later that the portrait had originally hung at Two Rivers. It was part of Mrs. Spence McGavock's estate. Mama and I had gone to the Spence McGavock auction sale, and we bought some things. I wish I had been in the antiques business then because the pieces were really cheap compared to today's prices. I remembered that her estate had been handled through First American Bank, so I called Bob Andrews at the bank's trust department, and they found who had inherited that portrait. The portrait did not go through the sale. We needed things to hang on the walls in Carnton, but we didn't think it was right that a portrait belonging at Two Rivers should be in Carnton. The portrait was of David McGavock, son of the original owner of Two Rivers. The portrait is now back in Two Rivers, hanging exactly where it had hung for more than one hundred years.

Sometimes my interest in history leads me into new territory. Madelyne Pritchard from Martin, Tennessee, is secretary to Governor McWherter. After I was appointed to the Tennessee Historical Commission, she asked me to speak to her study group about the Tennessee River.

That seemed to be a worthwhile mind-stretching exercise because I knew virtually nothing about the river. Most of my information came from Donald Davidson's book written on the Tennessee River in the forties. For example, the TVA tore up farms and flooded them, and TVA might not have needed to do as much of that as it did. I was told as a child that it was done to control floods and to bring cheap electricity to the area. There was a lot about Native American culture and what they brought to this area that we still live with today. They introduced corn, which has played a significant role in all our lives.

I took speech in college under the speech teacher my mother had at Lipscomb; no one was any better than Miss Ora Crabtree, and she gave me confidence. I credit her with giving me courage, but many times it takes a lot of courage for me to speak in front of a group.

Billy felt that we should create a chair at Lipscomb University because that was giving back to God and the school stressed Christian values and morals. We gave land and money to create the Caroline Jones Cross Chair. I've been raised and cut my teeth on real estate, and I never thought it would lose its value the way it did in 1988. Thank goodness, Lipscomb was willing to wait to sell it to get a fair price—$1,200,000. My grandfather and father were astute businessmen and made most of their money in real estate. To see what happened in 1988 to real estate was hard for me to fathom.

Education was important to both sets of grandparents and my parents, as I've mentioned, and it was for Billy and me too. On August 3, 1990, there was a Golden Circle Reunion at Lipscomb with the honorary family being that of Arch and Ettie Jordan, and all twenty of my first cousins and their spouses and Aunt Minnie attended. Lipscomb has been dear to the hearts of most members of my extended family, so I was honored to be asked to join the National Advisory Board. Although this board does not make the decisions for the school, those decisions are shared with us. Board members are from different areas of the country and different walks of life; it's a diverse group. Not all are alumni, but their parents or children attended Lipscomb. The national board brings issues to the administration's and the board of trustees' attention. For example, the school needs to keep enrollment up; it's not a problem now, but it was during my mother's and aunts' and uncles' days there.

Where is Lipscomb going? At a meeting with the new president, Steve Flatt, about the chair that Billy had established in my honor, he told me about the provost being appointed to fill the gap between administration and the chairmen of departments. The school has grown and has growing pains. Steve is putting some things into practice that needed to have been done. It's important for the school to maintain its homey atmosphere, especially since it is a church-related school emphasizing Christian principles. It's easier to get the message across when the school is smaller. Lipscomb and schools like it will always need money. Tuition is very inexpensive for the education offered. Nationally the school ranks high for getting a good education for a small amount of money; keeping high academic standards should always be a priority. Lipscomb is appealing to people no matter what their religion.

On the day of his inauguration as president, Steve Flatt met with the board and told us of school traditions that he wants to reinstitute. Such traditions build strong bonds between students and the school, and there needs to be an interested alumni association. Steve attended Lipscomb; then he went on for a Ph.D. and at one time worked for Lipscomb. Athens Clay Pullias, the president in Steve's day, saw the importance of having academically gifted young people come back to Lipscomb as teachers and administrators. The school paid for the students to get advanced degrees elsewhere, and the students pledged to return for a certain numbers of years and work at the school. Steve Flatt was one such young person, and he recognizes the significance of having a similar program again.

Leaders have vision, they show people what can be done in a community, and they get them excited about and involved in wanting to improve or start something new. Leadership requires energy and enthusiasm, and if a leader doesn't exert both, others will not follow suit. Making others think that the project is their idea from the beginning is important. For example, I told the committee for BGA's antique show that it was a compliment to me that they were taking my knowledge and experience and learning from what I had done the hard way; then they applied their ideas and made the project better. Starting the best project in the world can become a flop if there is no interest or follow-up from people other than the leader. Now I'm willing to offer rocking chair advice to people and trying to encourage them to be leaders while I remain in the background.

Whether a leader is in politics or business, keeping one's word is mandatory. Billy certainly knew that and lived up to what he said he would do, and he usually exceeded what he said he would do. He was not like some developers who develop an area and then never return. He lived here in the county that he did so much to develop, and he had the necessary strong personal interest in his project.

My strongest gift is organization in personal life, home, and business. Organizational abilities are vital to leaders. My energy levels are almost boundless, and my love of people makes me want to be around others. These gifts, though, sometimes make it hard for me to stop and step back and get perspective on where I'm going and who I am.

My children's gifts are organization and stick-to-itiveness. Billy was the same way, so they got a dose from each side of the family. Amy and Jim are now involved in many community projects. I can see Billy and me in them and their civic involvement. Perfectionism can be a blessing and a bane, and there is that tendency among all of us. Amy and Jim love people and they entertain in their homes. They were included in our projects, and we didn't neglect them because we were doing any of these things. Neglecting the family to do even good works is detrimental to the family and ultimately to the community.

Lipscomb has proposed a curriculum focused on servant leadership. The idea is based on Christ's teachings on leadership, especially Mark 9:35: "Whoever wants to be first must be last of all and servant of all." Leaders of Lipscomb, particularly Steve Flatt, want to implement measures to offset the selfishness, greed, and pride that seem too prevalent among businesspersons. Although my grandfathers never used the term exactly, servant leadership was what they were teaching by word and deed. Having the mind of Christ as a leader certainly has a positive impact on how that person leads and interacts with others.

I tell the people in our Leadership classes that when city fathers and others say it can't be done, you keep trying. Leadership Franklin started in 1995–96, and the second class met once a month from September to April 1997–98.

Leadership Nashville's first executive director was Corinne Franklin. Corinne had a house at Monteagle, and she and Billy worked together on the board there. Most of my information about the Leadership program came from reading about it, and Billy and I thought it was a wonderful thing for Nashville. Both of us wanted to participate in Leadership Nashville, but at that time only Davidson County residents were allowed.

Billy and I talked about the importance of having a Leadership program in Franklin, but we were waiting until the town grew a little more before doing anything about it. Finally we said it was time. He put out some feelers with the Chamber of Commerce, but there was no interest. I thought that he let the matter drop, but I found out later from Gordon Inman that Billy was actively working on it before his illness.

A sponsoring organization is helpful. After Billy died, I knew that I wanted to do things that we had done together, and I talked to Jim about the project because I knew he had a strong interest in seeing Franklin progress. I had gotten in touch with Janet Vogt from Dyersburg, who was that town's Leadership executive director. She came here two years ago while I was recuperating from my back operation and talked to Jim and me about this project and gave us some logistics about it. When I was able to travel, I went to a Leadership meeting in Dyersburg at Janet's invitation. The man who was taking a lead in it was Dr. Bob Smith, chairman of arts and sciences at UT-Martin. He was also the founder of Westar—Leadership in West Tennessee.

In the meantime unbeknownst to Jim and me, Richard Herrington, who is the CEO of Franklin National Bank, and Julian Bibb, who was a graduate of Leadership Nashville, had been talking. They realized a need for the same thing here. Julian had been an interim director for Leadership Nashville when Corinne Franklin died. With Jim being on the board of Franklin National, we all got together to cooperate on the idea.

Jim, Richard Herrington, and some other men started Franklin Business Leadership Council. They meet once a month, every second Tuesday, at Legends Golf Club for breakfast. They discuss issues such as I-840 and its impact, the courthouse's move and that impact, and so forth.

We of Leadership Franklin asked Gayle Moyer, a graduate of Leadership Brentwood, to be on the steering committee. In March of 1995 Jim, Gayle, Julian, and I met on the porch at Tuck-A-Way. People had told us that we couldn't pull the organization together by September. None of us accepted that, however, and we accomplished our mission.

The first class was composed mainly of members of Franklin Business Leadership Council. The goal is to have sixteen people from various parts of the community—education, medical, religion, etc. Only four of the sixteen in the first class were born and reared in Franklin.

As the volunteer executive director, I have a forty-hour-a-week job for a few months out of the year, raising money to underwrite the program, planning monthly agendas, and keeping things on schedule during the meetings. Participants have to commit their time solidly to the program, and they sign a confirmation that they will be there for those times. The participants paid $350 the first year; in 1997–98 the cost was $400. All the meals are donated by local restaurants.

The days are action packed. If we ask people to give up one whole day out of their work week, we had better have something with meat for them in the programs. One of our first speakers was David Rusk, the son of Dean Rusk, U.S. secretary of state from 1961 to 1969. David works for the city of Memphis as well as other cities in the U.S. and around the world on a consulting basis. David knew a lot about Franklin and talked to us about our affluence; Williamson is the most affluent county in the state of Tennessee per capita. The county has had a boom of building, and he talked about land use. He spoke of the twenty-year-old concept in Montgomery County, Maryland, in which the county integrated all prices of houses into one unit of subdivisions, even public housing, and made it law.

David touched on affordable housing and ways we could get more in the county. Firemen and police officers and teachers can't afford to live here if they are not a two-income family. The public servants put their lives at risk for us, and the teachers see children more hours per day than parents do; we have to do something about this housing issue. Living in public housing today are mostly single-parent families with the mother as the parent. If they could live in an area where there were intact families, they could see what family living is like by example. All the children in Montgomery County, Maryland, go to school together. Children from the single-parent homes get to see how children from two-parent families live too. This arrangement with all income levels of people living in the same area can solve social ills. That is the right thing to do, despite protests from some people.

David pointed out our county's lack of visionaries. That's one thing Leadership Franklin is trying to promote. We want men and women to run for offices where their vote and their expertise can be put into place. We're not teaching leadership per se. People are born with it or they're not, but the skills can be honed. We have much potential here in Franklin, and more wonderful leaders are going to surface.

Because of my involvement in economic development and the leadership program, Marie Williams, executive director of the Tennessee Quality Awards program, asked me if I would like to be an examiner. The state of Tennessee has actively pursued and successfully brought in industry to the state. The Quality Awards program is based on the Malcolm Baldrige criteria that President Reagan highlighted in his administration. It's good for companies to have themselves critiqued and see how they're doing: Are they viable? Are they making money? If businesses fail, the communities lose too.

However, our state doesn't need to give away everything the way Alabama has given away the country store to Mercedes for that plant. We gave a lot for Saturn, and it remains to be seen how good Saturn will be. Williamson County wouldn't have gotten Primus, which is a Fortune 500 company, if Governor McWherter and the state hadn't stepped in with widening some roads and providing infrastructure, which needed to have been done whether we had Primus or not.

Becoming an examiner has meant much hard work for me. In June 1997 I went to classes for three days, held at the Nissan Plant. The main teacher was a Federal Express employee; Federal Express has received the Governor's Award, which is the highest award for business. Nissan, Northern Telecom, parts of TVA, Caterpillar—all those companies have gotten awards. Examiners have to go to the school every year, no matter how many times they have been in the program. The instructor used words that weren't even in the dictionary that I had in college, and I had to learn the Malcolm Baldrige criteria too. There was so much new information, I was struggling. I left Friday night after the last session and drove to Monteagle, then slept almost around the clock because it literally drained me.

Each company writes up its business procedures in keeping with the Malcolm Baldrige criteria. Then the four of us on a team take what the company has written at face value and write our opinions. At this step we have not yet made an on-site visit. It is all totally confidential, and we can't identify the company we are critiquing.

I was assigned to one team for a company that had applied for a Level Four, and the company was almost a rubber stamp of our

Century Construction Company. We sign that we don't have conflicts of interest with these companies that we evaluate. I called Marie and said, "I don't know this company, and I'm not involved in Century Construction Company any more in the hands-on everyday running of it. I gave Century Construction to Jim four years ago, and since I can't ask Jim about the company I'm assessing, I'm wondering if I have a conflict of interest. If so, put me somewhere else." She said, "No, I put you on that review because you were so involved with your company for so many years. You will know how to critique it."

At the on-site visit with the other examiners, the meeting had just gotten started with introductions, and I introduced myself as the volunteer executive director for Leadership Franklin and indicated that all of my working life had been in the construction and development business with my husband. One of the owners of the company looked at me and said, "Are you one of those Crosses from Franklin?" I smiled and said yes. Then another man who worked for the company asked, "Are you Amy and Jim's mother?" That's another good example of the family's reputation preceding me.

We are asked to tell how much time we spent on each project, although there is no compensation for this work. On one evaluation I turned in twenty-five or twenty-six hours; the other evaluation took about twenty-three hours. We cite the strengths and weaknesses on one page, and areas of improvement needed go at the bottom of the page. There are seven categories (e.g., human resources and leadership). We say we think we've found an area that needs to be clarified on the site visit. (Site visits are not mandatory for all levels.) For the site visit we ask them to clarify, verify, or review the areas cited. We are taught how to assess the company. We don't go in and say, "We think everything you're doing is wrong." They receive a list of our questions in advance of the visit so they know the areas we want to discuss.

If I had been younger and started this a long time ago, I would love to have been involved in it on a full-time basis. This endeavor has been a healthy challenge, but I'm sure it won't be my last one.

CHAPTER 9

No Time to Weep

> *If God sends us on stony paths,*
> *he provides strong shoes.*
> *—Corrie Ten Boom*

Prepare for widowhood from the first day you marry," I told a group of young women who had asked me to speak to them at our church. That being said, I'm not sure that any woman is ever ready for widowhood, no matter the circumstances. I certainly could not have predicted the long path to widowhood that God would have me walk.

The night that Billy had his cardiac arrest in the show ring, I gathered the family around me in the hospital in Murfreesboro, and I had a prayer to let Billy live. That was unusual for me, a woman, to pray aloud in our family; it wasn't something we did at home, but we probably should have. That realization hit me much later, though, not while we were there in the hospital with Billy's life hanging in the balance. We told God that we would accept Billy in any way; we weren't ready for him to die. That was what we got. But was it the best answer for him?

God is arranging things in our lives for our best interests. We wonder how taking a mate away at a young age can be for anyone's best interests. It's not wrong to ask God why or question him. We need to learn what lessons there are to learn from all experiences. And we are told in James 1:2–3: "Consider it pure joy, my brothers, whenever you face trials of many kinds, because you know that the testing of your faith develops perseverance." I remarked to the children that other people would look at us to see how we handled Billy's illness. That came true. Days down the road, we found out that was what happened. As a direct result, at least one man got his financial affairs in order, and another man got his spiritual life in order. We don't know what the repercussions will be of our actions and words and how they will affect other people.

Up to that point, I had flitted through life with no real problems—well, no earth-shaking problems. Bad things had happened to Billy's brothers and my sisters but not to us as a couple that we couldn't get through. Then so many things piled on me at one time that it's a wonder I survived mentally and physically. I probably wouldn't have if it hadn't been for relying on my faith in God that had developed over all the years of my life and thinking of my parents and grandparents and how they would have survived the situation. My early teachings certainly came to mind each day for those five years.

My world came to an end when Billy had his cardiac arrest. The children and I were in limbo in more ways than one. Forget about my marriage and my personal life. I didn't know which way to go with the businesses. The children had their businesses, too, but they were there to help me. A big problem was a recession in the middle of Billy's illness. We couldn't give property away, and that was where most of our money was invested.

I wondered when something devastating would happen to me and why God had overlooked me and my family. I was thankful that he had until then. When things did go wrong for so long, there was a time that I said, "I can't take any more problems, God. Please quit sending them." I'm amazed at how hard it was to go through all those years with Billy being ill and with the business being uncertain, but I look back now and realize that it could have been much worse. God never gives us more than we can take. I kept thinking about the refiner's fire and how the gold was refined as a result of being through it (Malachi 3:2–3). I wanted us to come out better and not worse from the experience.

God gave me five years to get used to the idea of losing Billy. He was in various hospitals for six months, with doctors doing all they could to get him well. Then he came home with LPNs and RNs around the clock for four and one-half years. He looked the epitome of a healthy man before that eventful night, despite his diabetes and underlying heart problems. He had been in the hospital only to be born and have periodic physical examinations. He was such a strong man, it took him a long time to die. That's the truth of it.

The insurance company let me act as an agent to hire and fire nurses and aides, and we saved money that way. Having the nurses with him at home gave me a chance to get my life in order, knowing that death was inevitable. I was thankful that God gave me that time; maybe God did because he knew I couldn't have stood a sudden death. It would have been easier on Billy, though.

We were so close—he was my husband, my lover, the father of my children, my business partner all in one. Losing all that in one fell swoop and seeing his mind, which was so great, go down to nothing were almost more than I could bear. For a while he responded to his name and said, "Huh." He responded when I told him that I sold the airplane. That was it. We don't know if he was having little strokes or if he gave up. He might have thought, *What's the use?* There is no way to know. Injuries like his are still a mystery for the most part to the medical profession.

You can usually recognize the fighters among people with serious illnesses. In the latter years of his illness I told Billy that he didn't have to fight for us; we wanted him to be happy and free of pain. That might have been a bad thing to do, but I didn't want him to think that he had to keep struggling when I knew he couldn't succeed.

One friend asked me, "Do you think you have more faith because of this illness?" I said, "Yes, I have more faith and I'm more humble." We as a family had very little patience, and we had to learn patience. We had to wait on the Lord. Everything has its season and its time, and we have to wait for our fit into that season and time. We're taught about praying and living a good life, but unless you are faced with something like that, you don't know what prayer means. It's so good to lift problems off your heart and feel God lifting you up by the arms. One lesson I learned is that prayer is important, and prayer brings peace.

It never dawned on me *not* to stick with Billy throughout his illness. In her desperation at seeing her son in such a condition, my mother-in-law even mentioned that she hoped I would stay with him.

Abandoning Billy never, never entered my mind. She said, with her father being a doctor, he had seen people abandon seriously ill folks. My attitude goes back to my heritage. I took him for better or worse, in sickness and in health, and I meant every word of those vows. He would have done the same and more for me.

Another friend asked me why we didn't put away more money for his sickness. We weren't without resources, and we had insurance, yet his illness seriously drained those resources. I said, "Whoever dreamed we'd have to put this much away for five years? Catastrophic illness today can wipe out a family's resources. It's impossible to put that much money away, especially if you're in business and trying to use your capital to work on." The nurses were necessities because I couldn't physically care for Billy, who was a large man. With my back like it was—three vertebrae deteriorated—it was a wonder I could do anything. The best I could do was to turn him in bed with a sheet.

At the time of Billy's illness, members of the medical community were taught to save lives. Today I think they are taught to consider the quality of life. He happened to be in the transition phase. I'm not talking about euthanasia with Dr. Kevorkian standing by. People who have been through these things look at them a little differently from people who haven't had a loved one in such circumstances. I can't condone Dr. Kevorkian's activities. I don't think it's morally right for people to kill themselves, but because of our experiences resulting from Billy's prolonged illness, I have a better understanding of how people can come to such a point of despair that they seek out Dr. Kevorkian. I don't care whether it's legal to pull a plug; I have to look at what God would want me to do. We had few options open to us; today if someone has a family member in similar straits, there are more options.

Within a day or two after Billy's attack, Aunt Grace, Daddy's oldest sister, called me and said that Billy had told her about a week earlier that if he had to live like my parents did with sitters around the clock and not be able to go and do, he hoped that I would not let him linger, that I would pick up a gun and shoot him. That made Billy's attitude clear about long-term illness.

The family had hope for a long time that Billy would snap out of it. Looking back, I feel the doctors knew more about his condition than they wanted to tell me at the beginning of his illness because they knew I was not ready to accept the medical evaluation. Again, I'm telling things like I saw them. They gave me a straw of hope to keep me going. I was confident that he was going to get well because he was so big and strong and a fighter by nature.

The night of his cardiac arrest I was in the center ring of the International Horse Show. My job was working with the awards, the ribbons, and the giving away of them. Billy was sitting in our box eating a funnel cake, and I had to point to my watch to indicate to him that he was in the next class. He was dressed in his riding habit but needed to get his horse warmed up from the trainer. Both children were there that night, and for that I will be forever grateful.

Billy was showing in the fifty years old and over class, and I thought he was winning the class. He was in the ring, and the judges asked the riders to reverse their horses. David Welsh was on the rail right where Billy reversed. Billy's last meaningful words were, "David, is my horse's tail brace straight?" Not thirty seconds later he fell off the horse. Everybody thought that the fall hurt him, but he was very relaxed at the time he hit the ground. I ran out to him immediately. Because the judges in the ring and the other riders who had dismounted would not let me near him, I just knew that he was dead. Two doctors, Sarah Womack and Roy Harmon, were there, and they gave him CPR. There was no ambulance with oxygen; there was only a rescue squad ambulance. (After our experience, the next year I paid to have an ambulance and paramedic at the show.)

They took him to the hospital in Murfreesboro. I called Joe Ross to send a helicopter from Vanderbilt, but the helicopter was at Jamestown. They couldn't move Billy anyway until they stabilized him and found out more about what had happened. He had on an almost new tailor-made riding suit, and the hospital staff cut it off him and handed me what amounted to rags. The sinking feeling I had while holding the remains of his suit is something I never want to feel again.

After Billy was stabilized, they took him to St. Thomas. Sister Juliana, who was head of the Ladies of Charity then, had bought some land from us when her group wanted to build a satellite emergency center in the Cool Springs area. Sister was there when we arrived at the hospital. Carter Williams, our internist, had just recovered from open heart surgery and had been back in practice only a few days. He was there, too, with Dr. Barton Campbell, Billy's cardiologist who had earlier found a blocked artery. They said that had to be where the clot went through.

In January of that year Billy had had an arteriogram, and the doctors found blockage in a position in the heart on which they wouldn't operate if there was just one blocked artery. To this day, doctors don't operate on people with blockages similar to Billy's.

The doctors felt so sorry because of what happened; they had done what was medically indicated, yet they knew the possibility was there for the blocked artery to cause problems. Dr. Campbell had told me when Billy had his arteriogram that diabetes treats the arteries like cholesterol. It builds up plaque that sloughs off and causes clots. The damage was to his brain, not his heart, because of the lack of oxygen. The condition is called anoxia.

Billy stayed at St. Thomas for six to eight weeks. The insurance companies and the doctors researched his problem and recommended Lakeshore Coma Stimulation Unit in Birmingham. Nashville didn't have a facility like it then. Billy was placed in a part of an old hospital, which was in such a horrible neighborhood that policemen had to walk me to my car each night. My pocketbook was stolen twice from his room. I was there with him every day, and at night we had a sitter because I didn't want him by himself since he was unable to talk. He was there almost two months.

Billy talked a bit when he first got there. Jim was standing near the door of Billy's room as he was being wheeled in, and he called out, "What's happening?" That gave us some hope. Then he said something in the night to the sitter about Jenny, but the sitter didn't know who he was talking about. He never spoke directly to us. He was rambling but he spoke clearly. After he left Birmingham, he never spoke again.

He had apparently cut out an ingrown toenail before his attack. He had so many other problems that no one noticed it until the toe became irritated, then the nurses put a heating pad on it. I kept my hand on the heating pad to make sure it wasn't too hot, but one night after I left, the nurse brought in bags of hot water that scalded him.

The toe eventually had to be taken off. Some doctors wanted to amputate more than the toe, but I was having none of that. A plastic surgeon was the solution back home at St. Thomas.

Dr. Louis Kirschner at Vanderbilt was Billy's neurologist. Joe Ross and his wife, Isabelle, are family friends. Isabelle, Joe's brother and sister, and I went to Lipscomb together. Joe had been at Duke University Hospital before becoming vice chancellor in the medical school at Vanderbilt. Joe knew all of the avenues that we were taking to find a place for Billy, and he and Carter Williams flew down on our plane to talk to the doctors in Birmingham about Billy. Those two doctors and the doctors in Birmingham decided that Billy could come home and go to Vanderbilt for therapy.

The administrators and doctors at Vanderbilt were discussing building a facility to care for patients like Billy. When Vanderbilt was working on a certificate of need to present to the state of Tennessee, Joe asked me to write a letter to Vanderbilt telling of my experiences. Joe said that the letter helped; after all, our family had firsthand knowledge of the need. In the meantime a nephew was in a bad wreck and had a head injury, and there was no place appropriate for his treatment in the area. The state did issue Vanderbilt a certificate of need, and the Stallworth Rehabilitation Center was built. I am very fond of Dr. Michael Lewis, who came here from Mt. Sinai Hospital in New York to head Stallworth Rehabilitation Center. He and his wife, Betsy, have been assets to Nashville.

The advisory board appointments included me. I think I could be a help to families going through such experiences as we had, and I am ready and willing to be called on if I am needed in that capacity. Our dentist, Tom Covington, had a tractor accident and was paralyzed from his waist down. He was at Stallworth, and I visited him twice to find out what kind of care he was receiving. He said it was every bit and more of the care we had been told that people were receiving.

Words are inadequate to tell how much Carter Williams helped the family during Billy's illness. Carter and his wife, Caroline, are personal friends. Carter fished with us in Florida, and their daughter, Rachel, started in kindergarten at Ensworth with Amy and went to school with her all the way through Harpeth Hall.

In all sorts of ways I had to become Billy's advocate, such as fighting an insurance company over a claim. Thank goodness, I have the fight in me, and I want things explained to me. Accepting that the company wouldn't pay the claim was not in the nature that God gave me. The company wanted to deny the claim completely. I persisted in digging through the policy because I knew why Billy had bought it, and I knew that he was covered.

Most people in my generation treat doctors like gods. I found out that they're human, just like I am. Billy had good doctors, and they eventually told me that they didn't think there was any hope for him. They were at a loss for someone in his condition—and in many ways doctors don't know much more today about brain injuries. For a while I denied their conclusions and didn't want to believe what they said. I *knew* he would get better, but he didn't. In time I had to accept the reality of his condition.

When Billy was ready to leave St. Thomas for the second time and come home, I was working on the claim for the health insurance policy. The policy was to pay for skilled nursing in the home. Billy knew that my sisters and I had to have sitters around the clock for our parents and what a hassle it was, and he had purchased disability insurance and other policies. He became uninsurable when those policies were exhausted, however. The state of Tennessee had what was called the T-Chip—Tennessee Comprehensive Health Insurance Plan—which was quite expensive. (T-Chip is now under TennCare, so it's different.) Premiums were paid six months before anyone was eligible to receive the insurance.

There was no manual for dealing with all the insurance companies and even the doctors and seeing that Billy had the best care we could obtain for someone in his condition. It's like when you marry or have a child. There is nothing that says one, two, three. Believe me, when you go through all that and then become a widow, there is still no one, two, three. Because I'm so tenacious, about like a bulldog, I go on until I find an answer and pursue all possible avenues. When there is no answer or no answer that I want, it's hard to swallow.

The nurses who cared for Billy became a part of our family. They will always have a special place in my heart. They loved him and became attached to their patient. They were Edith Talley (night nurse), Debbie Huff, Fenis Sparkman, and Barbara Reed. Barbara had been the nurse at home with Mama when she had open heart surgery, and later she stayed with Billy's mother after her surgery and became her companion for several years. Word of mouth was my source for these wonderful people. These nurses, all LPNs, stayed almost his entire illness.

Finding ways to keep him from getting bed sores and ways to take care of his hygiene needs required research that discovered specialized products for persons in long-term care. The nurses turned him and kept him clean and kept his skin creamed. He never suffered from the dreaded bed sores.

We put Billy in the wheelchair every day and took him outside on nice days or into rooms where activities were. He was always with us. We had the van wheelchair equipped so that we could take him on outings and even to Monteagle. At the beginning of his illness I think he knew he was there at Monteagle, and he was much calmer than usual. We took two shifts of nurses, David, our house man, and Jim to move him.

At Monteagle the men who had served with Billy on the board came by to visit him. It was traumatic for them to see him so unlike his former self, and some of them even cried. Physically he looked pretty good for a while. Near the end he probably didn't weigh 130 pounds, and he had weighed 230 at the time of his attack.

The nurses had instructions to talk as if he was going to get well. Every evening I told him what had happened during the day. I even told him the bad things, thinking it might jolt him, but it never did.

We had to put Billy in Vanderbilt in April after his attack in August. He was so agitated, the nurses could hardly stand it. He seemed to be trying to get something out but couldn't. He was so agitated that the technicians couldn't even do an MRI. The doctors put him in intensive care and didn't let me stay with him. He hollered the whole time and had to be medicated to be calmed down.

From the minute Billy fell off that horse, I was fighting for him—seeking out the best medical solutions, seeing that the insurance companies lived up to their policies, hiring good nurses, scheduling hours for the nurses, getting friends to come on the weekends to move him when our household employees were off. I was also fighting for our businesses.

Jim and Amy tried to shield me from a lot of what was going on in the businesses. I couldn't have done it without them. My job was to be with Billy, and they knew that was where I wanted to be. That was a full-time job without everything else that needed attention in the businesses. Our many longtime employees and staff members carried on well, but the recession complicated things.

The bank didn't make life any easier for us or for other people, for that matter. Billy was on the board and had been to a board meeting on Wednesday, the day of his attack, and he knew what the bank had done to some friends. He told me that we had plenty of equity, and he said to keep the bank informed of what we were doing. We laid everything on the line to the bank, but that wasn't sufficient to smooth out the problems.

What happened with that bank went deeper than having problems with a business arrangement. I put my first paycheck in that bank when I started working at the age of sixteen; I trusted it and its employees. I felt betrayed, almost as if my daddy had betrayed me. Billy and I had friends who had been employees, and they were let go at a time when we needed people who knew us to offer assistance. It happened to me at the lowest ebb of my life. That's when you find out who your true friends are. My trust in some people has been terribly shattered. Being able to trust people again requires conscious effort, and working on overcoming bitterness about these business dealings is an almost everyday task. Nevertheless I emerged intact, and other people might not have. Allowing bitterness to take me down to a point that I became physically sick—or worse—was not an option.

If Billy had not been sick, all of this probably would not have happened with the bank. Some people think that maybe because I was a woman, things turned out the way they did. I don't think it was because I was a woman; I don't think the people at the bank thought I would fight because I had to care for him and the businesses. They probably thought I had no energy left.

No one cared how much we were spending to look after Billy. One bank board member said that I ought to put him on Medicaid. That hurt. He would never have done that to a member of his family.

Business and Billy's illness were two separate issues, and I fully recognized the difference. Yet I would have appreciated a little sympathy and empathy. It was a severe blow to have a plan worked out with the bank that I accepted in good faith but then to have the rug pulled out from me.

People today can't seem to sit down and work out their differences; they turn to the courts and sue each other. That's wrong and, I believe, sinful. My lawyer said, though, that when somebody sues you, you have to respond. Everybody is greedy, and jealousy has a part too. When you get to a point of success, there are hundreds to knock you off your pedestal as well as thousands to applaud you.

You can't let it get you down. You have to pick up the pieces and go on. God knows who is right. That's what I told my children about fighting when they were in school. I told them that I don't like to see fights, especially when boys pick fights. I said, "I'd rather you be slapped because it takes a man to stand up." The poem "If" by Kipling is a favorite. When all around you is going awry, you can remain with your head up. That's what I tried to do when the hard times came. I tried to remain as steadfast in what I believed as I could.

God got all the glory for looking after me and the children, and he continues to get the glory. My faith had to be instilled over the years. A reserve of faith and strength doesn't start in a moment of trouble. Without that I know I wouldn't have gotten through it, and as a family, we became stronger, not weaker. Having a relationship with God was important, so that I was accepting when death was inevitable. In the early years of his illness I prayed hard for Billy to live, and then later I prayed hard for him to die. All the time I knew it had to be God's will.

As time went on, it was harder for friends and family to come to our house. Billy's mother couldn't bear to see him, and she didn't come to the funeral. She died not long after Billy's death. I've always been in sympathy with her because she lost two sons before she died, and not long after her death, a third son, Maurice, was killed. To lose a child would absolutely be my undoing. You expect to lose your mate in the sequence of time, but you don't expect to lose a child.

One faithful friend to come over and help us with moving Billy was Brent Sanders. When we were developing Oakwood and selling lots to builders, the builders listed their houses with my cousin Dan of Folk-Jordan Real Estate. Brent was working for Dan. Daddy, being retired, would go into the sales office of the subdivision and shoot the breeze with Brent and others. He thought a lot of Brent, and that's how the family's relationship with him began. Before that we had known Mamie, who became his wife.

Billy got Brent interested in horses, and they went trail riding together; now Brent and Amy do horse-related activities as time permits. Brent just loved Billy, and the illness devastated him. To this day our families remain friends—well, Brent and Mamie are more like extended family—and they are kindhearted people who can't do enough for others. Brent and Mamie have McArthur-Sanders Realtors, and they have helped Amy in her business. Mamie and I have had fun decorating all the houses they have lived in; she has a good eye and likes beautiful things. One time, before she and Brent married, she went to England with Billy, Amy, and me, and she became interested in the process of buying antiques. After both of our parents died, my sisters and I sold their house to Brent and Mamie.

Church attendance has remained at the center of our family life. We go to Fourth Avenue Church of Christ, which is an old church with about eight hundred members. When Madeline and Will become Christians, they will be at least the sixth generation of members of the Church of Christ (and there could be more generations). Billy's will left money to the church. Part of the money we used to refurbish the chapel—paint, carpet, and plantation shutters. We bought some computers for the office. A book being published of the history of the church wasn't fully underwritten, so we helped with that. Some money is left over to be put into another project.

It was a very sweet and caring church while Billy was sick. I think it was hard for members there to accept his death also. One elder told us that they didn't know what to do for us. I kept saying, "I have so much family, my cousins and sisters. They are a help to me. You elders help someone else who has no family and needs you more."

A new preacher, Eddie Miller, had come to our church. After about a month of his being in that position, I called and asked him to visit us at the house. I said to him, "Eddie, you may have to preach a funeral for a man you've never known, but I want you to get to know us. I have turned Billy over to God many times. I told God, 'I can't get him well. I've done all I can do. You, God, just point me in the right direction and I will work my head off. But I don't know where to go or what to do.'" And God does point you. I had to totally give Billy up to God, but I took him back several times, thinking I could do better than God was doing. Peace comes when you know that God is in control.

The last days that Billy lived were very hard on the family because we could tell that the end was imminent. The doctors assured me that he was in no pain. We know nothing about the brain when we get right down to it. I'm hoping that there will be breakthroughs in brain research so that we can know more of what people in similar circumstances do know. Many questions weren't answered for me. Born July 24, 1932, Billy died August 9, 1993, one day short of five years from the day of his cardiac arrest.

Visitation was here at the house because that is an old custom. The family had done that with my grandfather, and I remember that vividly even though I was a child. Billy's father had home visitation with Billy's grandfather. It's a loving thing to do. Funeral homes are cold and impersonal to me, so I thought I would bring him home. We had space for the people and parking for the cars. There were so many people that they filled two register books at the house and another one at the church, well over one thousand people.

The obituary in the *Tennesean* called Billy a "businessman, land developer and Tennessee Walking Horse enthusiast." It continued,

> Gov. Ned McWherter described him as a "leader in the Tennessee Walking Horse industry and in the development of a better business climate in our state" whose "many contributions such as his leadership in establishing the Middle Tennessee Livestock Arena, will be greatly missed." . . .

> Much of the growth seen in Williamson County today is the result of his work. Among the major projects he championed were Ellington Park, Oakwood Estates, Buckingham Park, Maplewood, Laurelwood, Century Industrial Park, Harpeth Industrial Park, The

Maples, Royal Oaks Business Park, Royal Oaks Plaza, Stonebrook, CrossRoads/South Business Park, Windsor Park and the CrossRoads Executive Center.

"Headline News, Local Edition," on August 9, 1993, reported Billy's death. The news reader called him a prominent Williamson County businessman, who was considered a "modern pioneer" by businesspeople. The Cross Group was credited with several major projects. He made a "community commitment" and was considered an "ambassador for the county." Mayor Jerry Sharber said, "J. W. Cross will always be remembered in Franklin. . . . His ability to create a vision and transform that vision remains unsurpassed. His visions of the past are the realities of today. And many of our citizens are the beneficiaries of his dreams." His vision in the Moores Lane area with the sewer treatment plant—along with the help of two others—got Cool Springs going. County Executive Robert Ring was quoted as saying that Billy had "a vision rarely seen of what Williamson County could be." J. W. Cross saw to it that the county had a certain "quality of life." The services were held at the Fourth Avenue Church of Christ at 10:00 A.M. on August 11.

Billy had been a member of the Tennessee Historical Society, Tennessee Botanical Gardens and Fine Arts, Tennessee Polled Hereford Association, Nashville City Club, the Walking Horse Owners' Association, Nashville Chamber of Commerce, Williamson County Chamber of Commerce, Monteagle Sunday School Board, and the board of Brentwood Academy.

Shortly after Billy's death, the *Tennessean* ran the article "End of a Williamson County Era" (August 15, 1993), which focused on Billy, John Sloan Sr., and Reese Smith Jr. and called them the "Three Horsemen" of Williamson County. Billy's relationship with horses has been detailed in this book; John, who had died in 1988, was a founder of the Iroquois Steeplechase; and Reese, like Billy, was stricken while riding a horse during the 1991 International Show at MTSU, but died just days later. Each man contributed to developing the county; again, Billy's many contributions have already been explained; John "wrote the legislation that led to the creation of the city of Brentwood"; and Reese was a builder and developer. Perhaps the best tribute came in these comments: "The three had differing styles and differing ideas, but they helped make Williamson County what it is today: the place where many people want to live."

Woodlawn Cemetery went bankrupt during the Depression, and Uncle Bryan had bought some plots at the bankruptcy sale. When Uncle Bryan moved to San Antonio in the mid-1940s, Daddy bought the plots from him. Linda's little boy was buried there; then Mama and Daddy. Billy and I had never bought any plots. Billy seriously wanted to be buried on Tuck-A-Way Farm, but I couldn't bring myself to do it. I didn't know then what my plans would be; I might have wanted to sell the farm and move elsewhere. Family cemeteries are a lot of trouble for the people who end up on the land with them. His mother and daddy are buried in Clarksville, but I didn't want to take him back there either.

The children and I decided on Woodlawn. They wouldn't go with me to pick out the plots. Doing that task alone was hard, but I understood their feelings. My cousin Ann Whitley had buried her husband, Dave, just before Billy died. They had been living in several states before moving back to Middle Tennessee to retire. She picked out a beautiful plot in the Garden of the Cross. I didn't know the name of that garden until after I had bought our plots. Clive, my brother-in-law, at the burial of Dave had remarked that the area of the cemetery overlooked Nashville's skyline, and he liked that. He said to his wife, "Mary, you buy our plots here." (She hasn't done it yet.) I bought three plots—one for Billy, one for me, and one for Amy. At the same time I bought the marker and put my name on it. I told the children that if I do marry again, I still want to be buried as a Cross. All they have to fill in is the death year.

Grandma Jordan would take the man who worked for her and me and go to the cemetery and clean up Granddaddy's grave and place flowers on it. Now in the Smyrna Cemetery, there is perpetual care. I don't like to go to graves or put out those tacky plastic flowers. I have driven by Billy's grave several times because I was lonesome, I guess. But Billy is in a better place. As I explained to Madeline and Will: when you go to live with God, you don't come back.

At Billy's death most of the donations went to the scholarship in his name at MTSU for equine science. It is for a boy or girl in financial need who is to major in equine science, not necessarily related to Walking Horses. Some people gave to charities of their choice and to Brentwood Academy. The three designated charities were Brentwood Academy, MTSU, and World Christian Broadcasting. A memorial horse show at Ellington Agricultural Center—held soon after Billy died to raise money for the scholarship—raised $12,500. The committee of men who put on the show brought in all of the studs in the area, something that hadn't been done in a long time; parts of the barns were decorated and set aside for the studs with all their pedigrees. During a break in the classes, there was a parade of studs. We did it up right. The men wanted it to be an above-average show, and it was with white columns at the entrance displaying huge bouquets of red roses. The proceeds of this book are to be added to the MTSU scholarship so that more young people can benefit from it. The fund had enough in it so that in the last semester of 1998 a student was provided with room, board, and tuition.

Daddy died the morning of the rehearsal for Jim's wedding. We knew he was quite ill and close to dying, although his mind was active to the end. Both he and Mama had been ill for about three years. During that time we had sitters with them at their house, and I did the hiring and firing of them. We had two in the daytime and one at night. That prepared me for what I faced with Billy. My sisters and I had already gone to the funeral home and made arrangements for their funerals some time before. Mary and Linda helped with our parents throughout those years of illness too. Seven months almost to the day after Daddy's death, Mama died. After Daddy's death she became very depressed. I knew when one parent died, the other would soon follow because they were so close. We hadn't yet settled Daddy's estate when she died, and we were still in the process of dividing up the furniture and selling their house at the time of Billy's cardiac arrest, almost four months from the day Mama died. In eleven months I lost in effect three close family members.

I never had time to grieve for my parents, and I really didn't have time to grieve for Billy during those five years. His death was a relief. People shouldn't feel guilty for feeling that about loved ones. You know that they don't want to live the life they have.

A married woman needs to be involved in her husband's business, whatever that is. If her husband works for somebody, she needs to know all the benefits, the plans in the company. He needs to know the same about her and her business. Some women are overwhelmed by all the decisions they have to make after a spouse dies, especially the financial decisions. If a woman does this all along in a marriage, it's not dumped on her all at once. All the years I had worked with Billy at least prepared me to handle some of the financial decisions.

Tuck-A-Way Farm has been placed in a trust, and the children have received gifts of land on which they built their houses. Those decisions took time to reach. When I had a mate, I could discuss such issues. Making weighty decisions when your mate is gone is difficult. Having the children nearby is a comfort, and there is plenty of room in this house if I someday need someone to care for me because I am ill. I did research and bought the best extended care insurance that would pay for someone to come in and care for me—another lesson learned from Billy's illness.

After Billy's death I made up my mind that I wasn't going to crawl in a shell. Nevertheless it's hard to make another life as a single woman. For many functions, going alone is not for me, and it's agony for me to ask a man to go anywhere with me. I miss terribly having someone to accompany me; we used to do so many things together and have such fun. During Billy's illness, my involvement in civic functions ended, but immediately they picked back up after his death.

Trying to find your place in society alone takes a while. People assume you can do things as you were doing before, but you really can't. It is a change, and you're the odd man. Our friends—the Crowells, the Flaughers, and others—that Billy and I used to do things with have been wonderful to me and have made me feel not so much like an odd man.

Two widows and I do things together, and that has helped to fill the void for all three of us. I call us the "three merry widows." They are Mary Jo Loden and Deane Pigg, who are old friends but we rarely did things together when our mates were living. Mary Jo went to Lipscomb. Deane and I had known each other in Donelson after we both first married and were in a Sunday school class together. Both of them go to the Church of Christ too. Deane came in my shop one Memorial Day and hired Preservation Interiors to do the interiors of several rooms for her, so I got to know her and her husband, Joe, better. Joe died suddenly. Mary Jo's husband, who also had died suddenly, had been dead several years when Billy died.

Following Billy's death, Mary Jo and Deane called and asked me to join them for supper. Since then they've been to Monteagle with me; we go out every few weeks to eat; we take special trips or go to special events together. Deane and I went to Paris, and Mary Jo and I went on a cruise through the Panama Canal to South America and Central America. One year we all went to England and stayed a month in a cottage in the Cotswolds. We're very compatible and like the same things for the most part. We just like to *go!*

Widowhood—I don't like the word or the condition. I'd love to have had more years together with Billy. At least we took the advice of Aunt Evelyn, who told us not to put off anything; her husband, Uncle Herbert, had died young, so she knew what she was talking about. I would take nothing for all our experiences together.

Getting used to living alone has been an adjustment. While I was working after graduation, I briefly lived in an apartment in Clarksville, but a family lived downstairs. Other than that I've always lived with family—my parents or my husband. Various activities fill the day and people are around the house, but at night I miss having someone to go out with or talk to about all the daily events or eat supper with. Enjoying yourself enables you to be content alone. That's a blessing because too many widows sit and bemoan their situation and wait to be entertained.

A neighbor at Monteagle, Abbie Lou Reynolds from Tampa, Florida, lived to be more than one hundred years old and was a widow for many of those years. She loved to tease back and forth with Billy, and she often made him cookies. She told me that if I was ever a widow, I should set a real table with a place mat and silver and china as though I was setting the table for the family and sit down and eat my meal. She said, "Don't ever stand over the kitchen sink and eat." I followed that good piece of advice, and I cook regular, healthful meals for myself.

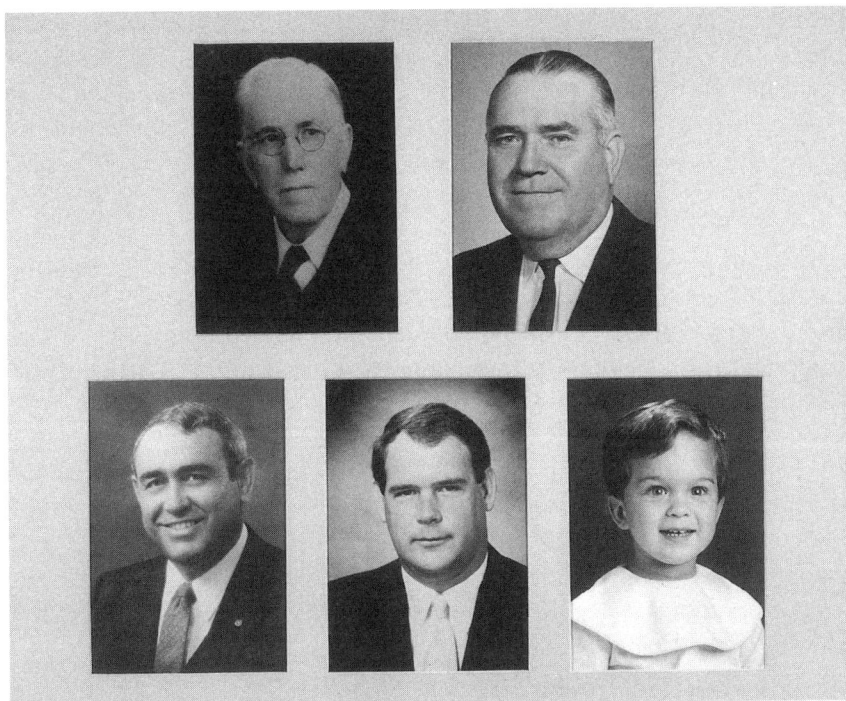

Five generations of Crosses: top left, James William Cross, top right, James William Cross Junior; Bottom left, James William Cross III, bottom center, James William Cross IV, bottom right, James William Cross V.

Many major events seem to happen in August in my life. I had back surgery in August 1995 because the last three vertebrae were deteriorated. The doctors put in two five-inch steel rods with clamps and about a pound of steel to reinforce the spine, and they took bone from my left pelvic bone to place between the vertebrae. For four months I convalesced and wore a brace; I was in and out of bed and also walking around. Sitting was not good for me.

During my recovery, I started thinking about the strength of character of my ancestors that was passed down to all of us. That's also when I knew I had to write this book and let my grandchildren know about their family. I've had many problems—and I know other people have had many worse ones—but I still believe that God doesn't put more on us than we can take. By that I think he has given us over the years opportunities to overcome some of the difficulties, but we don't think they're difficulties at the time.

When Billy was sick, the young people at church wanted to have a devotional at our house and wanted me to say some things about his illness. I brought Billy into the room in his wheelchair and told them: "You boys and girls may not have had a tragedy in your lives yet, but you will. You may have friends who will be killed in accidents. You may not lose your parents for a while. When life presents these difficult situations to you, you can't gather up all the courage. This comes from way, way back of getting yourself prepared for anything in life. I hope you don't have it in one lump sum like I did. But still I think the preparation from my parents and grandparents brought me to this situation with my ability to get through it."

For the first time since Billy's illness, I had time to think about where I was headed. I was a widow. That was something new. I didn't know where God was leading me. Sometimes you have to stop and wait and listen to God because he is trying to tell you something. I am the greatest one to break that rule because I go right ahead full force without stopping and listening.

My Monteagle home became a retreat for me to stop and listen and learn.

CHAPTER 10

Monteagle and
My Healing Process

> *There is no beautifier of complexion,*
> *or form, or behavior, like the wish to scatter*
> *joy and not pain around us.*
> *—Ralph Waldo Emerson*

fter Billy's death, I went to Monteagle to think. Before that I
had not taken time to evaluate my life or my self. I was content
with the direction of my life; I had no real problems; maybe I
was too busy doing to think about being. In my younger years my
parents had more or less set a path for me, and after our marriage,
Billy and I forged our path together and later with our children. The
careful plans we had laid screeched to a halt with his illness.

Now I spend more time doing things I want to do and choose to
do instead of things I have to do on a daily basis. My children live
away from this house and have their own lives. My husband is gone.
There are no other schedules to work around. In essence everything
I do is on my time schedule. My community activities are still satis-
fying, and I know I'm making a contribution to others through them.

As executive director of Leadership Franklin, I enforce attendance at classes for participants. Two class members have even
planned operations around Leadership classes in order to attend. I
told Jim that I would have to miss one month because of a trip, but I
felt guilty after my "you have to be there" stance. He said, "Mama,
it's not like you're getting paid." That is how seriously I take all
projects; I treat them as if they're jobs, and I've made a commitment
to them. I don't feel that I can ask others to do anything I'm not
willing to do.

A Delightful Life

The plan for my future didn't come to me like a bolt. I did a lot of reading and thinking. There was no heavenly vision. That quiet time—waiting and listening—sent me in my new direction. There is nothing like a steady rain to walk in, and even as a child, I found that soothing. Reflecting on my life showed me what had led me up to that point. God was leading me, but I didn't realize it.

During Billy's prolonged illness, thinking ahead was out of the question, and we couldn't make any plans. The family lived moment by moment, and that strain eventually became evident on all of us. The only trip I took while he was ill was to Russia; it was mostly business and some pleasure, and I stayed in constant touch back home. If he had died while I was away, I knew there was nothing I could have done here except make it easier on the children. I never left him for a pure pleasure excursion.

Monteagle has always been a special place to me. Time seems to stand still, and I can really relax there. I love to go in the fall and winter if weather allows me to get up the mountain. My first visit to Monteagle occurred in 1945. The opportunity came because of my uncle Ernest's generosity to a widow from Memphis named Jean Watson. She wanted to buy a house in Monteagle and turn it into a boardinghouse to make money to send her two children to college.

No one can put a loan on a house in Monteagle because it is leased land, owned by the Monteagle Sunday School Assembly. A lease runs for ninety-nine years, but an individual owns the building on the land. Mrs. Watson had gone to Murfreesboro looking for financing, maybe not knowing that was the way the Assembly had set up the legal arrangements, and she went to Uncle Ernest's bank (Murfreesboro Federal Savings and Loan, now Calvary Bank).

Uncle Ernest, being the kind heart that he was with his tendency for giving and sharing, felt sorry for her and personally loaned her the money to buy a house. Then he got to thinking, *What if Mrs. Watson doesn't have anybody to come and stay with her? Here she is with a big burden.* He told Aunt Amy to take one niece from his side and one from her side. Esther Woller, who was the friend of Aunt Amy's niece, went along too. Her mother, Frieda, was a friend of Aunt Amy. The nieces were Andrea Rogers (Aunt Amy's sister Sue's daughter) and me.

240

We left Murfreesboro on the train. There was no air-conditioning, of course, and it was coal driven. We had the windows up and the smoke blew in. We were almost black by the time we got to Cowan. My white eyelet pique dress was not the best choice I could have made for that trip. At Cowan an old train called the Mountain Goat went up the mountain and took the ice cream and the newspaper once a day. We elected to take Janey's Taxi up the mountain. That was the first time I had seen a woman taxi driver, and she went up that mountain like a bat shot out of hell and delivered us safely to the boardinghouse. We stayed a week. I enjoyed it so much that I could hardly wait to go back.

While she was in college, Amy did some research on Monteagle, and she offers this explanation about its origin (in 1882) and its purpose:

> Monteagle Sunday School Assembly [MSSA] was started by the Sunday School Society as a place for individuals to come for religious, cultural, and music education in a natural environment. It was a program for enhancement of their intellect and spirits. The Chautauqua movement was a reaction to the "springs" type places, which were considered very decadent and frivolous. The same purpose exists today. MSSA was different from other Chautauquas in that it was created as a church and had more religious organizations' interest and support. Cottages and boardinghouses and churches were built by missionary societies for teachers to come and study.

A brochure from 1945 described it this way: "The Monteagle Assembly is a Non-PROFIT ORGANIZATION governed by a Board of Trustees elected by its Members. It exists for the mutual benefit of the several thousand annual patrons and all the money taken into the treasury is expended for advantages with which Monteagle is not naturally endowed." It even had a resident doctor and dentist.

Monteagle is one of the few remaining places to preserve the tradition of Chautauqua. There were numerous activities: chamber music and classical recitals; individual coaching for school and college work; lectures daily on political, artistic, dramatic, historical, religious, and musical subjects; tennis; swimming; croquet; hiking; fishing; dancing in the gym twice a week; a golf course but not on the grounds; and movies (called "sound pictures") five nights a week. When we were there, we heard cellist Oscar Eiler, pianist Lawrence Goodman, and violinist Kenneth Rose. Twilight prayers, Sunday school, Bible lectures, and Sunday services were the religious offerings. We participated in every cultural event and all the twilight prayers. The water in the pool is spring fed, and it was one of the first swimming pools in the South. At first women bathed at one hour; men the next. No mixed bathing was allowed.

The cottages rented in 1945 for $100 to $400 a season; hotels and boardinghouses were also available. (A season is two months. In 1997 some cottages rented in the thousands of dollars *per week*.)

Aunt Amy wrote to her friend Frieda, Tuesday, July 17, 1945, "The children like the place so well they say they want to stay longer than a week but a week is a pretty good visit and we plan to leave Cowan at 2:40 [by train] Sunday afternoon and get home about 5:00."

Esther wrote several letters home to her parents and her brother, Norman. Here is one she wrote July 16:

> Went shopping this morning have only $6.00 left, owe Amy 11¢. Today at the bridge we saw a rattle snake. It was way at the bottom of about 20 yards down. We meet soom [*sic*] nice people, Mr. and Mrs. Peck. They came from Louisiana, they have a 10 year old dog Brownie. This morning we played with the Pecks shuffle board. We kept the score. Caroline & Mrs. Peck beat. I mailed your card the first thing this morning. Having to buy 3¢ stamp from Amy for your letter makes 14¢ I owe Amy. I am writing in my rest period (2 to 4). Going to play croquet after our rest period. Going to a concert tonight. It is 15 till 2 so I must quit and get to bed. (Ran out of ink just then.) Got to bed past 10. Goodbye don't forget to write to me.

Later in the week, she wrote about picking berries and buying paper dolls.

Some mornings families from the valley brought fresh fruits and vegetables, and Mrs. Watson bought produce from them for her boardinghouse. When Mrs. Watson rang the bell for a meal, you had to be in your seat or you didn't get fed. It was sort of like being in the army. The meals were good, though. If you received mail, she put it at your place at the table. I think the mail ran only once a day.

Billy and I implemented a piano concert at Monteagle dedicated in honor and memory of Aunt Amy, and she was there for the first one. She was a great pianist and vocalist who taught piano and voice, and she sang at women's clubs, weddings, funerals, and so forth.

At one of the concerts, Billy introduced the artist, and he said, "I do believe it was part of our marriage contract that I promised to have a house in Monteagle." The second year we were home from Germany we were already going to Monteagle for the Fourth of July picnic. We knew few people; we'd just go and have our picnic and stay at the Sewanee Inn. Mrs. Watson had sold her boardinghouse by then.

Quite a few people now stay in the Assembly year round. Our house is a year-round house. We put heat in it, which made it salable if necessary. We were always thinking of the future.

At the one hundredth anniversary of Monteagle, Caroline and Billy costumed for the event, standing in front of the gazebo on the mall.

When we first had the house, few people had phones. Most went to the Assembly office to call or receive messages. We knew that would be a burden with Billy being in business, so we put in a phone.

Much laundry, both clean and dirty, was carried up and down that mountain. We had no washing machine in the early years. We even took our food because there were no stores to speak of, and we'd have to drive to Cowan or Winchester to buy groceries. That is much different now.

Our house sits on two lots—18 and 19. The property committee later made it into one lot, which is lot 19. The house backs up to an open space, a park. I like that because the houses in the Cabbage Patch are crowded together, and living crowded up with others is not for me. We bought the lease from Mrs. Hyer, Frances Reynolds's mother, for five hundred dollars, and that was the going rate. We had to renew our ninety-nine-year lease before Billy died. We pay assessments and water and sewer fees to the Assembly, and we pay Grundy County property tax.

I remember the two houses that were on our lots originally. One faced Margaret McAlister's house, and the other faced the Bide-A-Wee, now called the Bridgeway House—the Reynolds from Tampa own it. The original two houses, which were up on pillars, burned during the war. The soldiers from Camp Forest in Tullahoma rented them. Monteagle Sunday School Assembly had its own fire department with hydrants years ago.

Irwin Crais used to be our across-the-street neighbor. He has since given that house to his children and bought a larger one for himself. He lives in Birmingham, and when Billy was in the hospital there, he came to see us at the hospital. That was very kind of him because I know it was very hard to see Billy in that condition. He and Billy had been on the Monteagle Sunday School Assembly board together.

We built the house in 1965 when Jim was one and a half. We started with three small bedrooms and one bath. There are a living room and a dining room in an el; the kitchen isn't big enough to cuss a cat, but many big meals cooked from scratch for many people have come out of that little kitchen. We had a screened porch on the back and later glassed it in. Seventeen people stayed once when we had only one bathroom. Needless to say, the bathroom time had to be scheduled, and each person was instructed to scrub the tub with cleanser after finishing. In 1977 we added three bedrooms and two baths. A bunk room, another bedroom, another living room, and a utility room were completed in the basement.

The basement is above ground in the back; therefore, it has daylight. A room and a bath there were initially for Geneva, our cook. Before she worked for us, she went to Monteagle with a family from Pulaski. She enjoyed going there and seeing old friends who worked for other families. They had "colored" Sunday school listed in the program because the blacks couldn't come to church with us even in the early 1960s. The "colored" service was held in the afternoon at the same chapel with the same preacher for the white service.

Fewer black people come to Monteagle now because there are virtually no black maids. There are some black nannies, however.

Jenny and soon-to-be-age-one Madeline at Madeline's first Fourth of July picnic at Monteagle.

Furnishings that went up to the Monteagle house in the beginning were early attic and leftovers from family. For instance, Aunt Minnie gave me twin beds with iron springs. The house was built with leftovers from construction jobs—items from a house being torn down, its windows, lumber. We didn't want to borrow money to pay for the house.

Billy was president of the board of MSSA for four years. He helped obtain a grant from the federal government for the city of Monteagle to have a better sewer and water system, and we tapped onto that. He was proud of that accomplishment. The president acts almost like a mayor and the board like a council, so it's like running a small town. The board is made up of members based on denominations, which depend on the denominations of home owners—Episcopalian or Baptist or Methodist or Church of Christ. They meet every two weeks during the season, which is the second week of June to the second week of August.

Our weekends when Billy was president weren't as restful as they had been, and I chose to be on two committees. One year a Mrs. Patterson who owned a Washington, D.C., newspaper wanted some money from her endowed fund to go toward making a better life for mountain children of Monteagle. Her editor was Frank Waldrup, and Frank and his wife, Eleanor, had a house at Monteagle.

Billy came home from a board meeting and told me that they were setting up an education fund with the Patterson monies. I really wanted to be on that committee, and I was made chairman. Meeting with the counselor at the Grundy County High School, I told her what the scholarship fund was all about. The school personnel needed to choose the scholarship recipients because they would know the children better than those of us on the committee. The goal was to give money to the seniors in high school so that they could go to college. My hope was that the young people would come back to Grundy County after they graduated and make life better for the mountain community. Unfortunately as yet, not many of them can come back because there are so few jobs; being a teacher or a doctor is about it. There is not much industry or business.

The scholarship recipients received five hundred dollars each, which in 1975 at a state school would go a long way to pay tuition for a year. Most of them went on for a degree, either two or four years.

246

There were four or five recipients each year, and it gave me much satisfaction to go to awards day and present the scholarships. I served as chairman on the committee until Billy got sick. For four years I also served on the Endowment Committee.

We all feel safe and protected during the season. Personnel are on duty at the front gate, and a fence surrounds the property. Members have codes to unlock the gate when the season is over. Madeline and Will love it because they can run free and ride their bicycles. I placed a limit on how far they can go from the house. I hope someday we can leave the cars outside the Assembly so that children can ride or walk without the fear of cars.

We still celebrate the Fourth of July at Monteagle with family and friends. Billy and I did a lot of things with Mary Ann and Jim Crowell and Pete and Paula Flaugher. We would go to UT ball games, especially the UT and Kentucky game since Pete went to Kentucky. We took trips together, and they came to Monteagle early on. Jim had a big recreational vehicle that we could eat and sleep in. It must have been the biggest gas guzzler in the world. Billy later on bought a van, and we went to the games in it.

When Jim was six or seven, we went three weeks to Europe. We were supposed to come home the day before the Fourth of July, and I had arranged with Mama and Mary Ann and Paula to get the food ready because I knew I wouldn't have time. It looked like we wouldn't be on time getting into New York because of late flights from Europe. Amy and Jim were so upset that they were going to miss the Fourth, they cried each time they thought of it. I called home from New York and told Mama we were going to be delayed. We did make it in time for the flag raising and the prayer. The only two Fourths we missed were while Billy was sick. We took him for two years along with the nurses, but we didn't take him to the picnic.

The three Batey sisters who live in the Nashville area—Ann, Sue, and Margaret—and my two sisters and I would go to Monteagle to get away for a while, usually before the season opened. We would talk about our parents and our grandparents and the legacies they left us. Next we asked the fourth Batey sister—Evelyn from Lake Charles, Louisiana. Then we decided that we wanted all the girl cousins to get together, including the in-laws. All of us used to get together at Christmas at Tuck-A-Way, but since Billy's illness and death, we

First cousins' reunion, 1995 at Monteagle. First row: left to right, Bonnie Tucker Batey, Sue Batey Baker, Linda Jones Biggs, Judy Jordan (wife of A. W.), Sarah Jordan Womack, Sue Jordan Rodarte, and Margaret Jackson Jordan. Second row: left to right, Frances Jordan Hearn, Mary Jones Anderson, Betty Jordan Lunn, Dorothy Jordan Balfour, Margaret Batey, Evelyn Batey Sigmund, Caroline, and Ann Batey Whitley. (Absent: Claire Huddleston Summers.)

discontinued that practice. We all missed that, so I sent a letter inviting the girl cousins and cousins-in-law to Monteagle. In 1997 the boy cousins wanted to come, too, so the three living in Middle Tennessee came up to spend the day and have lunch. We stay from Tuesday through Friday morning.

Here is an idea of what happened, from the 1995 reunion. The fifteen cousins in attendance were Linda Biggs, Mary Anderson, Bonnie Batey (wife of Tom), Judy Jordan (wife of A. W.), Margaret Jordan (wife of Dan), Betty Lunn, Margaret Batey, Ann Whitley, and Sue Baker (all of Nashville); Evelyn Sigmund (Louisiana); Dorothy Balfour (California); Sarah Womack (Woodbury, Tennessee); Frances Hearn and Sue Rodarte (Texas); and me. Sarah shot a video, and each of us received a copy in a presentation case. Sue Ann wrote this poem about our get-together:

Caroline Cross

Girl Cousin Family Reunion

We have an incredible family bond
Our memories are so very fond
We have gathered at Caroline's place
So we look upon the others face

Now Maggie had six and Roy had five
And all of them are still alive
Bryan had four, but one did die
We miss her so and I still cry

Now Ruth had three and Minnie had two
And Herbert, he only had one
And Ernest, he had none
Then there was Charlie, most of us never knew

The family was strong, the love was great
As Grandma and Granddaddy raised their eight
Each child they did educate
And their lives they did elevate

All of our parents have now gone
But we continue to sing their song
We know the tie that binds
We know our love endures the times

We share our tales and the fun we had
We seem to remember the good and not the bad
There have been times that were hard for us all
But those Jordan genes held us tall

When we needed to be lifted high
There was always family near by
So many times we can't deny
Our feelings say we need to cry

And now with each passing season
We come to know the very reason
Christ has been the center of our family
He has blessed those with him in eternity

As we leave and bid adieu
Show us how we can renew
Show us Lord, how to keep the bond

As we leave and travel beyond
Show us how to teach our children and their children too
The wonderful stories we once knew
How to keep the laughter and the love
And our connection with our Father above

Major activities were eating, talking and reminiscing, napping in the hammock out back, playing bridge, having Bible study on the front porch, playing basketball, and eating some more. Someone was in charge of food and called ahead of time to tell everybody who was responsible for which meal. They had some idea of what people were going to cook so that we didn't have the same thing at each meal. They brought so much food that even with two refrigerators we needed coolers to hold it all. We Jordans love good food and are all good cooks.

All of us expressed concern about how to pass on the family interaction to our children. There is a closeness among us that I'm not sure that our children do—or maybe can—understand. Each of us has been important in the others' lives in many special ways over the years.

Another common element that we discussed was the love of God taught and shown by our grandparents and each set of parents. Tradition and religion hold us together. We're not all in the same denomination, but we share a strong religious foundation.

One fun conversation centered on whether or not to iron sheets. We'd ask each one as she appeared for breakfast, "Do you fold or wad?" The usual initial reaction was a blank stare because we had to explain what we were talking about. Most didn't iron, but I was an exception. Ironed sheets look so much better in the linen closet and feel so good to sleep on.

Margaret Batey was the oldest, and we called her the matriarch. She remembered Christmas at our grandparents' house "as if going to heaven." The children could have all the delicious apples and oranges that they wanted because Grandaddy provided bushels of them.

Betty Lunn called the cousin reunion "a most unusual gathering" to get all of us together. She emphasized the values of the good Jordan stock.

Dot (Betty's older sister) and others mentioned that in hard times, without family they didn't know how they would have gotten through them. Dot also noted that Aunt Dixie's "style and flair" were passed on to her children. When Aunt Amy died, Dot inherited her

Our parents' fiftieth wedding anniversary, held at Tuck-A-Way Farm. Left to right, Caroline, Mary, Linda, Mama, and Daddy.

251

elegant hostess tea gown that was purchased at the French Shoppe in Murfreesboro.

Evelyn Batey Sigmund said that her husband fought in the war "with a microphone." He was in the control tower of an airport. She recalled baby-sitting me and Ettie Lu. Evelyn talked about our industrious Granddaddy Jordan and said that she wouldn't have missed the reunion at Monteagle if she'd had to walk.

Linda remembered Grandma living with us on Sterling Road and protecting Linda; Grandma didn't like for our parents to discipline Linda. She loved the Christmas Eve get-togethers and "didn't realize that other families didn't do that." When we all married, we learned that other families weren't as close as ours.

Bonnie Tucker Batey is married to Tom, and they lived in Saudi Arabia and Australia when he worked for Columbia/HCA as the

All the grandchildren at the anniversary. Front row (on the floor): Winn Biggs, Susan Anderson Burns, Sam Anderson, and Dan Anderson. Second row: David Anderson, Amy and Jim, Leigh Biggs Reames, and Tommy Anderson.

company's in-house architect. Her mother-in-law, Aunt Maggie, made her feel a part of the family from the beginning, she said. That made her an outlaw. In our family, as Margaret Jordan observed, outlaws are wanted.

Sue Batey Baker at one time lived in Washington, D.C., while her husband, Lamar, was a congressman from Chattanooga. Then she and Lamar moved to Atlanta, where Lamar was the southeastern representative for the Department of Transportation under Reagan. She said, "Our grandparents were better than Santa Claus. They took us to Nashville, the first movie, circus, other special events. Grandma always fixed special food when we visited her."

Frances Owen Jordan Hearn had memories of living next door to our grandparents. She went over there for "comfort and security." Grandma was churning, cooking, and crocheting, always busy.

Frances Owen's older sister was Ettie Lu. She died tragically when she was in her forties. She was living outside San Antonio then. She had two children, Karen and Crissinda. Crissinda lives in Texas. Karen, now age forty-four, accompanied me to London on an antique buying trip recently, and she lives in Lake Charles, Louisiana, where she met up with Evelyn, her mother's first cousin, and they have become close.

Mary, my sister, remembered Effie, the cook, in the kitchen at Grandma's house, the steamers for cooking the fruitcakes and the cutting the fruit at Christmastime, and washing clothes in the smokehouse. She recalled that Grandma later rented rooms to construction company managers to build the Smyrna Air Base because she had a big house and Smyrna had no motels when the air base opened.

Margaret Jordan (Dan's wife), another outlaw, was proud to announce that "the family has taken me in." She said that she felt closer to us than to her blood kin, and she really loved the family gossip.

Many stories were told of Aunt Maggie. Once she rode the bus to Enid, Oklahoma, to see her daughter Evelyn, and Mama went along. Mama wore a black wool dress that looked much the worse for the bus trip. She had packed a linen napkin with her lunch and the dress was covered with lint from the napkin—and she trailed a brand-new

Three granddaughters at their grandparents' home, standing in front of their mothers' portraits: Leigh Biggs Reames, Susan Anderson Burns, and Amy Cross Nance. Christmas 1985.

mink stole behind her in the dust. (Remember that Mama was not the clotheshorse.) Evelyn told about picking them up at the bus station, and Aunt Maggie had brought a suitcase full of turnip greens. Evelyn had a large red-haired neighbor called Lorraine who wore loud Lycra pants and was equally flamboyant. She didn't want her mother to meet Lorraine because Aunt Maggie would worry about Evelyn having such neighbors, but when they did meet, they hit it off from the beginning. I'm sure Aunt Maggie felt that she was going to help Lorraine or raise her standards. When Evelyn moved to Louisiana, Aunt Maggie told a neighbor there that her daughter "used to be right frivolous" but was better by that time.

Aunt Maggie was famous for mailing religious pamphlets to any of the relatives who had moved away from Tennessee. In addition she wanted to research the churches in the area where a family member moved. She was not one to leave religious instruction to chance.

Aunt Maggie was also known for sending turnip greens and fresh flowers on the bus all the way to Chicago to another daughter, Ann. The greens were inedible and the flowers were wilted and unusable

254

by the time they arrived, but her daughter didn't have the heart to tell her not to send any more. Ann lived outside Chicago in Oak Park and had to drive into the center of Chicago and pick up the "gifts" from her mother.

Uncle Herbert was commended for helping boys from TPS, in earlier days a home for children who needed care (not necessarily orphans). He clothed and educated many of them. He later set some up in business, and three became leading businessmen in Nashville. Men and women in the church he attended would go to TPS off Murfreesboro Road and teach Sunday school to the boys.

Sarah Jordan Womack was the baby of Roy and Katie, and Roy was the baby of his family. She admitted about the reunion, "I needed to get away and I needed our family." She told about going to Clinton's inauguration. That came about because of the Jordan family's relationship with the Gore family.

To understand the Gore connection, you have to know some background that goes *way* back. Mama's brothers and brother-in-law—Uncle Herbert, Uncle Bryan, and Uncle Alvis—decided they wanted to help Albert Gore Sr. run for office and try to break up the Crump machine in Memphis that was affecting us here in Middle Tennessee. They wanted Albert to run as the congressman from his district, which included Rutherford County. Pauline, his wife, had graduated from Vanderbilt Law School; she was—and is—a very astute woman. While my uncles were helping Albert, Aunt Minnie (Mama's sister) and Aunt Dixie took Pauline to Grace's, and they helped her buy clothes for the campaign.

Albert Sr. and Pauline had a daughter, Nancy, who was my age; she has since died. After Al was born, the children stayed with Aunt Minnie or Aunt Dixie while Pauline and Albert Sr. were campaigning. When Albert ran for the Senate, Uncle Herbert was treasurer of the campaign. At Uncle Herbert's death, Aunt Evelyn (Herbert's wife) received a call from Albert Sr. Aunt Evelyn had asked him to be a pallbearer, and he requested to be an active pallbearer and carry the casket. The family thought that was a humble request, but Aunt Minnie, who was the guardian of the manners, like to have died. She protested, "Evelyn, you don't have a senator as an active pallbearer." Mama told her, "You just be quiet, Minnie." Mama tried to be the peacemaker.

Anyway Sarah's husband, J. W. (Jubba) Womack, works for CBS News. When Al Gore Jr. was running for the presidential nomination, J. W. was assigned to Al's CBS TV crew during his campaign. On Al's first stop in his hometown to announce his candidacy, Sarah was there with her husband, and she told Al of her connection with the Jordan family. Upon her return home, she called Aunt Minnie and told her that if Al Jr. won the presidency, she would go to Murfreesboro, pick up Aunt Minnie, and take her to the inauguration. However, Bill Clinton, not Al Jr., was the Democratic presidential nominee and Al Jr. was the vice presidential nominee. CBS made J. W. part of the crew to follow the Clinton campaign. The Womacks were elated when Clinton won because after all those years of following candidates on their campaigns for CBS, one of J. W.'s candidates was to be inaugurated.

Unfortunately Aunt Minnie died before the inauguration. Sarah was not to be stopped; she asked CBS officials to reserve her two seats as close to the inaugural platform as possible because she had an important person to bring with her. She framed a picture of Aunt Minnie and took that and placed it in the extra chair. Aunt Minnie was there in spirit, and Sarah kept her promise.

The family has been pleased to call Middle Tennessee home for many reasons. David Halberstam, the writer and the historian speaking at a seminar on Albert Gore Sr. in Murfreesboro in the fall of 1997, pointed out one that we may take for granted. At one time Halberstam worked for the *Tennessean*, later he worked on political campaigns, then he moved to South Africa to take a job there, and his next move was to Poland. The diversity of his career and travels makes his an informed perspective. He commented that there is a tenderness in the rolling landscape of Middle Tennessee that goes back to the people. He observed that much of Middle Tennessee came through the trials of integration better than other southern states, and he attributed it to that tenderness. He saw a lack of hatred that was apparent in other areas of the South.

My grandfathers had the desire to want to do better even though they had little education. They didn't build church buildings. They built the inward churches of people they knew.

We came from a family that gave and gave. Some people don't understand that giving things to people is not showing off. Something in our family makes us want to give. We were taught that if we didn't give, that was wrong. The more we gave, God gave more increase with it. Both sets of my grandparents were givers. I am accused of giving too much at Christmas to my grandchildren, but it's a delight to do it. I want my grandchildren to have the same gift of giving, and example is the *main* thing. Today we don't really sacrifice in anything. I don't want to have bad times—I appreciate good times—but I'd like to see us sacrifice more.

Billy's family was not as giving as mine, but Billy himself was. He wasn't here to reap the rewards from some of the things he did for people, especially in this community. During his illness, many kindnesses done for me and the children resulted directly from his

The family all together with Billy watching over us: Jenny holding infant Will, four-year-old Madeline, Caroline, Jim, and Amy.

257

generosity to others. He was a giver to the family and to people outside the family. He loved to buy me gifts and was so generous that I quit mentioning when I thought something was nice or special because he would buy it for me.

At a party I saw some farmers I have known for years but don't see regularly any more because they no longer come to cut our alfalfa or buy some from our farm. They pulled aside the hostess of the party and asked if I had had a facelift. They thought that I looked too good not to have had one. The hostess, of course, replied that I had not had one. I had not done anything different from what I had ever done. I'm glad that my healing process was showing in my face. God's grace and peace must have been evident. After five years of what I had been through, my face could have shown something really grim.

Grandma Jordan always taught me, "Beauty is as beauty does," and I believe that. I now try to impress that truth on Madeline: "Being pretty on the inside means that you try to be a good person, you love people, and you love God." As Will gets older, I'll teach him the same thing but will probably have to couch it in somewhat different terms. Most boys don't want to talk about being pretty or beautiful. Aunt Amy was not considered a real beauty, but to people who knew her, she was the most beautiful woman they had ever known. Outward beauty is not nearly as important as inward beauty. If I can teach my grandchildren—and maybe someday my great-grandchildren—that lesson and some others I learned from my family, I will feel that I have truly accomplished something worth-while on this earth. Ralph Waldo Emerson summed up many of my feelings about what is involved in true success:

> To laugh often and much; to win the respect of intelligent people and affection of children; to earn the appreciation of honest critics and endure the betrayal of false friends; to appreciate beauty; to find the best in others. . . . To leave the world a bit better place, whether by a healthy child, a garden patch, or a redeemed social condition; to know even one life has breathed easier because you have lived. This is to have succeeded.

Appendices

Ties to Dr. Thomas Walker

Thomas Walker (1715 to1794) was the second son born to Thomas and Susanna Walker in King and Queen County, Virginia. Walker was a man of many talents: a physician, merchant, and land owner in Virginia. He was founder and trustee of the town of Charlottesville, Virginia, and probably was the first white man to enter Kentucky (in 1750). Dr. Thomas Walker State Park in Kentucky is near the present town of Barbourville. He built a cabin in 1750, the first building of record to be erected by a white man in Kentucky. That was twenty-five years before Daniel Boone built Boonesborough. Walker's Mountains in southwest Virginia were named after him. He was also a surveyor. He named Cumberland Gap and the Cumberland River in honor of the Duke of Cumberland (the son of King George II of England). A historic marker marks the site. He treated with the Indians upon appointment by the House of Burgesses, along with Jon Harvie. He was a member of the House of Burgesses.

Thomas had many children with Mildred Thornton Meriwether (her first husband was Nicholas Meriwether). Thomas Walker Jr. is the line through which my family comes. He was their fourth child. Thomas Jr. was a captain in the 9th Virginia Regiment in the Revolutionary War. In 1772 he married Margaret Hoops, daughter of Adam and Elizabeth Hoops of Philadelphia. They had eight children, and the third child was a daughter named Mildred, born in 1782. She married Tarleton Goolsby in 1797, and by 1810 they were in Kentucky.

Margaret Ellen Goolsby, daughter of Mildred and Tarleton, was born in 1838 in Johnson County, Indiana. She married Thomas Sturgeon. Margaret, daughter of Thomas and Margaret, married Daniel Dodd Elliott in 1860. They had these children by the 1880 census—Minnie, Ettie (my grandmother), Walker, Emma, and Maude—and were living in Jefferson County, Indiana. Daniel and Margaret came to Tennessee before Ettie married. They bought no land. When Daniel died, Margaret with her daughter Emma, who was also a widow and had small children, moved to what is now Clovis, New Mexico, and homesteaded. Margaret's granddaughter, Maggie Jordan Batey, remembers that Margaret "would always take the Bible and read" while on a visit to Tennessee.

Grandma used to say that Margaret Elliott would talk about everybody going West in covered wagons. On the sides of the wagons was written "To Texas or Bust." When the people came back to Tennessee, the sides of the wagons had "Busted by God." But Grandma always spelled out the last part as b-y-G-o-d. She couldn't bring herself to say it aloud; that would have been taking the Lord's name in vain. I was a senior in college before it hit me what she had been spelling out all those years because all of us in the family would repeat her story verbatim and spell it out too.

These are the children of Ettie Elliott and Arch Wood Jordan:

Birth Dates of the Jordans

Maggie—1891	*Minnie—1902*
Charlie—1893	*Herbert—1904*
Ernest—1894	*Ruth—1907*
Bryan—1896	*Roy—1909*

Newsom Family Connection

Nancy Newsom from Newsom Station in Davidson County went to Rutherford County and married James Morton. They had a daughter, Nancy Caroline Morton (Nancy Newsom's sister was Caroline), who married Constantine Jordan. Constantine was my great-grandfather; he was Arch's daddy. I have Nancy Newsom's lace cap that she wore when she had her portrait painted, and the portrait is now in the Louis Todd family in Nashville.

When Interstate 40 was first built, they had to dynamite the original Newsom family home, which the Ezzell family (Mrs. Matt Dobson's family) had purchased. It was a three-story rock house.

Obituaries

HLeo Boles wrote about A. W. Jordan in the *Gospel Advocate*, January 31, 1935:

> In the passing of A. W. Jordan, Smyrna, Tennessee, the church and community have lost a good man; his wife and children have lost a noble husband and faithful father; many others have lost a trusted friend. . . .

> Brother Jordan learned the truth and accepted it in early manhood. . . . The church in his community did not have a more liberal supporter nor a more loyal friend than was found in A. W. Jordan. . . . The writer enjoyed his kind hospitality many times. . . . Brother Jordan was not a public man in the sense of taking a leading part in church work, but his good, sound judgment and his encouragement were always sought. . . . He lived a faithful Christian life, and taught his family not only by word, but by his life, the reality that there is in Christianity.

> . . . If I were asked to give in a word our brother's dominating characteristics, I would say that it was his good judgment in business. . . .

> Many years ago Brother Jordan visited the old Nashville Bible School and spent one night there. He was there on business. . . . He

was so impressed with the idea of a Christian education at that time that he determined to give his children the advantages of such training. Soon after that he placed his oldest child, now Mrs. Maggie [wife of James B.] Batey, in school there. All eight of his children were trained in the Nashville Bible School, now David Lipscomb College.

Services for Tom Fox Jones were held at 11:00 A.M. at Fourth Avenue Church of Christ, Franklin, with Myron Keith, Paul Brown, and Jim Taylor officiating. Burial was at Woodlawn on September 14, 1987. He had died September 11, at age eighty-one.

Active pallbearers were Thomas E. Batey, John Butner Jr., Leslie R. Jones, A. W. Jordan, Dan H. Jordan, Donald R. Jordan, J. J. Redmon, Larry Redmon, Brent Sanders, Richard Stover, and Dr. Carl H. Stem.

He was a developer of commercial and residential property in Williamson County from 1964 until mid-1970s. The *Williamson Leader* called him a "pioneer land developer." He was also a charter member of the Tennessee Walking Horse Breeders' Association.

A memorial service for Ruth Jordan Jones was held at the Fourth Avenue Church of Christ, Franklin, 11:00 A.M., on April 20, 1988. She lived March 2, 1907, to April 18, 1988. She was interred at Woodlawn.

The speakers were Paul Brown, Dr. Mack Wayne Craig, and C. Myron Keith. The songs were "Consider the Lilies of the Field," "The Lord's My Shepherd," "In the Morning of Joy," and "Faith Is the Victory."

Honorary pallbearers included James B. Batey, Gene H. Cross, Geoffrey Ellis, Lawrence Glover, Curtis C. Green, Otis Henry, Paul

Kinnie, Richard Maddux, Willliam McBride, Charles Miller, John Pinkerton, James Preston, Cecil Vines, Robert Waller, and Dr. Carter Williams. Active pallbearers included Thomas E. Batey, John Butner Jr., Robert A. Huddleston Jr., Leslie R. Jones, A. W. Jordan, Dan H. Jordan, Donald R. Jordan, Dr. William B. Jordan, J. J. Redmon, Larry Redmon, Brent Sanders, Richard Stover, and Dr. Carl H. Stem.

Mama had been an active member in the Home Demonstration Clubs in Davidson and Williamson Counties. She went to national conventions all over the United States. She even went to Hawaii with a bunch of women from the clubs; there she and one other woman toured all the islands. She was really skilled at putting on demonstrations too.

Uncle Herbert had been one of the founders of Great Lakes Christian College in Beamsville, Ontario, Canada. When Uncle Herbert died, Mama took over his interests there. The college held a Ruth and Tom Jones Day.

Mama was a people person who never met a stranger in her life. She could always rake up kin or some kind of relationship wherever she went. For example, the family was driving to San Antonio from Tennessee to see Uncle Bryan. We stopped at a city cafe in Marshall, Texas, to eat supper. Daddy said, "You girls, remember that your mama isn't going to find anybody she knows here." We hadn't been sitting there very long before a Mrs. Johnson, who was one of the founders with A. M. Burton of Life and Casualty Insurance Company, stepped into the cafe. She never had children, so each year she took a group of students across the USA to see the country at her expense. Mama said, "Here is Grandma Johnson." (That was what they called her at Lipscomb.)

James William Cross died April 11, 1975, at the home of J. W. Cross III. He was a farmer and agent for Federal Crop Insurance. The funeral was held on Sunday, April 13, at 2:00 P.M. at Madison Street United Methodist Church. Rev. James Clark and Rev. Lexie

Freeman officiated. He was born in Montgomery County, September 8, 1907. His father was James W. Cross Sr., and his mother was Margaret Laughren Cross. His wife was Pearl Brandau Harris Cross. He had been a member of the National Disaster Committee, USDA Tennessee State Chairman, ASCS under Eisenhower administration, member of CCC Committee on Grain for Southeast Area, past president of the Montgomery County Farm Bureau, and past president and director of the Tennessee Farmer's Cooperative. He had been active in the Republican Party and was a delegate in the State Constitutional Convention. Interment was at Resthaven Memorial Gardens, Clarksville.

The Jones Family

The Jones family started with John Jones Jr., called Jolly. It was rumored that Jolly and an unknown brother ended up in Rutherford County, Tennessee, from North Carolina because they were orphans. Jolly was born about 1807 and died in 1879. His wife was Margaret Evans. They had eight or nine children. My family line descended from his child John Calvin, who was born in 1843 (he died in 1889). In 1879 John Calvin came back to Tennessee from Ennis, Texas, where he and his bride, Nancy Caroline Smith, had moved after their marriage. At Jolly's death there was a big sale of all personal property. His wife chose to move to Arkansas at his death; she and some of her children moved there and the town of Jonesboro is the result of that move. Jolly owned a lot of real estate and a general store. Apparently Jolly was involved in the buying and selling of real estate to make most of his money. He gave the rock for the toll road from Eagleville to Murfreesboro.

John Calvin Jones decided to stay in Eagleville, and he purchased a farm on Swamp Road. But he and Nancy Caroline lived in Eagleville across from the present high school. At his death he was buried in the Old Jones Cemetery, which is located on the farm of Jolly. He had married Nancy Caroline Smith in 1866.

They had seven children. Only three survived to long life—James Rutherford, Artemis Leslie, and Mary Margaret. Mary Margaret married Graves Jackson. Our family descended from Artemis Leslie, who inherited his father's farm and lived there until his death in 1941. He was a farmer and livestock trader. Artemis Leslie was born in 1876, and he and his wife, Bertha Era Moon, had ten children.

Artemis Leslie—Daddy Jones—and his mother moved after John Calvin's death to the farm on the Swamp Road in Eagleville. We're not sure how long they lived there before he met and married my grandmother, Bertha Era Moon. They were married on the riverbank on that farm. They had been to a protracted church meeting and had the minister come and marry them. She now has a granddaughter named for her, Ann Era Jones Ping. Bertha's father was Dr. John Robert Moon, who practiced in Eagleville most of his life.

The Jones children called their mother Mammy; we grandchildren called her Mama Jones. Daddy Jones had to be pretty industrious to take care of all those children. My daddy always said that Daddy Jones provided Mammy with the latest of any kind of household invention, such as a washing machine, to make her job easier. He was interested in such things.

Daddy Jones became the dealer for Delco lighting systems. He sold the systems to people on farms before TVA and electricity became prevalent. Delco systems income supplemented what he made on the farm. His sons helped install them, and that's where my daddy developed his mechanical ability.

The summer of 1997 Johnny Butner, my cousin, came from Winston-Salem for the Jones family reunion and stayed with me at my home. He and I picked up Uncle Buster to go to the Jones cemetery in Eagleville and the Moon cemetery in Unionville. We were coming in to Eagleville on the new road and saw an auction sign for Clive, my brother-in-law. He was going to auction Granddaddy and Grandmammy Moon's house. The house had gone out of the family some time ago, so Clive had no idea that it had once belonged to his wife's great-grandparents.

One summer his mother sent Johnny here from Winston-Salem to get a taste of working on the farm. Aunt Grace, the oldest of my daddy's sisters, lived in Vicksburg, Mississippi. She came in the summer with her two children to visit as well as assist with wheat threshing and picking cotton. Remember, a lot of cooking had to be done to feed the crews that came to the farm for the harvests. Aunt Grace would come out all prim and proper in her starched linen dresses every morning, and she'd say, "Johnny, you're going to weed the garden today." Johnny didn't know what a weed was. She proceeded to show him. Uncle Buster said, "That's just like Dad [Daddy Jones]. You could not sit around. He had you working. He never let his children sit. They were doing something the whole time." There were always women hired to help Mama Jones, but just overseeing the large family was an amazing feat.

On that outing to the cemetery I learned that as a young man, my daddy had a still in the silo and made white lightning. He was a prankster and a cut-up, but had an inquiring mind. Apparently my daddy had people coming to the farm to buy his white lightning, unbeknownst to my grandfather. And Daddy Jones being the pillar of the church. . . . I can imagine the dressing down my daddy received.

Daddy Jones had told his children that he wanted to be buried in the cemetery with his mother and father. Jolly, Daddy Jones's grand-father, owned huge tracts of land in the Eagleville area known as Versailles. The foundation ruins of his house are still in existence. There are no tombstones in that cemetery, however; there are only rocks. Daddy's brothers and sisters had put a fence around the area, but the cemetery ended up in the middle of somebody's field. Daddy didn't want to bury Daddy Jones there because tending the grave would have been hard to do. They buried Mama and Daddy Jones in Evergreen Cemetery in Murfreesboro. Billy and I had a tombstone placed at the family cemetery; we chose a rustic stone and put the name and birth and death date of all buried there—including the slaves and their children. At the home place that Daddy Jones inher-ited he put in a concrete sidewalk from the road to the house, and then he concreted the porch and steps. Before that, huge limestone pieces had been there for the steps; he moved them and made benches under the pair of maple trees out front. Billy and I moved those benches to the cemetery when the home place sold.

One day just before Daddy died, his siblings were all here for the reunion, and since Daddy was bedridden, they were in his bedroom visiting with him. They were talking about how much their mother had cooked because of the crews to work on the farm and the size of the family. They wondered how many biscuits Mammy had made in her life. They came up with a boxcar full. They had either cornbread or biscuits at every meal—three meals a day.

Aunt Sara's husband died young as a result of a mastoid operation; he had just graduated from UT. Aunt Sara was left a widow with three young children. Mama Jones was in the process of selling the farm, and she and Aunt Sara and the children moved to Nashville together. It was a good setup for both women. Near the end of her life Mama Jones had Carter Williams as her doctor; she was Carter's first patient in our family. He was my mother and daddy's doctor, our doctor, and now my children's doctor. He has ended up being a personal friend as well as our doctor.

Mama Jones had had cancer. When her condition worsened, she was to go to Vanderbilt Hospital. I had gone to her house to help Aunt Sara transport Mama Jones to the hospital. Mama Jones was "directing traffic" and telling us things she wanted done. When I arrived at Kirkwood Lane, she was working on a quilt top for Amy, my daughter, and she asked me to get it quilted for Amy. She was so industrious even then. She was a beautiful woman, the kindest, sweetest woman, but a strict disciplinarian. You knew where you stood with Mama Jones. The same way with Daddy Jones.

After she was admitted to the hospital that day, Carter Williams met us there and came out and said to Aunt Sara and me and my father, who had just arrived, "Well, Mrs. Jones doesn't want to be put on any support system. She said she is ready to die. Do you think she means it?" We said, "She knows exactly what she is saying. We knew her mind-set before we brought her here to the hospital." She lived only two or three days, and she was gone. I thought that was so wonderful—to look forward to death and not be afraid of it. She was such an organized and methodical woman. I think maybe a lot of my organizational ability came from that side of the house, not that my mother's side wasn't organized. That was a strong suit I got from them.

———•◆•———

Nona (the sister born before my daddy) went to Winston-Salem to teach school, and there she met and married John Butner, who was of German Moravian descent. Uncle Buster said that Daddy Jones was upset that Nona married a man far away from home. I am said to look like her. She died at age ninety or ninety-one. After their marriage, she and Uncle John bought a house built in the late 1700s and restored it and lived there until she moved to a Moravian retirement home. That is my first recollection of restoration. She had three children. But after she had her first two—Johnny and Jo—Aunt Nona wanted to come back to see her parents in Tennessee. Uncle John's work prevented him from driving them over, so he sent Gill, a black man who worked for Uncle John and Aunt Nona, to drive her over here.

Uncle Buster said that Daddy Jones was thrilled that his daughter had married a man who could afford to send her back in a chauffeur-driven car. Then Daddy Jones had Gill drive him wherever he needed to go. No matter who you were or how you arrived, you had to work around his house.

Ailene, who was born after my daddy, went to visit Aunt Nona. She stayed and married into the Kapp family, also a German Moravian family. Uncle Ernest, her husband, was a chemist for R. J. Reynolds. The Kapp family was one of the first families of Old Salem.

Both of my grandmothers made the clothes for all their children when the children were young; usually someone came in to help with the sewing. I've heard stories that Daddy Jones would take his daughters and buy their Easter hats or spring bonnets. The women also had to do or supervise all the cooking, make their own soap, and iron and starch everything. There were no washing machines early on.

Daddy Jones put a stove in the wash house so that it would be warm in the winter. Of course, it was hot as Hades in the summer because they had to boil all that water. I don't know how those women survived all that. And yet they raised good children with good habits, who were mannerly and well schooled.

A DELIGHTFUL LIFE

I can't say enough about my grandparents and that era. They were hard workers, trying to make things better for their children than they had themselves. They could see the opportunities that education would bring their children. My grandparents sacrificed much and worked very hard to better themselves, their children, and their future generations.

Life was hard on the farm. Using an old typewriter, Daddy Jones wrote letters to Grace, his eldest daughter, who was living in Vicksburg, Mississippi. In one letter Daddy Jones was bemoaning the fact that he could not get enough money together for Uncle Buster's second year at UT. Uncle Buster had gone to Oklahoma to work with wheat threshing crews to make money in the summer. This was in the Depression.

It was hard even on those young men and women who had two-year degrees from college. They could teach school anywhere, but there were no jobs. That is why two of them ended up in Winston-Salem and married into good German families there.

Daddy's second oldest brother was John. John was an accountant in Chicago (Daddy had followed him to Chicago and worked there for a time), but he lost his job during the Depression and came back to the farm. Later John went back to Chicago. Another brother, Uncle Jess, followed to Chicago but then went on to Niagara Falls, New York, and worked for the Nunn-Bush Shoe Co.

Daddy Jones saw to it that Uncle John was busy when he came home from Chicago. Daddy Jones had him plowing with the horse and a single-tree. Uncle John was a natty dresser who always wore a shirt and tie. No one ever saw him in casual clothes until many years later. He was out in the field plowing in his white dress shirt and had the collar turned up. He was always cold, even in spring and summer. He left the plow, went to the house, and put on his necktie. Then he went back to plowing. Someone asked, "Why did you put the necktie on, John?" He said, "I was cold."

Uncle John was a kind man. Daddy and Uncle John helped Aunt Sara in meeting the needs of her family. She was working, but with only one year of college when she married, her jobs were limited. Her husband died so young, they hadn't accumulated much. Carl and his sisters are a credit to their mother and father. Whenever anybody in the family needed assistance, other family members were always there for them. Aunt Sara worked at Vultee during the war, after the war she sold real estate, and later on she became a librarian in the Metro system.

Community Involvement of Nancy Caroline Jones Cross

1974—Chairman of second Heritage Foundation Ball at Carnton. Fund-raiser for Heritage Foundation to preserve historic structures in Williamson County.

1974—Founder of the first Candlelight Tour of Historic Homes in Williamson County as a fund-raiser for Carter House. APTA property tour still in existence today.

1975—Founder of the Spring Town and Country Tour of Homes for Heritage Foundation still in existence today.

1975—Second woman president of Heritage Foundation.

1975–79—Chairman of Carter House Antique Show APTA.

1975–85—In small group responsible for securing 1820s plantation house, Carnton, in Franklin as a historic property open to the public. Charter member as well as serving on board of executive committee from inception until 1985.

1975–88—Member of Endowment Committee of Monteagle Sunday School Assembly, Chairman of Education Scholarship Committee awarding college scholarships to Cumberland Mountain boys and girls.

1976—Fund-raising committee of first YMCA (Harpeth) in Williamson County—now known as Brentwood Y.

1977–79—Board of Carter House APTA—Franklin Civil War historic property owned by state of Tennessee.

1979—Awarded Distinguished Service Award of Williamson County by Franklin Jaycees.

1985–87—Belmont Mansion Board.

1987–present—National Advisory Board of David Lipscomb University.

1988—Chairman of International Grand Championship Walking Horse Show; a six-day event raising $75,000 for the Walking Horse Owners' Association as well as cerebral palsy riding program.

1990–91—Board of Directors of O'More College of Interior Design.

1992—Family was awarded National Distinguished Award from Walking Horse Owners' Association for promotion of the breed.

1993–97—Board of Vanderbilt University Stallworth Rehabilitation Center.

1994–97—Board of Franklin YMCA; chairman of Community Development.

1994—Chairman of Williamson County Economic Development Showcase; instrumental in formation of the showcase in 1991.

1994–present—Appointed by Dr. James Walker, president, MTSU, to the committee to plan the new John Miller Equine Arena at MTSU.

1994–present—Board of World Christian Broadcasting Company, broadcasting in Russia, China, and Philippines.

1994–present—Board member O'More College of Interior Design.

1996—Member of Franklin National Bank Scholarship Selection Committee for Williamson County seniors to attend college.

1996–present—Cofounder and volunteer executive director of Leadership Franklin.

1997—Tennessee Quality Awards Board of Examiners, a division of Tennessee Department of Economic Development.

1997—Governor Don Sundquist appointment to Tennessee Historical Commission.

1997—Founder of Battle Ground Academy Antique Show.

1997—Advisory Board of Visitors for Battle Ground Academy.

Organizations

Fourth Avenue Church of Christ
Charter and Life Member of Carnton Association
Life Member Carter House APTA
Magna Charter
Colonial Dames, Chapter 7
Daughters of American Revolution
Affiliate of ASID (Interior Design)
Association for Preservation of Tennessee Antiquities
Ladies Hermitage Association
Walking Horse Owners' Association